HAND OF GOD

PHILIP KERR is the bestselling author
of the Bernie Gunther series, for which
he received a CWA Ellis Peters Award.
He was born in Edinburgh and now lives
in London. He is a life-long supporter
of Arsenal.

Follow @theScottManson on Twitter

ALSO BY PHILIP KERR

Scott Manson

January Window
Hand of God
False Nine

Bernie Gunther

March Violets
The Pale Criminal
A German Requiem
The One from the Other
A Quiet Flame
If the Dead Rise Not
Field Grey
Prague Fatale
A Man Without Breath

Standalone novels

A Philosophical Investigation
Dead Meat
Gridiron
Esau
A Five Year Plan
The Second Angel
The Shot
Dark Matter: The Private Life of Sir Isaac Newton
Hitler's Peace
Prayer
Research

For Children

One Small Step

Children of the Lamp

The Akhenaten Adventure
The Blue Djinn of Babylon
The Cobra King of Kathmandu
The Day of the Djinn Warriors
The Eye of the Forest
The Five Fakirs of Faizabad
The Grave Robbers of Genghis Khan

PHILIP KERR

A SCOTT MANSON THRILLER

HAND OF GOD

HEAD of ZEUS

This book is for Adam and John Thynne

'A little with the head of Maradona
and a little with the hand of God'

Diego Maradona on his first goal against
England in the 1986 World Cup

PROLOGUE

Never mind the Special One; according to the sports press I'm the Lucky One.

After the death of João Zarco (unlucky) I was lucky to land the job as the caretaker manager of London City, and even luckier to keep it at the end of the 2013–14 season. City were judged lucky to finish fourth in the BPL; we were also judged to have been lucky to reach the Capital One Cup Final and the FA Cup Semi-final, both of which we lost.

Personally, I thought we were unlucky not to win something, but *The Times* thought different:

Considering all that has happened at Silvertown Dock in the last six months – a charismatic manager murdered, a talented goalkeeper's career cut tragically short, an ongoing HMRC investigation into the so-called 4F scandal (free fuel for footballers) – City were surely very fortunate to achieve as much as they did. Much of the club's good fortune can be attributed to the hard work and tenacity of their manager, Scott Manson, whose fulsome and eloquent eulogy for his predecessor quickly went viral on the internet and prompted the Spectator *magazine to compare him to none other than Mark Anthony. If José Mourinho is the Special One, then Scott Manson is certainly the Clever One; he may also be the Lucky One.*

I've never thought of myself as being lucky, least of all when I was doing eighteen months in Wandsworth nick for a crime I didn't commit.

And I had only one superstition when I was a professional footballer: I used to kick the ball as hard as I could whenever I took a penalty.

As a general rule I don't know if today's generation of players are any more credulous than my lot were, but if their tweets and Facebook posts from the World Cup in Brazil are anything to go by, the lads who are playing the game today are as devoted to the idea of luck as a witch-doctors' convention in Las Vegas. Since few of them ever go to church, mosque or shul, perhaps it's not that surprising that they should have so many superstitions; indeed, superstition may be the only religion that these often ignorant souls can cope with. As a manager I've done my best to gently discourage superstitions in my players, but it's a battle you can't ever hope to win. Whether it's a meticulous and always inconvenient pre-match ritual, a propitious shirt number, a lucky beard, or a providential T-shirt with an image of the Duke of Edinburgh – I kid you not – superstitions in football are still as much a part of the modern game as in-betting, compression shirts and Kinesio tape.

While a lot of football is about belief, there's a limit; and some leaps of faith extend far beyond a simple knock on wood and enter the realms of the deluded and the plain crazy. Sometimes it seems to me that the only really grounded people in football are the poor bastards watching it; unfortunately I think the poor bastards watching the game are starting to feel much the same way.

Take Iñárritu, our extravagantly gifted young midfielder, who's currently playing for Mexico in Group A; according to what he's been tweeting to his one hundred thousand followers it's God who tells him how to score goals; but when all else fails he buys some fucking marigolds and a few sugar lumps, and lights a candle in front of a little skeleton doll wearing a woman's green dress. Oh yes, I can see how that might work.

Then there's Ayrton Taylor who's currently with the England squad in Belo Horizonte; apparently the real reason he broke a metatarsal bone in the match against Uruguay was that he forgot to pack his lucky silver bulldog and didn't pray to St Luigi Scrosoppi – the patron saint of footballers – with his Nike Hypervenoms in his hands like he normally does. Really, it had very little to do with the dirty bastard who blatantly stamped on Taylor's foot.

Bekim Develi, our Russian midfielder, also in Brazil, says on Facebook that he has a lucky pen that travels with him everywhere; interviewed by Jim White for the *Daily Telegraph* he also talked about his recently born baby boy, Peter, and confessed that he had forbidden his girlfriend, Alex, to show Peter to any strangers for forty days because they were 'waiting for the infant's soul to arrive' and were anxious for him not to take on another's soul or energy during that crucial time.

If all of this wasn't ludicrous enough one of City's Africans, the Ghanaian John Ayensu, told a Brazilian radio reporter that he could only play well if he wore a piece of lucky leopard fur in his underpants, an unwise admission that drew a flurry of complaints from the conservation-minded WWF and animal rights activists.

In the same interview Ayensu announced his intention to leave City in the summer, which was unwelcome news to me back home in London. As was what happened to our German striker, Christoph Bündchen, who was Instagrammed in a gay sauna and bar in the Brazilian city of Fortaleza. Christoph is still officially in the closet and said he'd gone to the Dragon Health Club by mistake, but Twitter says different, of course. With the newspapers – especially the fucking *Guardian* – desperate for at least one player to come out as gay while he's still playing professional football (wisely, I think, Thomas Hitzlsperger waited until his career was over), the pressure on poor Christoph already looks unbearable.

Meanwhile, one of London City's two Spanish players in Brazil, Juan Luis Dominguin, just emailed me a photograph of Xavier Pepe, our number one centre back, having dinner at a restaurant in Rio with some of the sheikhs who own Manchester City, following Spain's game against Chile. Given the fact that these people are richer than God – and certainly richer than our own proprietor, Viktor Sokolnikov – this is also cause for some concern. With so much money in the game today players' heads are easily turned; with the right number on a contract, there's not one of them that can't be made to look like Linda Blair in *The Exorcist*.

Like I said, I'm not a superstitious man but when, back in January, I saw those pictures in the papers of a lightning bolt striking the hand of the famous statue of Christ the Redeemer that stands over Rio de Janeiro, I ought to have known we were in for a few disasters in Brazil. Soon after that lightning bolt, of course, there were riots in the streets of São Paulo as demonstrations against the country's spending on the World Cup got violently out of hand; cars were set on fire, shops vandalised, bank windows smashed and several people shot. I can't say I blame the Brazilians. Spending fourteen billion dollars hosting the World Cup (as estimated by Bloomberg) when there's no basic sanitation in Rio de Janeiro is just unbelievable. But like my predecessor, João Zarco, I was never a fan of the World Cup and not just because of the bribery and corruption and the secret politics and Sepp bloody Blatter – not to mention the hand of God in '86. I can't help feeling that the little man who was named the player of the tournament in Argentina's World Cup was a cheat, and the fact that he was even nominated says everything about FIFA's showcase tournament.

As far as I can see, about the only reason to *like* the World Cup is because the United States is so bad at football and because it's the one time when you'll ever see Ghana or Portugal beat the crap out of the USA at *something*. Otherwise the plain fact of the matter is that I hate everything about the World Cup.

I hate it because the actual football played is nearly always shit, because the referees are always crap and the songs are even worse, because of the fucking mascots (Fuleco the Armadillo, the official mascot of the 2014 FIFA World Cup, is a portmanteau of the words *futebol* and *ecologia* – fuck me!), because of all the expert divers from Argentina and Paraguay and, yes, you, Brazil, because of all the England 'we can do it this time' hype, and because of all the cunts who know nothing about football who suddenly have a drivelling opinion about the game that you have to listen to. I especially hate the way politicians climb on the team coach and start waving a scarf for England when they're talking their usual bullshit.

But mainly, like most Premier League managers, I hate the World Cup because of the sheer bloody inconvenience of it all. Almost as soon as the domestic season was over on 17 May, and after less than a fortnight's holiday, those of our players who had been picked for international duties joined their respective squads in Brazil. With the first World Cup match played on 12 June, FIFA's money-spinning competition gives no time at all for players to recover from the stresses and strains of a full Premier League season and affords plenty of opportunities for them to pick up some serious injuries.

Ayrton Taylor looked as though he was out of the game for two months and seemed certain to miss City's first match of the new season against Leicester on 16 August; worse than that, he was likely to miss City's Group B play-offs against Olympiacos in Athens the following week. Which – with our other striker now the subject of intense speculation as to the true nature of his sexuality – is just what we don't need.

It's at times like these I wish I had more a few more Scots and Swedes in the team as, of course, neither Scotland nor Sweden qualified for the World Cup in 2014.

And I can't decide what's worse: worrying about the 'light adductor strain' that stopped Bekim Develi playing for Russia in their Group H match against South Korea; or worrying that the Russian manager Fabio Capello was playing him against Belgium before he'd given Develi a chance to properly recover. You see what I mean? You worry when they don't play and you worry when they do.

If all that wasn't bad enough I have a proprietor with pockets as deep as a Johannesburg gold mine who's currently in Rio looking to 'strengthen our squad' and buy someone we really don't need who's not nearly as good as all the TalkBollocks pundits and callers insist he is. Every night Viktor Sokolnikov Skypes me and asks my opinion of some Bosnian cunt I've never heard of, or the latest African *wünderkind* who the BBC has identified as the new Pelé, so it must be true.

The *wünderkind* is Prometheus Adenuga and he plays for AS Monaco and Nigeria. I just watched a *MOTD* montage of the lad's goals and skills with Robbie Williams belting out 'Let Me Entertain You' in the background, which only goes to prove what I've always suspected: the BBC just doesn't get football. Football isn't about entertainment. You want some entertainment, go and see Liza Minnelli fall off a fucking stage, but football is something else. Look, if you're trying your damnedest to win a game, you can't really give a fuck if the crowd are being entertained while you do it; football is too serious for that. It's only interesting if it matters. Just watch an England friendly and tell me I'm wrong. And now I come to think of it, this is why American sports are no good; because they've been sugared by the US television networks to make them more appealing to viewers. This is bullshit. Sport is only entertaining when it matters; and, honestly, it only matters when it's all that fucking matters.

Not that there's anything very honest about the way football is played in Nigeria. Prometheus is just eighteen years old, but given that country's reputation for age-cheating he might be several years older. Last year, and the year before that, he was a member of the Nigerian side that won the FIFA U-17 World Cup. Nigeria has won the competition four times in a row, but only by fielding many players who are much older than seventeen. According to a large number of bloggers on some of Nigeria's most popular websites, Prometheus is actually twenty-three years old. The age disparities of some African players in the Premier League are even greater. According to these same sources, Aaron Abimbole, who now plays for Newcastle United, is seven years older than the age of twenty-eight that appears on his passport; while Ken Okri, who played for us until he was sold to Sunderland at the end of July, might even have been in his forties. All of which certainly explains why some of these African players don't have any longevity. Or stamina. And why they get sold so often. No one wants to be holding those particular parcels when the fucking music stops.

That's just one reason why I won't ever become the England manager; the FA doesn't want anyone – even someone like me, who's half black – who's going to say that African football is run by a bunch of lying, cheating bastards.

But it isn't the true age of Prometheus, who plays for AS Monaco, which is currently occupying the journalists grubbing around the floor for stories in Brazil – it's the pet hyena he was keeping in his apartment back home in Monte Carlo. According to the *Daily Mail* it bit through the bathroom plumbing, flooding the whole building and causing tens of thousands of euros' worth of damage. A pet hyena makes Mario Balotelli's camouflaged Bentley Continental and Thierry Henry's forty-foot-high fish tank look sensible by comparison.

Sometimes I think that there's plenty of room for another Andrew Wainstein to start a game called Fantasy Football Madness in which participants assemble an imaginary team of real-life footballers and score points based on how expensive those players' homes and cars are, and how often they get themselves into the tabloids, with extra points awarded for extravagant WAGs, crazy pets, lavish Cinderella-style weddings, stupid names for babies, wrongly spelt tattoos, daft hairstyles and off-menu shags.

I bought Fergie's book when it came out, of course, and smiled when I read his low opinion of David Beckham. Fergie says he kicked the famous boot in Beckham's direction when his number seven refused to remove a beanie hat he was wearing at the club's Carrington training ground because he didn't want to reveal his new hairstyle to the press until the day of the match. I must say I have a lot of sympathy with Fergie's point of view. Players should always try to remember that everything depends on the fans that help to pay their wages; they need to bear in mind what life is like for the people on the terrace a bit more often than they do. I've already banned City players from arriving at our Hangman's Wood training ground in helicopters, and I'm doing my best to do the same with cars that cost more than the price of an average house. At the time of writing, this is £242,000. That may not sound like much of a restriction until you consider the top-of-the-range Lamborghini Veneno costs a staggering £2.4 million. That's almost chump change for players making fifteen million quid a year. I got the idea of a price ceiling for players' cars the last time I looked in our car park and saw two Aston Martin One-77s and a Pagani Zonda Roadster, which cost more than a million quid each.

Don't get me wrong, football is a business and players are in that business to make money and to enjoy their wealth. I've no problem with paying players three hundred grand a week. Most of them work damn hard for it and besides, the top money doesn't last that long and it's only a few who ever make it. I'm just sorry I didn't get paid that kind of loot when I was a player myself. But because a football club is a business, it behoves the people in that business to be mindful of public relations. After all, look what's happened to bankers, who today are almost universally derided as greedy pariahs. Perception is all and I've no wish to see supporters storming the fucking barricades in protest against the disparity in wealth that exists between them and professional footballers. To this end I've invited a speaker from the London Centre for Ethical Business Cultures to come and talk to our players about what he calls 'the wisdom of inconspicuous consumption'. Which is just another way of saying don't buy a Lamborghini Veneno. I do all this because protecting the lads in my team from unwanted publicity is an increasingly important way of ensuring you get the best out of them on the football pitch, which is all I really want. I love my players like they were my own family. Really, I do. This is certainly how I talk to them, although a lot of the time I just listen. That's what most of them need: someone who will comprehend what they're trying to say, which, I'll admit, isn't always easy. Of course, changing how players handle their wealth and fame won't be easy either. I think that encouraging any young men to act more responsibly is probably as difficult as eradicating player superstitions. But something needs to change, and soon, otherwise the game is in danger of losing touch with ordinary folk, if it hasn't done so already.

You've heard of total football; well, perhaps this is total management. A lot of the time you have to stop talking to players about football and talk to them about other things instead; and sometimes it all comes down to persuading average men how to behave like gifted ones. In this job I have learned to be a psychologist, a life counsellor, a comedian, a shoulder to cry on, a priest, a friend, a father and, sometimes, a detective.

CHAPTER 1

I'd gone on holiday to Berlin with my girlfriend, Louise Considine. She's a copper, a detective inspector with the Metropolitan Police, but we won't hold that against her. Especially as she's extremely pretty. The picture on her warrant card makes her look like she's advertising a new fragrance: *Met by Moschino, the Power to Arrest.* But hers is a very natural beauty and such is the power of Louise to charm that she always reminds me of one of those royal elves in Lord of the Rings: Galadriel, or Arwen. That does it for me, anyway. I've always loved Tolkien. And probably Louise, too.

We did a lot of walking and saw the sights. Most of the time we were there I managed to stay away from the television set and the World Cup. I much preferred to look at our hotel room's wonderful view of the Brandenburg Gate, which is among the best in the city, or to read a book; but I did sit down to watch the Champions League draw on Al-Jazeera. That was work.

As usual, the draw took place at midday in UEFA's headquarters in Nyon, Switzerland. The club chairman, Phil Hobday, was in the bemused-looking audience and I caught a glimpse of him looking very bored. I certainly didn't envy him that particular duty. While the moment of the draw

11

drew near, I was Skyping Viktor in his enormous penthouse hotel suite at the Copacabana Palace in Rio. As we waited for our little ball to come out of one of the bowls and be unscrewed by the trophy guest – a laborious and frankly farcical process – Viktor and I discussed our latest signing: Prometheus.

'He was going to sign for Barcelona but I persuaded him to come to us instead,' said Viktor. 'He's a little headstrong, but that's only to be expected of a prodigious talent like his.'

'Let's hope he's not such a handful when he comes to London.'

'Oh, I don't doubt Prometheus'll need a good player liaison officer to advise him of what's what and to keep him out of trouble. The boy's agent, Kojo Ironsi, has a number of suggestions on that front.'

'I think it's best that the club appoints someone, not his agent. We want someone who's going to be responsible to the club, not to the player; otherwise we'll never be able to control him. I've seen this kind of thing before. Headstrong kids who think they know it all. Liaison officers who side with the players, who lie for them and cover up their shortcomings.'

'You're probably right, Scott. But it could be worse, you know. . . The boy's English is actually quite good.'

'I know,' I said. 'I've been reading his tweets ahead of Nigeria's match in Group F with Argentina.'

I wasn't entirely in agreement with Viktor about this being a good thing; sometimes it's actually better for the team if a player with a big ego can't make himself easily understood. So far I'd resisted the temptation to bring up the fate of the mythological Prometheus. Punished by Zeus for the crime of stealing fire and giving it to men, he was chained to a rock where his liver was eaten daily by an eagle only to be regenerated at night because, of course, Prometheus was an immortal. What a fucking punishment.

'Look, Viktor, since you've met him it might help if you could persuade the boy to stop tweeting about how talented he is. That will keep the British press off his back when he comes to England.'

'What's he said?'

'Something about Lionel Messi. He said that when they meet on the football field it will be like Nadal versus Federer, but that he expects to come off best.'

'That's not so bad, is it?'

'Vik. Messi has earned his chops. The man's a phenomenon. Prometheus needs to learn a little humility if he's going to survive life in England.' I glanced at the TV. 'Hang on. I think this is us now.'

London City were drawn to meet the Greek side Olympiacos in Piraeus, for the away leg of the play-off round, towards the end of August. I gave Viktor the news.

'I don't know, is that good?' asked Viktor. 'Us against the Greeks?'

'Yes, I think so, although of course it will be very hot in Piraeus.'

'Are they a good team?'

'I don't really know much about them,' I said. 'Except that Fulham just bought their leading striker for twelve million.'

'So that's to our advantage then.'

'I suppose it is. But I imagine I'll have to go to Greece sometime soon and check them out. Compile a dossier.'

Louise had kept quiet throughout my conversation with Viktor but when our Skype call was over, she said: 'You're on your own for that particular trip, I think, my darling. I've been to Athens. There was a general strike and the whole city was in turmoil. Riots on the streets, graffiti everywhere, the rubbish not collected, a vicious right-wing, Molotov cocktails in bookshops. I swore then I wasn't ever going back.'

'I think it used to be worse than it is now,' I said. 'From what I've read in the newspapers it seems to be a little better since the votes in the Greek parliament about the national debt.'

'Hmm. I'm not convinced. Just remember, the Greeks have a word for it: *chaos*.'

After the draw was over, Louise and I went to lunch with Bastian Hoehling, an old friend who manages the Berlin side, Hertha BSC. Hertha isn't yet as successful a club as Dortmund and Bayern Munich, but it's only a matter of time and money, of which there is plenty in Berlin. The recently renovated stadium was the venue for the 1936 Olympic Games. Seating seventy-five thousand, it is one of the most impressive in Europe. With people moving to Berlin all the time – especially young people – the club itself, recently promoted to the Bundesliga, is well supported. The English Premier League is without peer, and Spain may have the best two clubs in the world, but for anyone who knows anything about football the future looks decidedly German.

We met Bastian and his wife, Jutta, in the 'restaurant sphere' at the top of the old TV tower, and when we we'd finished talking about the spectacular view of the city and surrounding Prussian countryside, the excellent weather we'd been enjoying, and the World Cup, the subject turned to the Champions League and City's draw against Olympiacos.

'You know, when the World Cup is over, Hertha has a pre-season tour of Greece,' said Bastian. 'A match against Panathinaikos, Aris Thessaloniki and Olympiacos. The club owners thought it would be good for German–Greek relations. For a while back there, Germany was very unpopular in

Greece. It was as if they blamed us for all their economic ills. Our tour is hopefully a way of reminding Greeks of the good things Germany has done for Greece. Hence the name of our peninsular competition: the Schliemann Cup. Heinrich Schliemann was the German who found the famous gold mask of Agamemnon, which you can see in the National Archaeological Museum, in Athens. One of our club sponsors is launching a new product in Greece and this competition will help to oil the wheels. A *fakelaki*, I think they'd call it. Or maybe a *miza*.'

'I don't think it can be *fakelaki*,' said Louise, who spoke a little Greek. 'That's an envelope for a doctor to take care of a patient.'

'*Miza* then,' said Bastian. 'Either way, it's a means for Germany to help put some money into Greek football. Panathinaikos and Aris FC are both supporter-owned clubs, which is also something that Germans believe in strongly.'

'You mean,' said Louise, 'that there are no Viktor Sokolnikovs and Roman Abramovich figures in German football?'

Bastian smiled. 'No. Nor any sheikhs either. We have German clubs, owned by Germans and run by Germans. You see, all German clubs are required to have at least fifty-one per cent of their shares owned by the supporters. Which helps to keep the price of tickets down.'

'But doesn't that mean less money to spend on new players?' she asked.

'German football believes in academies,' said Bastian. 'In developing youngsters, not buying the latest golden boy.'

'And that's why you do better in the World Cup,' she said.

'I think so. We prefer to invest money in our future, not in player agents. And all club managers are accountable to their members, not to the whims of some dodgy oligarch.' He smiled. 'Which means that in a year or two's time, when Scott here has been fired by his current master, he'll be managing a German club.'

'I've no complaints.'

This wasn't exactly true, of course. I didn't much care for the way Prometheus had been bought without any consultation with me, or, for that matter, Bekim Develi. That would certainly never have happened at a German football club.

'You should come with us for the Olympiacos game, Scott. You could do your homework for the Champions League game as Hertha's guest. We'd love to have you along. Who knows? We might even share a few ideas.'

'That's not a bad idea. Maybe I'll do that. Just as soon as we've finished our own pre-season tour of Russia.'

'Russia? Wow.'

'We have matches against Lokomotiv Moscow, Zenit St Petersburg and Dynamo St Petersburg. It sounds odd, but I think I'll only really start to relax when I have all of our team safely back from Rio.'

'I know exactly how you feel, Scott. And it's the same for me. Even so, I thought we were taking a risk going to Greece. But Russia? Christ.'

I shrugged. 'What can go wrong with the Russians?'

'You mean apart from all the crazy racists who support the teams?'

'I mean apart from all the crazy racists who support the teams.'

'Look out that window. What you see down there used to be the communist GDR.' He grinned. 'We're in East Berlin, Scott. This question you asked – what can go wrong with the Russians? – we used to ask ourselves this question every day. And every day we would come up

16

with the same answer. Anything. Anything is possible with the Russians.'

'I think it will be all right. Viktor Sokolnikov has arranged the tour. If he can't ensure a trouble-free pre-season tour of Russia, then I don't know who can.'

'I hope you're right. But Russia is not a democracy. It only pretends to be. The country is ruled by a dictator who was schooled in dictatorship and advanced by dictatorship. So just remember this: in a dictatorship anything can happen, and usually does.'

Sometimes, with the benefit of hindsight, good advice can seem more like prophecy.

CHAPTER 2

From the very beginning things went badly for us in Russia.

First, there was the flight to St Petersburg aboard the team's specially chartered Aeroflot jet which left London City airport after a three-hour wait on the stand without electricity, air conditioning and water. Soon after take-off the plane developed a serious fault, which had most of us thinking we might never walk alone again. It was like being aboard a fairground ride, but, in an Ilyushin IL96, it was nothing short of hell. We dropped through the air for several thousand feet before the pilots regained control of this Russian-made Portaloo with wings and announced that we were diverting to Oslo 'to refuel'.

As we made our descent to Oslo Airport the plane was shuddering like an old caravan and had every one of us thinking about the Busby babes and the Munich air disaster of 1958 when twenty of the forty-four passengers died. That's what every football team thinks about whenever there's a problem on a plane with bad weather or turbulence.

Which makes you wonder why Aeroflot are the official air carrier sponsors of Manchester United.

All of this prompted Denis Abayev, the team's nutritionist, to try and lead everyone in prayer, which did little for the confidence of all but the most religiously minded that any of us were going to survive. Denis had a fistful of degrees in sports science and prior to joining City he'd advised the British team at the London Olympics while working for the English Institute of Sport, but he knew nothing about human psychology and he scared as many people as those to whom he brought comfort. After the longest twenty minutes of my life the plane landed safely to the sound of cheers and loud applause, and my heart started again; but as soon as we were in the terminal at Oslo Airport I took Denis aside and told him never to do something like that again.

'You mean pray for everyone, boss?'

'That's right,' I said. 'At least don't do it out loud. Short of shouting "*Allahu Akbar*" and waving a Koran and a Stanley knife I can't think of anything more likely to scare the shit out of people in a plane than you praying like that, Denis.'

'Seriously, boss, I wouldn't have done it unless they were already scared shitless,' he said. 'I'm afraid it just seemed like the right thing to do at the time.'

Denis was a tall, thin, intense-looking man in his late twenties with longish hair and the beginnings of a beard or, perhaps, just the end of a near-futile attempt to grow one; if you'd dribbled some milk on his stubble the cat could have licked it off. He was dark, with eyes like mahogany and a nose you could have hooked a boat with. If Zlatan had a nerdy little brother then he was probably the image of Denis Abayev.

'I understand that, Denis. But if you must pray, then please do it silently. I think you'll find that the airlines don't much like it when people start thinking that God can do what the pilot can usually manage on his own. In fact, I'm quite sure they don't; and neither do I. Don't do anything religious near my players again. Understood? Not unless we're a goal down at the Nou Camp. Got that?'

'But it was the hand of God that saved us, boss. Surely you can see that.'

'Bollocks.' Bekim Develi, who was standing behind us, had overheard Denis.

'It was the will of Allah,' insisted Denis.

'What?' exclaimed Bekim. 'I don't believe it. He's a fucking jihadi. A pie-head.'

'Bekim,' I said. 'Shut the fuck up.'

But the Russian was still pumped full of adrenalin after our narrow escape – I know I was; he pushed past me and jabbed a forefinger on Denis's shoulder.

'Listen, friend,' he said, 'by the same token it was the will of your Allah that put us in fear of our lives in the first place. That's the trouble with you people; you're quite happy for your friend Allah to take the credit when things go right, but you don't seem to want to blame him for anything when things go wrong.'

'Please don't blaspheme like that,' Denis said quietly. 'And I'm not a jihadi. But I am a Muslim. So what?'

'I thought you were English,' said Bekim. 'Denis. What kind of name is that for a pie-head?'

'I am English,' Denis explained patiently. 'But my parents are from the Republic of Ingushetia.'

'Shit, that's all we need,' said Bekim. 'He's an *arabskiy* – a fucking LKN.'

I later learned that an LKN was an abbreviation and one of the derogatory terms that Russians used to describe anyone from their southern and probably Muslim republics. 'Shut up, Bekim,' I said.

'You know, being a Muslim doesn't make me a terrorist,' said Denis.

'That's a matter of opinion. Listen, friend, I tell you now.

I know you're the team nutritionist. But don't ever give me any of your halal meat. I love all animals. I don't want to eat any animal that had its throat cut in the name of God. Fuck that. I only want meat from a humanely killed animal, okay?'

'Why would I do that? I'm not a bloody fanatic.'

'That's what you say now. But it was your lot who killed all those kids in Beslan.'

'Those were Ossetians,' said Denis.

'Fuck that.'

'That's enough, Bekim,' I said. 'If you say another fucking word I'll send you back to London.'

'You think I still want to go anywhere after that fucking flight?' Bekim placed a big hand on his own chest and shook his head. 'Jesus, I may never get on a plane again, boss. I used to think Denis Bergkamp was a pussy because he wouldn't fly. Now I'm not so sure.'

I'd never believed very much in fining players; you have to do it, sometimes, but it always feels a bit wet, like you're stopping a boy's pocket money. It's always better to work on the assumption that they want to play and to be part of the team and that if they don't behave and treat other people with respect, you'll take that away. Sending a man home from a training session or a match is usually a more effective punishment of last resort. That and the threat of a punch in the mouth.

I took a firm hold of the Russian's shoulders and looked him in the eye. He was a big man, with a red beard like a shovel, and a temper to match, which was why he was nicknamed the red devil. I'd seen him nut players in the mouth for doing less than I was doing now; but then I was quite prepared to nut him back.

'Just cool it, will you?' I said. 'You're still up in the air with my fucking stomach. You need to shut your mouth and calm down, Bekim. We've all had a very frightening experience and none of us is thinking straight yet. But you know something? I'm glad we went through that. It's only shit like this that makes us stronger, as a team. That means you, that means me and it means him. Yes, Denis, too. You understand me, Bekim?'

Bekim nodded.

'Now, I think you owe this man an apology.'

Bekim nodded again and, looking a little tearful, perhaps as he recognised what he had come close to losing, he shook hands with Denis and embraced him; and then, still holding Denis in his arms, the big man started to cry.

Feeling pretty satisfied with this outcome I left them to it.

CHAPTER 3

Prometheus joined the team in St Petersburg. He was a tall, muscular boy with a big smile, a shaven head, a nose as long and wide as a Zulu's shield and more diamond studs in his ears than the Queen of Sheba. He dressed like a star of gangsta rap and seemed to own more baseball caps than Babe Ruth – not an uncommon look among the lads at London City. But unlike some of our other players he showed no signs of fatigue after his World Cup; he worked hard in training, did exactly what he was told and behaved himself impeccably. He even stopped tweeting; and when he called me sir I almost forgot about my earlier reservations concerning his attitude to discipline. Besides, after the first match, I had a more pressing matter to worry about.

Dynamo St Petersburg are a relatively new team and the creation of its co-owners, Semion Mikhailov and Pushkin Kompaniya, a Russian energy giant that does everything from manufacturing huge power turbines to exporting oil and gas and, very probably, large quantities of cash. The Nyenskans Stadium, on the banks of the Neva River, is close to the Lakhta Center, the tallest skyscraper in Europe. It has a capacity of fifty thousand which, until Dynamo's older rivals, Zenit's, new stadium is finished, makes it the largest in the city. All of which makes St Petersburg sound sophisticated and modern. In reality, the roads are badly potholed, the people shockingly threadbare and all but the best hotels – of which there are perhaps three or four – are verminous.

No less verminous are a hard core of football hooligans who carry Nazi flags, give Hitler salutes, throw bananas at black players and generally cause mayhem whenever and wherever they can. Since Bekim Develi had left Dynamo St Petersburg in difficult circumstances just six months earlier I'd taken the decision not to play him in this, our first match, for fear that his presence would inflame the home fans. Plus, I figured his adductor muscles probably needed a few more days' rest. But I hardly wanted to rest our black players; that would have been giving in to intimidation, which is just what these racist bastards want. Perhaps because it was supposed to be a friendly match there were fewer monkey chants than usual and, at my request, our black players, of whom there are several, refused to be provoked. Predictably a banana was thrown onto the pitch but Gary Ferguson picked it up and ate it, which, if you've seen the condition of most fresh fruit in Russia, was brave.

The trouble, when it came, was from an unexpected quarter.

Dynamo defended well and they had one player, a centre back named Andre Sholokhov, who I made a note of for the future, but the star of the match was our own twenty-four-year-old Arab Israeli left-winger, Soltani Boumediene, who had started his career at Haifa and, like Denis Abayev, was a Muslim, albeit a fairly relaxed and secular one.

Soltani's goal, the only goal of the match, was scored just before the last minute, a brilliant swerving, dipping free kick from an almost impossible angle and something I'd seen him try in training but rarely pull off. It was what happened next that caused all the problems. Soltani ran towards the television camera and gave a four-finger salute in celebration that meant nothing to me or to almost anyone else in the stadium and, at the time, passed without incident. It was only when we came off the pitch at full time that the situation grew unpleasant.

We were in the players' tunnel on our way to the team dressing room when several members of the local OMON anti-riot police arrested Soltani and bundled him roughly into a police van. Volodya, our diminutive Russian minder, spoke to one of the policemen and was informed that the four-finger salute Soltani had made on camera was what was called a '4Rabia' – the symbol of those supporting deposed Egyptian President Mohammed Morsi and the Muslim Brotherhood, which is a banned organisation in Russia. Volodya also told us that the police had orders to take Soltani back to the Angleterre Hotel – where we were staying – to collect his things, and then drive him straight to Pulkovo International Airport from where he was to be deported immediately.

Viktor accompanied us back to the hotel and spent the next thirty minutes on the telephone to the Colonel General of Police at the Ministry of Internal Affairs in Moscow while the team waited in the lobby. The Muslim Brotherhood, so the Colonel General claimed, had approved of previous Chechen Muslim attacks in Russia, although it later transpired there was no real evidence to support this allegation. But it couldn't be denied that Soltani's Twitter account listed the following tweet: *Standing in love and soldierly Islamic brotherhood with friends and family in Tahrir Square #R4BIA and #Anticoup*. All of which meant that Vik's conversation with the Colonel General was to no avail and the deportation would go ahead as ordered.

As soon as we heard the news, the players and staff gathered outside the front of the hotel and watched as, handcuffed, Soltani Boumediene was driven away to the airport. No one said anything very much but the mood was subdued and several of the players told me they were in favour of us all following Soltani back to London on the next available plane. In view of what happened next, it might have been better if we had.

The press had got hold of the story by now and by some fluke this included BBC World, which hadn't had a scoop in two decades. Somehow they managed to persuade Bekim Develi to be interviewed about what had happened and Bekim proceeded to give the lucky reporter an even bigger story than the one he thought he was reporting.

Bekim was the only Russian in our team and took what had happened to Soltani very personally:

'As a Russian citizen,' he said, 'I feel deeply ashamed by what's happened here at the Nyenskans Stadium this afternoon. Soltani Boumediene is a friend of mine and has nothing to do with the Muslim Brotherhood. He does not support terrorism. He is one of the most democratically minded players I've ever met. How else could he have played for an Israeli football team for as long as he did? The Israelis never found cause to deport the man when he was with Haifa FC. But the Russian authorities think they know better than the Israelis. Of course this is merely typical of modern life in Russia: no one has rights and people can be arrested without trial as a result of a single phone call. And why does this happen? Because of one man who is above the law, who does what he likes, and who is accountable to no one. Everyone knows who this man is. He is Vladimir Putin, the President of Russia. He is of course just a man but I for one am fed up of Vladimir Putin behaving like he is the tsar or perhaps God himself.'

Bekim also announced that he was joining the Other Russia, an umbrella coalition of Putin's political opponents. He even suggested that Dynamo St Petersburg was affiliated with the Russian FSB – the secret police – just as Dynamo Moscow had once been a front for the old KGB.

'There are secret people in St Petersburg,' he told the BBC, 'members of the FSB who are in bed with certain businessmen who need to make their dirty money as clean as possible. A football club is a very useful way of laundering dirty money, which may of course be why these crooks started Dynamo St Petersburg in the first place. To wash their ill-gotten gains. Money that has been embezzled and stolen from the Russian people.'

All of which left Vik having to make several more calls in order to try to prevent Bekim Develi being arrested, too.

CHAPTER 4

In Moscow – the next leg of our tour – things went from bad to worse. And this time neither racists nor Russia's autocratic president had anything to do with it.

By now it was strongly suspected by almost everyone who knew anything about football that Christoph Bündchen, our young German striker, was probably gay. And in no way could Russia be described as tolerant of homosexuality, as the lead-up to the Sochi Olympics confirmed; it was not uncommon for Russian men to be beaten up on the streets of Moscow merely because they were suspected of being fond of flowers. All of which meant that as soon as Christoph touched the ball in the Arena Khimki, where Dynamo Moscow currently play their home games as they await the construction of the new VTB Arena, the crowd would wolf-whistle, make kissing noises and not a few even bared their pale, spotty backsides.

It was ugly and intimidating and while Christoph did his best to ignore it, scoring a peach of a goal that left Dynamo's otherwise brilliant keeper, Anton Shunin, looking about as agile as a Douglas fir that someone had planted in the goalmouth, I could see from the way he didn't even celebrate his goal that the crowd was getting to him. At the team captain Gary Ferguson's suggestion I took Christoph off at half time and told Bekim Develi to go and shut the crowd up with another goal; he did, twice, in the space of ten minutes.

Normally, when Bekim scored a goal at Silvertown Dock, he adopted a sort of spear-chucker stance that put me in mind of Achilles or the Spartan King Leonidas in the film *300*; sometimes he even pretended to hurl an invisible javelin at the away fans; but lately he had started biting his thumb, which left me puzzled.

'Is that some sort of Russian insult?' I asked our assistant manager, Simon Page.

'What?'

'Bekim biting his thumb like that. That's the second time he's done it today.'

Simon, who was from Yorkshire, and as blunt as a muddy tractor tyre, shook his head.

'I haven't a bloody clue,' he confessed. 'But there are so many fucking foreigners in our side that you'd have to be Desmond fucking Morris to know what the hell's going on out there sometimes, what with all these quenelles and fucking R4bias and cuckold horns. And giving people the bird, is it? In my day you flicked some bastard a V-sign when he tackled you off the ball and most referees were clever enough to look the other way. But nothing's missed these days; fucking telly sees everything. BBC's the worst for that. They love to stir the PC shit-bowl when they get a chance.'

'Thank you, Professor Laurie Taylor,' I said. 'I certainly wouldn't have missed that explanation.'

'Bekim doesn't bite his thumb when he scores,' said Ayrton Taylor, who was still recovering from his broken metatarsal and the disappointment of England's World Cup. 'He sucks it. Like Jack Wilshire.'

I hadn't seen Jack Wilshire score that many goals – certainly not for England – so I was still puzzled.

'What the fuck for?' asked Simon.

'Because of his new baby boy. It's his way of dedicating the goal to his son.'

'Fucking hell,' muttered Simon. 'You'd think a tattoo would be enough. I think I preferred the spear chucker he used to do. That looked a bit more becoming for a man. Sucking your thumb like that just makes you look like a twat.'

'I think I preferred the spear chucker, as well,' I said.

'He's stopped doing that because Prometheus said he didn't like it,' explained Ayrton. 'He said he thought it was insulting to Africans.'

'He said what?' Simon was appalled.

'Prometheus asked him to stop doing the spear chucker. He was very polite about it, to be fair.'

'Fuck him,' said Simon. 'Who's he? Just some Johnny-come-lately who's yet to prove he can hack it in English football. Bekim's the real deal.'

But the serious trouble began not on the pitch but in the dressing room after the match; and it wasn't the Dynamo supporters who caused it but one of our own players.

'Those Russkies blowing kisses, and showing us their bare arses,' said Prometheus. 'Do they think we're queer or something?'

'Forget it, son,' said Gary. 'They were just trying to needle you. To piss you off.'

'Makes a pleasant change from a banana, I'd have thought,' said Jimmy Ribbans.

'I'm not so sure about that,' said Prometheus. 'People want to call me a black bastard then that's okay. As anyone can see, I am black. And as it happens I'm a bastard, too. At least according to my mother. What's more I like bananas. But what I don't like, man, are batty boys. In my country you call someone a batty boy, that's enough to get you killed. Is it because we're an English side that they think we're queer?'

'Something like that, probably,' said Gary.

'And you're okay with that?'

'So who gives a fuck if they do think that?' said Bekim.

'I do,' said Prometheus. 'I give a very big fuck about that. In Nigeria there is a new law that says you can go to prison for fourteen years if you are married to a man.'

'My wife's married to a man,' said Ayrton Taylor. 'Last time I looked.'

'I mean one man marrying another man,' said Prometheus. 'Batty boys. Sharia law means gay people are whipped on the streets for having gay sex.'

'And you're okay with *that*?' asked Bekim.

'Sure I am. It's about the one thing that Muslims and Christians in my country can both agree on. But as it happens there are very few black Africans who are shirtlifters and bum bandits. Really, it only seems to be a problem in white countries.'

'I wish you wouldn't use these words,' said Gary. 'Live and let live, that's what I say. So why don't you zip it, sunshine, and get showered.'

'I'm just saying that it's only in big cities where this problem with batty boys seems to arise. In Africa it's not really a problem at all.'

During this exchange nobody was looking at Christoph Bündchen who was trying his best to pretend that the conversation wasn't happening, but clearly Bekim felt his acute discomfort almost as much as the young German did himself. The Russian glanced anxiously at Christoph before looking back at Prometheus.

'Where do you get your fucking ideas from?' said Bekim. 'That's the biggest load of crap I've ever heard. No gay people in Africa? Of course there are gay people in Africa.'

'Put a sock in it,' I said. 'All of you. I don't want to hear any more talk about gays in this dressing room. D'you hear?'

'I'd have thought the dressing room is where the matter needs to be discussed most of all,' said Prometheus. 'I don't want to share a bath with some homo who might touch me up or give me Aids.'

'Shut your mouth, Prometheus,' I said. 'And if you ever showboat in a match like that again I'll take you off and fine you a week's wages.'

Towards the end of the match he'd played keepy-uppy for several seconds, making an obvious chump of the defender before passing it to Bekim who'd scored. It wasn't such an egregious error in the light of the final outcome but I was desperately trying to change the subject.

'I think you're fucked up, sonny,' Bekim told Prometheus. 'You might have joined an English football team. But clearly you've yet to join civilisation.'

'That goes for you, too, Bekim,' I said. 'Put a sock in it.'

'And I think maybe you're standing up for batty boys because you're one yourself,' Prometheus told Bekim. 'Not to mention a racist. Me, uncivilised? Fuck you, Ivan.'

Bekim stood up. 'What did you say?'

'That's enough,' I said.

Prometheus stood up and faced him. 'You heard me, batty man.'

'*Ya toboi sit po gor loi,*' said Bekim, speaking Russian now. He always started speaking Russian when he got angry; he wasn't called the red devil for nothing. '*Ti menya zayebal. Dazhe ney du mai, chto mozhesh, me-njya khui nye stavit.*

32

Don't even think you can dis me like that, you fucking animal.'

'Will you two bastards behave yourselves?' shouted Simon.

By now I was standing in front of Bekim gripping his wrists, and Gary Ferguson was blocking Prometheus, but it wasn't going to stop these two powerfully built men from taking a pop at each other. Sometimes the dressing room is like that. There's too much energy, too much testosterone, too much frustration, too much mouth, too much attitude. You can't explain it except to say that shit happens. One minute they were shouting insults at each other, the next they were trying to punch each other in the face. I did my best to keep hold of Bekim's wrists but he was too strong for me, and there was a loud smack as the Russian's forearm connected with the side of the Nigerian's face and Prometheus collapsed like an overloaded coat stand. He was up again almost immediately, grabbing at the Russian's red beard and taking a swing himself. He missed and hit Jimmy Ribbans, who reeled away with blood pouring from his mouth before turning and flicking a hard jab square into the face of Prometheus.

I have to admit that there was a small part of me that was hoping some of this might knock some sense into the young Nigerian's head, but I have to admit it seemed unlikely that Prometheus was going to stop being a homophobe just because someone had punched him.

'You fucking hit me?' Prometheus yelled at Bekim as he was restrained for a second time. 'You fucking hit me?'

'You only got what's been coming for a long time, sonny,' said Bekim.

'I'll put the hex on you, batty man. You see if I don't. I know a witch doctor who'll fix your faggot arse good. I'll have you killed. I'll burn your fucking car. I'll rape your fucking wife and make her suck my cock.'

'Fuck you, *chyernozhopii*. Fuck you and the chimp that gave birth to you.'

This second exchange of insults initiated another flurry of fists and kicks.

'Cool it,' I yelled again as the rest of the team and playing staff pulled the three combatants apart. 'The next person who throws a punch is suspended. The next person who insults someone else is suspended. I mean it. I'll suspend you both without pay and then I'll fine you a week's wages; and when I'm good and ready and you've sat on the subs bench for the whole season I'll fucking sack you both. I'll make sure that every club in Europe knows what a pair of twats you are so no one will buy you. I'll make sure you never work in football again. Is that clear?'

'And if that's not enough I'll beat the living shit out of you both,' said Simon. 'And I'm not talking about the handbags we just had in here.' There were few who would have doubted he could have done it, too. There was nothing bluff about the big Yorkshireman's threat. When he took his glasses off and removed his upper plate he was one of the most frightening men in the game. 'It'd be worth the sack just to beat some sense into your fucking heads. I've never heard the like. Call yourself team mates? I've seen Old Firm matches that were more cordial than what just happened in here. What a pair of cunts.'

CHAPTER 5

In spite of my terrifying experience aboard an Aeroflot Ilyushin jet, I dislike flying in helicopters even more than in Aeroflot Ilyushin jets, and this included Vik's luxurious Sikorsky-92 which, following the team's return from Russia, left London's Battersea Heliport one Tuesday morning in August, bound for Paris. Aboard were Viktor Sokolnikov, City chairman Phil Hobday and me.

Whenever I fly in a chopper all I can think about is not the time we're saving but Matthew Harding, the millionaire vice-president of Chelsea FC who was tragically killed in a helicopter back in 1996 after an away game with Bolton Wanderers. It's an old wives' tale that helicopters are any less aerodynamic than an airplane – a helicopter's blades will continue to rotate, despite a stalled engine (or so Vik told me); but it's a fact that helicopters do more dangerous things than planes, such as take-off and land in closely built-up areas, and what's more in parts of the world with very poor weather. To be killed in a helicopter would be bad enough, I think; but to be killed in somewhere like Bolton really would be bloody awful.

We were flying to Paris to have lunch with Kojo Ironsi who, as well as being the agent and manager of Prometheus Adenuga, was the owner of the famous King Shark Football

Academy in Accra, Ghana. Vik already owned a stake in King Shark, but Kojo – who was rumoured to be short of cash – was looking to sell him a bigger share and I was along to help City's billionaire club-owner evaluate just how much the academy might be worth. Or at least that's what I thought. I had player reports from an independent African-based coach, which I was supposed to bring into play if Vik decided that Kojo was asking too much.

All of the players who had come through the King Shark Academy – including Prometheus and several other big names – had a contractual relationship with KSA which meant that they and the football clubs who acquired them paid a percentage of their transfer fees and wages to KSA. Kojo claimed to be a philanthropist and that what he did was to the advantage of talented young Africans who might otherwise struggle to find opportunities to play for the top clubs, but from the outside it looked like these players were indentured to Kojo and KSA for the whole of their professional lives.

'How much is too much to pay?' I asked Vik somewhere over the English Channel.

'Whatever he's asking is too much,' said Phil. 'That's a given here. It'll be like trying to buy a carpet from a Moroccan snake.'

'There are good players on that list, though,' said Vik. 'Wouldn't you agree, Scott?'

'Certainly. Several of the top Africans now playing in Europe seem to have come through KSA. At least that's what Kojo claims.'

'According to my lawyers all of those contracts are watertight,' said Vik. 'And you can't argue with all of the juicy fees from top clubs that continue to be paid into KSA's Swiss bank accounts. I already own a twenty-five per cent stake in KSA. My guess is he'll want me to take more equity, up to forty-nine per cent of the company. For which I might be prepared to pay him ten million euros. Of course, he'll ask twice that. Maybe more.'

'Then it beats me why you need me along,' I said.

'I don't want to wake up one morning and find myself accused of part-owning a company that's trafficking in children. You might ask him about that.'

'I can easily do that. I have quite a few doubts there myself.'

'Assuming I'm satisfied and I do decide I want to buy an increased share, I'll need you to help Kojo see sense, from the perspective of someone who knows players and their real value on the market. And one player in particular: our young friend Prometheus. We should use the boy's on-going disciplinary problems as a stick with which to beat Kojo down. Understood?'

'I think so. You want me to tell this guy that Prometheus has been disappointing, so far.'

'Which is true,' said Phil. 'Frankly, he's a pain in the arse. I've spent more time dealing with that stupid bloody car of his than I care to remember.'

Almost as soon as Prometheus had arrived in London he had spent four hundred grand on a Mercedes McLaren SLR, but there was just one problem, which the Met had quickly identified: the Nigerian didn't actually have a driving licence. This hadn't been a problem in Monaco where he only ever drove from one end of the mile-long principality to the other, and rarely faster than thirty miles per hour – frankly, it isn't possible to go much faster than that in Monaco. But things were different in London. Prometheus was already facing losing a licence he didn't yet have, and the confiscation of his car, which was something of a record at any London football club.

'He's a good player though,' said Vik. 'I'm sure Scott can get the best out of him.'

'I wish I shared your confidence, Vik.'

'How are things with him and Bekim?' he asked.

'Not much better than since we were in Russia. Prometheus has kept his mouth shut in training. But several times he's re-tweeted some Catholic bishop of Nigeria who's publicly thanked the country's president, Goodluck Jonathan, for making a law against homosexuality. Which doesn't help the situation.'

'As long as Bekim doesn't follow Prometheus on Twitter then I can't see what the problem is,' said Vik. 'You can only be offended by someone tweeting something if you're following them, right?'

'The problem, Vik,' said Phil, 'is that whatever Prometheus re-tweets gets picked up by the tabloids. Which, like anyone else, Bekim does read. Not to mention Christoph Bündchen. And of course they haven't forgotten what happened to the German boy in Brazil. The newspapers are trying to stir up trouble like they always do.'

'*Is* he gay?' Phil was asking me, but it was Vik who answered him.

'Of course he's gay,' he said. 'Not only that but he's living with a man.'

'To be fair,' I said, 'Harry Koenig is just a flatmate. A German player from QPR reserves that the liaison officer fixed up for Christoph to live with, so that he wouldn't get lonely.'

'Maybe so. But actually Harry is gay, too.'

'How do you know that?' I asked.

'Because I had them drone-hacked.'

'Drone-hacked? What's that?'

'I own a military drone company,' said Vik, matter-of-factly. 'The smallest ones are about the size of a pigeon. You just have a drone follow someone around, sit on their window ledge, record what you want. They can recharge themselves on telephone lines.' Vik was unapologetic about this. 'I've drone-hacked all our players. I'm not paying the kind of money I pay to our players without knowing everything about them I can. Relax, Scott, it's not illegal.'

'Well, if it isn't, it sounds like it ought to be.'

I wondered if I'd been drone-hacked; it made phone-hacking sound very old-fashioned.

'I've also had them all given psychiatric evaluations. Did you know that three of our players are psychopaths?'

'Which ones?' I asked.

'That would be telling. Don't look so shocked, gentlemen. Psychopaths can be useful, especially in sport. It doesn't mean they're going to kill someone.' He chuckled. 'At least not right away.'

I wondered if he was unconsciously referring to our helicopter pilot, who was circling our improbably small landing site like a bee considering the charms of an unusual yellow flower with an H-shaped stigma. I closed my eyes and waited for us to put down.

'Cheer up, Scott,' said Vik. 'It might never happen.'

'I sincerely hope not.'

CHAPTER 6

A small fleet of black Range Rovers was waiting on the helipad to take us into the centre of the city. Twenty minutes later we were speeding up the Champs-Élysées. It all looked very different from the last time I'd been there in May 2013 when, as a guest of David Beckham, I'd visited Paris to see PSG's win over Lyon, which secured them their first French title since 1994. The day after there had been a riot as the celebrations turned ugly and I'd hurried back to the George V Hotel to escape the sting of tear gas. Shops were looted, cars burnt out and passers-by threatened with violence, with thirty people injured, including three police officers. Whoever thinks English fans don't know how to behave should have been there to see it. There's nothing the French can learn from us when it comes to having a riot, which is probably why there are always so many police in Paris. Paris has more cops than Nazi Germany.

The restaurant was Taillevent, in rue Lamennais. It was a rather cool austere room of light oak and beige-painted walls, and catered to those who wouldn't dream of spending anything less than one hundred and fifty euros on lunch. They greeted Vik as if he had climbed down from a golden elephant with a diamond on its forehead. Kojo Ironsi was already there as was Vik's other guest, an American hedge fund manager called Cooper Lybrand.

I liked Kojo more than I expected to; I liked Cooper Lybrand not at all. Kojo talked about his boys and his clients. Cooper only talked about the chimps and muppets he'd taken advantage of in one business deal after another. But both of them were after the same thing: Vik's cash.

Kojo was smartly dressed and politely spoken, with a well-deserved reputation for looking after his KSA clients. He had an easy laugh and hands as big as shovels; once a goalkeeper for Inter Milan and an African Footballer of the Year it was easy to see why players had confidence in him. It was said there was nothing he wouldn't do for some of his bigger-name clients on the grounds that if they couldn't play they couldn't pay. Rumour was he'd once taken the rap for a very famous striker in the English Premier League who'd almost been caught in possession of cocaine.

It wasn't long before he'd introduced the subject of the developing feud between Bekim Develi and his own client, Prometheus.

'Why don't you sort those two out?' he asked Vik. 'Speak to your friend, Bekim. They ought to shake hands and make up, don't you agree? For the sake of the team.'

'Certainly they should. But I leave that kind of thing to Scott here. He is the manager, after all.'

'I should have thought the solution to the problem was obvious,' said Kojo. 'I mean how you can get them to shake hands.'

'I'm glad you think so,' I said. 'Right now they just want to shake each other by the throat. But I welcome any suggestions you might have for how we might establish diplomatic relations.'

'Easy. Sell Christoph Bündchen. Buy another striker.'

I smiled and shook my head. 'I don't think so, Mr Ironsi.

Christoph is a very talented young footballer. One of our best players. With an extremely bright future.'

Kojo was a tall man with a bald head and an easy smile. He shrugged. 'Well then, can *you* speak to Bekim Develi? Reason with him so that good sense can prevail.'

'I'll reason with Bekim if you can reason with Prometheus. To be honest with you, that's not so easy. What's more, the boy's attitude to gay people is going to make him very unpopular with the media, if it hasn't done so already. I think it would be best if he was to make some sort of statement expressing regret for any offence caused to the LGBT community.'

'I agree,' said Kojo. 'I'll call him this afternoon, before I fly to Russia. See what I can do.'

'I'm very glad to hear it. If all that happens I'm sure I can get those two to shake hands.'

'I'm glad that's settled,' said Kojo.

I wasn't so sure it was but I was willing to give Kojo's talents as a fixer the benefit of the doubt.

'You're going to Russia?' asked Vik.

'Yes. It's possible that someone there might want to take a stake in King Shark, if you don't.'

If Kojo thought this was a way of sharpening Vik's interest, then Vik certainly didn't show it.

'If you're going into partnership with Russians then you'd best be careful,' was all the Ukrainian said. 'Some of those redfellas are pretty tough customers.'

'Not particularly ethical, eh?'

'That's right.'

'Thanks for the tip. I certainly appreciate it.'

'Since you mentioned ethics,' said Vik, 'Scott has got some reservations about the very existence of African football academies. Isn't that right, Scott?'

I shrugged. 'I suppose I do, really. I think we both know that there are many unlicensed football academies in Africa.'

'In Accra alone there are at least five hundred such places,' said Kojo, 'most of them run by unscrupulous men with no experience of the game. Nearly all demand fees from the children's parents who take them out of school to enable them to concentrate on football full time. The idea being that having a professional footballer in the family – at least one who plays in Europe – is the equivalent of winning the lottery. Some even sell their family homes in order to pay these fees. Or to pay for boys to come to Europe for a trial with a big club. Which of course never transpires. Yes, it's very sad what happens.'

'I don't say that yours is one of these unlicensed academies,' I said carefully. 'But I do ask myself about the way KSA players are contractually tied to you for life.'

Kojo shook his head. 'A certain amount of due diligence will satisfy you that the King Shark Academy is one of the best academies in Africa. The Confederation of African Football has described the KSA as a model for all football academies. We take no fees, and we offer a proper education alongside football, which is why we have almost a million applications a year from all over the continent for, perhaps, just twenty-five places. So we can afford to take only the most promising boys. But since we ask no fees it seems only fair that we should expect some return on our investment. And to be fair I don't think you will hear complaints from anyone in the game today who is a product of KSA. Or for that matter any of the three or four academies like it. In fact, Manchester United has just bought a controlling stake in Fortune FC, one of our rival establishments in South Africa. Dutch clubs like Ajax and Feyenoord are looking to do the same in West Africa. The question is, can London City afford *not* to own a half share in King Shark? You know my price, Vik, and you know what the opportunity amounts to. The future of professional football is in Africa. Those boys are hungry for success. Hungrier than anyone in Europe. Almost by definition.'

Vik nodded. 'Thank you for your candour, Kojo. And I'll certainly think about what you've said. Listen, I've an idea. We have a Champions League match against Olympiacos in Piraeus on 19 August. Why don't you and your wife come out to Greece as my guest? You can stay on *The Lady Ruslana*, in the harbour at Piraeus. I'll give you my decision then.'

'Thanks, I'd love to,' said Kojo.

'You, too, Cooper.'

'Thanks, Vik,' said Cooper. 'I'd like that, too. I've never been to a soccer match.'

Kojo, Phil and I left Vik with Cooper Lybrand to discuss an investment in his hedge fund, which Vik's company was considering. Like many of the people that Vik knew, Cooper was the sort of man I'd have been happy never to see again, especially since he had used the dread word: 'soccer'. I love America. I even love Americans. But whenever they call football 'soccer' I want to kill them. And Cooper Lybrand was no exception to this rule.

CHAPTER 7

I'd eaten far too much and I was glad to be outside.

It was a beautiful warm afternoon and Phil and I strolled up to the Champs-Élysées where he went into Louis Vuitton and bought a bag for his wife, or perhaps his girlfriend. With Phil you could never tell: he was as smooth as the Hermès silk handkerchief that was spilling out of his pocket.

'Kojo's a complete crook, of course,' said Phil. 'But he's quite right. We can't afford not to take a controlling interest in his academy.'

'I thought he was only willing to sell enough to make Vik his equal partner.'

'Maybe, but that's not the way Vik likes to do business. He likes to own things.'

'So I'd noticed.'

'He likes to be in control.'

I let that one go. I was beginning to see just how much control Vik wanted to have, over everything.

'Kojo's also right about Christoph,' said Phil. 'I'm afraid we shall have to sell him before the end of August, Scott. It's the quickest way to patch up this stupid disagreement between Bekim and Prometheus.'

'Sell him? You're joking, aren't you, Phil? The boy is a future star.'

'We both know that the only reason Bekim is so persistent about this matter is because he knows that Christoph is gay. Which is perfectly understandable. It's the comradely thing to do – stick up for a younger player, like that. Admirable, even. Just not practical. We have to make sure that those two get on at all costs.'

'Why not sell Prometheus? He's the one who's caused all this trouble. He's the one with the attitude problem. Mark my words, if it's not this it'll be something else. You said yourself that he's a pain in the arse. All that business with the car. It's just the beginning. There'll be a lot more of that from Prometheus. He makes Mario Balotelli look like the teacher's pet from the Vienna Boys' Choir. Vik should never have bought him.'

'I, for one, should be very happy never to see him again. But we can't sell him, Scott. Vik wouldn't hear of it. And so early on after we bought him people would smell a rat. We'd be lucky to get half of what that boy is worth. Christoph is a different story. After some of the goals he's scored for us and for Germany we stand a very good chance of selling him for a considerable profit. Don't forget we paid FC Augsburg just four million for him last summer. If we can make the sale before his homosexuality becomes known we might get twenty million quid for him. Perhaps more. Given the situation in the dressing room I don't think you'll have too much problem persuading the boy to put in for a transfer. Good for him, and good business for us. Actually this could work out quite well, really. It gives us a real chance of meeting UEFA's Financial Fair Play guidelines.'

'I assumed that Vik's accountants would find a way around those. After all, everyone else's accountants have done, so far.'

'Until we've maximised the club's commercial revenue with

sponsorship deals,' said Phil, 'we're going to need to make a profit of ten million pounds over the next two years, just to meet the UEFA guidelines. Or, put another way, those same guidelines will allow us to lose thirty-seven million pounds over the next three seasons.'

'But we didn't really need another striker; not with Ayrton and Christoph on the team; surely not buying Prometheus would have helped.'

'You might think so. But under the terms of Vik's arrangement with Kojo, Prometheus was free.'

'What terms? I don't understand. Either we bought him or we didn't.'

'We did and we didn't, you might say. Officially yes, unofficially no. He's what you might call a sale-or-return. A loan deal.'

'It all sounds suspiciously like the kind of third-party ownership arrangement that was banned by the Premier League in 2008.'

'Banned, yes; enforceable, no. Threepios are actually quite common in Europe and South America. And because they are it's easy enough for a good accountant to get round them, even an English accountant. On paper Prometheus cost us £22 million from which Kojo might ordinarily have taken a fee of £11 million. But Kojo already owed Vik £10 million so his actual fee was just £1 million; and because the balance of the transfer fee is actually performance-related then all Vik has to pay is a hundred grand a week to Prometheus, from which Kojo takes fifty per cent. In fact we pay the boy even less than that because a quarter of Kojo's cut comes back to Vik anyway.' Phil shrugged. 'So you see Prometheus costs us hardly anything at all. It's actually a little more complicated than that, but in essence that's how it works. The real reason Vik bought Prometheus was because he was as cheap as chips.'

'So, that's how we beat Barcelona to his signature.'

'Precisely.'

I swallowed uncomfortably. The temptation to tell Vik and Phil to fuck off was strong, and getting stronger by the day. Somewhere in my ears I could hear Bastian Hoehling back in Berlin: 'In a year or two's time, when Scott here has been fired by his current master, he'll be managing a German club.' I was beginning to think it might not take that long.

'What's up?' asked Phil. 'You look a bit sick.'

'The beautiful game,' I grunted, bitterly. 'Christ, that's a laugh. Sometimes it seems like the only thing that's straight in the game are the fucking lines on the pitch. Everything else seems as bent as Pakistani cricket.'

'Football is a business, like any other, Scott, especially off the field. And in the boardroom there's nothing beautiful about it.' He shook his head. 'It's a game, but it's a zero-sum game, with buyers and sellers, supply and demand, and profits and losses.'

'Just don't tell the fans,' I said. 'Look, Phil, *I* can just about forgive you for being a slippery fucking bastard. But they certainly won't.'

CHAPTER 8

'Peter,' said Bekim. 'After Peter the Great. As a child he had red hair, too.'

'He's another red devil, all right,' I said. 'Just like his father.'

I was staring at a picture on an iPhone of a very small baby with red hair.

'Yes, Peter is very lovely,' I added quickly, for fear that the Russian might take offence at my calling him a devil. 'You must be very proud, Bekim.'

'Very proud,' he said. 'To be a father is to be blessed, I think. Perhaps one day, Scott, you too will have children. I hope so. I'd like you to feel the way I feel now.'

I nodded. 'Perhaps I will. But at the present moment I've got my hands full looking out for my players. I really don't know where I'd find the time to be a father.'

'It's true,' he said. 'You are a bit like our father. Only not as old.'

'I'm very glad to hear it,' I said.

'Sometimes we're like little children. This stupid business between me and Prometheus. You must think we're idiots.'

'I don't think you're an idiot, Bekim. Let me make that quite clear. I don't hold you responsible for what happened at all.'

Bekim nodded.

'And now the German boy is leaving,' he said. 'I can't believe it. It's such a pity. Because I think Christoph's one of the most talented players at this football club.'

'Agreed,' I said. 'I was very much opposed to selling him; and told Vik and Phil that a sale would be over my dead body. But now he's asked for a transfer.'

'Can't you talk him out of it?'

'Believe me, I've tried. But his mind is made up.'

'You know why he wants to go, of course.'

'Yes.'

'Because of that stupid gay-hating bastard, Prometheus.'

'Yes. I know.'

'My agent has asked me to make the peace with him. To shake his hand.'

'I know. And will you?'

'I suppose so. If Christoph is determined to leave the club then I can see no reason not to. For the good of the club, you understand. Not because I like this man. I don't like him at all. Or what's in his heart. But I think the feeling is mutual, don't you? He hates me, too.'

I let that one go. There seemed little point in discussing an enmity I hoped was now over.

'Prometheus has tweeted his regrets about offending gay people,' I said. 'Which is helpful to this whole affair, don't you agree?'

'I just wish that it would make Christoph change his mind.'

'It doesn't look like it, though. Anyway, we're not short of offers for the boy so far. Barcelona has offered thirty million quid.'

'Then he should take it. Barca is a great club. And Gerardo Martino is a great manager. Although it's still difficult to be a *maricón* in some parts of Spain.'

We were at my flat in Chelsea. Bekim lived not very far away, in St Leonard's Terrace, in a beautiful, seven-million-pound nineteenth-century Grade II listed building set back behind a private carriage drive with fine views over the rolling lawns of Burton's Court. Inside there were red walls and red furniture as might have been expected from a man nicknamed the red devil; even the flowers in the vases were red.

'Did you come by to talk about Christoph, Bekim? Or was there something else?'

'There was something else, yes. I hear you're going to Greece. To check out Olympiacos, in Piraeus.'

'Yes. The Berlin side Hertha FC has a pre-season friendly with them. They've invited me along to see them play. I'm also going to check out their number two goalkeeper, Willie Nixon. Now that Didier Cassell is out of the game we're going to need to buy a reserve goalkeeper, and soon. If Kenny Traynor gets injured we're screwed.'

Didier Cassell had been City's first choice goalkeeper until an accident had forced him to quit the game; he'd hit his head on the post in a match against Tottenham the previous January. He wasn't long out of hospital after making an only partial recovery.

'You know I have a house in Greece,' said Bekim. 'On the island of Paros. As a matter of fact it's not so very far from the place in Turkey where I'm originally from. Before we moved to Russia.'

I shook my head. 'I didn't know that.'

'I bought it when I was playing for Olympiacos. It's just a thirty-minute hop on a plane from Athens. Very quiet. When I'm there the local people leave me alone – in fact, I think they really don't know who I am at all – you can't imagine how wonderful that is. I go there several times a year. By the way, you must stay at the Grande Bretagne Hotel; it's the best hotel in Athens. And while you're there – yes, this is the reason I came here today – you must meet this woman I know and take her to dinner. Her name is Valentina and she is the most beautiful woman in all Athens, although originally she's from Russia. I'll text you her number and email. Seriously, Scott. You won't be disappointed. She makes every other woman look quite ordinary and she's great company. You should take her to Spondi, the best restaurant in Athens. I know she likes it there.'

I knew Bekim's reputation as a ladies' man. Before meeting his current girlfriend and the mother of his child, Alex, he'd had a string of glamorous girlfriends, including the Storm supermodel Tomyris, and the singer Hattie Shepsut. In an interview with GQ magazine he'd admitted to sleeping with a thousand women, which, if it was true, meant he was basing his opinion of his friend Valentina on a fairly significant statistical sample and was perhaps something that needed to be taken seriously.

He took out his iPhone again. 'Here,' he said. 'I've got a picture of her on my phone.'

He swiped his way through several photographs until he found the one he was looking for.

'There. What do you think?'

'I'm going to watch a football match, not check out the local hookers.'

'She's not a hooker. Believe me, you won't forgive yourself if you don't at least take her out to dinner. I wouldn't recommend her to you if I didn't think you'd find her the most delightful company. She's very sophisticated, very well read. And she knows about art. Every time I see her I learn something new.'

'If she's so sophisticated, how come she knows a sod like you?'

'Does it matter? Look at her, man. She's properly fit. A face to launch a thousand ships, eh?' Bekim grinned. 'Sometimes I read this phrase in the newspapers. Writers talk about a country's best-kept secret. Well, she's Attica's best kept secret.'

'Attica?'

'The historical region that encompasses Athens.'

'I see. So, when I'm in Attica, I'm going to look up Helen of Troy, is that it?'

Bekim grinned. 'That's right. It couldn't do you any harm, could it?'

'No, I suppose not.'

'Life is more than just football, Scott. Even for you. You have to remember that.'

'You're right. I forget that sometimes. But with two games a week – three if we get through the play-offs for the Champions League – there's not much time for life.'

'In this game of ours, it's easy to forget everything else.'

'Yes. It is.'

'I'll tell her you're coming, shall I? And that you're staying at the Grande Bretagne on Syntagma Square. The rooftop bar and restaurant has the best view in all of Athens. Take her there before you go to Spondi and put the bill on my tab.'

'Why not?'

I agreed just to humour him, as if he really was a child, and then forgot all about it.

'But be careful, Scott,' he added, 'and I don't mean with lovely Valentina. There are two teams in Attica. Olympiacos and Panathinaikos, and they are bitter rivals. They hate each other. They are eternal enemies, Greeks say. Sometimes when these two sides play they don't even finish the game because the crowd violence is so bad. When you go to Olympiacos, keep away from Gate 7, okay? Those are the real hard-core fans. Very violent. Like Glasgow Rangers and Celtic. Only worse.' Bekim grinned. 'You raise your eyebrows. I can see you don't believe me. Yes, I know you're part Scottish and you think that nothing could be as bad as the Old Firm. But what you have to remember is that half of all the men in Greece under the age of thirty are unemployed; and where there is such mass unemployment, you're always going to have bad hooligans. Same as Weimar Germany. Same as South America. There is also match fixing because there is a football mafia. To be an honest sportsman is difficult in Greece, Scott. And if you are interviewed by a newspaper just remember to keep your mouth shut. Because the people who talk about this kind of thing get hurt. Just be careful, is all. Please be careful, Scott.'

There was real concern in Bekim's voice and, after he'd gone, I wondered if this might actually have been the real reason that he'd come to see me. That would have been typical. In many ways he was a very secretive man, as I later discovered.

CHAPTER 9

I flew to Athens the night before Hertha's match with Olympiacos. It was past 1 a.m. when a taxi dropped me in front of the Grande Bretagne Hotel, which was every bit as impressive as Bekim had told me it would be. The huge marble-floored lobby was spacious, elegant and above all, wonderfully cool; outside, in Syntagma Square, the temperature was still in the mid-twenties. The people inside the hotel were well-dressed and looked prosperous and it was easy to forget that Greece was a country with 26 per cent unemployment and a debt that amounted to 175 per cent of its total economy; or that Syntagma Square had seen some of the worst riots in Europe as the Greek parliament voted on austerity measures that would, it was hoped, satisfy the European central bank and, in particular, the Germans who were contributing most of the money that was needed to bail them out. All that seemed like a long way off as I walked towards the front desk.

The receptionist on duty checked me in and then handed me an envelope that had been in my pigeonhole. Inside the envelope was a handwritten message on scented stationery:

Bekim told me what time you were arriving in Athens and since I was in the vicinity of your hotel I thought I would stop by and say hello. I am in Alexander's

Bar, behind the front desk. I shall wait until 2.15 a.m.
Valentina (00.55)
PS, If you're too tired from your journey, I shall quite
understand, but please send this note back via the
bellboy.

I went up to my room with the porter and pondered my
next move. I wasn't particularly tired: Athens is two hours
ahead of London time and having scorned the plastic in-flight
meal, I was now hungry for something more substantial
than a handful of peanuts from the minibar. Greeks tend to
eat quite late in the evening and I was sure I could still get
some dinner, but I felt less certain about eating on my own;
an attractive dining companion would surely be a pleasant
alternative to my iPad. So I cleaned my teeth, changed my
shirt and went back downstairs to find her.

In spite of what Bekim had said I still suspected that I
was about to meet a hooker. For one thing there was his
own priapic reputation to consider, for another there was
her nationality. I don't know why so many Russian women
become hookers but they do; I think they feel it's the only
thing that will get them out of Russia. After our pre-season
tour I never wanted to see the country again either. I've never
minded the company of prostitutes – after you've been in the
nick for something you didn't do, you learn never to judge
anyone – it's just sleeping with them I object to. It doesn't
make me better than Bekim – or any of the other guys in
football who succumb to all the temptations made possible
by a hundred grand a week. I was just older and perhaps a
little wiser and, truth be told, just a little less pussy-hungry
than I used to be. You get older, your sleep matters more
than what's laughingly called your libido.

Alexander's Bar looked like something out of an old Hollywood movie. The marble counter was about thirty feet long, with proper bar stools for some serious, lost weekend drinking, and more bottles than a bonded warehouse. Behind the bar was a tapestry of a man in a chariot I assumed was Alexander the Great; some attendants were carrying a Greek urn beside his chariot that looked a lot like the FA Cup which probably explained why everyone looked so happy.

It wasn't hard to spot Valentina: she was the one in the grey armchair with legs up to her armpits, coated tweed minidress and Louboutin high heels. Louboutins are easy to identify; I only knew the minidress was a three-grand Balmain because I liked to shop online and it was a rare month when I didn't buy something for Louise on Net-a-Porter. The blonde hair held in a loose chignon gave Valentina a regal air. If she was a hooker she wasn't the kind who was about to give a discount for cash.

Seeing me she stood up, smiled a xenon headlight smile, took my hand in hers and shook it; her grip was surprisingly strong. I glanced around in case anyone else had recognised me as quickly as Valentina had done. You can't be too careful these days; anyone with a mobile phone is Big Brother.

'I recognised you from the picture Bekim sent me,' she said.

I resisted the immediate temptation to pay her a dumb compliment; usually, when you meet a really beautiful woman, all you can really hope to do is try to keep your tongue in your mouth. I remembered Bekim showing me her picture on his iPhone. But it was hard to connect something as ubiquitous and ordinary as the image on someone's phone with the living goddess standing on front of me. All my earlier thoughts of dinner were now gone; I don't think I could even have spelt the word 'appetite'.

We sat down and she waved the barman towards us; he came over immediately, as if he'd been watching her, too. Even Alexander the Great was having a hard job keeping his embroidered eyes off her. I ordered a brandy, which was stupid because it doesn't agree with me, but that's what she was drinking and at that particular moment it seemed imperative that we should agree about everything.

'I live not far from here,' she explained.

'I had no idea that Mount Olympus was so close,' I said.

She smiled. 'You're thinking of Thessaloniki.'

'No,' I said. 'I'm thinking of Greek mythology.' I was having a hard job to restrain myself from pouring yet more sugar in her ear; she probably heard that kind of shit all the time.

'Have you eaten?'

I shook my head.

'There's still time to go to dinner,' she said. 'Spondi is a five-minute cab ride from here. It's the best restaurant in Athens.'

The waiter returned with the brandies.

'Or we could eat here. The roof garden restaurant has the best view in Athens.'

'The roof garden sounds just fine,' I said.

We took our drinks upstairs to the roof garden restaurant. The rocky plateau that dominated the city and which was home to the Parthenon, now floodlit, is one of the most spectacular sights in the world, especially at night, from the rooftop of the Grande Bretagne, when you're having dinner with someone who looks like one of the major deities who were once worshipped there; but I kept that one to myself because it's not every woman who likes that much cheese. And frankly, after a couple of minutes, I barely even noticed the Acropolis was there at all. We ordered dinner. I don't remember what I ate. I don't remember anything except everything about her. For once Bekim had not exaggerated; I don't think I'd ever met a more beautiful woman. If she'd had any skill with a football I'd have offered to marry her right there and then.

'What time is the game tomorrow?' she asked.

'Seven forty-five.'

'And how were you planning on spending the day?'

'I thought I would see the sights.'

'It would be my pleasure to show you the city,' she said. 'Besides, there's something I want you to see.'

'Oh?'

'It's a surprise. Why don't I come back here at eleven and pick you up?'

'Sounds like a plan.'

Sweet dreams, she said as we parted on the steps of the hotel and I knew that this was almost a given. I don't usually remember my dreams but this time I was kind of hoping I would, especially if Valentina featured in any of them.

CHAPTER 10

The following morning I caught a taxi down to Glyfada, just south of Athens, to have breakfast with Bastian Hoehling and the Hertha team at their hotel, a sixties-style high-rise close to the beach but perhaps a little too close to the main road north to Piraeus. Apparently Olympiacos supporters had spent all night driving past the hotel with car horns blaring to prevent the Berlin side from sleeping. The Hertha players looked exhausted; and several of them were also suffering from a severe bout of food poisoning. Bastian and the club doctor had considered summoning the police to investigate, but it was hard to see what the police could have done beyond telling them the Greek for lavatory.

'You really think it was deliberate?' I asked, choosing now to ignore the omelette that the hotel waiter had brought to our table.

Bastian, who was feeling unwell himself, shrugged. 'I don't know, but we seem to be the only ones in the hotel who've gone down with whatever this thing is. There's a party of local car salesman having a conference here that seems to be quite all right.'

'That certainly clinches it, I'd have thought.'

'If this is a friendly,' he said, 'I can't imagine what it's going to be like when you play these guys in the Champions

League. You'd better make sure you bring your own chef and nutritionist, not to mention your own doctor.'

'Our present team doctor is just about to take up a new position in Qatar.'

'Then you'd better find a new one. And quick.'

'Perhaps you're right.'

'I wouldn't put anything past these guys,' said Bastian. 'The newspapers seem to be treating this whole competition like Greece versus Germany. The Olympiacos manager, Hristos Trikoupis, referred to us as Hitler's boys.'

'That surprises me,' I said. 'Hristos was at Southampton with me. He's a decent guy.'

'Nothing surprises me,' said Bastian. 'Not after Thessaloniki: the bastards threw rocks and bottles at our goalkeeper. We had to warm up in a corner of the pitch well away from the crowd. I couldn't feel less popular in this country if my name was Himmler not Hoehling. So much for the home of democracy.'

'You're Germans, Bastian. You must be used to that kind of thing by now. The first thing you learn in the professional game: there's no such thing as a friendly, especially when there are Germans involved. There's just war and total war.'

Because I was speaking German I used the phrase *totaler Krieg* famously coined by Josef Goebbels during the Second World War, and some of the Hertha team glanced nervously my way when they heard it, the way Berliners do when they hear that kind of Nazi shit.

'If I were you, Bastian,' I added, 'I would play tonight's game the same way. It's the only language these Greek guys understand and respect. You remember the rest of what was written on Goebbels's banner? *Totaler Krieg – kürzester Krieg.* Total war – shortest war.'

'I think maybe you're right, Scott. We should fucking run over them. Kick the bastards off the pitch.'

I nodded. 'Before they do the same to you.'

After breakfast I went back to the Grande Bretagne Hotel, in the centre of Athens. At exactly eleven o'clock I was sitting on a large, biscuit-coloured ottoman in the hotel lobby, texting Simon Page about our first game of the new Premier League season, an away match against newly promoted Leicester City, on 16 August. Simon was just about to take an eight o'clock training session at Hangman's Wood and I was telling him not to make it a hard one as I was concerned that some of our players were still tired after their World Cup duties, not to mention our disastrous and entirely unnecessary tour of Russia.

'Did you sleep well?'

I glanced up to find Valentina standing in front of me. She was wearing a plain white shirt, tight blue J-Brand jeans, comfortable snakeskin sandals and black acetate Wayfarers. I stood up and we shook hands.

'Yes, thanks.'

'Ready?' she said.

'Where are we going?'

'To see someone you know.'

We took a taxi to the National Archaeological Museum, a five-minute drive north from the hotel. The museum was designed like a Greek temple, a little less run-down than the one on top of the Acropolis, but not far off being a ruin; and like many public buildings in Greece – and quite a few private ones – it was covered in graffiti. Beggars drifted around the unkempt park that was laid out in front of the entrance like so many stray cats and dogs and I handed one old man all of the coins that were in my trouser pocket.

'It's something I always do back home,' I said, seeing Valentina's sceptical look. 'For luck. You can't get any if you don't give any. Football's cruel, sometimes very cruel. You have to make sure the capricious gods of football are properly appeased. You shouldn't even be in the game unless you're an optimist and to be an optimist means you cannot be a cynic. You have to believe in people.'

'You don't strike me as the superstitious sort, Scott.'

'It's not superstition,' I said. 'It's just pragmatic to take a balanced approach to good luck and to careful preparation. It's actually the clever thing to do. Luck has a way of favouring the clever.'

'We'll see, won't we?'

'Oh, I think Hertha will win. In fact, I'm sure of it.'

'Is that because you're half German?'

'No. It's because I'm clever. And because I believe in *totaler Krieg*. Football that takes no prisoners.'

Inside the museum were the treasures of ancient Greece, including the famous gold mask of Agamemnon that Bastian Hoehling had mentioned, back in Berlin. It looked like something made by a child out of gold foil from a chocolate bar. But it was another treasure that Valentina had brought me to see. As soon as I saw it I gasped out loud. This was a life-size bronze statue of Zeus that many years before had been recovered from the sea. What struck me most was not the rendering of motion and human anatomy but the head of Zeus, with its shovel beard and cornrow haircut.

'My God,' I exclaimed, 'it's Bekim.'

'Yes.' Valentina laughed delightedly. 'He could have modelled for this bronze,' she said. 'Couldn't he?'

'Even the way he stands,' I said, 'mid-stride, in the act of throwing a spear or hurling a thunderbolt, that's exactly the way Bekim always celebrates scoring a goal. Or nearly always.'

'I thought it would appeal to you.'

'Does he know?'

'Does he know?' Valentina laughed again. 'Of course he does. It's his secret. He grew his beard so he would look like this statue; and when he scores he always thinks of Zeus.' She shrugged. 'I'm not sure he actually thinks he's a god, but I wouldn't be at all surprised.'

I walked around the statue several times, grinning like an idiot as I pictured Bekim adopting this same pose.

And yet, perfect as the statue was, there was something wrong with it, too. The more I looked at it the more it seemed that the outstretched left hand was wrong, that it was attached to an arm several inches too long; later on, I bought a postcard and measured the approximate length of the arm, and realized that the hand would actually have reached down as far as the god's knee. Had the sculptor got it wrong? Or had the original display angle of the figure required an extended arm to avoid a foreshortened look? It was hard to be sure but to my critical eye, the hand of God appeared to be reaching just a little too far.

She nodded. 'I've been thinking about what you said earlier, about being lucky.'

'Yes? What about it?'

'I think you're going to be lucky,' she said, and taking my hand she squeezed it, meaningfully.

'When?'

'Tonight.'

I lifted her hand to my mouth and kissed it. The nails were short, but immaculately varnished, while the skin on the palm of her hand was like soft leather, which struck me as strange. 'And I thought you were talking about the football.'

'Who says I'm not?'

I smiled. 'I suppose that means you're coming to the game.'

CHAPTER 11

The Karaiskakis Stadium, in the old port of Piraeus, looked like a half-sized version of the Emirates, in London, with a capacity of just 33,000. The impression was bolstered by the fact that Emirates Air was an Olympiacos team sponsor and because of their red and white strip, although the shirt was more like Sunderland's than Arsenal's. The match was not well attended, but it was enthusiastically supported. The Gate 7 boys, or Legend as they liked to call themselves, made their calculatedly intimidating presence very loudly felt behind the German goal. They had bare chests and big drums and a sort of director of operations who kept his back to the pitch for almost the whole game so that he might properly orchestrate the obscene songs and low, Neanderthal chants. From time to time bright red flares were let off in the stadium but these were ignored by the police and security, who kept a low profile to the point of near invisibility. I was surprised at how unwilling the local police were to interfere in what took place inside the ground; they were forbidden to use the security cameras inside the stadium to identify potential troublemakers, a result of some obscure privacy law.

Valentina and I were seated in a VIP area immediately behind the German dugout. At eighty euros a ticket in a country where the average monthly income was just six hundred and fifty euros you might have expected these mostly middle-aged and elderly supporters to be better behaved. Not a bit of it. I don't speak any Greek but thanks to Valentina I was soon able to distinguish and understand words that would certainly have had the users of their Anglo-Saxon equivalents quickly removed from almost any ground in England. Words like *arápis* (nigger), *afrikanós migás* (coon), *maïmoú* (monkey), *melitzána* (eggplant), *píthikos* (ape).

The man in the seat beside me must have been in his late sixties but every so often he would leave off smoking his Cohiba cigar or eating his cardamom seeds, leap onto the top of wall, bend over the edge of the German dugout and bellow, '*Germaniká malakas*,' at the unfortunate Bastian Hoehling.

'I keep on hearing that phrase, *Germaniká malakas*,' I said to Valentina. 'I get the *Germaniká* part. But what does *malakas* mean?'

'It means wanker,' she said. 'That's a very popular word in Greece. You can't get by without it.'

I found it hard to condemn the man for his choice of language. As I'd discovered, there are worse things to be called at a Greek football match. It's a passionate game and stupid people watch it just as often as clever ones; you can encourage respect in football, and I was all in favour of that, but you can't stop people from being ignorant.

The match was keenly contested but the Greeks seemed genuinely surprised that the Berliners should have come at them so aggressively. Although Olympiacos competed strongly for every ball, they were quickly behind thanks to a superb header from Hertha's talented Adrian Ramos that made me understand why Borussia Dortmund were so keen to secure the Colombian's services after their own top striker,

Robert Lewandowski, had left to join Bayern Munich in the early summer. But oddly the Gate 7 boys didn't even pause; indeed, they carried on shouting as if the German goal had not happened.

Meanwhile, trying my best to ignore the crowd, I made tactical notes in an ancient Filofax I always used for this kind of thing:

> *Greeks weak at defending set-pieces. Muscular and fit-looking, but small of stature which makes them less equipped to compete in the air when good crosses swing in. Bekim Develi or Prometheus can give anyone problems if they get the right service. Develi tends to drift naturally to the right and this should probably be encouraged as Miguel Torres, likely Olympiacos's right left-back, plays more like a right-winger than a defender – especially if Hernán Pérez isn't playing, which he wasn't today. If Develi does find space, or drags out Sambou Yatabaré (most likely centre half), he is more than capable of putting Jimmy Ribbans through. I hope our referee will be better than the one here today. I wouldn't be surprised if the penalty earned him a small bonus.*

'It's ages since I went to a football match,' said Valentina as the Gate 7 hooligans, with arms extended in Nazi salutes, started another nasty song: '*Pósoi Evraíoi ékanes aério símera?*' – How many Jews did you gas today?

'I can quite understand why.' I glanced around. 'You're about the only woman here, as far as I can see.'

With Hertha's number one keeper, Thomas Kraft, feeling too ill to play, I had a good chance to assess their second string keeper, Willie Nixon, an American. I've always admired

American goalkeepers: they're usually great athletes and Nixon was no exception, pulling off a couple of saves that kept his team in the game. He was young, too.

A few minutes later, I thought I would have a chance to see what Nixon was really made of when Olympiacos won a penalty so unbelievable it looked as if the referee had pulled it out of a top hat. The German defender, Peter Pekarik, brought down one of the Greek players just outside the box – except that the big-screen replay showed he was at least a foot away when Kyriakos dropped to the ground, apparently suffering from a fractured tibia. That was bad enough but the improbably named Pelé, who took the Greek penalty kick, put the ball so high over the crossbar he must have thought he was Jonny Wilkinson; his effort was greeted with a loud and derisive chorus of boos and whistles and, around me, several shouts of *ilíthia maïmoú* (stupid monkey).

I used to wonder exactly why Socrates had felt obliged to drink hemlock; I guess he must have missed a penalty for Olympiacos, too.

By half time the Berliners were two goals up; they scored again immediately after the break, and that was how the game finished: 3–0. Hertha had won all three games of its Greek peninsular tour and the Schliemann Cup, put up by Hertha's sponsors, was won by the Germans themselves, which seemed a very German outcome. But it wasn't Willie Nixon the goalkeeper who had impressed me most, but Hertha's charismatic team captain, Hörst Daxenberger. Strong as a racehorse and 193 centimetres tall, he looked like a blond Patrick Vieira.

The Schliemann trophy ceremony, like the earlier warm-up, took place in a corner of the field far removed from Greek insults and missiles and Valentina and I joined Hertha for the muted champagne celebration in the players' tunnel. In spite of the futility of the competition in which they had taken part I was glad for the German lads; they'd had a pretty tough time of it one way or another and were glad to be going back to Berlin. I almost envied Bastian Hoehling returning to a football club that was owned and managed in such an egalitarian way. You might say that Germans have had quite enough of autocrats and dictators. But they couldn't get enough of Valentina who, it turned out, spoke quite good German; glasses of champagne in their hands, they were round her like wasps at a picnic. She had that effect on men. Perhaps she wasn't the most beautiful woman in Greece but she was certainly one of the most attractive.

An hour later we returned to the hotel in a limo kindly provided by Hertha FC.

A little to my surprise no money was ever asked for and none offered; and it was only after I arrived back in London that I learned how my night with Valentina owed nothing to good luck and everything to Bekim Develi, when the red-haired Russian let slip that he had paid five thousand euros for me to have Valentina, in advance of me going to Athens.

CHAPTER 12

It was a warm Saturday afternoon in August when we arrived at the King Power Stadium in Leicester for our first match of the new season. Just to the west of the main entrance single sculls were going up and down the River Soar like hi-tech swans. Full of misplaced optimism at being in the Premiership once again, Leicester's supporters were noisy but hospitable and a far cry from the kind of hostile welcome we could expect when we travelled to Greece the following week. I wondered just how good-humoured these fans would remain when they were faced with the cost of supporting their club at away matches in London and Manchester. It was high time that TV companies like Sky and BT started to insist on ring-fencing a proportion of the money paid to the Premiership to subsidise ticket prices: there's nothing worse for your armchair fan than seeing empty terraces.

I still hadn't resolved our goalkeeping crisis – we still needed to replace Didier Cassell – and if there was one player of Pearson's I really envied it was Leicester goalie Kasper Schmeichel, son of the more famous Peter. Kasper had played for Manchester City and for Leeds United before joining the Foxes in 2011; he'd also played for his country, Denmark, on several occasions, and I had the feeling that, like his father, who had played for Man U until the age of thirty-nine, Kasper's best years as a keeper still lay ahead of him. With fourteen days left before the summer transfer window closed I was seriously considering asking Viktor Sokolnikov if we could make an offer for the twenty-seven-year-old Dane.

Any doubts about Schmeichel's ability were swiftly squashed when, just five minutes into the game, we were awarded a penalty. Prometheus powered the ball straight for the bottom right corner of the net, and how Schmeichel got a hand to it seemed nothing short of miraculous. That would have been impressive enough but, having batted the ball straight back at Prometheus, Schmeichel then launched himself across the whole width of the goalmouth, to the very opposite corner, where he just managed to prevent the Nigerian scoring on the rebound. Almost as important as the Dane's agility was the way he cleverly managed to psych out our man even before he took the penalty kick. After Prometheus had placed the ball on the spot, Schmeichel had calmly walked out of his goal, picked the ball up, dried it on his shirt, and then cheekily tossed it back at the African, who angrily waved Schmeichel back into his goal. Some referees might have given a keeper a yellow card for doing that, but on the first day of the season? It looked like mind games and if it was, it worked.

A team's overall psychology is never helped when you miss a penalty; and this was dealt a further knock when our captain, Gary Ferguson, scored an own goal which left the home side one-up at half time. Shit like that happens; you learn to shrug it off. What worried me more was seeing Prometheus berate his own team captain. I'm no lip-reader but I think Gary gave the kid a few choice words back, although how he restrained himself from smacking the boy in the mouth is beyond me. Generally speaking, when you're the captain a smack and a curse tends to work better than just a curse.

'Forget it, Gary,' I told him, loudly, in the dressing room. 'This is football not fucking Quidditch. If you're a defender and you're doing your job properly there are always going to be occasions when you're going to score an own goal. It's just statistics. A ball you'd clear from your box, nine times out of ten, will go the wrong way because this isn't snooker and there are no perfect angles. You got your knee to it; and it came off your knee, that's all. Nobody with a brain in his head could blame you for a goal like that.'

I looked at Prometheus who was busy changing his pillar-box red Puma evoPOWER boots for a pair that looked like they'd been made from an old tabloid newspaper: *Why Always Puma?* said the red headline on the side of the boot.

'Are you finished pissing around with those fucking boots?'

At last I'd caught his eye.

'Everyone in football makes mistakes,' I said. 'It's that kind of game. If nobody made those mistakes the game would be as boring as England's group for Euro 2016. And there's nothing more boring than that. What I don't ever want to see is anyone else in this team thinking that they have the right to apportion blame. Especially when they're not without fault themselves. Finding fault, chewing ears off, arse-kicking and handing out bollockings – that's my fucking job. Or Gary's when the match is in actual progress. And if I ever see it happening in this team again I will bite the guilty party on the arse like a fucking hyena. I like my job and I don't need anyone's help to say what needs to be said. Clear?'

'Why you pickin' on me, man?' asked Prometheus. 'I didn't do nuthin'. All I said to the cap here was that those big, hairy, white Scotsman's knees of his was goin' to lose us the game if he wasn't bloody careful. It was like, a joke, y'know?'

It was no wonder Fergie threw boots around the dressing room; at that particular moment I wanted to take that ridiculous boot out of his hand and ram it down his throat. Gary was muttering, 'Shut the fuck up,' while Bekim was shaking his head, silently. Others just turned away as if they didn't want to see what was going to happen next.

I smiled. 'It was like a joke, yes, except that it wasn't fucking funny. You don't make jokes to your colleagues when they just scored an own goal for the simple reason that they might be feeling a little sensitive. It's never funny when someone scores an own goal, unless it's the other team that scores it. I shouldn't have to spell this out for you, sonny – and don't ever interrupt me again or I'll tell Gary to shove one of his big, hairy, white Scotsman's knees into your small, hairless, black Nigerian balls. That is if you've got any balls. Understood?'

Prometheus said nothing which seemed to indicate that he'd got the message. I rocked back on my heels for a moment and glanced around the dressing room. There was no one else I felt deserved any particular criticism; Leicester had ridden their luck, and that was all there was to it.

'It's a fact,' I said, 'that on the first weekend of the football season, newly promoted clubs often do well. They fancy their chances against one of the big boys. And why not, when they finished the season with – what did they get in the Championship – eighty-six points? They deserve to be in the Premiership and if they can't give us a good game today, when they're all fit and rested because only a couple of them saw any international duty, they never will. I guarantee if you play this same team at the end of the season you'll walk all over them. So, don't be surprised if their tails are up today.

But keep your shape, and keep the ball; pass it around. Toblerone football, like we practised in training. Let them lose themselves in the magic triangles. If necessary, make them so fucking impatient to get on and win the game that they come to you. That's when you open them up.'

It ought to have worked out that way, too. But it didn't. We lost 3–1, following a brace of goals from Jamie Vardy and David Nugent who looked as potent a strike partnership in a newly promoted side as I'd seen in a long time. At 4.40 p.m. Leicester went top, on goal difference.

London City was third from bottom.

CHAPTER 13

PA (Performance Analysis) software is so useful. I often wonder what managers used to do without a tablet; edited footage of a game's key events on an iPad are an essential tool for any manager and I like to view these with just two or three players on the coach home because I don't always want to do it in front of the whole team. In my experience a player who makes a mistake doesn't need to see it endlessly replayed on a screen in front of his mates to know that he fucked up. I know from experience how humiliating that can be. But this time I sent the pictures from my iPad up to the TV screens on the coach so that everyone could listen in to what I had to say. Sometimes a little humiliation is good for the soul.

'Let me have your attention here,' I said into the microphone as our coach drove away from the King Power Stadium. 'Shut the fuck up, okay? What are you talking about? How good they were? How quick that guy Vardy was? How good their goalkeeper was? How like his daddy he is? Fuck you. That isn't why we lost today.

'Over there, to the west of the King Power Stadium, is the River Soar. And I'm now pointing right for all those of you who don't seem to know your right from your left, or your arse from your elbow. It used to be said that after the Battle of Bosworth in 1485, the victorious Tudor side threw the body of King Richard III into that shitty-looking river. Although obviously that can't be true as they recently found his skeleton underneath a car park in the centre of Leicester. I guess the poor bastard lost his ticket and couldn't get out. Either way I'm sure a lot of you now know what old Richard must have felt like. I know I do. It's no fun losing in fucking Leicester city.

'Everything happens for a reason and sometimes the reason isn't always immediately bleeding obvious because small actions can have large consequences. It's what scientists call chaos theory. Or what lawyers and philosophers call causality or causation. Historians do this shit too: the cause of the First World War isn't just that the Archduke Ferdinand got himself shot in Sarajevo; that was only the straw that broke the camel's back. You see? When you play professional football you get a fucking education. Something some of you are clearly in need of. I'm here to help. That's right, guys. You want to know stuff: come to me.

'Being a football manager is a bit like what those other guys do; it's even a bit like being a detective – if what we're doing here on the coach is looking at the already stinking corpse of that match, in search of an explanation for why we lost. Because it's never as obvious as you think. Let me show you *why* we lost. We can forget about the own goal. Like I said before, that was just unlucky. So, instead, we'll take a closer look at the first goal they scored; James Vardy's goal. The guy's always full of running and when he plays he takes a lot of the pressure off Nugent. Gary found Vardy a handful today; so did all of our back four. Vardy's a striker but to me he looks more natural on the left, where the goal came from. Frankly, he was playing out of position, which is why you found it hard to mark him. It was a good goal and he struck it well, but he scored because none of you thought he had the room to shoot. We know different now. I've said it before and I'll say it again: the longer you stand off a striker like that the more tempo he builds, and the more tempo he builds the more chance he has of scoring. Don't try to match him turn for turn. You won't, because he's thinking faster than your body can move. There's nothing faster than the speed of thought. So, keep your eye on the ball and commit to the tackle and, if necessary, a trip to an orthopaedic surgeon.

'But if we reverse the action and go and look at what happens a whole minute or two before he scores Kenny rolls the ball out to Gary, who passes to Kwame, who can't think of anything else to do with it but square it John – only there's just not enough pace on the ball for that to happen safely, which means John is stretching for it, and his pass to Zénobe isn't going to get there in a month of Sky Super Sundays. Nugent intercepts the ball and chips to Vardy, who turns one way, and then the other, and then again, with everyone standing off him like he's got the fucking plague, until the moment when you all think he hasn't got room for a shot, and you relax a little; only it turns out he has got just enough room, and he scores.

'Looked at again, before Vardy even had a sniff of the ball, what I'm saying is this: Kenny, before you rolled that ball out, did you not see that Prometheus had acres of space in midfield? You've got better eyesight than a Comanche Indian; you're also one of the most accurate kickers in the game; you could easily have reached him, so why did you roll out? Rolling out like that only works when their striker has got concrete in his boots; this one was like a fucking whippet today. No, wait, let me finish.

'And, Kwame, this isn't pass the parcel we're playing here. When you're making a pass you have to think what the other guy is going to do with the ball when he gets it. That's fine if you're trying to create space, but here you don't know what to do with the space you already have.

'And John, you're not expecting the ball – that much is obvious – but why not? Every one of you, at every moment of the game, should be expecting the ball. A – E – T – F – B. Always expect the fucking ball. But here, because neither of you is thinking on the ball, you're just trying to get rid of it, so the pass to poor Zénobe is nothing short of fucking desperate.

'Remember what I said before the match, what I say before every match: creative thinking on the ball means knowing what you're going to do with it before you even get it. And that means reading the other players around you like they're chess pieces, seeing the space around them and what they can do with it better than they can. R – T – P and F – T – S. Read the players and find the space.'

I waited another second before springing my surprise.

'But here's the real reason why we fucked up and Jamie Vardy scored. And for this we go right back to when Kenny rolls out to Kwame. A second before, he looks up and sees Prometheus in all that space and he's clearly going to punt that ball up to him. He's found the player in space. But then he changes his mind. Why? Because with his Comanche Indian eyesight he reads the player and sees that Prometheus has his back to him; when I freeze the action and move the picture you can see it for yourself; there's Prometheus. See? There's the back of his head, and it's pointed at Kenny for how many seconds – let's see now. Jesus Christ, it's ten seconds.

'A – E – T – F – B. Always expect the fucking ball. *Always* expect the fucking ball. But, Prometheus, you're watching – I

79

don't know what the fuck you're watching for ten seconds – but it isn't the fucking ball. So what, asks Kenny, would be the point of firing the ball up the pitch to him? He's enjoying the sunshine. Thinking about his pet hyena. That's why Kenny rolls out. Because he doesn't have a choice. And that, gentlemen, is the true story of Jamie Vardy's fucking goal.'

Prometheus stood up in his seat, arms flapping like an angry penguin. His face was quivering so much that one of the diamond studs in his ears was flashing like a little flashlight.

'It's my fault that he scored?' said Prometheus. 'I was miles away from that geezer when he scored.'

'Maybe you weren't listening to what I was saying. Maybe there's something wrong with your ears as well as the muscles in your neck.'

'Why is it always me who fucks up in this team?'

'You tell me, sonny.'

Prometheus shook his head.

'It's not fair,' he bleated.

'You're right. It's not fair to the men on this team that you should let them down so badly. I don't know what else to call it when you're not even looking to see where the ball is going. A – E – T – F – B. Always expect the fucking ball. But maybe you're different, kid. Maybe you're the one person on this planet who has developed eyes in the back of your head. Maybe you can watch the ball while seeming to look the other way. That's a good trick although I can't see how that helps your team mates. Because that's what this game is all about.'

Prometheus sat down heavily and punched the seat in front of him which, fortunately, was unoccupied.

It's a two-hour drive from Leicester City to east London. I waited until we were halfway down the M11, just north of

Harlow, before I left my seat and went and sat down beside him. There was a strong smell of aftershave and liniment. On his iPad Air a game of Angry Birds was in progress. He was wearing in-ear Monster Beats and the bright red cables that trailed from them looked like blood streaming out of his skull and down his neck. Certainly the big bass punch seemed loud enough to have made anyone's ears bleed.

Seeing me he sighed, plucked the in-ear buds from his lugs like a weary adolescent and waited silently for the one-on-one bollocking he assumed was coming.

'You know,' I said, 'life is full of conflict. That's what keeps it interesting. People have bust-ups all the time and because football is a high-intensity game, the bust-ups are pretty intense, too. When I was playing at Arsenal I remember our team captain, Patrick Vieira – big guy – taking me by the scruff of the neck and telling me that if I didn't shape up he was going to sort me out. He meant it, too. He was from Senegal and in Senegal you don't make that kind of threat unless you mean it. Frankly, he was the best player in his position I ever met. I mean, he had so much talent – much more than I ever had. But I was scared of him, too, so I did sort myself out. It was just what I needed at that time. Someone like him, who was prepared to talk to me like my big brother and point out my defects.

'But the important thing in life is that we learn from our mistakes and get on with each other afterwards. That's what a team is all about. It's like a big family, all brothers. Lots of testosterone and lots of fighting. Only we fight and then we forgive each other's errors and mistakes. Because we're brothers.

'When we were back in Russia you said your mother never knew your father. You referred to yourself as a black bastard; I'm guessing that you actually believe that. I think that it's your default position. You think you're bad. Maybe you think you'll be a better player if you're even badder. But I'm here to tell you that this isn't the best way. Not for a true professional. Now I've been lucky. My dad is still around. But Patrick wasn't so lucky. His parents divorced when he was very young and Patrick never saw the guy again. But Patrick didn't let it affect him. I tell you, I never met a guy with more discipline than Patrick. Hugely talented, like I said, but even more disciplined.

'You're one of the most naturally gifted young players I've ever seen. And I don't think you're nearly as bad as you seem to think you are. You can be a great player at any club you choose to go to. But talent isn't enough. You're going to need discipline to make the most of your talent, just like Patrick Vieira. Like we all do, frankly.'

I nodded. 'Here endeth the lesson.'

'Thanks, boss.'

I held out my hand.

Prometheus grinned and shook it.

'A – E – T – F – B,' he said.

I grinned back at him. 'Always expect the fucking ball. Damn right.'

CHAPTER 14

On the following Monday morning the team flew to Athens where the temperature was as high as when I'd been there. Tempers were even higher: the teachers were on strike; the courts were on strike; even the local doctors were on strike. Fortunately we'd brought our new quack from London. His name was Chapman O'Hara and he'd stepped up from the ranks of City's growing medical department to take charge of the team's health issues. We'd also brought Denis Abayev, the team nutritionist, and our travel manager, Peter Scriven, had hired a special team of local chefs who were all Panathinaikos fans and therefore bitter rivals of Olympiacos, because I certainly hadn't forgotten what had happened to Hertha at their team hotel in Glyfada. The last thing I wanted close to a Champions League match was a team brought down with food poisoning.

The hotel Astir Palace occupied a beautiful, pine-dotted peninsula in Vouliagmeni, the heart of the Athenian Riviera, about half an hour south of the city of Athens. Peter Scriven had chosen well: the only access was along a private road with a security barrier and constantly manned guardhouse which meant that any over-enthusiastic Olympiacos fans bent on driving by our hotel with car horns blaring couldn't get near the place. The hotel itself had seen better days, perhaps. It lacked the class of the Grande Bretagne, not to mention the historic views; food was simple and the bar poorly stocked; and although numerous, the service staff were slow and indifferent. The facilities were, however, ideal for accommodating a bunch of grown-up adolescents: an individual bungalow for each player; a large and well-equipped Technogym; a nice swimming pool that overlooked the sea; several private beaches. There was even a five-a-side football pitch. In front of the hotel were a heliport and a small marina where Vik's helicopter and yacht-tender were already in constant attendance of *The Lady Ruslana* which was anchored in the sea about a hundred metres offshore, and facing the hotel. It looked like a small pearly-white island.

Naturally the team were all banned from heading into Athens or Glyfada to explore the city's night life. And I'd slipped the guys manning the hotel security barrier some cash to make sure that not one female was allowed to come and visit any of the team. But before dinner I took Bekim Develi and Gary Ferguson into Piraeus where a press conference had been arranged in the media centre at the Karaiskakis Stadium. At first most of the difficult questions came from the English press which was not so surprising after the 3–1 defeat at Leicester; then the Greeks chipped in with their own agenda and the situation became a little more complicated when someone asked why Germany seemed to have it in for Greece.

'What do you mean?'

'Why do the Germans hate us?'

Choosing to ignore the behaviour of the Greek football fans towards the lads in Hertha FC, I said that I didn't think it was true that Germans hated Greeks.

'On the contrary,' I added. 'I have lots of German friends who love Greece.'

'Then why are the Germans so hell-bent on crucifying us for a loan from the European Central bank? We're on our knees already. But now they seem to want us to crawl on our bellies for the central bank's loan package.'

I shook my head and said that I wasn't in Piraeus to answer questions about politics and ducking an honest answer like that would probably have been fine. But then Bekim – Russian-bred, but born in Turkey, the ancient enemy of Greece – jumped in and things really deteriorated when he proceeded to make some less than diplomatic remarks about public spending and how perhaps Greece really didn't need to have the largest army in Europe. The fact that he was speaking in fluent Greek only made things worse because we could hardly spin what he said and blame his answer on Ellie, our translator. Asked if Bekim was worried about a big demonstration planned for the night of the game outside the parliament, Bekim said it was about time some of the demonstrators put their energies into digging Greece out of the hole it was in; better still, they could start cleaning the city which, in his opinion, badly needed some TLC.

'You've been living beyond your means for almost twenty years,' he added, in English, for the benefit of our newspapers. 'It's about time you paid your bill.'

Several Greek reporters stood up and angrily denounced Bekim; and at this point Ellie advised that it might be best if we cut short the conference.

In the car back to the hotel I cursed myself for bringing Bekim to the press conference in the first place.

'Once was unfortunate,' I said. 'But twice looks like downright fucking carelessness on my part.'

'Sorry, boss,' he said. 'I didn't mean to cause you any problems.'

'What devil possessed you?' I asked. 'Christ, their fans are bad enough when it's a friendly. You've made sure that tomorrow's going to be extra rough.'

'It was going to be rough anyway,' he insisted. 'You know that and I know that. Their supporters are bastards and nothing I said is going to make the way they behave any worse. And look, I didn't tell them anything they don't already know.'

'We're a football team,' I said, 'not a lobby group. Not content with pissing off the Russians when we were in Russia, you now seem to have managed to do the same with the Greeks. What is it with you?'

'I love this country,' he said. 'I hate seeing what's happening here. Greece is such a beautiful country, and it's getting fucked in the ass by a bunch of anarchists and communists.'

He shrugged and looked out of the window at the graffiti-covered walls of the streets we were driving through, the many abandoned shops and offices, the piles of uncollected rubbish, the potholed roads, the beggars and the squeegee guys at the traffic lights and on the grass verges at the roadsides. Greece might have been a beautiful country but Athens was ugly.

'I love it,' he whispered. 'I really do.'

'Fuckin' beats me why,' said Gary. 'Look at the state of it. Full of fuckin' jakey bastards and spongers on the social. I'd never have believed it if I hadn't seen it with my own eyes. Christ, I've seen some fucking squallies in my time. But Athens – Jesus, Bekim. Call this a capital city? I reckon Toxteth is in a better state than fucking Athens.'

'Hey, boss.' Bekim laughed. 'I've got a good idea. After the match, why don't you let Gary do the press conference, on his own.'

CHAPTER 15

The following morning, before breakfast and while the temperatures were still in the low twenties, we had a light training session. Apilion was located in Koropi, a twenty-minute drive north from the hotel, and on a wide expanse of very rural land at the foot of Mount Hymettus which towers over three thousand feet over the eastern boundary of the city of Athens. In antiquity there was a sanctuary to Zeus on the summit; these days there's just a television transmitter, a military base and a view of Athens that's only beaten by the one out of a passenger jet's window.

A green flag with a white shamrock declared that Apilion was the training ground of Panathinaikos FC. Surrounded with olive and almond trees, fig-bearing cacti, wild orchids and flocks of ragged sheep and goats, the air was clear and clean after the congested atmosphere of Piraeus and downtown Athens. From time to time one of the local farmers fired a gun at some birds, scattering them to the wind like a handful of seeds and startling our more metropolitan-minded players. In spite of that and the presence of several journalists camped alongside the carefully screened perimeter fence, Apilion felt like an oasis of calm. Nothing was too much trouble for the people from Panathinaikos; as the other half of the city's Old Firm all they cared about was that they might assist us in sticking it to their oldest rival, Olympiacos. Football is like that. Your enemy is my friend. It's not enough that your own team succeeds; any victory is always enhanced by a rival's failure, no matter who they're playing. Panathinaikos would have supported a team of Waffen-SS if they beat the red and white of Olympiacos.

'Fucking hell,' exclaimed Simon Page, staring up at the flag as we got off the bus. 'Are we in bloody Ireland, or what?' He clapped his hands and shouted at the players. 'Hurry up and get on that training ground, and watch where you're putting your feet in case you tread on a four-leaf clover. I've a feeling we're going to need all the luck we can get here.'

I could hardly argue with him since our new team doctor, O'Hara, was returning to London after his wife had been taken ill. Antonis Venizelos, our liaison from Panathinaikos, was still trying to find us a replacement doctor in case of emergency.

'The doctors' strike doesn't make this easy,' he explained a little later on. 'Even doctors who don't work in the public sector are reluctant to work today. Operations have been cancelled. Patients sent home. But don't worry, Mr Manson. The Karaiskakis Stadium is right next to the Metropolitan private hospital. Even though it is in Piraeus this is a very good hospital.'

He lit a menthol cigarette with the hairiest hands I'd ever seen and stared up at Mount Hymettus.

'I have some other news that might have an important bearing on the game.'

'Oh? What's that?'

'I just heard on the telephone,' he said. 'The Olympiacos team were paid their wages today, and in full. This will put them in a very good mood. So tonight I think they will try very hard.'

'When do they normally get paid?'

'I mean that it might be two or three months since those American bastards last got their wages.'

'Bloody hell,' I said.

Antonis grinned and popped some seeds in his mouth that he chewed like gum and which sweetened his breath. He was a handsome man with an Alan Hansen-sized scar on his forehead that travelled across his left eyebrow like tiny tramlines, lending him a vaguely Cyclopean aspect.

'Exactly. It's hell for everyone right now. At least it is in Greece, my friend. Nothing that happens in this country is like anywhere else. Remember that. Your boys get paid at the end of the month, just like other people in England, yes? But in Greece, the end of the month and payday might be several more weeks in coming – perhaps longer – if you know what I mean. Our university teachers haven't been paid in months.'

'I can't see our lot going without their wages for very long,' I said as Simon and some of the City players returned to the team coach. 'They're coin-operated; like everyone else in the English game right now.'

'You got that right,' Simon grumbled.

'Sometimes,' said Antonis, 'the people in this country work for months without pay only to find out at the end of it that their employer has gone out of business and doesn't have the money to pay them. In Greece getting paid what you're supposed to be paid is like winning the lottery.'

'But why do you call Olympiacos American bastards?' I asked.

Antonis sneered. 'Because American navy warships used to dock in the port of Piraeus. You see, when their sailors came ashore they used to sleep with the whores of Piraeus. Which is why we call them the sons of whores or American bastards, although quite frankly all of the women of Piraeus are whores. It's not just us. Everybody in Greece hates Olympiacos. They're a bunch of cheats and liars.' He shrugged. 'Believe me, my friends, they say much worse things about us.'

'That's a little hard to believe,' said Simon. 'But what *do* they say?'

Antonis shook his head as if what anyone from Olympiacos thought could be of no real account. 'They think that because we're Athenians we think we're better than them. That we're snobs. Which of course we are when it comes to Olympiacos. They call us *lagoi* – rabbits, because they think we run away from a fight. Which is just wishful thinking on their part. That is no surprise. They're just a bunch of *gavroi*.' He smiled. 'This a kind of very small fish you find in the harbour that eats the shit from all the ships docked there.'

Simon and I exchanged a look of surprise at the level of enmity from a man who otherwise seemed perfectly civilised and urbane. I knew what the big, xenophobic Yorkshireman was thinking just by looking at his face. Since we'd arrived in Athens, he'd said it often enough: 'Bloody Greeks. They're their own worst enemies. I might feel sorry for the bastards if they weren't so fucking bolshie.'

'Good footballers, though,' was what Simon actually said now. 'How many times have they won the Greek League? Thirty-six times, is it? And the Greek Cup twenty-three times? And they'd have won the league this year again, if they hadn't been docked all those points by the Hellenic Football Federation. Which is how we come to be playing them now, in the play-offs.'

Antonis pulled a face and looked away. 'You can teach anyone to play football,' he said simply. 'Even a *malakas* from Piraeus. That is why they have to cheat. You might be the favourites for this match but don't underestimate the capacity of the *gavroi* for low tricks. Tonight, it won't just be eleven men you are playing. It will be sixteen, if you include the five match officials. And the crowd, of course; don't forget the so-called Legend. They're like another player, and a vicious one. There will be nothing friendly about the place you're going tonight. And you can forget all your English ideas of the beautiful game. There's no beautiful game in Greece. There's no beautiful anything. There's just – anger.' He nodded. 'In Greece it's the one thing of which we have an unlimited supply.'

CHAPTER 16

Whenever you see a football manager pacing up and down his technical area shouting encouragement and making signs at his team like a demented on-course bookmaker it makes for compelling television – the cameras love to see 'the pressure written on the manager's face'. In truth, the players shouldn't even be looking at the manager but at the ball and, above the noise of the crowd, they seldom hear anything but the ref's whistle, unless you're Sam Allardyce. Most of the time you patrol your lonely ten yards of space only for the sake of appearances; your suffering shows that you care. Plus, it's harder to sack a manager who is soaked to the skin, with mud on the knees of his Armani suit, not to mention some gob on his back.

Occupying a technical area in Piraeus is even more intimidating with thirty thousand baying Greeks at your back, and frankly it could be something more lethal than a bit of gob that's coming your way. Just ask the Greek assistant referee who got hit with a flying chair during the Greek Cup in 2011. Venturing from the dugout at the Karaiskakis on a sweltering hot night in August, it felt like I was leaving the safety of the walls of Troy to duel with Achilles; not recommended. But at Olympiacos it isn't just crazy fans you have to watch out for: in 2010, despite winning the game 2–1 following some questionable refereeing decisions, the Olympiacos owner, Evangelos Marinakis, attacked Panathinaikos players Djibril Cissé and Georgios Karagounis at the end of the game.

So after just five minutes of the first half, when Bekim Develi scored from twenty-five yards with a shot that looked like a diagram from an artillery officer's trajectory chart, I wasn't that surprised that I should be hit on the shoulder with a banana as I threw off my linen jacket which was already damp with sweat and ran to the edge of my technical area to interrupt his thumb-sucking tribute to his new baby son, with a simple handshake.

It had all started so nicely, too, with both teams trooping calmly to the centre of the field, hand in hand with twenty-two local mascot children to the tune of Handel's 'Zadok the Priest'. What could be more calculated to create an inspiring image of UEFA's family values and the honourable pursuit of victory in competitive sport? Even so, I sometimes wonder if any of these European football sides are aware that Handel's music was composed especially for the anointing of an *English* king. This was followed by a minute's near silence for the death of some Greek sportsman of whom I confess I'd never heard. But what the hell? A minute's silence before a football game *for anything* strikes me as a good idea, especially in Greece – anything to stop those fucking drums and the warlike chants of the Gate 7 ultras. To listen that awful, masculine sound, brimful of aggression and testosterone, you would think yourself back at Rorke's Drift in 1879, facing ten thousand Zulus.

I ignored the banana which – a later replay showed – must have come from the VIP seats. I guess VIPs are just as racist as anyone else. It didn't hurt; not as much as a chair might have done. You can ignore almost anything when you're a goal up after five minutes in the Champions League; the way I felt at that particular moment I could probably have ignored a spear between the shoulder blades. I turned back to the dugout and bicep-curled both arms, triumphantly.

The banana was almost immediately forgotten in the disaster that swiftly followed. Because no sooner had the game restarted than Bekim Develi missed a simple pass from Jimmy Ribbans, fell to his knees as if in penance for his mistake, and then collapsed face down in the centre circle, to the loud disdain of the Greeks. Seconds later, both Zénobe Schuermans and Daryl Hemingway began waving frantically towards our dugout. The club physio, Gareth Haverfield, didn't need prompting from me; he snatched up his bag of tricks and sprinted onto the pitch.

'What's up with him?' said a voice next to me. It was Simon. 'Heat too much for him, do you think?'

I nodded. 'He's fainted, yes. It is incredibly hot in here.'

'Twenty-nine degrees Celsius,' said Simon. 'I don't know about him but I feel like a fucking chicken vindaloo. I hope he hasn't fainted. If he's fainted he'll have to come off. Perhaps he got hit with something. A coin, perhaps.'

'Could be. They've been throwing money away in this country for years. Makes a change from a banana.'

Risking another banana perhaps, I walked anxiously to the edge of the technical area. I put my glasses on; I am just a little short-sighted – more so at night, when I'm feeling tired. But what I could see now made little sense; Bekim Develi appeared to be trying to head-butt the ground and Gareth was trying without success to turn him onto his back. I knew this wasn't good when the referee ran to the Olympiacos dugout and said something that made their whole medical team sprint onto the pitch; instinctively, without waiting for the ref's permission, I followed, slowly at first, as if not quite sure of what I was doing, and then a little more quickly as I began to realise just how serious things were.

By now Develi had stopped moving altogether, and one of the Greek medicos had cut off his shirt with a pair of scissors and was giving him chest compressions; Gareth, our own physio, was doing mouth-to-mouth as a paramedic frantically unrolled an oxygen airway tube. Even the crowd seemed to have realised what was happening and fell silent.

Seeing me, Gary Ferguson stood up from his team mate's side and came towards me. His cheeks were wet, but not with sweat.

'What is it?' I asked, already feeling sick to my stomach. 'What's wrong with him?'

'He's dead, boss. That's what's fucking wrong with him.'

'What? He can't be. How?'

'I dunno. One minute he's running around like he's the dog's bollocks; the next he's on the floor. The way he went down I thought he must have been shot.'

The referee, an Italian called Merlini, came over and for a minute I thought he was going to tell me to leave the pitch; instead, he shook his head sadly.

'I'm so sorry,' he said. 'But it doesn't look good, I'm afraid. They're bringing a defibrillator to the pitch now. They would take him to the hospital across the road, but they're worried about moving him.'

'Jesus,' muttered Gary.

Out of the corner of my eye I saw Kenny Traynor with his head in his hands, and Soltani Boumediene with his face buried in Xavier Pepe's shoulder. Prometheus was talking animatedly to one of the Olympiacos players. Jimmy Ribbans appeared to be kneeling in prayer for his stricken colleague. I might have knelt down to pray myself but I knew Bekim's girlfriend was probably watching at home and the last thing she needed now was to see me looking like I'd given up hope.

I glanced up at the television display screen and then at my watch.

Merlini seemed to read my mind.

'He's been like that for several minutes, now,' he said. 'I don't know what to do. I think I'd better speak to the other officials. And to the guys from Olympiacos. I should tell them what's happening, too.'

'I'd better speak to the rest of the lads,' said Gary after Merlini had walked away. 'If he wants to restart this match we're going to have to pick ourselves up pretty quickly. And who are we going to bring on to replace him?'

'Iñárritu,' I said, numbly.

Gary walked away as one of the Greek medicos finished attaching two large sticky defibrillator pads to Bekim's now motionless chest.

'Do not touch the patient,' said a female American woman's voice from inside the yellow machine, which looked more like a child's toy than something that could revive a man like Bekim Develi. And then: 'Shock advised. Charging. Stand clear.'

'Stékeste,' said one of the Greeks loudly; everyone sat back from Bekim.

'Press flashing shock button,' said the machine voice.

'Stékeste,' repeated the Greek medico and then pressed the shock button.

Bekim's body jerked momentarily but otherwise he remained motionless.

'Shock one delivered,' said the machine voice. 'It is safe to touch the patient. Begin CPR, now.'

The Greek translated for some of the others attending Bekim and then, together with Gareth, he started chest compressions, while Gareth gave Bekim mouth-to-mouth, thirty and two, like you're supposed to. The men were drenched in sweat not just from the heat in the stadium, but from the sheer effort of what they were now doing: trying to bring a man back from the dead. And this in full view of more than thirty thousand spectators.

'Continue for one minute thirty seconds,' said the machine.

'Christ,' said Simon who was now standing alongside me in the centre of the pitch. 'Has he had a heart attack, or what?'

'Worse than that, I think,' I said. 'It seems like his heart has stopped beating altogether. They're trying to get it going again now.'

'It can't be,' said Simon. 'Not him. Not Bekim. The lad's only twenty-nine and as fit as a flea.'

'Right now it doesn't look as though he's going to make thirty,' I said.

'Stop CPR. Stop now. Do not touch the patient. Analysing heart rhythm. Do not touch the patient. Shock advised. Stand clear.'

'*Stékeste*,' said the Greek medico.

'Press flashing shock button.'

Once again Bekim's body jerked spasmodically and then remained motionless. Some others came onto the pitch with a scoop stretcher to pick the man up just as soon as he could be safely moved. It was already beginning to look pointless.

'He needs to be in hospital,' said Simon. 'Someone needs to call a fucking ambulance.'

'They're doing the right thing,' I told him. 'If they stop with the defibrillator then there'll be no point in taking him to the hospital.'

'No point anyway if the fucking doctors are on strike,' said Simon.

By now the news that Bekim was in serious trouble had reached the small contingent of English supporters who were somewhere in the stadium and they began to sing his name.

'BEKIM DEVELI! BEKIM DEVELI!'

'BEKIM DEVELI! BEKIM DEVELI!'

To my amazement the Greeks joined in and for almost a minute the whole crowd was as one in its attempt to let the stricken Russian know that they were rooting for his recovery.

'BEKIM DEVELI! BEKIM DEVELI!'

I swallowed hard, and in spite of the heat shivered a little with emotion, trying to keep it together, but inside I was in complete turmoil. What about his baby son? I kept asking myself. What if he doesn't make it? Who's going to look after Peter? What will happen to Alex? Football, bloody hell!

Bloody hell, indeed.

CHAPTER 17

As six pairs of hands lifted Bekim onto the stretcher and hurried him off the pitch, I followed Gareth to the mouth of the players' tunnel. The air was as warm as an open oven but I felt cold and empty inside. The audience started to applaud the man now fighting for his life.

'Is he alive?' I asked him.

'Only just, boss. His heart's all over the place. Maybe they can do something for him at the hospital. His best chance now is a massive shot of adrenalin. Or if they open him up and massage his heart. But we've done all we can for him here, I think.'

'But what happened? What caused this?'

'I'm not a doctor, boss. But there's something called SADS – Sudden Arrhythmia Death Syndrome, or what the newspapers call Sudden Adult Death Syndrome – but that's just what doctors call it when they have no fucking idea why people keel over and die. Except that they do. All the time.'

'Not when they're twenty-nine,' I said. But Gareth didn't hear me; the stretcher had halted briefly so that he could help to give Bekim CPR again.

'Go with them,' I told Simon. 'Go with them to the hospital. And stay in touch.'

'Yes, boss.'

I turned to find Gary standing behind me. He looked pale and drawn.

'Drink something,' I said, almost automatically. 'You look like you're dehydrated.'

'Is he dead?'

'I don't know. No, I don't think so. But it's not looking good right now.'

'We can't play on tonight,' he said. 'Not in these circumstances, boss. The lads need to know Bekim's all right.'

'I think you're right.'

'Christ, it makes you think what's important, eh?'

I walked towards the touchline where Merlini, a UEFA official and several guys from Olympiacos were in conference. Merlini had both hands clasped as if he'd been praying too; he was biting his thumbnail anxiously as he tried to decide what to do. The Olympiacos manager, Hristos Trikoupis, put a hand on my shoulder.

'How is your man?'

I shook my head. 'I really don't know.'

'They're taking him to the Metropolitan,' he said. 'It's a two-minute walk from here. It's a very good hospital. A private hospital. Not a public one. Try not to worry too much. It's where all our own players go. I promise you, they'll give your guy the best treatment available.'

I nodded dumbly, a little surprised at this turnaround in his attitude to me; before the match he had said some very unpleasant things about me in the Greek newspapers; he'd even brought up my time in prison and had joked that that was where I belonged, given my record as 'a very dirty player'. Mind games, perhaps. All the same, that had hurt. You don't expect that kind of behaviour from someone you used to play alongside. It had been all I could do to shake hands with Hristos Trikoupis before the match without trying to break his arm.

'Look,' I said eventually, 'I don't think my boys can play on. Not tonight.'

'I agree,' said Trikoupis.

Merlini, the referee, pointed to the tunnel. 'Please, let's go inside and have a talk there,' he said. 'I don't feel comfortable deciding what to do in front of the television cameras or all these people.'

He blew his whistle and waved at the players on the pitch to come off.

I grabbed my jacket and then we went into the officials' room; Merlini, the UEFA official, Hristos Trikoupis, the two team captains and me.

We sat down and for almost a minute nobody said a thing; then Trikoupis offered around some cigarettes and everybody took one, me included. There's nothing like a cigarette to help draw yourself together; it's as if, when you inhale smoke into your lungs, you're pulling something back into yourself that had been in danger of escaping.

Gary smoked like a hard-bitten soldier in a trench on the Somme. 'I used to think these would kill me,' he said. 'But after what's happened here tonight, I'm not so sure.'

Trikoupis handed me a glass of what I thought was water and it was only after I'd downed it that I realised it was actually ouzo.

'No,' I said, firmly. 'We can't play tonight.'

'I agree,' he said.

'So do I,' said Merlini. He seemed relieved that the decision had been made for him. 'The question is, when is the match to be finished?'

The UEFA official, a Belgian called Bruno Verhofstadt, who

looked like Don Draper wearing Van Gogh's beard, nodded. 'Very well,' he said. 'That's agreed. I'm sure we all hope and pray that Mr Develi will make a full and speedy recovery. Obviously I'm not a doctor but I trust Mr Manson and Mr Ferguson will forgive me if I state a very cruel and unpalatable truth: that it seems to me whatever happens now there can be no question of Bekim Develi playing for London City in the very near future. Not after a heart attack.'

I nodded. 'That's fair, I think, Mr Verhofstadt.'

'Thank you, sir. I hope you will also forgive me if I suggest that we use this opportunity to try to find the best way forward from where we are now. By which I mean the situation as it exists, from UEFA's point of view.'

'Which is?' I asked.

'I'll understand completely if you don't feel you want to talk about this now, Mr Manson. I wouldn't like you to feel that I'm putting you under pressure to make a decision about what to do next.'

'No, no. Let's talk about it. I agree, I think we have to do that now. Makes sense. While we're all here.'

'Very well. So then, given we are agreed that Mr Develi is unlikely to play any further role in this cup tie. . .' Verhofstadt glanced at me as if awaiting confirmation.

I nodded.

'Then according to UEFA a match which has begun must be completed as soon as possible. UEFA rules also forbid domestic games taking place in Europe on the same night as the Champions League or Europa League games. Tomorrow night is also a Champions League night. There are no domestic games anywhere else. From a scheduling standpoint it would seem to make sense that we complete this match at the earliest available opportunity that is convenient to both teams.'

'You mean tomorrow,' I said.

'I do mean tomorrow, Mr Manson.' He sighed. 'Come what may.'

I knew exactly what Verhofstadt meant by that. He meant that we would have to play the game even if Bekim Develi died; but I hardly wanted to admit out loud that this was a possibility, even though I knew in my heart of hearts that this felt like something much more than just possible.

'Come what may. That also makes sense. It's not like we had many travelling fans here tonight. I think most of our supporters were already here on holiday.' I nodded. 'I mean, we're all here in Greece. If we don't play tomorrow then it's hard to imagine when we are going to be able to play this cup tie. We've got Chelsea on Saturday, and then we're supposed to have the home match of this cup tie, next week.' I glanced at Gary Ferguson. 'It's either that or we withdraw from the competition. What do you think, Gary?'

'We can't withdraw,' he said firmly. 'No, boss. If we have to play we have to play. I don't know of any circumstances under which Bekim would want us to withdraw from the Champions League – not on his account, anyway. Especially not now we're a goal up.' He took a superhuman drag on the cigarette and then used it to reinforce the point he was now making. 'Look, I don't know how to say this, boss, except to mention an old movie I once saw, with Charlton Heston. Bekim Develi is your *El Cid* kind of guy. I mean, dead or alive, he'd want us to be there tomorrow. To play, you know?' He shrugged. 'Just for the record, I'd feel the same way. My club, do or die, okay?'

Verhofstadt looked at Trikoupis.

'Yes,' he said. 'I agree. We can play tomorrow, as well.'

'Thank you, gentlemen. Thank you all for being so accommodating in an extremely difficult and tragic situation.'

I shook hands with Hristos Trikoupis and then with Mr Verhofstadt.

'Then that's settled,' he said. 'This match will be postponed until tomorrow.'

As Gary and I left the officials' room, Trikoupis drew me aside.

'I didn't want to say this in front of the UEFA guy,' he said, suddenly much less amicable. 'After all, you're a big boy now, Scott. But do you really know what the fuck you're doing? I don't think so. You think it was tough out there tonight? That was nothing compared to how it will be tomorrow. Don't think that we're going to go easy on you just because you have a player who had a heart attack. A player, I might add, who was not much loved after what he said about this country at the press conference the other night.'

'Like I said earlier, I don't think we have any other choice but to play.'

'If you like. But you can depend on this. Tomorrow night, we're going to fuck you in the ass. We're going to comprehensively destroy you all. And then we're going to tie your bodies to our chariots and drag you around the walls of this stadium in triumph. And however bad you feel now you will certainly feel worse tomorrow. My advice to you is this. Go home now. While you still can.'

I was still feeling too numb about what had happened to Bekim otherwise I might have told Hristos Trikoupis to go and fuck himself, especially after what he'd said about me in the newspapers. But things were quite bad enough without me starting a fight with another manager under the eyes of the local police. So I turned away without another word and went back to the dressing room where I told the players of what had been decided.

Not long after that Simon Page returned with the news that several of us had expected and all of us were dreading: Bekim Develi was dead.

It took me several moments before I could respond. When I finally did, I said:

'We'll leave it to the people in the media to idealise the man and enlarge him in death beyond what he was in life. That's what they like to do but it's not what Bekim would have wanted. I know that because last night, after that disastrous press conference, I asked him why he'd said what he said. And he replied: "The truth is the truth. I say it when I see it and that's just the way I am." Those of us who loved Bekim Develi, for who he really was, we'll just leave it at this: we will remember him as a man who always tried, as a man who never gave up, as a man who defended fair play for all, but above all we will remember him as a truly great sportsman. When one of your team mates dies like this, I don't know – this is about as bad as it gets. But tomorrow we'll have the opportunity then as a team to show him how much we valued the time we had with him.'

I stood up. 'Come on, lads. Have a shower and let's get on that coach.'

CHAPTER 18

Of course I'd never wanted Bekim Develi at the club. It had been Viktor's idea to buy him from Dynamo St Petersburg. But Bekim had quickly impressed us all with his discipline and absolute commitment to the football club, not to mention his enormous technical ability. More importantly, he'd been lucky for us, which is to say he'd scored goals, more than a dozen goals in less than four months, important goals that had enabled us to finish fourth in the table behind Chelsea, Man City and Arsenal; if I had to single out one player who had helped us to qualify for Europe it would have been Bekim Develi. Yes, there had been times when I could have wished for him to be less outspoken but that was the red devil for you: mischief was hard-wired into his DNA. It was a part of him, like the red beard on his face.

Now that he was gone I wondered which of us – me or Viktor Sokolnikov – was going to telephone Bekim's girlfriend, Alex, back in London and tell her the bad news. Vik had already spoken to her several times to assure her that everything that could be done was being done. The fact was Vik had known them both for longer than I had and, much to my relief, he volunteered to make the call himself. I'll say one thing for our Ukrainian proprietor: he never shirked a difficult job.

'Besides,' he said, 'she's Russian and she ought to hear this terrible thing in her own language. Bad news is always less kind in translation.' Vik shook his head. 'Please, excuse me. Help yourself to a drink and make yourself comfortable. I may be a while.'

He went away and was gone for almost forty minutes.

We were on Vik's yacht, *The Lady Ruslana*. His helicopter had flown me from the landing pad in front of the hotel onto the ship soon after my arrival back in Vouliagmeni from the Karaiskakis Stadium. He'd offered me dinner on-board, which I declined. I had no appetite for food although the same could not be said of his other guests on the yacht – Phil Hobday, Kojo Ironsi, flicking mosquitoes away with one of those African fly-whisks, Cooper Lybrand wearing an immaculate white linen suit that made him look like Gatsby, a couple of Greek businessmen who had lost their razors, and several pretty girls – who even now were loudly tucking in to dinner on the outside deck that would not have disgraced the table of a minor Roman emperor. Even close to the death of someone I was sure he had cared a lot about, Vik lived well; perhaps that's the only way to be: with an eye not to the future, or the past but only on the present. *Tempus fugit* and all that.

The yacht's red ensign flag at half-mast was a nice touch but I could have done without Kojo's big, booming laugh; or the fireworks and lightshow on another yacht – bigger than the Vatican State and just as opulent – moored about a hundred metres away.

'That's *Monsieur Croesus*,' said Vik when he came back to the stateroom where he'd left me, 'Gustave Haak's boat; the investor and arbitrageur,' as if that was all the explanation needed for such a conspicuous middle finger to the cash-strapped Greeks who must have watched what was happening from the shore with something like astonishment. 'It's his birthday. Haak likes to enjoy his birthdays. Me, I prefer to forget them. There have been too many, and they come too often for my liking.'

'How did she take it?' I asked. 'Alex?'

Vik sighed. 'Stupid question.'

'Sorry. Yes, it was.'

'Actually, it so happens I'm very good at giving bad news. But then, as a Jew coming from Ukraine we've had generations of practice.'

'I didn't know you were Jewish, Viktor.'

'So was Bekim. I don't suppose you knew that either.'

'No, I didn't. Why didn't I?'

'Jews in football. This isn't something to shout about like some stupid Haredi with a *kolpik* on his head. It's like being gay: best kept quiet about in front of the great British public with its strong sense of sporting fair play.'

'You got that right.'

He grimaced. 'I'm worried about Alex. According to Bekim she's suffering from post-natal depression. That's normal, of course. But when I first got to know her she was addicted to cocaine. It's at times like this that people – weaker people, such as her – reach for the wrong kind of help. I told her to leave all of the arrangements for Bekim's funeral to me, but perhaps it would be better for her to be busy. You see, I know he wanted to be buried in Turkey, where he was born. In Izmir.' He pointed at one of the windows. 'Which is just across the Aegean Sea, in that direction. So it makes sense that I should do it. Don't you think?'

'Yes. And I, for one, am very glad you're doing it. I'm not sure I can handle the Champions League and the local undertakers in the same day.'

'Scott, really.' Vik smiled and rubbed his beard. 'You're being a little melodramatic. What you do, you do very well, but honestly it's nothing compared to what I have to do.'

'No?'

'No. You're an intelligent man. But sometimes I wonder if you have the least idea of what it's like to run a twelve-billion-pound business. The responsibility. The effort required. The number of things I have clamouring for my attention. I have thirty thousand people working for me. All you have to do is get eleven men to play football.'

I nodded silently. I already felt sad but now I felt small, too. On *The Lady Ruslana* Vik was the master in a way he never was on land; he only had to nod to make things happen around him. The crew of the boat wore orange polo shirts and shorts and were so young they looked like a high school gym class in Australia, which was where they were from, mostly; once or twice I thought he'd nodded at me only to discover that he'd ordered himself a drink, or a snack, or sent some flowers to Alex, or summoned the launch that would take me back to the hotel.

'I'd forgotten that helicopters make you nervous, Scott,' he explained.

'I don't think I ever mentioned it, did I?'

He shrugged. 'A man doesn't have to say anything at all for him to be just as eloquent as Hamlet,' he said. 'Sometimes, his body says everything for him. Besides, I think you've had more than enough stress for one day, my friend. I know I have. So then. Take the launch. Go back to the hotel. Eat something. Try to get a good night's sleep. And like I said before, leave everything other than tomorrow's football match in my hands. But before you do all that, forgive me please. I'm sorry I put you down like that earlier. I made

109

you feel insignificant and unimportant and that really wasn't necessary. My apologies.'

It was perhaps a modest demonstration of omniscience; all the same it was a touching one.

And then he embraced me warmly.

When I got back to the hotel I found the police waiting for me in the lobby; they explained that there would have to be a post-mortem and that for legal reasons Bekim Develi's possessions could not be removed from his bungalow at the hotel, which was now closed until further notice.

'It's the coroner's office,' they explained. 'When a man of just twenty-nine drops down dead there are procedures that must be observed.'

'I understand,' I said.

It looked as though any funeral plans that Viktor Sokolnikov might have had for Bekim Develi to be buried in his home town of Izmir were now on hold.

CHAPTER 19

We resumed the match abandoned the previous night with eighty-three minutes still to play. And the game started well. How could it not? We were already a goal up. This was an away goal too, the best kind in UEFA's *Animal Farm* world where some goals are more equal than others. Our players seemed anxious to win the game, for Bekim's sake if nothing else. The sports page of every English newspaper urged us on to victory over the Greeks and – with one Cassandra-like exception, the always-prescient Henry Winter at the *Daily Telegraph* – predicted that City would surely prevail.

Unfortunately no one had shown Olympiacos the script of how this particular revenge tragedy was supposed to play.

Our evening began to break up like the Elgin Marbles almost as soon as the City players stepped onto the pitch. It was as if, having lost Hector, our doom had been sealed for we were uncertain in defence, clueless in midfield, and impotent in attack. Schuermans and Hemingway were both outplayed by the thirty-two-year-old Argentine Alejandro Domínguez, who proved that his team had no need of centre forward Kostas Mitroglu – sold to Fulham for £12.5 million – to score goals. He equalised with just fifteen minutes on the clock, running on to a fantastic through ball from Giannis Maniatis, Olympiacos's captain and central midfielder, whose pass looked as if he might have called Jesus Christ's bluff and got a camel through the proverbial eye of the needle. Why our own midfielders didn't close him down was one mystery; but it was wrapped up in the enigma of how our almost sedentary defenders didn't manage to stop Domínguez from finding space to take a shot that Kenny Traynor ought to have saved easily. Unsighted and wrong-footed, our goalkeeper dived one way and Domínguez neatly flicked the ball the other. The ball crossed the line with an almost cartoonish lack of pace, as if Jerry the mouse could have stopped it, adding to Traynor's obvious distress. He slapped the ground several times and shouted at the pitch, as if blaming the gods of the underworld below our feet.

The Legend fired off several red flares behind Traynor's goal, which only served to underline the Scotsman's infernal performance and filled the air in the stadium with a strongly sulphurous smell.

'Fucking hell,' exclaimed Simon. 'I've seen some daft defending in my time but those two twats take the biscuit. The way they ran at the lad Domínguez you'd have thought they were trying to do a scissors in fucking rugby. Do you want to shout at them or shall I? Because I am so fucking angry about that, boss. I am so fucking angry.'

'Be my guest,' I said.

Simon spat out his extra-strong mint like a loose tooth, marched to the edge of the technical area, gesticulated furiously at our back four and let rip with a stream of obscenities that made me glad the Greek supporters were so loud. All I heard were the words 'stupid cunts', and in truth, when you come right down to it, those were the only two words he really needed. I wasn't sure if FIFA could have envisaged what Simon was doing as 'an element of the game' within the change it had made to the laws in 1993, bringing technical areas into existence, but I doubted this kind of thing really did 'improve the quality of play'. Of course, I was guilty of this sort of intemperate behaviour myself; indeed there were a couple of times when I'd been sent to the stands for what the referees' association called 'aggressive coaching'.

By now our goalmouth had disappeared in the cloud of red smoke from the Greek flares, which spared our goalkeeper's blushes, and wisely, the referee waited a full minute before restarting the game.

'Simon,' I called, 'come back here. You'll give yourself a fucking heart attack.'

He didn't hear me. Brick-faced and full of rage, the big Yorkshireman continued to shout and wave his arms about like a madman conducting an orchestra of deaf musicians and suddenly it occurred to me, after what had happened to Bekim Develi, that his having a heart attack wasn't so very improbable. And as the game restarted I got out of my seat and, leaving the dugout, went to fetch him back. Out of the corner of my eye I saw Hristos Trikoupis complaining to the fourth official that I had stepped in his technical area, which wasn't true, of course, but, at that particular moment, I had other things to worry about.

'Leave it, Simon,' I repeated, taking hold of his arm. 'They can't even see you, cos of the smoke.'

He was about to take my advice when a high ball came our way and, immediately in front of us, Daryl Hemingway and Diamntopoulou both jumped to head it. The Greek seemed to mount up on the Englishman's back in an almost gymnastic attempt to reach the ball. Neither man quite making contact, but in the wrestling match that ensued the Greek suddenly fell clutching his face in pain, as if Daryl had deliberately straight-armed him to the ground. It was patently obvious to me and to Simon – and must have been equally clear to the linesman standing right beside us – that Daryl's back-swinging arm had done little more than brush Diamntopoulou's girlish top-knot of hair. But with the Greek still rolling on the pitch in agony as if he had been stabbed in the eye with a red-hot poker, we were astonished to see the lino raise his flag and Merlini, the referee, already striding towards Daryl and reaching for the card in his top pocket.

A yellow would have been bad enough; the red was an outrage. Daryl Hemingway stood there as if he could hardly believe what was happening. Nor could Simon and I. How we restrained ourselves from further comment at that moment, I shall never know. I put a hand on Daryl's shoulder and started to walk him to the dugout but not before changing our own formation from 4-3-3 to 4-4-1. If we dug in, we might hold on to a draw, which was at least something we could build on back in London.

'I didn't fucking touch him, boss. Honest.'

'I saw the whole thing, Daryl. It wasn't your fault. One of these bastards has been bought. That much is now obvious, anyway.'

I looked back to the pitch in time to see Diamntopoulou get back to his feet, without a mark on his face, and Simon, still on the edge of the technical area, sneer: 'You cheating, fucking bastard. He never touched you. Call yourself a sportsman? You're a fucking girl, that's what you are, son. A fucking girl.'

Diamntopoulou was barrel-chested, with more tattoos than a Scottish regiment, and under the Yorkshireman's obvious derision he bristled, visibly.

'You call me a girl?'

'Well, you're not a man, that's for sure.'

114

'Fuck you.'

'No, but I'll fuck you, if you like, girlie. That's all you're good for, you Greek *malakas*.'

'You need to learn some manners, fat man,' shouted Diamntopoulou, squaring up, as two Olympiacos players intercepted, and it was fortunate that the fourth official was there to put his body in front of the Greek's.

'Any time you're ready to try, *malakas*, I'll be fucking ready.'

Unsurprisingly, Simon found himself sent back to the dressing room; to be fair to the Greek officials, in all normal circumstances they might have sent him to sit in the stands, but these were hardly normal circumstances. It wasn't judged safe for Simon to sit among the Olympiacos fans; and of course they had a point. Anywhere looked safer for Simon than the Olympiacos stands.

Reduced to just ten men we had a hard job containing the Greeks, especially Perez on their left wing. We held out bravely with Gary Ferguson rescuing us a couple of times and Kenny Traynor on his best form with three top-drawer saves, but now doubly demoralised it was an impossible task.

As soon as the second half restarted Perez escaped from Jimmy Ribbans to curl in a left-footer that was their second. Ten minutes later Schuermans failed to dispossess Perez who ran into more space than he could have imagined was possible and hammered in his second one of the match.

The ruins of our evening might fairly have been compared with the Acropolis when Dominguez was substituted in the 79th minute and Machado, who came on in his place, scored immediately with a scrambled millipede of a goal that came about because they just had more fucking legs to kick the ball than we did. The final score was 4–1.

I went to shake hands with Hristos Trikoupis and was more than a little shocked to see him grinning back at me and holding up four fingers. Under different circumstances I might have made something out of it; instead I turned away and then clapped my players off the pitch. They hardly needed another bollocking.

'Come on, lads. Hurry up and get changed. We've a plane to catch. The sooner we get out of this madhouse and back to London the better.'

I wasn't looking forward to the television interview I'd agreed to do immediately after the game; I certainly wasn't going to tell their reporter, what I really thought of it: that this was a night of confusion, duplicity, disorder and defeat. That wouldn't play well with anyone, even though it was the truth. Instead I'd already decided to be a bit Italian about it; Italian football managers are masters at dissembling and they have a saying that comes in useful at times like these. *Bisogna far buon viso a cattivo gioco*: 'It's necessary to disguise a bad game with a good face.'

Of course, it's one thing putting on a good face when it's only ITV waiting to speak to you in the players' tunnel. It's another thing altogether when it's the fucking cops; it's always more difficult putting on a good face for them.

CHAPTER 20

Two uniformed police officers and a third man wearing a grey linen suit met me outside our dressing room. The man in the grey suit was tall with fair hair and a little tuft of hair under his bottom lip that I suppose was a beard but looked like some baklava that had missed his mouth. I'd seen better beards growing on a toothbrush. I might have ignored him altogether but for the credentials wallet he was holding up in front of my face. His teeth were very white but even at a distance his breath could have done with freshening.

'Are you Mr Scott Manson?'

'Yes.'

'My name is Chief Inspector Ioannis Varouxis, from the Special Violent Crime Squad, here in Athens.' He put away the wallet and handed me a business card with English on one side and Greek on the other. 'Could I speak with you, sir? In private.'

Under his arm was an iPad in a rubberised cover that matched the colour of his suit and I caught a scent of a rather nice aftershave. His shirt was clean and neatly pressed and he didn't look like the Greek policemen I had seen in movies.

I frowned. 'Now?'

'It is important, sir.'

'All right. If you insist.'

He led me along the corridor to the officials' room where I'd gone the previous night following Bekim's death; my mind raced through the reasons why someone from a special violent crime squad should want to speak to me. Had Simon Page hit someone? Had a Greek assaulted him? Were the Olympiacos supporters planning to attack us as we left the Karaiskakis Stadium? The two uniformed policemen took up positions either side of the door which one of them closed, leaving me alone with the Chief Inspector.

'First of all, let me say that I am very sorry about Bekim Develi.'

I nodded silently.

'To die so young was a terrible tragedy. And that it should happen in Greece, during a match like that, was most regrettable. Actually, I wanted to speak to you earlier today but my superior, Police Lieutenant General Stelios Zouranis, felt that this might interfere with your preparations for tonight's game. Indeed, that you might think this to be a crudely partisan attempt to influence the result.'

'I'm not sure that anything would have affected our performance tonight. We were awful.'

'Under the circumstances, it's hardly surprising that you lost. For the record I should tell you that I am a Panathinaikos supporter. So, it makes my skin crawl even to be here. Your player, Hemingway, he should never have been sent off. But that was just typical of a match against Olympiacos. Somehow they always contrive to win.'

I looked at my watch. 'You'll forgive me if I ask you to come to the point, Chief Inspector. We have a chartered plane waiting to take us back to London. It seems that your air-traffic controllers are going on strike at midnight. And we really don't want to miss our take-off slot.'

'I know. And believe me this is most regrettable also, sir. But I'm afraid that none of you will be permitted to leave Greece.'

'What?'

'Not tonight, at any rate. Perhaps not for several days.'

'You're kidding.'

'Not until we have completed our inquiries. The Minister of Culture and Athletics has spoken to the manager of your hotel and he has generously agreed to extend your stay until this whole matter has been resolved.'

'What matter? Your inquiries into what?'

'I am in charge of investigating a violent crime, Mr Manson. Specifically, a homicide. Perhaps even a murder.'

'Murder? Look, with all due respect, Chief Inspector, what's this all about? Bekim Develi had a heart attack. In front of thirty thousand people. I can easily understand that there will have to be a post-mortem into his death; that's normal in any country. But I fail to understand the need for a police investigation as well.'

'Oh, it's not Bekim Develi's death I'm investigating, sir, although I believe there will have to be an inquest – standard procedure.'

'Then whose death are we talking about? I don't understand. Has something happened to someone on my staff?'

'No sir. Nothing like that. The body of a young woman was found in the harbour at Marina Zea, near Piraeus, this morning. Some boys discovered the body in ten feet of water, with a heavy weight tied to her feet. Our investigations revealed that this woman had a plastic room key for the Astir Palace – your hotel – in the pocket of her dress. This afternoon we went to your hotel and found that the room key had been issued to Mr Develi. We also checked the hotel CCTV and, er. . . well, see for yourself.'

Varouxis opened up his iPad and tapped the Video icon to show me a grainy-looking piece of film.

'This is her arriving at Mr Develi's bungalow, on Monday night. As you can see, the time identification shows it to be 2300 hours. You will agree that this is surely him saying goodnight to her at the door, yes?'

'Can I please view that clip again, Chief Inspector?'

'Certainly sir.'

I watched the clip several times, but it was not to verify what Varouxis had said regarding Develi – clearly it was Bekim. Instead I wanted to establish if the girl entering and leaving the dead man's bungalow was Valentina, the escort to whom he had introduced me; it wasn't, which was a relief as it absolved me from having to tell the Chief Inspector that I had slept with the dead woman. The girl in the film was good-looking and given Bekim's predilection for renting late-night female company it didn't take a detective to guess her profession. His hands were inside the girl's knickers as he was still saying hello to her.

'Yes, that's him all right,' I said. 'For obvious reasons I'd ordered a player curfew on visitors that night which Bekim Develi seems to have ignored. The girl I don't know.'

'You'll admit then that it's possible Bekim Develi might have been one of the last people to see this girl alive. You see there's CCTV of her going into the bungalow; but none of her leaving.'

I nodded. 'Yes, I suppose so. But to be fair to Bekim, she might have left by the back door, to the terrace.'

'Yes, that's possible. But certainly if he himself was alive now we should want to speak to him very urgently, in which case I would be having this conversation not with you but with him. Where did you meet her? What time did she leave? That kind of thing.'

'I guess you would at that. Just to clarify one thing. Does this injunction on travel back to London apply to Mr Sokolnikov and his guests on Mr Sokolnikov's yacht?'

'No. Only to those of you who were staying at the Astir Palace, which is where the dead woman was last seen alive.'

I nodded. 'All the same, to detain a whole team for the behaviour of one man – a man who's now dead – it seems a bit excessive.'

'On the face of it, it might seem that way. But look here, we both have difficult jobs to do, Mr. Manson. Me, I have to balance what's right from a procedural, investigative point of view with what's legal and fair in this situation. And you, well, I should think it's an impossible task you have, sir. Trying to police the behaviour of young men with wallets as large as their egos and their libidos. Perhaps you'll also admit that it's possible Bekim may not have been the only City player in that bungalow when she came through the door. That he was not the only player to break your curfew on visitors.'

'Look, Chief Inspector, I've already agreed that it's Bekim Develi in the film clip. But there is no proof in that footage that anyone else was there.'

'No, not in the footage. You see, if I can't speak to Bekim Develi then perhaps I can speak to someone else who might also have met this unfortunate young woman. Perhaps they had – in Greek we call this a *trio*.'

'A threesome,' I said.

'Precisely so. I'm a married man, but one reads about such things. In books and newspapers.'

'Is there any evidence of a threesome?'

'Some, perhaps. The DEE – that's our forensics team – they went to Mr Develi's room this afternoon. They found indications that some kind of party occurred, perhaps. I don't want to go into too many details but traces of cocaine were found although it's impossible at this stage to say if the drugs were his or hers.'

'Bekim Develi would never have taken cocaine on the night before a match,' I said firmly. 'I'm certain of that. He wouldn't have taken the risk.'

'I'm sure you're right, sir. I dare say you've warned all of your players about the foolishness of such behaviour, on repeated occasions. Then again, it was you who ordered them not to entertain any girls in their rooms on the night before the match. An order that we now both agree that Bekim Develi flagrantly disobeyed. I would not insist that you remain here in Greece if I didn't have a good reason to do so; and since I think I have at least two good reasons, I'm hoping you'll see things from my point of view. That I can count on you to cooperate with my investigation.'

'While I can of course see things from your point of view, Chief Inspector, I wonder if you can see things from mine. The free movement of EU nationals is a fundamental principle of the Treaty under article 45. It might be argued that the whole team will suffer economic damage if it is prevented from leaving here tonight.'

This was pathetic, of course, but I really didn't know what the fuck else to say. I had to say something and the Greek detective was at least polite enough not to laugh.

'Plus, we have an important match against Chelsea on Saturday. I think any lawyer might be able to show that we will suffer real damage if we can't play that game. At the very least we'll be contacting the British Ambassador and asking him to speak with your minister at the earliest opportunity.'

'Oh, I don't think we'll have any problem in preventing you from leaving Greece, Mr Manson. The Minister of Public

Order and Citizen Protection, Konstantinos Miaoulis, has already approved my request. Being under investigation as a potential suspect is always a very good reason to prevent any EU citizen from exercising their right to leave a country. Even a whole football team. But if I might offer a word of advice: legal arguments involving the European Union are not popular in the Greek courts right now, for obvious reasons.'

'Thanks for the tip, Chief Inspector. Of course it's not up to me but to our proprietor and to our club chairman, Mr Hobday; however, I suspect we'll probably be engaging some local lawyers as well as asking our ambassador for his assistance.'

'Of course, of course. And you'll want this telephone number.' Varouxis took out a pen and wrote a number on a piece of paper. 'It's the British embassy, on Ploutarchou Street. 210-7272-600.'

'Thank you. I'll call him just as soon as we've finished talking.'

'Anticipating your objections it was also my superior's suggestion that we should meet again, tomorrow morning at the GADA. That's the police headquarters on Alexandras Avenue, in Athens. You really can't miss the place; it's opposite Apostolis Nikolaidis, the Panathinaikos stadium. You, your proprietor, your lawyers, the ambassador – whoever you like – can put questions to the minister, Lieutenant General Zouranis, and to me, of course.'

'All right. Shall we say three o'clock tomorrow afternoon? The sooner we can clear this matter up, the sooner we can all fly back to England.'

'Three?' Varouxis winced. 'Generally we stop work at two. Let's say ten o'clock.'

'Ten it is.' I paused. 'I have a question. You keep talking

about the dead woman, the unfortunate girl. Doesn't she have a name?'

'Not yet. But given the hour of her arrival as well as some forensics in Bekim Develi's bungalow, I think it's fair to assume that she may have been a prostitute. I don't suppose you recognised her?' He winced again. 'Forgive me. What I mean to say is, did you see her hanging about the hotel, sir? In the bar, perhaps?'

'I'm afraid not, Chief Inspector. You know, my own bungalow was right next to Bekim's. If I'd heard him up to something, I'd have put a stop to it. For a serious breach of discipline like that I'd have fined him a lot of money, probably.'

He nodded. 'I have another question for you.'

I shrugged. 'Fire away.'

He reached into his jacket pocket and withdrew a pendant on a piece of leather string – an amulet depicting the palm of an open right hand. It reminded me of something I'd seen recently but what I couldn't quite recall.

'They removed this from around his neck at the hospital and gave it to the coroner's office. Did you know he was wearing it?'

'No,' I said. 'And if I had I'd have told him to remove it immediately. FIFA forbids players to wear any kind of jewellery during a football match. You can get booked for that kind of thing.'

He tugged at his experimental beard for a moment, which gave me a better understanding perhaps as to why he had grown it: to give him pause for thought. 'In view of what you've just said – that wearing such a thing is forbidden, can you imagine why he would have run the risk of wearing such a thing?'

'No. Is this Greek?'

'I believe it's Arabic.'

'What is it, anyway?'

'This is supposed to provide defence against the evil eye. Christians call it the hand of Mary. Jews call it the hand of Miriam. But Arabs call it a *hamsa*: the hand of God.'

CHAPTER 21

'This can't be allowed to stand,' said Vik. 'We have a game against Chelsea on Saturday and we have to be back in London to beat him.'

To Viktor Sokolnikov, beating Roman Abramovich was more important than almost anything, as evidenced by the fifty grand bonus he'd previously offered every City player if we won. Every Russian billionaire probably measures himself against the Chelsea owner although quite a few – for example, Boris Berezovsky – are found wanting.

We were in the royal suite at the Grande Bretagne Hotel in the centre of Athens which Phil Hobday had taken to use as our team offices while we remained stuck in Greece; and at eight o'clock the next morning it was there we met the lawyers from Vrachasi, one of the top firms in Athens, that Vik had engaged to fight what amounted to the team's open arrest.

'I want a petition filed before the Greek court today,' he insisted. 'And I don't care what it costs.'

Dr Olga Christodoulakis, the senior partner from Vrachasi, was a large brunette in her forties with a pretty face and a manner as brisk as her own handwriting. She wore a bright green blouse that did little to restrain her enormous bosom and a tight black skirt that wasn't so much a pencil as a decent-sized fountain pen. She spoke excellent English with an American accent, but her bag-carrier of an associate – a younger man named Nikos something – was more fluent and just occasionally she said something in Greek and he chipped in with a swift translation.

'That's going to be difficult,' she said. 'The Greek courts are on strike at the moment. Which means that we're going to have to ring around the city and try to find a sympathetic judge who's prepared to break the strike to hear our case.'

Phil Hobday was horrified. 'Judges going on strike? I never heard of such a thing.'

'If the state doesn't pay what they owe you then there's not a lot of incentive for you to go to court,' she said. 'But right now that's not your biggest problem. I gather from the police that they intend to wait on the pathologist's report on the dead girl before deciding what to do next. The trouble with that is that the doctors handling all of the police autopsies are on strike, too.'

'Jesus Christ,' exclaimed Vik. 'This is like being back in Russia.'

'Can't another hospital do the autopsy?' suggested Phil. 'A private hospital. Like the Metropolitan Hospital in Piraeus. That's where they took Bekim Develi, wasn't it? They're not on strike.'

'I'm afraid that would never happen,' said Dr Christodoulakis. 'The Laiko General Hospital of Athens, on St Thomas's Avenue, has been handling police autopsies in Athens since 1930. This is not about to change just because of one strike. The doctors there are owed money by the state, the same as the lawyers. And to try to go around that would cause more trouble than it's worth. Even if we wanted to I doubt we'd find any pathologist who would dare to take this job.'

'I'm afraid she's right. These are the unfortunate facts of life in Greece right now.' Toby Westerman, from the British Embassy in Athens, looked pained, although that was probably his default expression. His thinning brown hair was combed from the back to the front which lent him the look of an unruly schoolboy, an effect that was enhanced by an old school tie and a pair of glasses that were almost opaque with fingerprints.

'It's like something out of Kafka,' said Vik. 'At this rate, the guys might be stuck here for weeks.'

I hadn't read any Kafka but I had read *Catch-22*, which was what the situation reminded me of. And I had another concern: discipline. Keeping a rein on eighteen players in a city like Athens during August was going to be difficult. Just the night before several of them had slipped out from the hotel complex in Vouliagmeni to visit a lap-dancing club on Syngrou Avenue.

'Who was this girl that she can cause so many problems?' demanded Vik.

'A hooker,' said Phil. 'That much seems certain.'

Vik got up from the table and walked around the dining area before helping himself to coffee from a silver pot on the sideboard. With the suite's expensive draperies, crystal chandeliers, gilt mirrors, bronze sculptures and original oil paintings, he looked quite at home. Beyond the drawing room and through the door you could see a bed big enough for any self-respecting oligarch and a couple of mistresses. Or hookers.

'I mean, just because she might have shagged Bekim doesn't mean he knew anything about her. Since when did that make you responsible for the rest of someone's life?'

He stared out of the window but his temper was not assuaged by the fine view of the Acropolis and Constitution Square.

I didn't blame Vik for being upset. The Greek constitution and its poorly functioning legal system was depressing. I was feeling upset myself but not about our catch-22 situation in Athens so much as what had happened back in London. Bekim's girlfriend, Alex, had taken an overdose of cocaine the previous night and was now at Chelsea and Westminster Hospital where her condition was officially described as 'poor'.

'Your policemen,' Vik asked our buxom lawyer. 'What are they like?'

'What he means is can they be bought?' asked Phil.

'Exactly, so,' said Vik. 'Well, why not? This is a heavily indebted country in its seventh year of recession. According to the annual Corruption Perceptions Index this country is the most corrupt country in the EU.'

Dr Christodoulakis shifted uncomfortably on her large backside.

'Ordinarily I might answer yes,' she said carefully. 'But with two government ministers involved, and the press already invested in the story, the possibilities for a *miza* or a *fakelaki*...' She glanced at the bag carrier.

'A backhander,' said Nikos.

She nodded. 'They are limited. For such a public case it would not be wise for anyone to take a backhander. But even if you did manage to bribe the investigating police officers you should also be aware that the Greek police are not to be trusted. They're closely related to the Golden Dawn – right-wing neo-Nazis.'

'I don't see that their politics matter very much,' said Phil. 'A bent fascist can be just as useful as a bent communist.'

Toby Westerman put his hands over his ears theatrically, and managed to look like one of the three wise monkeys. 'I don't think I should be listening to this kind of talk,' he said.

'Rubbish,' said Phil. 'What do you think the Germans have been doing since the beginning of the recession? They've been bribing the Greek government not to bring down the whole edifice of the EU temple. When the European Central Bank is involved a very large bribe is called a bail-out.'

Vik laughed.

'You've met him, Scott,' he said. 'This Greek Chief Inspector. What was your impression of him?' He looked at Dr Christodoulakis and grinned. 'Our manager, Mr Manson, knows all about bent cops, let me tell you. Being an ex-con you might say he's an expert on the subject. Isn't that right?'

I answered politely – more politely than the abbreviated biography Vik had just given of me might have led the two Greek lawyers to expect. 'It was my impression that Varouxis is a man who takes his responsibilities very seriously. And in spite of the sheer bloody inconvenience of what he had to tell me, he struck me as a fair sort of man.'

It all seemed a very long way from football; and I thought I'd better try to fix that since it was the only thing I really knew about.

'He even went to the trouble of telling me that he's a Panathinaikos fan which means he holds no love for Olympiacos. He didn't have to do that. And he could have given us the bad news *before* the match last night. The fact that he didn't speaks for itself. And don't let's forget this: it's not just Chelsea we have ahead of us but Olympiacos again, at home: the second leg of our Champions League match, next week. The Chelsea game can be postponed. I imagine Richard Scudamore is already expecting your call, Phil. But the situation with UEFA is going to be harder to fix. If we can't play the home leg against Olympiacos then we stand a good chance of going out of the competition at the first hurdle.'

'Christ, yes,' said Phil. 'He's right, Vik. Just to stay in the Champions League is worth anything up to fifty million quid.'

Vik nodded. 'At the very least,' he said, 'I think we need to know what the police know. Can this be done?' He was looking at Dr Christodoulakis now.

'Yes,' she said. 'I'm sure we can find out what they know and what they manage to find out. That much is possible. My instincts tell me that the dead girl's the key to everything. The more we know about her the greater the possibility that we can find someone who knows what happened to her in the moments that led up to her death, which might put your team in the clear. You might consider posting signs around Piraeus and the Marina Zea where her body was found, offering a small reward for information about the dead woman. You're right about one thing, Mr Sokolnikov. In Greece money doesn't just talk; it shouts in a voice of thunder from the top of Mount Olympus.'

CHAPTER 22

The GADA – the Attica General Police Directorate – was immediately across the road from Apostolos Nikolaidis, where we
parked our fleet of cars. Bedecked in Panathinaikos's shamrock green, the stadium looked as if it belonged in Glasgow or
Belfast. After Silvertown Dock and the Karaiskakis Stadium,
the AN Stadium was a bit of a third-world ruin; to say that
it had seen better days was something of an understatement.
On the crumbling walls were the mainly English slogans of
Panathinaikos, *Last End Fan Club*, *Mad Boys Since 1988*,
Victoria 13, *East End Alcoholics*, and crudely painted scenes
celebrating the club's former glory, daubed years before by
naïve, inexpert hands. It was hard to believe that these 'mad
boys' could be the descendants of the proud Athenians who
had built the Parthenon.

'Jesus Christ,' exclaimed Phil. 'What a slum.'

'Isn't it?' said Vik. 'Reminds me of home. Kiev, not London.'

'No wonder they hate Olympiacos,' said Phil.

But seeing it had given me an idea.

'I've been thinking more about what we were discussing
with Dr Olga What's-her-face,' I said as we crossed the busy
main road where another car was now depositing our new
lawyer and her bag-carrier.

'Christodoulakis,' said Phil.

'If the lawyers' and doctors' strikes last for any length of time,' I said, 'we're going to need a plan of how to make the best of things here, in Athens. The longer we stay in Greece the bigger the problem we're going to have keeping our lads in check.'

'You're the boss,' said Phil. 'Team discipline is down to you, Scott. Hand out a few fines. Kick a few backsides. Remind them that they're diplomats for English football and all that crap.'

'I don't think that's the right way to handle it,' I said. 'We may need to offer them a diversion. In case these bastard government ministers and police lieutenant generals prove to be as intransigent as the Chief Inspector I met last night. And I want your backing if I suggest it.'

Toby Westerman and Dr Christodoulakis joined us in front of the GADA building as I outlined my idea.

'Of course we'll need to get permission from UEFA. And perhaps Vik will have to put his hand in his pocket. From the look of this place they could use a couple of new turnstiles. But I was thinking that perhaps we could strike some sort of a deal with Panathinaikos to treat their ground as the home fixture for next week's match.'

'You mean us? Play in there?' Phil laughed. 'I hope they've all had their injections.'

'Sure, why not? And we could even let the Greens have the gate. What's the capacity of a place like this? Fifteen, twenty thousand? Looking at this place I bet they could use the money. The important point is that we know that, whatever happens, we're going to have a return match against Olympiacos. I can keep the team all pointed the same direction: towards training sessions at Apilion, just like before; followed by a match here next Wednesday night.'

'That might work,' agreed Vik. 'What do you think, Phil?'

He nodded. 'If we're stuck here for any length of time it might be our only chance of remaining in the Champions League. It might even assist us in building some local support on our side.'

'I hope it doesn't come to that,' I said. 'But we ought to have a plan, just in case we're stuck here. And I'll bet this culture and athletics minister will be just the person to help us make it happen. We should be ready to take advantage of his willingness to help while we have him. It might not be so easy to get hold of him again. He might go on strike. Or get voted out of government.'

'Actually the minister is a she,' said Dr Christodoulakis. 'Dora Maximos. She was a famous athlete and then an even more famous singer.'

'I get it,' I said. 'A bit like John Barnes.'

Phil laughed. 'God, you're a bastard, Scott.'

'Yes, but that's what I'm paid for, isn't it?'

The GADA was an unremarkable office block with an entrance like a bomb shelter. Near this was a small white marble shrine to the many Greek policemen who'd fallen in the line of duty; Michael Winner might have appreciated it but no one in Greece did. According to Dr Christodoulakis, the police in Athens were much hated. Gathered outside the front door were several newsmen – some of them English – who appeared to have been tipped off about our meeting; like everything else in Greece, information had its price.

In the conference room on the top floor where we met them you could easily see the football pitch across the road. And it was clear from the many plastic shamrocks and green ashtrays we found about the room that there was little support here for Olympiacos and plenty for Panathinaikos. But how much support there was for us in government remained to be seen.

The Minister of Public Order and Citizen Protection, Konstantinos Miaoulis, took charge of the meeting and, apologising profusely for detaining us in his country, he assured us the investigation would proceed with all possible haste in what were extraordinarily difficult circumstances, by which I assumed he meant the plain fact of the country going to hell in a handcart.

Dr Christodoulakis answered him quietly but firmly. 'Just to clarify the matter. It's my understanding that my clients – by which I mean every one of the London City staff and players who were staying at the hotel on the night that this young woman met her death – are forbidden to leave the country until the following has occurred: first that they have been questioned by the police as to what they might know about this young woman and Bekim Develi's involvement with her; and second that an autopsy shall have taken place to determine whether there is any forensic evidence linking her with anyone other than the late Bekim Develi.'

Chief Inspector Varouxis lit a cigarette and nodded. 'That is correct.'

Like everywhere else in the EU Greece had banned smoking in indoor public spaces back in 2010, but that didn't seem to matter at police headquarters.

'Given that the pathologists at the Laiko General Hospital are on strike,' argued Dr Christodoulakis, 'would it not be fairer if the return of the whole team to Athens from London was secured with the payment of bail, this sum to be set by a judge in chambers? That way the team might fulfil its own contractual arrangements which its continued detention in Greece could seriously damage, thus leaving the Greek government open to a civil action in the courts.'

Konstantinos Miaoulis was a fit-looking man, with a

military bearing, and while he may not have resembled a politician, he certainly sounded like one: 'I disagree. It's the government's opinion that to bring so many people back to Greece would prove enormously difficult. Suppose that one of the City team players is sold to another club before the transfer season closes? What guarantees could London City give the Greek government that they could make such an individual return? We take the pragmatic view that it's better to try and resolve this matter now, while everyone is here to assist the police. It's to be hoped that the strikes in the courts and among our medical profession will end very soon, enabling Chief Inspector's investigations to proceed with all possible speed.'

'Might I remind you,' said Toby Westerman, 'that as a signatory to the Schengen Agreement, the Greek government is technically in breach of its obligation not to observe *any* border or passport controls between this country and other member countries. Strictly speaking, the team don't need anyone's permission to leave the country. Legally, they're within their rights just to go to the airport and leave.'

'I wouldn't put that to the test if I were you,' said the Police Lieutenant General. 'The United Kingdom is not a signatory to the Schengen Agreement. The British government's complicity in the practice of extraordinary rendition hardly gives its representatives the right to lecture Greece on proper legal procedures.'

'On behalf of the British government,' Toby Westerman said, 'I protest the decision of the Greek police to detain the London City team, in the strongest possible terms'; but after that he remained silent for the rest of the meeting, which we all took to mean that the British government intended to do nothing.

'With the permission of Mr Manson, Mr Hobday and Mr Sokolnikov,' said Varouxis, 'I should like to question the players and playing staff at the earliest opportunity. And take their fingerprints.'

'Very well,' Dr Christodoulakis agreed. 'However, I must insist that the police keep us fully informed of any and all developments in this case, as soon as possible.'

'Of course,' said Varouxis. 'I should also like to take possession of Mr Develi's mobile phone, and any computers he might have. To help us identify the dead girl.'

These were still in Bekim's kitbag, now safely back in my room, but I wasn't in a hurry to hand these over.

'No, that won't be possible,' I said, 'but I'll be happy to let you have sight of them in my presence. Although, I don't think his laptop or phone will help you. I had a look at them myself last night when I got back to the hotel. I can assure you that the only calls he made and received on his mobile were to his girlfriend, Alex.' This was true; Bekim hadn't called anyone other than Alex. Nor had he sent or received any emails from anyone in Greece either and I explained this to the police. 'I even checked what websites he browsed. I was searching for escort agencies he might have looked at. But I drew a blank there as well. I should say you'd be better off seeing what calls came through the hotel switchboard. Or perhaps having a look at the PCs in the business centre.'

'Did you check those, too?' There was a note of sarcasm in the Chief Inspector's voice.

'No,' I said. 'Although I would have done if I'd thought of it at the time.'

Varouxis sighed irritably and lit another cigarette. By now I wanted one myself. My normal rule of just one fag a week was beginning to weigh rather heavily on me.

'This is a murder investigation, Mr Manson,' he said, stiffly. 'I'm well within my rights to force you to hand them over.'

'I understand that, Chief Inspector. However, there may be confidential information on those devices. We shall need to check this first. For the sake of his family. Perhaps you've seen the news? His girlfriend is in hospital. She took an overdose of cocaine and is now in a coma.'

'I'm afraid that is not acceptable, Mr Manson.'

'Then I suggest you get a court order,' I said. 'Perhaps at the same hearing we can petition the judge to leave the country. That is, if you can find a judge.'

Varouxis looked at Lieutenant General Zouranis as if seeking further guidance.

'I could order your arrest for this,' said Zouranis. 'I wouldn't need a judge for that. Obstructing the police is a serious offence.'

'I don't think Mr Manson is obstructing your investigation,' said Dr Christodoulakis. 'He didn't say he wouldn't let you see Mr Develi's electronic devices. Only that he wanted to be there when you did it.'

'Correct,' I said. 'How about this afternoon at three o'clock? We're currently using the royal suite at the Grande Bretagne Hotel as our office.'

Now Lieutenant General Zouranis looked at his minister for guidance; the minister nodded.

'Very well,' said Lieutenant General Zouranis. 'It shall be done as you have suggested.' He looked at Varouxis who shrugged his own compliance.

'In an attempt to help you identify the dead girl, Mr Sokolnikov intends to offer a reward for any information that leads to an arrest,' said Dr Christodoulakis.

'Good idea,' said General Zouranis.

Dr Christodoulakis looked at me and shrugged as if she too had done all she could. Recognising that we were stuck in Athens until further notice, I tossed onto the table my idea about playing the home leg of our draw with Olympiacos at the Apostolos Nikolaidis Stadium, which Dora Maximos, the Minister of Culture and Athletics, took up with alacrity.

'That is also a good idea,' she said.

'Yes and no,' said the Minister of Public Order and Citizen Protection. 'It's fair to say that by playing your home leg across the road you'll be perceived to have made yourselves the allies of Panathinaikos. You will have put yourself into the middle of the two eternal enemies, with all that this entails. It's a match that will require some very careful policing.'

'If they can handle it,' said the Police Lieutenant General, 'so can we.'

CHAPTER 23

'Christ,' said Phil when he and I and Vik had got rid of the embassy guy and our lawyer and were back to the Grande Bretagne Hotel. 'You were a bit leery with that Chief Inspector, Scott. I'd forgotten how much you dislike the police.'

'Actually, I don't mind Varouxis all that much. He's only doing his job. But then so am I. Looking after my players, dead or alive, is what this job is about. At least, that's the way I see it. And while I don't see Varouxis taking cash from a tabloid, I can't say the same for any of the people who work for him. If you're a Greek cop a bit of extra money would come in handy, I bet. Premier League footballer scores home and away and everywhere in between. That's the kind of story the English papers would love to run.'

'All the same,' said Phil, 'I still think you were a bit sharp with him.'

'As a matter of fact, Phil,' said Vik, 'it was me who told Scott to deny the cops access to Bekim's iPhone and his laptop until I've seen if he had any emails from me. You see, a few months ago Bekim bought some property in Knightsbridge on my behalf I'd rather no one knew about.'

'Sorry,' said Phil. 'I didn't realise.'

'As soon as Pete Scriven has brought them over from the team hotel in Vouliagmeni I intend to erase anything there that might connect me with the Knightsbridge deal. With Scott watching, of course. I wouldn't like either of you to think I'm up to no good here.'

'Of course not,' said Phil.

'The thing is, though,' added Vik, 'Scott is right. Bekim always did like escort girls a little too much for his own good. It's probably best we try to keep a lid on that as well, if we can.'

Phil shrugged. 'All right. I get that, too. But what I don't get is why the cops are making such a fuss about this. I should have thought that getting murdered was an occupational hazard for a prostitute. I mean, that's the risk you run when you go with a man you've never met before, isn't it?'

'That's no reason to write her off, Phil,' said Vik. 'She was a human being, after all.'

'I wasn't writing her off so much as making a comment on the Greek police. Why are they taking the death of one little tart so seriously? There are thousands of tarts in this city. Since the recession hit Greece back in 2009, it's about the only growth profession there's been in this bloody country.'

'It sounds a lot like you're writing her off,' said Vik. 'Look, Phil, she might have been a prostitute but murder is murder and the death of a prostitute creates its own peculiar, not to say lurid, sensation. Dropping a beautiful girl in the harbour with a weight tied around her feet is just the sort of dramatic detail than the newspapers love.'

'I don't think she was a prostitute,' I said. 'More like a high-class escort. It's splitting hairs perhaps but I think that's something different from a common prostitute. Bekim may have been many things, but he was extremely picky when it came to women. My guess is that she was expensive and probably quite picky herself. For a girl like that I should think the chances of a client bumping her off are quite slim, really. All of which means she ought to be easier to identify.'

Vik laughed. 'I must say, you sound remarkably expert about this sort of thing, Scott. It makes me wonder what you get up to in your private life.'

'Maybe Scott thinks he could find out who killed her,' said Phil. 'After all, he does have some form in this area. As an amateur sleuth, I mean.'

'Maybe I could,' I said. 'Maybe I should try, in any case. For the sake of Bekim.'

Why not, I thought; following my previous trip to Athens I was actually possessed of a significant line of potential inquiry although it wasn't one I wanted to share with the police or anyone else. Valentina didn't deserve that; and nor did Bekim Develi. I didn't know how much Bekim's girlfriend knew about the dead girl's connection with him, but I had a shrewd idea that there would have been plenty of speculation about it on Twitter. This would hardly have helped her state of mind and might even have been the reason why she'd taken too much cocaine.

'At the very least I might be able to accelerate the police inquiry. The Greeks don't look like they're in any great hurry to get this case solved, in spite of what they said back there. And if the cops are half as unpopular as Dr Christodoulakis said they were, local people might be a bit slow coming forward with information. They might need some help.'

'What about team discipline?' said Phil. 'And next week's match?'

'Simon can take charge of the training sessions,' I said. 'If they're training at eight in the morning to avoid the heat then they can hardly be out late at night. He'll soon find out if anyone's been breaking the curfew. And if they have, well, no one's better at handing out bollockings than him.'

'If you do decide to play cop then make sure you do it discreetly,' said Phil. 'Pissing off the Met is one thing. Pissing these Greek coppers off is something else. From what I've seen of them on the telly they're not exactly known for their tolerance. They like cracking skulls.'

'Sure, I'll be careful.'

'I was going to fly back to London for the day,' said Vik, 'to see Alex. But under the circumstances I think I'll stick around. Besides, I still have some business here in Greece. With Gustave Haak and Cooper Lybrand.'

'And Kojo?' said Phil. 'Did you make a decision?'

'Let's not discuss that now.'

'As you wish.'

'I like this idea, Scott. You playing the sleuth again. You know, after the way you found out what happened to Zarco while the Metropolitan Police were still playing with their whistles, I thought about this a lot. I mean, the way you worked out what had really happened. And I said to myself, maybe it's true, perhaps to be an effective manager you have to be a little bit like a detective: able to look at men, read them like paperbacks, and find the clues as to who they really are and not who they seem to be. But most of all I think they both have to be patient. That's what I mean. And Scott is a very patient man.'

'A few months behind bars will do that to anyone,' I said. 'All you've got in the nick is patience.'

'Well, don't worry,' said Phil, 'if you can't find out who killed her, then you can always do what every other manager does: you can blame the referee.'

CHAPTER 24

'I think it's only fair you should know what I'm looking for,' explained Vik as he scrolled through Bekim's Inbox and Sent file in the suite at the Grande Bretagne. 'I wanted to buy the penthouse at One Hyde Park and I didn't want my wife to know about it. So, Bekim agreed to be a cut-out and to purchase the penthouse using his own company.'

'It's really none of my business,' I said.

'Yes, it is,' said Vik, 'when we might be erasing something on a computer the police are about to examine forensically. People go to prison for this kind of thing. And since you've been in prison, you have a right to know what the hell I'm doing here.'

'Lying to the police isn't a crime,' I said. 'Not in my book. No more than it's a crime to tell your wife that her bum really doesn't look big.'

Vik grinned. 'She asked you, too, huh?'

As things turned out, Vik didn't have to erase any of the emails and messages from Bekim's computer or on his iPhone because he found nothing that looked as if it might expose something confidential.

Not that I would have known if there had been anything compromising. Half of Bekim's emails were written in Cyrillic which meant that after Vik had gone I felt obliged to telephone

Chief Inspector Varouxis and inform him of this, so that he might bring someone with him who spoke, and more importantly read, Russian.

'Look, I wasn't lying to you this morning,' I said when I called. 'There really isn't anything on his phone or his laptop. If there was, I'd have told you. We're keen to get home, remember?'

'All right. Say for the sake of argument I believe you. How did he contact this girl?'

'There could have been a hundred different ways. Perhaps they spoke on the phone in London. Or he used the computer in his office there. Or maybe he called the girl with someone else's mobile phone while he was here in Athens. Or phoned from the lobby. Perhaps he used a web-based email service that didn't even show up on his computer. Like Hushmail.'

'Hushmail?'

'It offers authenticated, encrypted messages in both directions. Just the thing for a promiscuous man with a nosy girlfriend back in London.'

'Yes, I take your point. Okay, I'll ring you back when I've found someone who speaks Russian. Thanks for letting me know.'

'No problem.'

'This reward you're posting for information. Please keep me informed if you discover anything. Anything at all.'

He sighed and I almost felt sorry for him until I remembered that he was the bastard keeping my team in Greece.

'Of course. Right away.'

When Varouxis had hung up I tried calling Valentina but she wasn't answering her phone so I sent her an email and a text asking her to contact me urgently. I had a shrewd idea that the dead girl might be known to her; that something had prevented Valentina herself from going to Bekim's bungalow at the hotel, and that the dead girl had gone in her place. I couldn't imagine that Bekim would have settled for second best so I decided that the dead girl, whoever she was, must have been a beauty like Valentina otherwise Valentina would never have sent her along to Bekim.

But by the afternoon I must have called Valentina at least a dozen times and left as many texts without receiving a reply. This was quite the opposite of how she had behaved when last I'd been in Athens and I was forced to admit the possibility that Valentina knew she herself had escaped the other girl's Plenty O'Toole fate and, in fear of her life, was now lying low. I didn't blame her for that but without an address this all seemed to stymie my plan to steal a march on the Athens police. I could hardly follow up on my lead without the cooperation of the lead herself. Yet I was still reluctant to hand over her name and number to Chief Inspector Varouxis. It wasn't just that I had little wish for my own behaviour to come out in public, or that I was trying to look out for Valentina or Bekim, but if the police were as right-wing as Dr Christodoulakis had said they were, I didn't want the cops brushing the whole thing under the carpet and suggesting to the press that because Bekim and Valentina were both Russian this was nothing to do with Greeks.

Without much of a clue how else my so-called investigation was to proceed, I had Vik's driver take me to Piraeus and the Marina Zea where Varouxis said the girl's body had been found. I was already regretting my own arrogance in imagining that just because I knew something the cops didn't, I could perhaps solve the dead girl's murder. The main road took us close to the Karaiskakis Stadium and, next to this, the Metropolitan Hospital where Bekim had died. I hadn't really looked at the hospital before; it was a strangely modern building constructed of blue glass and looked more like a Ladbrokes casino than what was supposed to be the best private hospital in Greece. It was hard to think of Bekim dying in a place like that.

Marina Zea was a large harbour full of expensive Tupperware boats and overlooked by a hillside encrusted with numerous beige-coloured apartment buildings of mostly poor quality. The police were still in evidence on the furthest side of the marina and it was not yet permitted for anyone to go there, so I amused myself walking around and looking at the floating palaces, the largest and most opulent of which was a modestly named vessel called *Monsieur Croesus*, and which I seemed to recognise, although I have no interest in boats. One floating apartment building looks much like another and to me spending tens of millions of pounds on something like a yacht always seemed the height of folly; boats sink, after all.

I walked on a bit. I don't know what I was looking for beyond a sense of how difficult it would be to bring a girl here and drop her into the water with a weight tied to her feet. At night, I decided, it would not be difficult at all. There was ample parking; of course, if she'd been on a boat it would have been even easier. I chucked a couple of stones into the water to test the depth and stirred up a little school of quite reasonable-sized fish; these, I supposed, were *gavroi* – the shit-eating fish to which our liaison from Panathinaikos had compared the players and supporters of Olympiacos.

It was a hot, sticky afternoon. Some of the city's ubiquitous, mostly Roma, garbage pickers were going through the wheelie bins and open skips on the marina. Several boys were diving in and out of the harbour, and climbing on the guy ropes of another, untended boat. It looked more fun than picking garbage and I almost envied the boys their carefree pastime until I remembered that it had been some boys diving in the harbour who'd found the dead girl's body. Which gave me an idea.

They were about eleven or twelve years old, tanned and skinny, the very image of urchins, as if they had been truly dredged off the sea floor.

'Speak English?' I asked one of them.

He shook his sleek black head.

I went back to the car and fetched my driver to translate and when I came back I asked the boys if it had been them who'd found the dead girl's body.

Two of the boys looked at each other and then nodded.

Holding up two twenty-euro notes I sat down on the wall of the harbour and asked them to tell me what they'd seen, in as much detail as they could remember. The two boys sat beside me and I handed over the cash, while the others looked on and listened as my driver, Charilaos, squatted behind us and translated what was said and offered around his cigarettes, which helped almost as much as the money.

'It was yesterday morning when they found her,' he said. 'Maybe ten o'clock in the morning. She was on the Koumoundourou side of the harbour, where the police are now, in about four metres of water.'

'Was it near to any boat in particular and if so which one?'

'Between two boats,' said Charilaos. 'Both for sale, as it happened. And the owners were not aboard. They know this because they went aboard each boat to try and get help.'

'Tell me what she looked like, this girl.'

'A very pretty girl with long blonde hair and wearing a dark blue dress. The water isn't very clear as you can see

148

and but for the blue dress they might have found her earlier. She gave them quite a shock.'

One of the boys looked embarrassed as he spoke again.

'But she wasn't wearing any knickers, he says. Her dress was floating under her arms.'

'Were her hands tied?'

The same boy spoke again and then Charilaos said, 'No, her hands were floating in the water, above her head. It was only her feet that were tied to a big orange weight. Of the type you see in a gym.'

'Any gag?'

'No gag.'

'Was she wearing shoes?'

'No. No shoes.'

I took out my notebook and asked the boy to draw a picture of what the weight looked like and he drew what looked to me like a kettlebell. I nodded.

'Were there any other injuries on her body that they saw?' I asked. 'Cuts, bruises, any blood?'

'No,' Charilaos translated, 'but the fishes were feeding on her private parts.'

'No bumps on her head? No cuts on her hands?'

'The boys says her hands were very nice. Her nails, too. Like her toenails. I think he means she had a manicure.'

'What colour?' I asked.

'They think purple.'

'Any jewellery?'

The boys looked a bit shifty.

'He insists she wasn't wearing any jewellery,' said Charilaos, 'but I don't believe him. For sure they stole it.'

'Forget it. Anything else that might distinguish or identify her?'

One of the boys said something and Charilaos asked him to repeat it.

'*Tatouáz*,' was the word he used.

'She had a tattoo,' said Charilaos.

'What kind of a tattoo?' I asked. 'And where?'

'On her shoulder. A sort of geometrical design, in black. It sounds to me like he means a *lavýrinthos*. You know? Like the story of Theseus and the Minotaur.'

'A labyrinth?'

'That's right. About the size of a teacup.'

'Did he tell that to the police?'

Charilaos laughed. 'I don't think so,' he said. 'I don't think the police were offering forty euros in cash. Besides, people in Athens, in Piraeus—'

'I know. They hate the police.'

Our walk back to the car took us past *Monsieur Croesus* again and this time I was surprised to see someone I knew standing on one of the upper decks; not only that but someone who recognised me, which was perhaps more unusual. It was Cooper Lybrand, the hedgie. He wasn't wearing the white suit any more but he still looked like a cunt.

'Hi there,' he said. 'What brings you down here?'

'Curiosity,' I said. 'They fished a dead girl out of the water on the other side of the marina. Apparently she spent the night with one of our players. So now we're forbidden to leave Athens. I just wanted to take a look at the spot for myself.'

'I heard about that,' he said. 'And about Bekim. I'm sorry.'

'I thought you were staying on Viktor's boat,' I said.

'I was. But I had some business with the guy who owns this one. Gustave Haak. And now here I am. We only docked here an hour ago so I guess that puts us in the clear, huh?'

'If you say so.'

'I'd invite you on board but it's not my boat. Gustave is a very private person.'

'Who says I am?'

Another head appeared on deck. Older and taller than Cooper Lybrand, he had a full head of longish grey hair, a face like a hawk and almost invisible glasses.

'Gustave. This is Scott Manson. He manages Vik's football club.'

'Of course, I know who Scott Manson is,' said Gustave Haak. 'Do you take me for an idiot? Forgive our manners, Mr Manson, and please come aboard. We're just about to have a glass of wine.'

I looked at my watch. 'All right. As a matter of fact I could use a drink.'

I told Charilaos I'd see him back at the car and went aboard.

By this time, Cooper Lybrand had told Haak what I was doing in Marina Zea and Haak was full of questions about the dead girl, most of which I was unable to answer.

'But you're quite right to come down here and take a look for yourself,' he said, ushering me into a spectacular drawing room that looked like it had been designed by a man with no children: everything was white. 'I find that the best, most original ideas come to me when I'm not behind a desk. It's the same when I'm investigating a company with a view to taking it over. You have to have good intel to know what the right move is going to be. Without that, you have nothing.' He smiled and waved at one of the many cartoonish blondes wearing very fetching white uniforms – which is to say they were all wearing white swimsuits and white sneakers.

'Will you have some of this excellent German Riesling, Mr Manson?'

'Thanks, I will.'

One of the blondes handed me a glass of liquid gold while Haak continued talking.

'I love the game of football,' he declared. 'And the thing I appreciate about football managers is that, unlike most managers in most businesses, you always know what they do. They manage football teams. And they're either good or they're bad. Most companies are full of managers who do nothing. No, that's not quite true. Most of them fuck things up, which is worse than doing nothing. I spend most of my time trying to find out who they are so that I can fire them. As soon as you do, the value of the company always goes up. It's uncanny. Anyway, that's my job, Mr Manson. The elimination of managers who are redundant in all but name.'

He was Dutch, I think, because his accent reminded me of Ruud Gullitt. Fortunately for him he had a better haircut.

'Vik tells me that you're a good manager, Mr Manson. But do you think it's wise to get involved in this? Wouldn't it be better to leave things to the police?'

'Have you met the police here in Attica, Mr Haak?'

'No, I can't say that I have.'

'The way I see it, Mr Haak, I can do one of two things in a situation like this. I can look to see if I can do anything, anything at all to help sort it out; or I can do nothing. I'm generally the kind of person who likes to do something, even if that something turns out to be not very much. For all I know that might push me into the category of manager you don't like, the kind who fucks things up. But, you know, I never mind fucking up just as long as I learn something.

In that respect at least I'm just like the police. They fuck up all the time and it never seems to deter them.'

'Good for you,' he said. 'And now because I'm a Dutchman, let's talk about something more important. Let's talk football.'

CHAPTER 25

Back at the Grande Bretagne I had a light dinner on my own in the Winter Garden restaurant next to Alexander's Bar and contemplated my next move. The only people calling or texting me were journalists and someone called Anna Loverdos from the Hellenic Football Federation – the Greek equivalent of the FA – offering her assistance, as well as several other managers sympathising with London City's plight, including José Mourinho, which struck me as a little out of character.

I watched a guy talking to a girl in the bar at the same table where I'd first met Valentina and after a while I knew I recognised the barman serving them as the same one who'd served us. After I charged my dinner to Vik's suite, I went and sat at the bar under the sceptical eye of Alexander the Great who knew a thing or two about murder himself having connived at the death of his own father, Philip.

The guy with the girl at my old table was working hard to seem like a regular sort; he was from Australia, one of those impeccably casual, sockless types, with stubble that never seems to grow beyond a certain uniform length. But I figured he was on the wrong side of five feet six inches and while he was doing his best to seem relaxed, he wasn't. Short guys are always bustling around like terriers to make up for their lack of inches; it's fine if you're Messi or Maradona but for most guys it's a problem. Especially when they're with a girl as tall as this one was; she looked like a Trojan prince's wet dream with beanstalk legs, plenty of big black hair, and a bow mouth that was probably too big for Cupid but looked just right for me.

The barman came over and I ordered a Macallan 1973. At three hundred and ten euros a glass that got his attention; and it was his attention I wanted more than I wanted the Scotch. When he brought the bill, I put four crisp one hundred euro bills into the maroon leather folder and told him to keep the change. As he reached for the folder I covered it with my hand.

'Maybe you remember me?'

He shook his head. 'Sorry, sir, I don't.'

'I was here a few weeks ago when Olympiacos played the German side, Hertha FC. I was in here with a girl. A Russian girl. Blonde. She wore a tweed minidress and Louboutin high heels. Her name is Valentina and I got the feeling you certainly remembered her from another time. On the Richter scale I would say she was at least an eight point nine. The kind of girl that causes major structural damage, even to earthquake-resistant wallets and credit cards. You remember her?'

I removed my hand from the folder, sat back on the stool and sipped some of the Scotch. The barman was looking at the folder and trying to work out if a ninety euro tip was more than he was making in salary that evening; we both knew it was.

'Come on. Aloysius Alzheimer would remember a girl like that.'

With a pimp moustache, a dinner-plate waist and a Derby winner's teeth, the barman looked like Freddy Mercury. He took the folder and laid it under the counter. 'Valentina? Yes. I remember her. I wouldn't say she's a regular in this bar, but maybe once or twice a month she comes in here.'

'With a different guy?'

'Not every time. But always with someone like you. A foreigner with plenty of money.'

'A working girl.'

He shrugged. 'This is Greece, sir. Any work is good work, nowadays. Who can afford to be proud about such things? Look at me: I used to be a university lecturer, in Chemistry. Now I mix cocktails for fifteen hundred euros a month. For fifteen hundred euros a night, who knows what I would do? But a *poutána* she was not. The doorman would never have allowed her in here. Excuse me for one minute, please.'

He went away to make some drinks for a few minutes and then came back.

'Did you ever see her with Bekim Develi, the footballer?'

'I liked him,' said the barman. 'And now that he's dead I wouldn't like to cause his family any distress. He was almost as good a tipper as you are.'

'I'm his family,' I said. 'As good as. I'm the manager of London City. My boss, Viktor Sokolnikov, is renting the royal suite. You might say we're trying to do a bit of damage limitation. Damage to Bekim's reputation, that is. The whole team is stuck in Athens until the police have satisfied themselves that there's no connection between Bekim and the death of another working girl.'

'This was in the newspaper, yes, I know.'

'We don't know this girl's name, yet. But perhaps she was a friend of Valentina's. That's what I'm trying to find out. Another hair-salon blonde with a labyrinth tattoo on her shoulder. I figure the best way of us getting home is to prove that Bekim had nothing to do with her death, but we can only do that if we can identify her. And to do that I need to find Valentina. Valentina and the dead girl – they both had Bekim in common, you see.'

'I understand, sir. I'm *prasinos*, myself. Green through and through. I have no love for Olympiacos. The way that bastard Hristos Trikoupis behaved after the game was a disgrace to this country. I'm surprised you didn't hit him. So I would enjoy it very much if you beat those bastards when next you play them. I tell you, it was the best moment of my life when the Greek Football Federation stripped the *gavroi* of all those points and took the championship away from them. So, I will tell you what I know.

'Valentina – I don't know her surname – but this was a nice woman, for a Russian. She always left me good tips, you know? Her Greek was very good. As was her English. She liked going to art galleries and museums. And she always carried a book, which is unusual. Also I think maybe she lived close to this hotel because one time when I was going home on my scooter I saw her walking in the street. She looked like she was also going home. Where was this now? Around the corner. Somewhere between Akademias and Skoufas.'

'Why do you think she was going home?'

'The streets are very steep there and she had her shoes off. The way women do when they've finished for the evening. Like they don't mind if they get their feet dirty.'

I nodded. 'Fair enough.'

'In here I never seen her with any other guy I recognised. But I did see her with another girl. Not a girl with a labyrinth tattoo on her shoulder. Another girl.'

'Do you have a name for this other girl?'

'No. But I can tell you who this girl is. I can even tell

you where to find her.' He looked across my shoulder and nodded at the girl with the beanstalk legs who even now was leaving the Alexander bar with her diminutive friend. 'It was her. I'm sure of it. This girl was a friend of Valentina's. She's Russian, too.'

I finished my Scotch and was about to follow them when the barman took me by the arm.

'The guy with her is staying in the hotel. And I expect they're going upstairs to his room. You wait there, and I'll make sure.'

He followed them out of the bar and was gone for a couple of minutes. When he came back he collected the leather folder and the bill off the table where the girl with the legs had been seated.

'Mr Overton went up to room 327 with her.'

'How do you know?'

The bar man grinned and flipped open the folder to reveal the bill with the Australian's name and room number written there by him.

'I followed them to the elevator,' he said. 'Now all you have to do is wait for her to come down again.'

I looked at my watch; it was just eight thirty. 'It's kind of early,' I said. 'They could be a while, don't you think?'

The barman shook his head. 'A girl like that costs a lot of money,' he said. 'My guess is that she'll be back down here in the lobby just before ten. You can set your watch by some of these girls. Tell you what: I'll speak to the concierge and get him to send her up to your room when she's through with the other guy. Until then, relax. Have another drink.'

I ordered a beer. The Macallan 1973 was good, but it wasn't worth three hundred and ten euros a glass. Nothing is.

CHAPTER 26

My iPhone rang in the royal suite. It was Peter Scriven, the team's travel manager.

'The hotel manager is already asking me how long I think we're going to be here. He's got other guests who are arriving at the weekend. The Ministry of Culture is trying to find us another hotel but it's high season and things are tight.'

'They can't have it both ways. They can't forcibly detain us in their country and throw us out of our fucking hotel. Can they?'

'I wouldn't put it past them, boss. This is Greece. From what I've read about us in the papers we should count ourselves lucky they're not demanding the Elgin marbles back before they let us go.'

The doorbell rang.

'I've got to go, Pete. Talk to you later.'

The girl standing at the front door smiled broadly when she saw that the occupant of the royal suite didn't actually look like a royal and said, 'Hi, I'm Jasmine. Panos said you were looking for company.'

'Panos?'

'The barman downstairs.'

'Yes, of course. Come in, come in. '

'Thank you.'

'I'm Scott,' I said, closing the door behind her. 'Pleased to meet you, Jasmine.'

'Are you here on business?'

'In a way.'

She stalked slowly around the suite like a girl holding the round card for a fight at the MGM Grand. In the wine cellar she squealed; and in the dining room she let out a gasp. Then, for a moment, she stood up on tiptoe by the fifth-floor window, looking one way and the other, like a beautiful meerkat.

'Great view,' she said.

'It is from where I'm standing,' I muttered, then added, 'This suite is a little fancy for my taste, but then I'm not royal.'

'Oh, I like it. I like it a lot.' She sat down on one of the many sofas and arranged her legs, carefully, which is to say what I was now looking at was a perfect geometry of flesh and high-heels that Euclid never dreamed of – for which the only algebraic formula could be $S=EX^2$.

I offered her a drink from the extensive bar. She asked for a Coke. I fetched us both one from the fridge and sat down beside her on the sofa. Her hair was nicely combed and she smelt lightly of scent; it was hard to believe that she'd just come from another guy's bed. But then some of these girls can scrub up in less time than it takes for a scally to steal a car.

'Can we get the business out of the way first of all?' I asked, like a real John.

'I'm glad you mentioned that,' she said. 'It's five hundred for an hour. Eight for two. And two thousand for the whole night. Nice suite like this. Be a shame to waste it sleeping.'

I took out my wallet and counted four new one hundred Euro notes onto the coffee table. 'Listen, Jasmine. All I want to do is talk.'

'All right,' she said. 'What do you want to talk about, Scott?'

'Jasmine,' I said. 'You're Russian, right?'

She nodded, suspiciously. 'You're not a cop, are you?'

'This is the royal suite, not police headquarters. And that's cash on the table, not a bailout from the European Central Bank. Really, I'm not a cop. I hate the cops.'

Jasmine shrugged. 'Some of them aren't so bad.'

'Do you know a girl called Valentina, Jasmine? And please don't say, no, because I know you do. Your friend Panos told me. All I really want from you is some information about her. You tell me what you know about her, you take the money and then you go. Simple as that.'

'Is she in trouble?'

'No. Not yet. As a matter of fact that's what I'm trying to save her from. It's important that I speak to her before the cops do. Really, you'd be doing her a favour. Nobody wants cops in their life. Not if they can help it. I had a brush with them once, in London, and it's left me badly scarred. Cops are like herpes: once you've had them, they always come back.'

'You want her phone number? Her email? I can give you this. For free.'

She opened her bag and took out a little notebook and after consulting it for a minute or so, she wrote a number and email on a piece of paper.

I glanced at it. I knew the number by heart, I'd already called it so many times; and her email was almost as familiar.

'Any other contact numbers? A postal address? A Skype address, perhaps? Only I've been ringing this number all day and she hasn't called back.'

Jasmine shook her head. 'That's all I have. Sorry.'

'Pity.'

I didn't suppose for a minute that Jasmine was this girl's real name; I imagined she'd chosen it because she thought the name made her seem more alluring; it didn't. I was doing my best to be brisk and businesslike, but it wasn't working very well, at least not for me. She couldn't have seemed more alluring to me if I'd been tied to the mast of the Argo.

'All right. Let's try something different. Did you ever work together? You know, for a client who wanted to see two girls. That kind of thing?'

It was a pleasant thought; and one that would have been all too easy to have made a reality.

'I asked her to do this once. But she said no. She preferred to work alone. Without an agency. And to pick and choose who her clients were. She could have made much more money than she did, I think. Have you met her?'

'Yes.'

'Then you know what I'm talking about. She's so beautiful. And clever, too.'

'What else can you tell me about her?'

'She is from Moscow. A graduate in Russian literature. She likes going to art galleries and museums. She's into sculpture, I think.'

'How did you meet?'

'In the bathroom downstairs. She spoke to me. I guess I looked a bit more obvious than she did back then. She gave me a few tips on how to tone it down a bit so I wouldn't get thrown out of places like this. Once or twice I saw her in here, at the Intercontinental, or the St George. We would say hello and sometimes have a drink if we were waiting for someone. I liked her.'

'Can you think of anyone else who knew her? Other girls, perhaps?'

'No. Like I said, she didn't work through an agency or from a website. She relied on word of mouth.'

'What about a girl with a tattoo on her shoulder? A tattoo of a labyrinth.'

Jasmine frowned. 'I've seen a girl like that talking to Valentina, perhaps. But I didn't know her name.'

'Was she Russian, too?'

'I think so. A lot of the girls working in Athens are Russians these days.'

I decided to level with Jasmine in the hope that what I told her would jog her memory, or even scare her into remembering something.

'The reason I'm asking is this, Jasmine: the girl with the labyrinth tattoo was found drowned in the harbour at Marina Zea sometime yesterday morning. As yet she hasn't been identified. All I know is that she might have known Valentina and that Valentina might be able to identify her.'

'But why? You said you weren't a cop.'

'I'm not. When did you last see Valentina?'

'Not for a while.' She shrugged. 'There are so many girls doing this kind of thing in Greece since the recession that it's hard to keep track of anyone. People drop out of the business all the time. But there's no shortage of girls to take their place.'

'One last question. Valentina's clients. Did you ever see her with one?'

'Maybe. But it's not the kind of thing you talk about.'

'Come on, Jasmine. It's important.'

'All right. I saw her with two clients. One was at a restaurant here in Athens called Spondi, with that footballer who died the other night: Bekim Develi. The other time she was getting into a man's car. Outside here, as it happens. A nice car. A new black Maserati.'

'Expensive.'

She shrugged. 'Believe me, this guy – he can afford it.'

'You recognised him? The client?'

Jasmine hesitated. Her eyes were on the money. 'If I tell you who it was, you won't say it was me who told you.'

I placed another fifty on the table. 'Not a word.'

'It was Hristos Trikoupis,' she said.

'The Olympiacos manager?'

She nodded.

'Are you sure it was Hristos Trikoupis?'

'Yes,' she sneered. 'It was him all right.'

'You're not a fan then?'

'Of Olympiacos? No.'

'Why? Because you support Panathinaikos?'

'No,' she said. 'My boyfriend supports PAOK. He's from Thessaloniki. Believe me, they hate Olympiacos just as much as those bastards from Panathinaikos.'

'Football,' I said. 'Ninety minutes of sport and a Trajan's Column of hatred and resentment.'

'Is it any different in England?'

'No.'

'I'm sorry I couldn't be more help.'

'No, you've helped me a lot. Really, you have. You can take your money and go if you like.'

She gathered up the money and left.

CHAPTER 27

The next morning I was outside the hotel at seven o'clock to find several journalists and TV crews waiting for me on what was left of the hotel's marble steps. These looked as if someone had attacked them with a hammer.

'What happened here?' I asked the doorman.

'Some people decided to throw some rocks at parliament last night,' he explained. 'So they used bits of our steps.'

'You're never getting the Elgin Marbles back. All right?'

I pushed my way through the scrum of microphones and cameras to where Charilaos was parked in the black Range Rover Sport, without giving any of the comments that first sprang into my mind.

'Morning, Charilaos,' I said. 'It looks like the press have tracked me down again.'

'Where are we going?' he asked as I closed the door.

'Apilion,' I said. 'Training session. Then Laiko General Hospital. Then back here at twelve for a meeting with Chief Inspector Varouxis.'

'Okay, sir. And call me Charlie. Everyone does.'

We drove off. In the back seat were some of the Greek newspapers and on most of the front pages was a likeness of the dead girl as drawn by a police artist. He or she had managed to make her look like the princess from a Disney cartoon and it was hard to imagine that a member of the public seeing this sketch would be prompted to call the police – except to recommend another artist.

I tossed the Greek papers aside and, for a while, read *The Times* I'd downloaded onto my iPad. There were plenty of column inches about City's plight in Athens. And now that UEFA had agreed for us to play our home match against Olympiacos at the ground of Panathinaikos, the story held even more interest that it had before.

'Will you need me this afternoon, sir?' asked Charlie.

'I'm afraid so. I thought I'd go and see my opposite number. Hristos Trikoupis. To discuss next week's match. I don't suppose you'd know where I could find him this afternoon.'

'You could always ring him up and ask,' suggested Charlie.

'I'd prefer him not to know I was coming.'

'Olympiacos have a match on Sunday evening. Against Aris. Right now he's probably at their training centre, in Rentis. You'll find it's very different from Apilion. Those red bastards have much more money.'

'You're not a fan, then, of Olympiacos.'

'No, sir. I've been always been Panathinaikos. Ever since I was a kid.'

'I envy you that, Charlie. You lose that devotion to just one team when you enter the world of professional football. Once you start playing for money you're a gun for hire and it's never the same again. Sometimes I think it would be nice just to follow a team; to be able to go and watch a game and be like everyone else, you know?'

'Right now it looks like it's us being followed, sir.'

I turned around in my seat.

'That silver Skoda Octavia,' he said. 'It was parked outside the hotel when I arrived this morning. And I've been around the block twice just to make sure.'

'Fucking journalists,' I said. 'When there's a piece of shit around there's always one of them there to peck at it.'

'More like cops,' said Charlie.

I turned around again.

'How do you work that out?'

'Because no one else in Athens wants to drive the same shitty car as the Hellenic Police. And because there are just two of them.'

'If they're cops, why the fuck are they following me?'

'Without wanting to alarm you, it's probably for your protection, sir. Now that it's been announced in the news-papers that you're playing the next leg against those red *malakes* in our stadium, there will be plenty of them who think you've made common cause with their most mortal enemies: the Greens. You might actually be in danger of being attacked yourself.'

'That's a comforting thought.'

Ten or fifteen minutes later we saw Mount Hymettus. The only clouds in the otherwise blue sky were collected on the undulating summit as if to shield the gods from the impor-tunate eyes of men. I could have wished for such privacy; the press were also in full force outside the training ground and Charlie was obliged to slow the car to a crawl as we approached the gate.

The training session was already in progress; and Simon Page's voice carried across the playing fields like a Yorkshire zephyr. No matter how many times I heard him explaining the purpose of a particular training exercise he always made me smile; this was no exception:

'It was Edson Arantes do Nascimento, more usefully known to us as Pelé, who first described football as the beautiful game. Now in Brazilian football the sole of the foot is used to control the ball much more often than in England. Like this. Left to right. To left, to right. If it feels odd to you that's good; that's why we're practising this. You can pass with the sole, you can dribble with the sole, you can check the ball with the sole. Most of what you see from Cristiano Ronaldo involves the sole of the boot. That boy can do more with the underneath of his foot than a fucking chimpanzee. So what I want to see now is you passing the ball from one sole to another, left to right to left. Slowly at first with one leg planted on the floor, and then, running on the spot, left to right to left. Nice and wide. Okay. Off you go. Don't look at the fucking ball, Gary. Keep your heads up. If this was a fucking game you'd be looking for someone to pass to. Even a greedy bugger like you, Jimmy.'

Seeing me, Simon walked over to the touchline and with arms folded watched our players as they continued with their technical training.

'If you can get Gary Ferguson to play like a Brazilian I'll eat your England cap,' I said. 'He's got the ball skills of Douglas fucking Bader.'

'Aye, but he's got the best eye for the ball of any centre back I've seen. Not to mention shin bones like a couple of crowbars. Gary could take the legs off a bloody dining table.'

'He's certainly a fearsome-looking figure. Especially with his plate out. He always gives a new meaning to the phrase "man marking".'

For a moment we were silent as we watched the players.

'Prometheus is probably the most gifted player on the park right now,' said Simon. 'Everything he does comes naturally.'

'Including being a cunt.'

'True. Although he's not been nearly so arrogant of late. Maybe it was Bekim's death. Or maybe it's just this place.' Simon took a deep euphoric breath of air and nodded. 'Smashing here, isn't it?'

'Apparently this training ground is named after a Greek poet.'

'Aye, well, that's easy to understand. If I had to look at that view every day I might write a poem myself.'

'I think I'd like to read a poem by you,' I said, wondering how many rhymes you could get for 'fuck' and 'cunt' which were, after all, the most frequent words in Simon's Yorkshire vocabulary. 'What's the mood like without Bekim?'

'Aye, well, that's a question.'

He went back on the pitch for a minute, organised another exercise and then came back.

'Now that we've lost our team Jesus,' I said, 'the other disciples are going to need inspiration.'

'You what, boss?'

'All teams need their own Jesus. Someone who can turn water into fucking wine, cure lepers and the blind, and raise the team from the dead when we're having a mare. Bekim was ours. So, who's the new team Jesus? That's the real question, Simon. Gary is a good captain, but he's not an inspiring figure. He's a discipline. And as last lines of defence go, he's the best. But he's not someone who can look you in the eye and persuade you that he's the answer to your prayers.'

Simon hummed and hawed an answer but in truth I already knew the answer to my own question. Before the pre-season window closed on 31 August I was going to have to persuade Vik to pay top money for the Hertha team captain, Hörst Daxenberger. With his long blond hair, blue eyes and beard,

Daxenberger was the nearest thing to Jesus I'd seen outside a crappy Hollywood movie. But to get him to come to City we were going to have to beat Olympiacos and qualify for Champions League; if we could do that, it'd be the one thing we could offer him that Hertha couldn't.

After the session was over I gathered the team and the playing staff around me in the warm sunshine and spoke to them.

'I know you all miss your families so let me say right away that Vik's lawyers haven't given up trying to persuade the police to change their minds about keeping us here in Athens. But unless a miracle happens it looks like we're remaining here for now. And let's face it, things could be a lot worse. The lads from Panathinaikos couldn't be more helpful and let's make sure they always know how grateful we are to them. Meanwhile, the sun's shining, the food is good and there's a nice beach at the hotel. I suggest you get a nice tan, download a book, use the gym and lay off the duty-free because we have the small matter of a Champions League match next week. Not to mention a three-goal deficit.

'So, I'll tell you what we know and then I'd like to invite anyone who can shed some light on any aspect of this sad affair to speak up – without fear of discipline or me grassing them up to the local filth. I promise you there will be no fines and no bollockings for anyone who can add to the store of what we know. Because I believe our best chance of getting out of here is to approach this like a team. To pool any information that we might have. I know the cops have already asked you about this and I don't know what you've told them, but I imagine it's not much. Bekim was your team mate and you're still looking out for him. I respect that. So am I. But this is me asking the questions now, not the cops. I want some answers.'

'Are you planning to play the amateur sleuth again, boss?' asked Gary. 'Like at Silvertown Dock when you helped find out who killed Zarco?'

'That's one idea. The cops are still trying to find their arseholes right now, so why not? It can't do any harm, can it? Now, as I'm sure you all know, Bekim rented girls like other people rent Boris bikes. Against team orders he had a girl back to his bungalow on Monday night, before the match. He fucked her six ways to Sunday, and the next day she was found at the bottom of the harbour with a kettlebell roped to her ankles. That's why we're being held here. The cops still don't know who she was. The question is, do any of you? Did he offer to spit-roast her with you? Did you hear anything? Did you see anything? As far as I can see she was a blonde, with a blue dress, and a tattoo of a labyrinth on her shoulder. Russian probably. Liked footballers, fuck knows why.'

'He told me he had a girl coming over to his bungalow,' said Xavier Pepe. 'And that she was something special. That she was Attica's best-kept secret and the most beautiful woman in Athens.'

'He actually used that phrase?'

Xavier nodded.

It was how Bekim had described Valentina before I had gone to Athens to see Hertha play Olympiacos.

'Can you remember what time it was when he said this?'

'It was after dinner,' said Xavier. 'About nine thirty.'

I took out my notebook and wrote this down, calculating that Bekim might actually have been expecting Valentina right up until the very moment when the other girl showed up

171

– according to Chief Inspector Varoúxis – at eleven o'clock.

'I think I might even have reminded him that his bungalow was next to yours, boss. And that he'd better be careful or you'd have his bollocks for breakfast.'

'And I would have done. So be warned. Anyone who thinks he might like a bit of local legover while we're here had better think again. Local cunt is definitely off menu until this thing is resolved.' I paused. 'Is that it, Xavi?'

He nodded.

'Anyone else?' I paused. 'What about this amulet that was found around his neck? Does anyone know anything about that? The detective I spoke to called it a *hamsa*. Apparently it resembles an open right hand. I'm pretty sure I never saw Bekim ever wear such a thing in England. And in spite of his attitude to my orders I'm quite sure he wouldn't have taken lightly the risk of falling foul of a UEFA official in Greece. They've handed out yellow cards for less.'

'I gave it to him.' It was Denis Abayev, the team's nutritionist – the man who had tried to lead everyone in prayer on the flight to St Petersburg when the plane had made an emergency landing.

'But you're the one Bekim accused of being a Muslim jihadi.'

'Only because he was scared,' explained Denis. 'Besides, he apologised for what he said almost immediately, didn't he? The *hamsa* is a good luck sign in the Middle East. It's also supposed to provide protection against the evil eye. I've been meaning to mention it to you before but I didn't like to, because you told me not to do anything religious near the players.'

'So why did you?'

'I gave him the *hamsa* to make him feel better. He might not

172

have believed in God, but Bekim was superstitious. He told me he thought someone was trying to put the hex on him.'

'What the fuck do you mean, "the hex"?'

Denis held up a little blue pendant that looked like a glass eye and handed it to me. 'He found this hanging on the handle of the French windows outside his bungalow, the night we arrived.'

'What is it?'

'It's a *mati*,' said Denis. 'An evil eye. They're very common here; you can buy them on any street corner in Athens. As an evil eye against the evil eye. Or just to mess with someone's head. And it did. Bekim was upset by it.'

I tossed the little blue eye back to Denis.

'Look, lads, the only evil eye I've ever seen that fucking works belongs to Roy Keane,' I said. 'That Irishman could stare down a Gorgon.'

'Nevertheless, Bekim Develi is dead, boss,' said Gary Ferguson. 'There's no getting away from it. This particular evil eye looks like it worked.'

'That's bollocks, and you know it, Gary. Look, this was just someone pissing around, right? A member of the hotel staff having a laugh. All the same, I'm beginning to see why the guys from Panathinaikos hate Olympiacos so much. It seems there's nothing these bastards won't do to try to put you off your game. Did you mention this to the cops, Denis?'

'No, boss.'

'Then let's keep it that way, shall we? We've got enough on our plate without the Greek cops thinking that someone wanted Bekim dead as well.'

'Too fuckin' right.' Gary shook his head. 'Sooner we get out of this shithole the better. When that cunt Inspector

Verucca was interviewing me, every time he breathed near me I almost passed out.'

I nodded. 'That career in television you were planning, Gary. After retirement. I think you're going to have to work on your media skills.'

CHAPTER 28

On my way back to the hotel to meet with Chief Inspector Varouxis I stopped at the Laiko General Hospital. I'd arranged with him that I could see Bekim's body and pay my respects, but mostly I just wanted to see that they were taking proper care of him. What with the strike I was concerned that they'd have my friend wrapped in a bin bag underneath some *keftedes* in the freezer.

It was a pink-coloured building in the city's northeast with little to distinguish it from any other public buildings in Athens. The word *dolofonoi* was graffitoed on one of the exterior walls near an entrance that was behind a line of orange trees. I'm fond of orange trees, but in Athens you find oranges lying on every street like fag-packets, which struck me as a little sad.

'*Dolofonoi*. What does that mean?' I asked Charlie, who'd come in to help me find the pathology department.

'It means "murderers".'

'Christ, I bet that fills the patients with confidence.'

'Anarchists,' he said. 'They think that by undermining everyone's morale they can bring down the state.'

The state didn't look too healthy to me but I kept my opinion to myself. I liked Charlie.

The doctors – and more importantly, the pathologists – were on strike, but the hospital orderlies were in a different union and so they were on duty; one of them led me down a long, badly lit corridor that looked like a left-luggage office, with dozens of refrigerated cabinets of the kind everyone's seen on *CSI*. The orderly was smoking a cigarette which, such was the cloying smell of human decay, might easily have been regarded as necessary for the job as the green scrubs he was wearing. A stepladder was standing in the middle of the floor as if someone had started to try to fix the faulty strip light on the ceiling, which was blinking like Morse code, and then changed their mind. The orderly checked a number on his clipboard and then moved the ladder with a loud tut and a sigh. He managed to make everything he did look like such a bloody inconvenience that I wanted to clout him on the back of his absurdly permed head. No less absurd was his flourishing black moustache which looked like a pair of spent Brillo pads.

Just as the strip light stopped blinking the orderly opened a door and drew out a drawer – the wrong drawer, that much was immediately apparent, for the toenails on the foot were neatly varnished with a pale shade of lilac.

'Perhaps if you took the fag out of your face you might see what the fuck you're doing,' I said under my breath.

But even as the orderly tutted again and closed the polished steel drawer, I knew I was now much more interested in the lady with the toenails than in Bekim's dead body. I'd remembered what one of the boys diving off Zea Marina had said: that the body they'd found in the water had a purple manicure. Of course to a boy, lilac looks the same as purple.

I let the orderly find the correct door and spent a sombre minute staring at Bekim Develi's body – it was hard to believe he was dead – before indicating with a curt nod that I was finished with him. But I wasn't finished in the mortuary. I needed to look at the girl's body too, if I could, for this had to be the girl from Marina Zea. How many dead bodies did they have with such perfectly varnished toenails? It hadn't occurred to me that they would have put the body of the girl who'd drowned in the same mortuary as Bekim Develi. And yet it made perfect sense, too.

Of course, being Sherlock Holmes is easier in Greece than it might be in other countries. When everyone looks as if they know by heart the words to 'Brother Can You Spare a Dime?', it's relatively straightforward for someone with money – someone like me – to buy exactly what he wants, more or less. But I was already learning not to be so absurdly generous. When the average monthly wage is just a thousand euros a nice new fifty is almost two days' pay. I held it up in front of him like a cup final ticket and told Charlie to tell him he could have it if he showed us the girl with the lilac toenails again.

The orderly hesitated only long enough to remove the cigarette from his mouth and then stub it out on the side of the stepladder. He pocketed the rest of it to smoke later, I supposed.

'I speak English,' he said, and took the note which he stuffed into the same pocket as his half-smoked cigarette. It looked like a metaphor for all of the EU's financial problems: the euro, in danger of going up in smoke because of Greek fecklessness.

He opened the previous steel door, pulled out the drawer, and swept back a grubby green sheet to reveal the stark-naked body of a girl. At the same moment the strip light started to flicker again and now I understood the purpose of the ladder, because the orderly mounted it and began gently flicking the fluorescent tube with a finger until it settled down again.

'*Eínai polý ómorfi,*' breathed Charlie. 'She's beautiful.'

'That she is,' I said. 'Quite stunning.'

Immediately I knew that I was looking at the right girl. She was in her mid-twenties, I supposed, with large breasts that looked fake, and a blonde pussy that was waxed to the point of non-existence – just a little bit of fluff to put on a show for a client, or for one to get rough with. More importantly there was a neatly done tattoo of a labyrinth on her left shoulder and, certain that the power of my fifty might not last for very long, I took out my iPhone and started to take pictures.

'No pictures,' said the man on the stepladder.

I ignored him.

'Don't worry,' I said. 'I'm not about to Instagram these. I'm hoping to find out what her name is. Not sell pictures of her muff.'

The orderly stopped tapping the light – which was working again – and came back down the ladder.

'Please, stop what you're doing – if these pictures get in the newspapers I could lose my job. That's a risk I can't afford. Even a job that doesn't pay money is still a job.'

I stopped taking pictures and found him another fifty from inside my pocket.

'Who said it doesn't pay money?' I said.

Reluctantly he took the fifty.

'But look,' I added, 'I give you my word you won't see these pictures in the newspapers. You know who I am, you must have read about this. The police are holding my team here in Athens while they investigate the death of this girl. On Monday night she had sex with Bekim Develi. And until they know her name and exactly what happened to her that night we're stuck here. Meanwhile the pathologists are on strike so there can't even be an autopsy. And the cops might as well be on strike for all the use they are.'

'You have my sympathies, sir; no one likes the cops in this town.' He nodded. 'So I will not insist that you erase these pictures you have taken on one condition.'

'What is it?'

'You're training at Apilion, aren't you? With Panathinaikos.'

'That's right.'

'Have they told you what animals the people who support Olympiacos are? That they are all the bastards of Yankee sailors and whores.'

'As a matter of fact they have.'

'Then my condition is this, Mr Manson. That whatever happens next week, when you leave my country you don't think too badly of my team. My name is Spiros Kapodistrias and all my life I support Olympiacos. But what Hristos Trikoupis said about you before the match was very shameful, sir. And the way he held up four fingers for four goals instead of shaking your hand? This was also very bad. Things are terrible in my country right now, it's true; but Greece is the home of European civilisation and, in my opinion, this is not how the game should be played. Our team deserves better than this man. We're not all like him.'

'It's a deal,' I said. 'And I'm grateful.'

He pointed at the body lying on the open steel drawer. She looked like she was waiting for someone to switch on a sun lamp.

'Please, Mr Manson,' he said. 'Take as many pictures as you want.'

I turned on my iPhone again and clicked away for a whole minute. To my surprise there were no marks around her ankles, and I remarked on this.

'Then it would seem she did not struggle very much,' said Spiros. 'Perhaps she was drugged, or intoxicated. Better for her if she was. Of course this is something that only Dr Pyromaglou will be able to determine.'

'Who's Dr Pyromaglou?'

'She's the senior pathologist here at Laiko; it's her who's been given this case by the Chief Medical Officer. It will be Pyromaglou who carries out the autopsy on this poor woman when—'

'She stops being on strike.' I pulled a face. 'Whenever that might be.'

'Pyromaglou does not want to be on strike, you understand. But it's been many weeks since any of us were paid in this hospital.'

'So why isn't your union on strike, Spiros?'

'Because it's not our turn to be on strike. Anyway, someone has to be here to care for the bodies. There would be a risk to public health if there was nowhere to put them. As it is, all of the other bodies in here are sharing a mortuary drawer with someone else.'

'That sounds cosy.'

'On police orders, these two – your player and the girl – are the only ones in here who rate a drawer to themselves.' Spiros nodded. 'Are you finished looking at her?'

'Yes.'

'Dr Pyromaglou,' he said, as he covered the body, returned it to the darkness of her steel sepulchre. 'I could give her your telephone number if you like.'

'Meaning what?'

'Only that if she wanted to make a private arrangement with you, then that would be her choice.'

'You mean to break the strike? To carry out an autopsy?'

Immediately, I took out my wallet and gave him my business card. I also gave him a card for the Grande Bretagne Hotel.

'She can call me anytime,' I said. 'And obviously I could make it worth her while.'

'The government could not ask such a thing, you understand,' said Spiros. 'That would be politically unwise for this particular coalition. And Pyromaglou certainly wouldn't do such a thing for the police. She hates the police. Her son got his skull broken by one of those thugs in the MAT. But yes, it's possible she might help you out.' Spiros shrugged. 'Besides, there are more ways to identify this girl and to say what might have happened to her than doing a full autopsy.'

CHAPTER 29

Back at the Grande Bretagne Hotel I spent an uncomfortable hour with Chief Inspector Varouxis. He and a Russian-speaking woman sat in the royal suite's capacious dining room examining Bekim's laptop and iPhone at one end of the table while, like their unwilling chaperon, I sat at the other end reading my newspaper on my iPad and enjoying a medium-sweet Greek coffee. It was probably the only thing I'd enjoyed so far that day. Some people call it Turkish coffee but don't expect anyone to bring you a Turkish coffee in Greece, or the other way around. Between two countries that hate each other even coffee has its politics.

Occasionally Varouxis called me over to explain something in the laptop's mailbox, and I would find myself in uncomfortable proximity with his breath. After the last explanation, I breathed in the flower arrangement on the mahogany sideboard to get the smell of his breath out of my head.

'Did you find anything useful?' I asked after the translator had left.

'No. You were right. However this girl contacted him, it wasn't by email or cell phone. At least not on this computer or phone.'

'Any leads yet on who she was?'

'We think she must have been working at the expensive end of the escort business. Her dress was by Alexander McQueen and retails at about two thousand euros. Her brassiere was Stella McCartney. About a hundred and fifty euros. Both were made for Net-a-Porter so we're hoping we can connect a garment number to a name. But these things take time. With any luck your reward will turn something up before then. There are signs all over Piraeus offering a reward for information so your lawyer, Dr Christodoulakis, will have her hands full. I expect there are a lot of people who would like to get their hands on ten thousand euros. Me, included.'

He probably knew that this was also the daily rate for the royal suite because he glanced around for a moment and then nodded. 'Everything is all right for you? Here in Athens?'

'It wouldn't seem right to complain,' I said. 'Not in this suite.'

'Perhaps not.'

'I'm just borrowing it. The club owner, Mr Sokolnikov, has taken it, to use as the team's base here in Athens.'

'You know, Mr Sokolnikov is worth almost twenty billion dollars. About a hundredth of the Greek government debt. It doesn't seem right that one man has so much when everyone else has so little. What do you think, Mr Manson?'

'So steal the soap if it makes you feel any better.'

'I was only making an observation.'

I shrugged. 'It's been my own observation that I'm being followed.'

'For your protection, it was thought best that some officers from the EKAM be assigned to you, Mr Manson.'

'But why me in particular?'

'Mr Sokolnikov already has several bodyguards, as you know. And your team stay safely out of trouble in their hotel on the peninsula at Vouliagmeni. It's only you who are in circulation, so to speak. And of course you were on television the other night.'

'It's not because you suspect me of murder?'

Varouxis tugged at the little beard he wore under his bottom lip; it reminded me of the tuft of pubic hair I'd seen on the dead girl's pussy earlier.

'I'm a policeman, Mr Manson. I have a suspicious mind. But no, as it happens, I don't suspect you of murder. One gets a feel for these things, the way you do about a player, perhaps. You're a hard man, I think, but not a murderer. However, I do wonder if you might perhaps be trying to do here in Greece what the newspapers said you did in London, with João Zarco. If you're planning to play detective again.'

'Why would you think that?'

'Because you are here in Athens and not back at the hotel with your team. Because you are almost certainly frustrated by the pace of this investigation; and if you're not, then Mr Sokolnikov will be: Russian oligarchs aren't known for their patience. And you are half German, so you probably think all Greeks are feckless and lazy, that we couldn't investigate our own arseholes. But in this case, I would strongly advise you to leave things to us, Mr Manson. Athens is a very different city from London. It's full of unexpected hazards.'

'Thanks, Chief Inspector, I'll bear that in mind. But right now, I'm planning to be a spy, not a detective.'

Varouxis frowned.

'I thought I'd take a drive over to the Rentis Training Centre,' I explained, 'to see what the opposition are up to, ahead of our return match next week.'

'They won't let you in,' said Varouxis. 'And there's a screen to stop nosy parkers. Besides, I happen to know that Olympiacos finish training at one on a Friday, after which

184

Trikoupis always goes to the same restaurant for lunch with his wife, Melina.'

'Oh well, thanks for the tip.' I looked at my watch. 'Perhaps I'll go and have some lunch myself. What's the name of this place Trikoupis goes to, so I can avoid it?'

'It's an old family place called Dourambeis. But don't avoid it altogether. It's probably the best fish restaurant in the city.'

'Thanks.'

'Don't mention it.'

He wasn't a bad guy, I decided, and I already regretted suggesting he steal the soap.

'What are you doing tomorrow afternoon, Chief Inspector? Only I have some spare tickets for the match. Panathinaikos versus OFI. Whoever they are.'

'Heraklion. A good team. This will be an excellent match. And I'd really love to go. But I regret I cannot. If my general found out I was going to a football match instead of investigating this murder he would be angry, I think.'

'Well, if you change your mind, give me a call. Most of my team are going to the game. You never know. One of them might say something useful. You know that's why football was invented, don't you? So men could talk to each other? Women had to invent book groups to do that. Talk, I mean.'

CHAPTER 30

This time, when I went outside the hotel, I saw them – two guys in their thirties leaning nonchalantly on the bonnet of a silver Skoda Octavia, smoking cigarettes and getting a little early afternoon sun on their unshaven faces.

'Where are we going now, sir?' asked Charlie.

'A restaurant in Piraeus called Dourambeis.'

'I know it.'

'Only see if you can get us there without our police escort,' I told him. 'For what I want to do this afternoon, I'd rather I didn't have any cops watching. Besides, I don't like being followed. It makes me feel like I'm being man-marked. I get antsy when I've got someone on my tail.'

Charlie nodded. 'Sure, sir. No problem.'

He started the engine and drove slowly away from the front of the hotel.

'*Can* you lose them?'

'This is Athens, sir. We have the worst traffic in Europe. In this city I could lose Sebastian Vettel.'

Charlie accelerated hard and, at the bottom of Syntagma Square, he turned sharply right and sped along a narrow shady street before making a swift left up a hill and then reversing into a small car park. Charlie made the big Range Rover feel like a Mini and it was immediately clear to me he was a professional driver. That shouldn't have surprised me, I suppose. Nearly all of the guys who drove for Vik had been on evasive driving courses; Vik took evasion in all its forms very seriously indeed: drivers, his wife, tax lawyers, not to mention a whole host of electronic countermeasures rumoured to have been installed on his private jet.

Charlie waited long enough to see the Skoda speed by in a futile attempt to catch us up – and then, when they were past, accelerated forward across the street and down another hill.

'We won't see them again for a while,' said Charlie.

'Neatly done,' I said.

At the top of the street he turned left, and drove south on the main road to Piraeus.

'Dourambeis is one of the best restaurants in Attica,' said Charlie. 'It's an old family place. Usually they're on holiday until the end of August. So I hope you checked that it's open.'

'You mean they close for the summer? When all the tourists are here in Athens?'

'Only for part of the month of August, sir.'

'But that's just crazy. Surely winter would be the time to close.'

'They close then, as well.'

'No wonder you've got a fucking recession. You're supposed to stay open during the tourist season, not bugger off on holiday. That's like a restaurant closing for lunch.'

Charlie grinned. 'It's Greece, sir. In this country people do things not because they make sense, but because they've always been done that way. Anyway, at Dourambeis I think you should have the scorpion fish. Off the fish counter inside the restaurant. It's the best in the city.'

'I'm not actually planning on eating,' I said.

'That's a pity.'

'At least not today. Hristos Trikoupis is having lunch there. I want to find out who he's with and perhaps follow him when he leaves. You see, I need to have a talk with him, in private.'

Charlie grinned. 'I like driving for you, sir. It's quite like the old days for me.'

'Meaning?'

'Before I went into private security, I used to be a cop.'

'What was your patch? Your speciality?'

'Low-level detective work. Nothing special. Burglaries, theft.'

'Why did you leave?'

'The money. In Greece it's always about the money. For everything.'

'I don't suppose you know Chief Inspector Varouxis.'

'Everyone knows Ioannis Varouxis,' said Charlie. 'He's the most famous detective in Athens. He was the cop who caught Thanos Leventis, a local bus driver who murdered three prostitutes in Piraeus, and attempted to kill at least three others. Apparently he cut off their nipples, fried them in salt and then ate them. The Greek newspapers called him Hannibal Leventis.'

'I wonder why Varouxis never mentioned this.'

'He's a very modest man, that Varouxis.'

'No, I meant I wonder why, when Varouxis is investigating the murder of a prostitute who probably had sex with Bekim Develi, that he never mentioned the deaths of those other prostitutes. It seems kind of relevant. Have the newspapers mentioned it?'

'No, sir. And they probably won't. At least not until – God forbid – another woman should be killed. You see, one of the women Leventis attacked was an English tourist, sir. It's not the sort of the thing that the Ministry of Tourism likes to remind people about. Especially at this time of year. It would be very damaging to the Greek economic recovery. Which is very fragile at the best of times. Tourism is one of the few industries we have got left.'

'Tell me, Charlie, this Hannibal Leventis – I suppose there's no chance they could have caught the wrong guy?'

'He admitted it, sir. In court. Although there was some talk of an accomplice who was never caught. The English woman who was attacked, she said there were two men who abducted her. One did the driving and the other one raped her. But none of the three victims who survived mentioned a second man, so her allegations were dismissed.'

'See if you can find out her name, Charlie, will you?'

'Sure. No problem, sir. I make a call when we stop the car.'

He drove in silence for a while; and then he said: 'A couple more things about Leventis, I just remembered.'

'Yes?'

'Sometimes he drove the Panathinaikos team bus. Sometimes.'

'And he used that bus?'

'Not that particular bus, sir. But another quite like it. That's why the girls got on in the first place. They thought it was a regular city bus.'

'And the other thing?'

'You have to remember about Panathinaikos and Olympiacos – they are the eternal enemies. This is a typical story for Athens and Piraeus since the Peloponnesian War, in four hundred BC. So then. On the Reds' website, they have a fan forum called the Shoutbox. And many Reds fans say the same thing: that the Athens police protected someone who was also involved in these murders because they support the Greens. That Hannibal's accomplice was allowed to go free.'

Charlie shook his head. 'Of course, that's a load of crap. Varouxis would never have done such a thing. I know this man. He is honest. Very honest.'

A few minutes later we pulled up outside a fairly unremarkable if large restaurant a stone's throw from the Karaiskakis Stadium in Piraeus. Several cars were parked outside, including a black Maserati Quattroporte, which, I presumed, belonged to Hristos Trikoupis.

'Is that it?'

'That is Dourambeis,' said Charlie. 'So, what now?'

I told him what Jasmine had told me about the Maserati.

'Okay,' he said. 'Wait here, sir. I go and take a look.'

He got out of the Range Rover, walked across the road to the restaurant and then went inside. A minute or so later he came outside again, bent down to look through the windows of the Maserati, and then trotted back to the passenger window of the car.

'I couldn't see him in the restaurant,' he said through the open window. 'But there are lots of private rooms in that place so he could be in one of them. There's a pass for the car park at Agios Ioannis Rentis on the windscreen. And a copy of Sir Alex Ferguson's autobiography on the front seat. It must belong to Trikoupis.'

'All right. Now we wait.'

Charlie lit a cigarette and made a phone call after which he told me that the English woman who had been attacked by Hannibal Leventis was called Sara Gill, and that she was from a place called Little Tew in Oxfordshire. This prompted me to make a phone call of my own.

To Louise.

'It's me. Can you talk?'

'Yes. But not for long. I miss you, Scott.'

190

'I miss you, too, angel.'

'You're in all the English newspapers.'

'Me, or just the team?'

'Mainly the team. And Bekim. Some people have said some very nice things about him. It almost makes me believe what you say, Scott: that it's more than just a game; that it's a way for people to come together.'

Except in Greece, I thought. And perhaps Glasgow.

'But you look tired in the photographs.'

'I could be worse. How's Bekim's girlfriend?'

'In a coma, probably brain-damaged. The cocaine stopped her heart and her brain was starved of oxygen for at least half an hour.'

'Jesus.'

'I'm glad you've called. I was just about to text you. I've got a friend – an ex-copper called Bill Wakeman – who works for the Sports Betting Intelligence Unit. It's part of the Gambling Commission. He's asked me for your number. Can I give it to him, Scott? He's a good man and you can rely on him.'

'If you say so.'

'He reckons they're investigating a series of big bets on your match against Olympiacos. A big punter in Russia won an awful lot of money betting against you the other night.'

'What's that got to do with the Gambling Commission if it happened in Russia?'

'Some of the bookmakers who might be affected are based here in the UK.'

'So what does he want from me?'

'To talk. Pick your brains. I imagine he wants to know if the match could have been fixed.'

'Not by me. But look, given what happened, is that the same thing as asking me if Bekim Develi could have been murdered?'

'I don't know. Is it?'

'I watched him die in front of me, Louise. It was a heart attack. The same thing happened to Fabrice Muamba when he was playing for Bolton against Spurs, in March 2012. I don't know how you can bet on something like that.'

'Just speak to him, will you? For me?'

'All right. Look there's something you can do for me, as it happens. I want you to find a woman called Sara Gill. Last known to be living in Little Tew in Oxfordshire. It seems that about four or five years ago she was attacked here in Athens by a fellow named Thanos Leventis. He's now doing life on three counts of murder. I'd like to know everything she can remember about what happened that night. And in particular if anyone else was involved.'

She tutted loudly. 'You're not playing detective again, are you?'

'Why do people always call it "playing"? I'm not playing at anything. It's a serious business, detective work.'

'You're telling me.'

'Besides, the sooner I find out what happened here the sooner I can come home to you, baby.'

'Just as long as you do. I'll see what I can do.'

I finished my call with a sigh and chucked the phone onto the seat.

'You can put the radio on, if you like, Charlie.'

'I've got a better idea, sir. Why don't you go to sleep, sir. I'll keep watch. Remember, I'm Greek. I have fourteen eyes.'

I wasn't exactly sure what this meant; but I settled back in the seat of the Range Rover and closed my eyes as instructed, and let my mind turn to thoughts of a perfect football world in which the future was always better than the past. I dreamed of Bekim Develi scoring audacious goals that were composed of absolute sorcery, and then celebrating in his primal, triumphant way – not that thumb-sucking tribute to his son, but, like the great god Zeus that sometimes he seemed to be, about to hurl a well-deserved thunderbolt at visiting fans.

CHAPTER 31

At Southampton, Hristos Trikoupis and myself had both played in defence, first for Glenn Hoddle and then wee Gordon Strachan. I don't know why Glenn isn't managing a club these days. Glenn kept the Saints in the Premier League against all odds; he bought me from Palace, and more controversially he bought Hristos Trikoupis from Olympiacos. Controversially because Hristos had led a player revolt against the manager of the Greek national team before Euro 2000. By all accounts he made Roy Keane and Nicolas Anelka look like teacher's pets. We played well together; I won't say we were Steve Bould and Tony Adams but we were pretty solid. Hristos was everything you'd want from a right back: tall, with a head like a hammer, and the unquestioning and ruffianly air of a professional hit man. I was always surprised that it should have been me who went to Arsenal and not him. Maybe that's what's driving how he feels about me now; I don't know. I went to Arsenal; he went to Wolves. I never asked how he felt about me going to the Gunners. And after I left the Saints I didn't speak to him again until the night Bekim died.

He was better groomed now; he'd let his fair hair grow and put on a little bit of weight which looked good on him. He walked out the restaurant, wearing a navy blue suit and a crisp white shirt open to his hairy navel; the woman with him was very thin with long brown hair and wore a layer-effect dress that made her look like Victoria Beckham. I recognised her: Nana Trikoupis, singer and former Eurovision contestant. She came sixteenth with a song called 'Play a Different Love Song' which Terry Wogan had amusingly renamed, 'Sing a Different Song, Love.'

They got into the black Maserati and drove off.

'That's him,' said Charlie, starting the car. 'And that's her, too. Queen Sophia. It's what the Greek newspapers call his bitch of a wife. Because she's such a terrible snob.'

'We've met. I went to their wedding. She threw a glass of champagne over the best man when he'd finished his speech.' I grinned. 'I guess back in 2002 WAG wasn't such a common term. Apparently she thought he'd called her a wog.'

We followed them east, down the main highway, and hugged the coast south, towards Vouliagmeni and the Astir Palace Hotel where all of the City players were staying. About halfway there he turned onto Alimou, and then right.

'It looks like he's heading towards Glyfada,' announced Charlie. 'The Beverly Hills of Athens. It's where you live if you're a millionaire. Everyone from Christos Dantis to Constantine Mitsotakis.'

I assumed these were some famous Greeks although I'd never heard of them.

'Every Greek dreams of winning the lottery and moving to Glyfada. You won't see any graffiti, the streets are clean, there are no empty shops and the cars are all new. I can never understand why, when there's a big demo and people want to have a riot, that they do it in Syntagma Square and not in Glyfada. If they burnt a few houses down here the government would soon pay attention.'

The Maserati pulled up in front of a set of electronic gates close to the Glyfada Golf Club and then disappeared up a short drive.

'This is as good as it gets in Athens,' said Charlie. 'A house on Miaouli. I'll bet he's even got a private entrance to the golf course.'

I nodded, remembering the house Hristos had once owned in Romsey, on the outskirts of Southampton – a nice six-bedroomed family home in Gardener's Lane; this house was something else. Even through the gates it looked like the dog's bollocks.

At the gate I got out of the car, pressed the intercom button on the gatepost and waited for the security camera to focus on my smiling mug and thumbs up. Then an electronic voice – quite obviously Trikoupis himself – asked me to state my business, in Greek.

'I want to see Hristos Trikoupis.'

'He's not here.'

'Come on, Trik. I know it's you.'

'Look, I don't want any trouble. If this is about what happened the other night after the game then I already told the newspapers that I was sorry. I got a bit carried away.'

I knew very well that no apology had been offered by Trikoupis for showing me four fingers for the four goals they'd put past us; instead he'd uttered some bullshit about how touchline confrontations were the inevitable result of having the technical areas too close together; and while this might have been true I also knew that Trikoupis had called me a 'black Nazi', a 'sore loser' and a 'cry baby' – as if the death of my player was already irrelevant to the way I'd handled myself that night.

'Hey, forget about it,' I said, coolly. 'Look, I was in the

area and I thought I'd drop by. To clear the air between us without all the football press there to watch us.'

'I appreciate that you did this. But the thing is, Scott, it's not very convenient right now. We're just about to have a late lunch.'

'That's all right, Trik. I understand, perfectly. But can I ask you one question?'

'Of course, Scott.'

'Are you alone? By the intercom? I mean, can anyone hear you at this present moment?'

'No, no one can hear me.'

'That's good. You see, I'm here because I wanted to speak to you about a mutual friend of ours. A Russian lovely named Valentina.'

'I don't know anyone by that name.'

'Apparently she knew that poor girl who was found at the bottom of Marina Zea the other night with a weight around her ankles. And I don't mean boots by Jimmy Choo. In fact, I think it was Valentina who sent her along to Bekim in her place. Which makes it very important I speak to her.'

'Like I said, I don't know anyone by that name,' insisted Hristos.

'Of course you do. You picked her up in your lovely black Maserati one night outside the Grande Bretagne Hotel. And knowing her, I bet you took her to Spondi. She's fond of that restaurant. As was Bekim. He went there with her, too. Sounds like quite a place. While I'm here I'll have to check it out myself. Perhaps I'll go after the Panathinaikos game tomorrow. Chief Inspector Varouxis's coming with me – he's a fan of the Greens. Perhaps I'll him about her then. You see, he doesn't know about Valentina. Not yet, anyway. Although to be honest with you, Trik, I'm not sure he *ought* to know about her. Not for her sake but for yours and mine. Now I can probably take the heat for something like that, I think. I'm not married. But I should think it's very different for you.'

There was a longish silence.

'So what's it to be? A little chat with me now or a longer chat downtown with the law? Not to mention an uncomfortable audience with Queen Sophia afterwards.'

Hristos sighed. 'What do you want, Scott? Specifically?'

'I want all the contact details you have for Valentina: mobile phone, addresses. Everything. Plus, the name of anyone else that knew her: pimp, clap doctor, other punters. Everyone. I'm doing you a favour. You talk to me or you talk to Varouxis. It's as simple as that.'

'All right, all right. Wait there. I'm coming down to the gate.'

'Okay.'

I waited, staring at the three-storey modern villa that stood at the end of the drive; it resembled the wing of an expensive clinic, or a small boutique hotel. The lawn was so perfect it looked as if it had been painted.

Then I saw him walking quickly down the drive. He came to the gate and handed me a sheet of paper through the railings.

I shook my head.

'This is the way you really want to do it? Like I was your Fedex guy? You know, I expected more of you, Trik. After all we went through together at St Mary's. This insults me. At the very least I expected you to be a man. Not someone who would hide behind his security gates.'

I looked at the sheet of paper, recognising the same typewritten telephone number and email address that were now printed almost indelibly on my mind.

'And I have these details already. Tell me something I don't know.'

Hristos Trikoupis was looking shifty and embarrassed. 'That's all I have. Look, what do you want me to say? I met her just the one time.'

'I don't believe you.'

'It's true, I tell you.'

'You just printed this off. So the details came easily to hand. Which doesn't speak of someone you only saw once. What's her surname? Did you file her name under V for Valentina, or something else?' I crushed the sheet of paper in my hand and threw it back through the railings. 'Like A for Adultery. Or perhaps C for Cleaners because make no mistake, that's where Nana's going to take you when she finds out that you've been a naughty boy. You forget, I came to your wedding. I've seen her temper. It's almost as terrifying as the way she sings.'

'Come on.' Hristos shook his head with exasperation. 'Who gets a surname from a girl like that? None of these girls show you their passport. Besides, they all have working names. Like Aphrodite and Jasmine.'

I let that one go. Maybe he knew Jasmine and maybe he didn't, but I wasn't interested in her relationship with Bekim Develi.

'Please, Scott. I really don't know anything about her. You're right. I took her to Spondi. Maybe they knew her there. I'd really like to help you here. But I really don't know anything.'

'Where did you fuck her? I mean after dinner.'

'I have a small apartment near the training ground.'

'How did you meet?'

'I met her at a charity evening arranged by the Hellenic Football Federation in the Onassis Cultural Center. On

199

Syngrou Avenue. In aid of disabled sport.'

'Who introduced you?'

'You won't say it was me who told you?'

'I will tell your wife if you don't spill the beans, you bastard. I just want to get home.'

'It was a woman called Anna Loverdos. She's on the International Relations Committee of the HFF.'

'Yes, I know. She keeps calling me to offer her sympathies about Bekim. I've been avoiding her calls but now I think I'll get back to her. Maybe tonight.'

'As a matter of fact I'm pretty sure Anna introduced Valentina to Bekim Develi, too. Really, Scott, that's all I know. Only please, don't let any of this get out. Anna could lose her job.'

'And I know how keen you all are to keep your jobs.' I nodded. 'On one condition.'

'Yes?'

'That when you and I see each other again, at next week's game, you'll shake my hand. Before and after the match. Properly. Because that's the example we're supposed to give those who watch the game. If we don't have respect for each other we don't have anything. And I'm fed up with the British press hunting for reasons why we don't get on.'

As he nodded I grabbed his shirt collar through the gate, and pulled him towards me quickly so that he banged his head hard on the railings.

'And if you ever call me a black Nazi again, you cunt, I'll fucking have you up before a FIFA disciplinary committee.'

I got back in the car and Charlie drove off.

'Speaking as a Green, sir,' he said, 'that was nicely done. Very nicely done indeed. I'd have paid money to see that bastard head hit something harder than a football.'

On the way back to the hotel I saw a tattoo parlour and had Charlie pull up outside so I could get an expert opinion on the dead girl's tattoo, now on my iPhone. But here – and at another tat parlour closer to the hotel – the SP was that while the labyrinth was well-drawn, the design wasn't unusual, not in Greece, where the idea of labyrinths got started, more or less.

About the only thing I knew for sure about labyrinths was that there was always a monster waiting at the end.

CHAPTER 32

When I arrived back at the Grande Bretagne I found Vik having a meeting in the royal suite dining room with Phil Hobday, Kojo Ironsi, Gustave Haak, Cooper Lybrand and some more Greeks I didn't recognise. I went into the bedroom, closed the door, picked up the telephone and called Anna Loverdos who sounded more English than Greek.

'I'm so glad you called me back,' she said. 'And I'm so, so sorry about what happened to Bekim Develi. How is his poor wife?'

'Not good.'

'If there's anything I can do for you and your players while you're in Athens, Mr Manson – anything at all – then please don't hesitate to get in touch.'

'Well, there is something,' I said. 'But I hardly like to talk about it on the telephone. I was wondering if we might meet up sometime and have a drink.'

'Of course. And I was going to suggest that myself. Where are you staying?'

'At the Grande Bretagne.'

'The Federation is just a ten-minute drive from there. Shall we say six o'clock tonight?'

'See you then.'

I went into the media room and switched on the widescreen TV, looking for some football. There was a repeat of a UEFA Europa League play-off match from the previous evening, between Saint-Étienne and Stuttgart.

The door opened and Kojo came in, flicking the air with his fly-whisk like an African dictator.

'Oh, good,' he said, 'you're watching the match.' He helped himself to a beer from the minibar and sat down.

'What are they talking about in there?' I asked.

'Money, my friend, what else? It's all those people ever talk about. Don't get me wrong. I like money as much as the next guy. But to me it's a means to an end and not an end in itself. I swear, all these fellows talk about is what they can buy and what they can sell and how much profit there is. It's like hanging out with the International Monetary Fund. Numbers, numbers, numbers. It's making me crazy, Scott.'

'That's why the rich stay rich, Kojo. Because they're interested in that shit. All those little fractions they're fond of add up and mean something – usually that the rest of us have been fucked over while we were looking the other way.'

'Maybe.' Kojo drank some of his beer. 'Anyway, I only came here today to watch the game. They don't get this channel on the boat.'

'It must be the only thing you can't get on that boat.'

'And I've got a client who's playing for Saint-Étienne, Kgalema Mandingoane: the South African boy who plays in goal.'

'I suppose he's one from your academy.'

'That's right.'

'You're as bad as the guys next door. Just watch the fucking game, will you?'

I grinned, but we both knew I meant it.

My phone rang; it was Bill Wakeman from the Gambling Commission and for a moment I left the room. We talked for a while, but I didn't have much to tell him.

'Is it possible that Bekim Develi was nobbled?' he asked.

'I suppose it's possible,' I admitted. 'We won't know for sure until the pathologists end their strike and someone can give him a post-mortem. But from what I saw, it looked like natural causes. Frankly, it reminded me of what happened to Fabrice Muamba back in 2012. Besides, we were very strict about what the team ate before the match. Our team nutritionist made sure of that.'

I told him about the food-poisoning incident involving Hertha. 'But it's hard to see how anyone could have nobbled Bekim and not everyone else,' I added. 'If anything he was twice as particular as anyone else about what he ate while he was here.'

'What about the other players?' he asked. 'Could one of them have intended to throw the match?'

'It would be stupid of me to say that couldn't happen, since it obviously does happen. But now you're asking me which of my players is bent enough to throw a football game.'

'And?'

'I can't think of one.'

'Really? Some of them you hardly know at all. Prometheus has just arrived at London City.'

'He may be a lot of things,' I said. 'But a cheat, I'm sure he isn't.'

'He's African, isn't he? Nigerian? Half the phishing scams in the world originate in Nigeria. They're all dodgy. And from what I've read about him, he's dodgier than most.'

'I'll pretend I didn't hear that, Mr Wakeman.'

'I'm sorry if I misspoke, Mr Manson. I certainly didn't mean to offend you. But you know, one particular punter in Russia – someone nicknamed the Russian bear – made a killing on this game. They won't say how much, but the bookies reckon that game might have cost them as much as twenty million pounds.'

'My heart bleeds for them. Look, I'd like to help. But I don't see what I can do from here. Right now all I really care about is that I get my team back to London as soon as.'

I ended the call and went back into the media room.

'You know, you really should think about buying this boy, Scott. You're going to need another goalkeeper now that Didier Cassell isn't coming back to the game. I happen to know Mandingo – that's what the French call him. . .'

I went to the fridge and helped myself to a Coke.

'I'm glad I've got this opportunity to be alone with you, Scott. There's something else I want to talk to you about. It's about Prometheus.'

I sighed. 'Why is it that every time I hear that boy's name I want to rip someone's fucking liver out?'

'It was Prometheus who hung that evil eye trinket on the door handle of Bekim's bungalow. The night before he died.'

'I might have known he'd have something to do with it.'

'The boy meant it as a stupid joke. Only now he's worried sick that it actually worked. And I do mean sick.'

'Come on, Kojo. That sort of thing. It's bollocks.'

'Not to him. He's African, Scott. You'd be surprised how many of them still believe in this stuff.'

'In fucking witchcraft, you mean? The next thing you'll be telling me is that he believes in fairies and fucking voodoo dolls. Bekim Develi had a heart attack, Kojo. Like Fabrice Muamba. Sudden Adult Death Syndrome. That's the medical description of something that the ancient Greeks used to say: "Those whom the gods love die young." It's sad, but that's just how it is.'

'The question is, what are we going to do about it? The boy won't eat. He can't sleep. He really thinks Bekim's death is down to him.'

'Why didn't he tell me himself? This morning, at the training session?'

'He wanted to, but he lost his nerve.'

'If he ever had any. I might have respected him even a little if he'd had the guts to tell me himself.'

'In front of all the others? It's bad enough he thinks he killed Bekim without some of the others thinking it, too. He's not the only superstitious idiot in your team.'

'You've got that right, anyway.'

'You're going to talk him out of this mindset he's got himself into, aren't you? Before the return match against Olympiacos. I mean, it's not the sort of thing you can leave to a man like Simon Page. I doubt that he can even spell psychology.'

'Oh, he can spell it. But his idea of a mental function is getting pissed at the Christmas party.' I nodded. 'I'll speak to him, okay?'

'Thanks, Scott. He respects you. He needs guidance, that's all.'

'I'll speak to him.'

Just at this moment, Mandingo – Kojo's client – pulled off a spectacular top-drawer save. Even I was impressed.

Kojo grinned. 'See what I mean? Mandingo's just twenty-two and already he's been picked for his country.'

'If he really is twenty-two, that's remarkable on its own.'

'I'm telling you, Scott, that boy is the next David James.'

I didn't know if that was good or bad but I shrugged and said I'd think about it; and fortunately for me, Phil put his head around the door soon afterwards and asked me to dinner on the boat. Frankly, I was relieved to find an excuse to leave the room.

'Eight thirty,' said Phil. 'There'll be a tender at Marina Zea at eight to pick people up.'

'People?'

'I think there are some girls who are coming aboard.'

I might have said I was busy, except I wanted to ask him and Vik if we could buy Hörst Daxenberger as a replacement for Bekim Develi.

'I'll be there,' I said.

My phone rang again and this time it was a Greek number I didn't recognise.

'Mr Manson?'

'Yes?'

'My name is Dr Eva Pyromaglou.'

CHAPTER 33

Anna Loverdos crossed her bare tanned legs and handed me her business card. Like her it was Greek on one side and English on the other. But the legs were shapely and certainly more interesting than what was printed on the card. When they're crossed a good pair of legs can distract a man from almost everything.

'My mum is from Liverpool,' she explained. 'She met my dad on holiday in Corfu. It's very *Shirley Valentine*. I was born here and then went to a girls' boarding school in England.'

Anna was in her thirties; attractive and well-spoken, she wore a wrap-effect pink satin skirt, a white silk blouse, and leather wedge sandals. The glass of champagne in her hand was the same colour as her hair.

'Then I came back here. That was before the economy went pear-shaped, of course. I had a business entertainment company. Events management for multinationals, that kind of thing. Then I worked in PR for the Investment Bank of Greece. And now I'm running the International Relations Committee of the Hellenic Football Federation. Which is a lot more fun.'

'I can imagine. So, what team do you support, Anna?'

'I don't. In my job it's best to avoid any possibility of partisanship. Greeks take the matter of what team you support very seriously.'

'So I've noticed. It's like entering a war zone.'

'Because my mum is from Liverpool I always say I'm an Everton fan. Which is always the right team to support in Greece because it's not Greek and they're never in the Champions League. Better safe than sorry in this country. But I'm sure I don't have to tell you about that.' She shook her head. 'Some of what's been said in the local press about you and your team has been awful, Mr Manson. Especially in view of what happened to Bekim Develi. This used to be a kinder country. But lately the rhetoric in football has become rather more poisonous in a way I've not seen before. These days Greeks tend to think all sport is venal and corrupt, like everything else.' She smiled. 'But you don't want to hear about that. My job is to make sure the remainder of your stay in Greece is as pleasant as possible. Yours can't be an easy job, right now. Let's face it, even at the best of times it's not easy keeping discipline among so many young and eligible men.'

I grinned. 'I've already had to fetch them out of a strip club on Syngrou Avenue called Alcatraz. Footballers and strippers. Footballers and escort girls. They're all tabloid stories just waiting to happen. You don't know the half of it.'

She laughed and drained her glass.

'Then again,' I added, 'perhaps you do.'

'No, but I can guess,' she said.

'I'd say you can probably do a lot more than guess, Anna.'

'All right, perhaps you're right,' she said, sheepishly. 'As a matter of fact I did go to Alcatraz once.'

'I thought so. Did you know Bekim Develi very well?'

'Reasonably well, poor man.'

'And was it you who introduced him to Valentina?'

'Who?'

'Oddly enough, that's what Hristos Trikoupis said, when I asked him. No, don't say anything yet. You know the old lawyer's principle that you should never ask a question to which you don't know the answer? That's the kind of question I just asked you, Anna. Only I'm not a lawyer. And you're not on trial. Hold up, no one is accusing you of anything. But there's no point in denying you know her.'

'What's all this about?' she asked.

'Just answer the question, please, Anna.'

She slouched back in the armchair as if someone had loosened her brassiere; her eyes looked down uncertainly at the table. I realised she was looking at her own business card.

'All right. But to be quite accurate it was Bekim Develi who introduced Valentina to me.'

I breathed a sigh of relief which wasn't entirely for dramatic effect. At last I felt like I was getting somewhere.

'But what of it? I get introduced to lots of people.' She picked up the business card and handed it to me a second time. 'That's what it says on the card, okay? "International Relations." Generally speaking that requires a little more than an exchange of emails.'

'Have another drink. You look as though you need it.'

I waved the waiter over and ordered two glasses of champagne.

'Look, all I want is to get my team back to London. I don't want to hurt anyone or cause them to lose their job. Least of all you. I can see you're a nice girl, but I need to know what you know. So. Tell me about it. Tell me everything you know and then you'll never hear about this again.'

'I want to know why you're asking.'

'All right. If it makes you feel any better. I figure Valentina introduced Bekim to the escort girl now lying in the chiller

210

cabinet at the Laiko General Hospital. She and Bekim had a little party in his room at the Astir Palace Hotel on the night before he died. As yet that girl remains unidentified. And I'm assuming Valentina can name her.' I paused. 'Look, you can talk to me or you can talk to the police. It's your choice. Just remember, I don't bite like they do.'

She sighed, wearily.

'What you've got to understand,' she said, 'is that it's not unusual for FIFA and UEFA officials to solicit the company of girls in Athens. I just do what I'm told, right? As it was explained to me – and I won't say by who – the important thing is to look after our VIP guests and to keep them out of trouble. Looking after our VIP guests means shepherding them away from the hookers on Omonia Square. Frankly, it's dangerous down there. There are lots of drug addicts and homeless people. The police have been cracking down. In Sofokleous Street there are over three hundred brothels and many of the girls have HIV. A decision was taken to steer our more important sporting guests away from these places and to introduce them to high-quality girls. I decided to recruit one girl to handle everything for me: Valentina. She was perfect for the role. Whenever there's a FIFA official or a top footballer in town, I have her contact him. If it's a FIFA official we pay her. If it's a footballer, then we let her negotiate her own fee. Sometimes she looks after the VIP herself but just as often she recruits someone else to take care of them. I suppose it was Valentina who provided Bekim with a girl. I know she liked him, and normally she looked after him herself, but on this occasion she must have been busy so she found someone else for him. I don't know who that was. But Valentina's real name is Svetlana Yaroshinskaya and originally she is from Odessa, in the Ukraine. I think she was originally an art student. She's got a flat somewhere in Athens; I don't know where. I used to Skype her when I wanted to speak to her. Her Skype address is SvetYaro99. But she hasn't been online of late. And she hasn't returned any of my calls. Which is unusual.'

The waiter came back with the champagne. I wrote down the Skype address and had Anna check it.

'Was she – was Svetlana the only girl you had any dealings with?'

'Yes.'

'You're sure about that?'

I took out my iPhone, tapped the Photos app, and called up the pictures of the dead girl's tattoo I'd taken at Laiko General Hospital.

'What about this tattoo? It's not quite Lisbeth Salander's dragon, I know, but it's still quite distinctive, I think. No?'

'No. Look,' she said nervously, 'you're not going to mention my name, are you? No one cares about the police very much. But I'd rather my name didn't appear in the newspapers. Especially the ones back home. My mum lives back in Liverpool these days.'

'FIFA officials accepting free sex from high-class call girls?' I shook my head. 'Where's the story there? I should think most people think that happens all the time.' I swiped the screen to the next photograph, a picture of the dead girl's face. 'Have you seen her? It's not a good likeness, but under the circumstances. . .'

'No, I've never seen her,' said Anna.

'Take another look.'

'I don't know her. What's up with her anyway? She looks like she's asleep.'

'Didn't I say? She's dead. That's what's up with her. This

is the girl who was found drowned in Marina Zea. The one who screwed Bekim Develi.'

Anna's jaw dropped and her eyes filled with tears.

I drank some of the champagne, stood up and tossed a fifty onto the table in front of her.

'That's for the drinks.' I peeled off another twenty. 'And there's a little something for your time, Anna.'

'You fucking bastard.'

I grinned. 'We'll make a real football fan out of you yet, love.'

CHAPTER 34

That night I didn't go to dinner on *The Lady Ruslana*. There wasn't time. Besides, I wasn't hungry and I knew I wouldn't be good company, not in view of what I had planned for later on that Friday evening. The discussion with Vik and Phil about buying Hörst Daxenberger to replace Bekim Develi was going to have to wait. This was one of those rare occasions when the dead take precedence over the living.

As soon as I left Anna Loverdos I Skyped the number she'd given me, without an answer; then I called our lawyer Dr Christodoulou on her mobile and found her still in the office at nine o'clock.

'Working late?'

'Unsurprisingly, the reward notices we posted around Piraeus have generated a very large response,' she said. 'It's going to take us all night to separate any genuine leads from the time-wasters.'

I told myself she was probably used to that; in Greece, wasting time seems to be a national pastime. And I didn't feel sorry for her; lawyers love work and not because they love work *per se* but because the more they do the more fees their clients pay.

'I hate to add to your workload,' I lied, 'but I'd like you to check out a name and see what it throws up: real name

214

is Svetlana Yaroshinskaya, goes by the working name of Valentina. She's a high-class escort. Possibly a friend of the murdered girl. Born in Odessa. I've got a Skype number, a mobile number and an email address. See what you can find out about her. Criminal record. Tax number. Bra size. Everything.'

'All right. I'll see what I can do. Anything else?'

'Not yet but watch this space.'

I didn't tell Dr Christodoulou where I was about to go. A descent into the underworld is always best kept secret. I was beginning to realise that you have to be a bit of a pilgrim to solve a crime; you must first say to yourself what you would know and then do what you have to do, though all may be against it. Not to mention anyone to whom you've behaved like a fucking bastard. I shouldn't have shown the pictures of the dead girl to Anna Loverdos; that had been rough of me. Yet a little part of me said it was right that she should share in some of the guilt I was feeling. It was men like me who'd fucked and murdered the girl in the mortuary at Laiko General Hospital; but it was a woman like Anna who'd helped to bring that situation about.

I took a shower to freshen up and clear my head, and put on an old T-shirt. I snatched up a handful of cash and a couple of whisky miniatures, and went downstairs to the hotel basement. I felt bad about leaving Charlie in the car out front but I needed a decoy and I didn't think my police escort would be so easily lost again. It's surprising how quickly cops learn things.

Having found my way through a few dingy, humid corridors and featureless passageways, I emerged through an anonymous door at the back of the Grande Bretagne onto Voukourestiou where the evening heat hit me like a big warm sponge. From there I walked a short way west onto Stadiou, and caught a taxi that took me around the square, then north, past the beleaguered Greek parliament building where a mixture of tourists and demonstrators were watching the Evzones – a ceremonial unit of Greek light infantry – changing guard at the tomb of the unknown soldier.

Tombs and their morbid contents were very much on my mind but this didn't stop a smile spreading on my face as I watched some of the floodlit ceremony from the back seat of my taxi. The changing of the guard in any country is always a ridiculous piece of nonsense; in Greece, it reaches a new level of absurdity: with their pom-pom shoes, white party dresses, big moustaches and tasselled red hats, the Evzones themselves resemble the clowns from some obscure Balkan circus, but all this is as nothing compared to the farcical drill which makes the poor soldiers that carry out this clockwork pantomime look as though they work at the Ministry for Silly Walks.

I arrived in St Thomas's Square, close by Laiko General Hospital, not long before eleven o'clock. Dr Pyromaglou had said that she would come and take a look at the body with me as close to midnight as possible when there were fewer people around in the hospital, to try to avoid being accused of breaking the strike.

'I won't perform an actual autopsy,' she had explained on the telephone, earlier that day. 'But from what I understand I might not need to. Wear an old shirt and bring a clean one to wear home because we can't be seen in scrubs or white coats. That will give the game away.'

Spiros, the mortuary orderly I'd met earlier, had called Eva Pyromaglou at home and given her my phone number. It seemed that he was going be there, too, if only to keep a lookout.

There was an outdoor restaurant under the orange trees next to the Greek church with the many roofs, and it was there I'd arranged to meet her. She was sitting alone, a copy of Sir Alex Ferguson's autobiography on the table to identify her. It was Mr Pyromaglou's copy apparently. I certainly couldn't have imagined his wife enjoying it. Mind you, I can't imagine anyone actually *enjoying* it. That book tried to settle more family business than the last fifteen minutes of *The Godfather* and you don't have to be Roy Keane or Steven Gerrard to feel that way about it. Reading the book, I learned that Fergie has always collected Kennedy assassination documents and artefacts and it struck me as a little odd that he even had a copy of Kennedy's autopsy. Then again I was hardly one to talk; meeting Dr Pyromaglou like this was more than a bit weird – like something out of an old Frankenstein movie – in which she and I were planning to interfere with a young woman's corpse at the stroke of midnight.

The doctor was in her forties with very pale skin, an almond-shaped face, long auburn hair and worry-lines on her forehead. She wore a hospital pass on a bead-chain around her neck, heavy-framed glasses, a black polo shirt, jeans and a pair of sensible shoes, and looked as if she'd been conceived and born in a library. We shook hands.

There was still half an hour before the new shift came on duty so we ordered some coffee.

'I know you've seen a dead body before,' she said. 'Spiros told me that you were okay with that. But looking at a body is different from what I intend doing. I shall probably need your assistance to take some swabs and perhaps to cut her a bit. So if you're sensitive to the sight of blood then you'd better say so now. I don't want you fainting while we're in there.'

'I'll be all right,' I said bravely. 'When you've played football alongside Martin Keown you get used to the sight of blood.'

It was a joke, but she didn't laugh. I brandished the two whisky miniatures I'd brought from the hotel and then drank one immediately. 'Anyway, I brought some courage from home.'

'We'll be working in quite a tight space,' she said. 'Did you bring a clean shirt, just in case of accident?'

I indicated a plastic bag by my leg.

'Thank you for helping me, doctor,' I said. 'And her. The girl in the drawer, I mean. The police seem to be taking their time about everything.'

'They're only quick when it's a matter of cracking heads.'

'Spiros told me about your son. I'm sorry. Is he all right?'

'As well as can be expected. But thank you for asking.'

That never sounds good, so I didn't ask more.

'Please understand that nothing is going to be written down tonight,' she insisted. 'At least not by me. Is that quite clear?'

I nodded.

'You won't be able to rely on what we find in a court of law because what we're doing is illegal. And another thing, I'm helping you, Mr Manson, not the police. This is a private matter between you and me. I figure that if everyone else in this country can work off the books then so can I.'

'Sure, I understand.'

'Do you have something for me?' she said.

I handed over a hotel envelope containing five hundred euros.

She nodded. 'If someone speaks to you just answer them in English and then they'll know for sure you're not breaking the strike.'

I nodded. 'What's the strike about, anyway?'

'Money,' she said. 'There isn't any. At least not for Greek public services.'

'So I gather.'

'There seems to be plenty for footballers, however. Even here in Athens.'

I drank my coffee silently; it's never a good idea to try to justify the salaries in football to anyone, least of all those in the medical profession. And it was a good job that before I could try, my iPhone chimed: Maurice had emailed me a link to an article in the *Independent* that said Viktor Sokolnikov was planning to fire me at the end of the season. I wasn't worried by this; no one ever reads the *Independent*.

'If it was just picking a team I'd hardly be here now, would I?'

Eva Pyromaglou nodded down at the grimly smiling face on the cover of her book. 'I certainly couldn't see him turning policeman to solve a crime.'

She looked at her watch. 'Come on,' she said briskly. 'It's time we were moving.' She picked up her phone and quickly texted Spiros, to let him know we were on our way.

CHAPTER 35

Laiko General Hospital was as dark as a church inside and almost as quiet. The hospital had a policy of switching off most of the lights at night, to save money on electricity.

'That's also in our favour,' she said, leading the way through dim corridors. 'But you should be careful where you're walking. You wouldn't want to have an accident in a Greek public hospital.'

I smiled; I was starting to like Eva.

Spiros was waiting for us around the next corner. He wasn't alone. Under a sheet on a trolley in front of him was the body of a woman and you didn't have to be a detective to work that out; her breasts stood up like a couple of sandcastles on a beach.

'This way,' he said and, pushing the trolley ahead, he led us along another dim corridor and through the open doors of a large and brightly lit elevator. Inside, he turned a key quickly, to operate the car, and then stepped outside, leaving Eva and me alone with the dead body. She pressed one of the buttons, the doors slid shut and the lift started to move. Almost immediately she turned the key again and the elevator stopped between floors, with a jerk.

As she threw back the sheet covering the dead girl's body

it was now plain to me that she was planning to examine the body right there, in the lift.

'Pity,' she said. 'She was very beautiful.'

'You're going to look at her in here?' I asked.

'Yes. In here we can be sure not to be disturbed. Spiros will text me when it's safe to bring the car back down.'

'Why do I get the feeling you've done this before?'

'In the elevator? No, you're the first; and I hope the last. I can't afford for this strike to go on much longer. It might even get violent, too. Towards the end strikes in Greece always become bloody-minded. You certainly wouldn't want to get caught in the middle of that.'

'Now you tell me.'

In a bag between the body's feet was everything Eva would need: scalpels, swabs, scissors, evidence bags, suture needles, antiseptic hand gel and latex gloves. She put the bag on the floor and then proceeded to examine the girl's body, meticulously, as if searching her flesh for the smallest blemish. For a while I let her work in silence, admiring the care and respect with which she treated the cadaver.

'I'm looking for bruises,' she murmured. 'Needle marks, abrasions, cuts, scratches, anything.' After several more minutes she shook her head. 'But there's not a mark on her.'

'To my eye she looks like she was pregnant,' I said, helpfully.

'No, that's not pregnant.' Eva grunted. 'You say she drowned? In Marina Zea?'

'That's what the cops told me.'

'Then we'd better make quite sure. Ordinarily I would just cut her open and see what's in her lungs but we can't do that. This is not a post-mortem, after all. However, a little superficial cutting will be permissible. Help me turn her onto her stomach, with her head hanging over the edge of the trolley.'

We rolled her over and Eva fetched a cardboard tray from her carrier bag that she positioned under the dead girl's lower jaw.

'Now what?'

'I want you to lean across her body, with all your weight. But I suppose I ought to warn you first that with all the gas that's built up inside her, it's possible she might misbehave. But I'm looking for any seawater that might be left inside her lungs.'

'Oh, of course.'

When Eva was ready I leaned across the dead girl's back and, at first, nothing happened.

'Harder, man. You can't hurt her now. Do it like you're a sports physio. Take your feet off the ground. Come on. Really let her have it.'

I did as I was told and a few seconds later, a loud and very smelly fart emanated from the cadaver's nether regions.

'Whatever happened to silent witness?' I said, turning my face in the opposite direction.

Finally, a trickle of liquid slid out of the cadaver's mouth and into the cardboard tray. Eva transferred this to a bottle which she placed in her carrier bag.

'Good,' she said. 'Now let's turn her onto her back again.'

We wrestled her over and then I stood back from the trolley, panting a little. It was getting very warm and malodorous in the elevator car. I was already glad I was wearing an old T-shirt.

'What's next?'

'We take a closer look at those tits, of course. Just look at them.'

'I did. I am. It's hard not to look at them when they're like that. I imagine they looked rather better when she was walking around. Maybe a little more natural.'

'That's your opinion.' Eva laid out her instruments at the foot of the trolley, as neatly as she was able.

'But they do stand to attention, don't they? Much more than yesterday, I think.'

'When silicon becomes cold it hardens a bit. Sometimes it gets smaller.'

'I know the feeling.'

Eva picked up a scalpel and then took hold of the dead girl's breast and moved it from side to side, as if judging where to cut.

'At least this one's still got her nipples,' she murmured. 'That's something, I suppose.'

'Yes, I heard about that. Hannibal Leventis, wasn't it? The Athenian bus driver who murdered those other girls?'

'You're well informed.'

'Not by the police, I'm not.'

'Believe me, this is a very different box of cakes.'

'You sound like you have some knowledge of those cases.'

'I do. It was me who sectioned them.'

'There was talk of Leventis having an accomplice, wasn't there?'

'Yes, there was. And he did, I think. But the police decided Leventis acted alone. Because that's what Leventis said. And it suited them to believe him.'

'I see.'

'All right, now pay attention. This is what you've paid for. You see this almost invisible scar here, under the breast? That's where the breast implant went in; and it's where we're going to take it out again.'

'We are? Why?'

'Has that phone of yours got a voice memo app?'

'Her tits are big but I don't think it was them that made her sink to the bottom of the marina. It was a large weight tied to her feet.' I fumbled the phone from my pocket, and tapped the app.

'With any luck this little girl's tits will tell us her full name and address. So you'd better start recording.'

I winced a little as Eva sliced the flesh deep along the scar under the breast and then pulled out her implant.

'Doesn't this count as invasive?' I asked.

'It may sound like splitting hairs to you but no, it doesn't, because we're going in and out through an existing scar. Everything will look like it was before. More or less.'

Wiping the implant with a length of paper towel she turned it over like a jellyfish and palped it for a moment.

'It's already more softer and more pliable just from the heat of my hand. And this is just what I was hoping for. On the back surface of the implant you will see an imprint that contains the name of the manufacturer, the style and size, as well as a serial number. When the device was placed, a copy of this serial number and the other details were sent back to the manufacturer so that it can be tracked for quality assurance and research purposes. This particular implant was made by Mentor. All I have to do is telephone Mentor in the morning and they'll tell me what I need to know.' She read out the serial number and the device size into the mike on my iPhone. 'And that's it. Unless we're very unlucky we should be able to identify this girl in less than twenty-four hours.'

Eva replaced the implant device and quickly stitched up the dead girl's breast again.

'Jesus, it's as simple as that?'

'Mmm-hmm. After Spiros told me about her tits, I had an idea that we could do this. These days, implant devices are as good a means of identification as the microchip in a cat or a dog.'

'Brilliant.'

Having finished her suture, Eva covered the stitching with a layer of body butter and then some foundation colour. By the time she'd finished the stitches were more or less invisible.

'Impressive,' I said.

Eva took a sample of blood from the girl's arm using a syringe.

'Do I need the voice memo any more?'

'No, you can switch that thing off. But we've not finished yet, Mr Manson. I'll do some blood work on her at home to determine what drugs and alcohol were in her system at the time of death.'

'Right.' I put the phone back in my pocket.

'I shall also need to take some swabs from her vagina, mouth and anus. If there's any that doesn't match her own blood type it will give us a useful means of identifying who she had sex with. And perhaps her killer. If killer there was. I must say there's no evidence to say that this girl put up much of a struggle. I've seen more violent-looking cot deaths.'

'Perhaps she was drugged after all.'

'If we find anything on the swabs it will enable us to eliminate players in your team. Of course, to do that we'll need to take samples from them, too. Including you, of course.'

'Of course.'

'The sooner we eliminate you the better, I think, Mr Manson.'

I helped her bag the swabs; she also took a lock of the hair on the girl's head and a few strands of her pubic hair.

According to Eva Pyromaglou, our post-mortem lite had been successful.

'What happens now?' I asked.

'Now we hope the elevator starts when we turn the key. I'd hate to be trapped in here all night.'

Right on cue, the corpse farted again.

'I see what you mean.'

Eva was about to cover her with the sheet when I stopped her.

'Wait,' I said, looking at the dead girl's face. 'The police sketch doesn't look anything like her; and the photo I took before doesn't look right. Her eyes are closed. Nobody looks like themselves in a picture when they have their eyes closed. Do you think you could open them?'

'I can do better than that,' said Eva.

She produced her make-up bag again and in just a few minutes, with a little bit of foundation, eyeshadow, mascara, blusher and lipstick, she had transformed the dead girl into a real person; she even sprayed her open staring eyes with some Optrex Actimist to bring a little brightness back to them.

'Fantastic,' I said, and took several pictures on my iPhone.

'No.' Eva shook her head. 'I think I was a bit too heavy-handed with the blusher. I've made her look like . . . like a whore.'

'No, she's not that bad. Not that bad at all.' I looked at the picture I'd taken on my iPhone and frowned. 'It's strange but now that you've tarted her up a bit, she looks exactly like my ex-wife.'

226

CHAPTER 36

Reading the sports pages on my iPad and watching *Football Focus* on BBC World, I felt like a fish out of water. I'd have given anything to be back in London preparing for our big game with Chelsea. I always liked going to Stamford Bridge, especially in August. Chelsea always feels special in summer. I guess that's why I live there.

Would we have beaten the Blues? At the beginning of the season, when your whole team is fit, anything is possible; for the same reason it's the newly promoted teams, like Leicester City, that you have to watch out for. It's only as the season wears on that beating the top sides becomes progressively more difficult. If, like the Blues, you've got a team composed of twenty-five international players, then it stands to reason you're going to be in the running for a top-four spot at the end of the season. It also stands to reason that if you have a squad like that and you're not top four then you're going to get the sack.

It was very early in the season for a manager to get the sack but according to the papers, that's what had happened to an old mate of mine. Nick Broomhouse had been manager at Leeds United for just two months and, after a dismal start to the season that saw them losing 6–0 to newly promoted Wolves and then 5–0 to Huddersfield, the new club chairman and owner declared he had no confidence in the manager. The match against Huddersfield was one of those derby matches that any Leeds manager just has to win. My guess is that he was just looking for an excuse to be rid of the previous owner's man. I had my own problems, of course, but these didn't stop me from sending a text offering my sympathies to poor old Broomhouse.

Of course, any manager always expects to get the sack, the way a burglar probably expects to get caught and go to prison. It's hardwired into your psyche that the sack is an occupational hazard; probably it's one of the reasons some of us are paid so much in the first place. But the money is never sufficient compensation for having your team taken away from you at a moment's notice. It hasn't happened to me, yet, but I don't doubt that my turn will come. Sometimes football management is just revolving doors. A six-year contract like mine would make some managers feel safe. Not me. A guy as wealthy as Viktor Sokolnikov would hardly notice paying five million quid to get rid of me. I'm not quite as cheap as chips to a man like Vik, but I'm something pretty close to it.

I was still musing upon my own disposability when Louise rang from my flat in Chelsea. We proceeded to have one of our more typically playful conversations, the way two people do when they think they might be in love but don't want to admit it before the other has.

'I miss you,' she said, plaintively.

'I miss you, too,' I said.

'I'm lying in your big bed, naked, with all the newspapers, and wishing you were here.'

'As long as it's just the newspapers you're in bed with, then that's okay.'

'I just want you to know exactly what you're missing here, Scott.'

'Believe me, I know. For one thing there's that game against Chelsea. Not to mention some big bonuses if we'd beaten the bastards. Which we could have done. Even without Bekim.'

'That's not what I meant.'

'I know what you meant, darling. But since you were teasing me, I thought I'd tease you back.' I laughed. 'That's why football was invented: to make women believe that we don't think about sex all the time.'

'Does it work?'

'Sure. For exactly forty-five minutes. Until half time when we can start thinking about sex again, for just fifteen minutes.'

'Don't you ever think about me during the match? Not once?'

'Maybe once or twice.'

'Really?'

'But that's only until your own side scores. Putting three past Man U, when Fergie's in the stands with a face like a slapped arse. That's better than sex in any manager's book.'

'It's not in your book.'

'You read it?'

'There are ten copies on your bookshelf. I could hardly avoid it.'

'But you only read the one, right?'

'Funny. I read it thinking it might give me an insight into you.'

'You certainly won't get anything like that from my book.'

'You think not?'

'You want insights into my way of thinking? Read the match-day programme.'

'I can tell you wrote it, Scott. The book, I mean. Some of the phraseology. . .'

'Of course I wrote it. Who do you think I am? Wayne Rooney?'

'It told me a lot that I didn't know.'

'That's what Wayne said.'

'It told me that you have a habit of getting yourself into scrapes. That maybe I should fly out to Athens. That you needed me to keep you out of trouble.'

'That was in the book?'

'To keep you company in the royal suite.'

'I'd like that, too. So, see if you can get a flight. Why not? I'll start running the bath. It's a big one.'

'All right, I will. I won't cramp your style? There must be a lot of Greek girls dying to go to bed with you.'

'Not since breakfast.'

'You can, you know. I don't mind.'

'I know.'

I tutted loudly and changed the subject. 'I spoke to your friend, Wakeman.'

'How was that?'

'He was a little insulting. For a start, I think he believes that all Africans are crooks. A lot of them are, of course. But nobody likes to be reminded of that. It's not so very long ago I was from Africa myself.'

'Sorry.'

'Not your fault, baby.'

'Well, *I* spoke to Sara Gill.'

'Who?'

'The woman from Little Tew in Oxfordshire? The one who was attacked by Thanos Leventis. The killer the Greek newspapers dubbed Hannibal. I'll text you her mobile and her Skype number.'

'She's willing to speak to me? About what happened to her?'

'Yes, she'll speak to you. She'll speak to anyone about what happened. It's getting people to listen that's been her problem until now.'

'I'll listen to her. I'm a good listener.'

Louise laughed. 'You think you are. But you're not. You get paid to talk, Scott. To talk at the right time and to say the right things. Which means you tend to say only what you want others to think that you're thinking, which isn't always the case, of course. It's quite a skill you have: the art of talking judiciously.'

'Is that what you think about me?'

'You don't want to know what I really think about you, darling.'

'Of course I do. That's why I go to bed with you, my lovely. So I can listen to what you're mumbling about me in your sleep.'

'I think you're actually quite a lonely man. Like a lot of football managers. It's you versus the world. You versus the next team. You versus the crowd. You versus the guy in the other dugout. You versus your father. You versus the newspapers. You versus the Metropolitan Police. And now it's you versus the Greek police. You're someone who needs to prove something, Scott. Because you're a survivor. Because you're driven. That's why you've turned detective again. Because you can't leave things alone. Because you want to be right.'

'And here was me thinking it's because I want to help clear Bekim Develi's name, and to get my lads back home to London.'

'You think that's why you're doing it, I know. But it's not true. You're doing it because, like most men, deep inside that inflated ego you call your heart you believe that you're just a born detective. This is just another kind of contest for you.'

I grinned. Louise had me pegged all right. It was one of the reasons I was so fond of her. 'Maybe.'

'But I've got news for you, my love: nothing in this world gets solved the way you think it should. To your satisfaction, I mean. Nothing in this job ever finishes up the way it ought to. The sooner you learn that the better.'

CHAPTER 37

Charlie drove me down to the Astir Palace hotel in Vouliagmeni. I didn't mind that the cops followed us this time. I wasn't about to do anything I preferred them not to know about.

As arranged with Kojo Ironsi the evening before, Prometheus was standing outside the front door of the hotel. He was wearing a blue denim shirt, a pair of jeans that looked like he'd been hit with shrapnel, pink S Dot sneakers, Alexander McQueen sunglasses and more gold chains than the mayor of Hatton Garden. He snatched the red Dr Dre beats out of his diamond-encrusted ears and came down to the window of the car in a haze of cologne and ill-temper. If I had any doubt about what I was potentially dealing with, the word DOPE was helpfully printed in white on the front of the lad's baseball cap.

I told him to put the bag in the back of the Range Rover and get in.

'How was training this morning?'

He shrugged. 'All right.'

We drove down to the Astir Marina. I'd arranged to borrow Vik's yacht tender for a couple of hours, so that I could drive the two of us out into the Saronic Gulf – a patch of blue sea on the edge of the world before it turned magically into a place where heroes did battle with gods and monsters; where Aristotle might have tried to teach Alexander an important life lesson; where there were no phone signals and we couldn't possibly be interrupted.

The boat was a thirty-three-foot Regulator with a centre console and a couple of outboards with a top speed of around fifty-two knots. It had been a while since I'd driven a boat so I hugged the coastline for a while, getting a feel for the conditions and the boat, before picking up speed and heading northwest out to sea. On the way we caught sight of *The Lady Ruslana* which stood off the coast like some ironclad Argo. I could just make out the crew members; against the dark blue hull, their orange shorts and polo shirts made them look like figures painted along the surface of a large Greek vase.

'Are we going to Mr Sokolnikov's yacht?' asked Prometheus.

'Not today,' I said.

'Pity. I heard it's pretty cool. I'd like to see that sometime.'

'I dare say you will. But on this occasion we're going for a short history lesson.'

'I never was much good at history,' admitted Prometheus.

'It's not the history that's important so much as the lesson,' I said.

After about fifteen kilometres the sea began to narrow between two points of land and I throttled back to a crawl before putting the engine into neutral. I didn't drop anchor. It wasn't going to be a long lesson. Besides, I needed to manoeuvre.

'We're here,' I said.

'Where's here?'

'This is where the lesson is going to take place.'

Prometheus nodded and with his phone still in his hand he leaned over the side of the boat, staring down into the watery blue depths as if expecting Poseidon himself, or perhaps a sea monster. There was quite a swell and it wouldn't have surprised either of us if something large had appeared in the water. A tuna perhaps or even a shark.

'Listen, boss,' he said, still looking down into the water, as if he didn't dare to meet my eye. 'I'm sorry about what happened, what I did to Bekim. That was wrong and I feel very bad about it. I put the evil eye on that man and I'm all messed up inside because of that, see? I only meant to spook him a little, and that's God's truth. If I'd known that it might really work I'd never have done it, you've got to believe me. I can't sleep and I can't eat for thinking about it. If I could turn the clock back, I would, yeah? I'd give anything. Anything at all. Honest.'

'That's all bullshit,' I said. 'There's no such thing as the evil eye. You behaved like a twat, that's all.'

'Seriously, I don't think I'm ever going to feel good about myself again, boss.'

'Well then, you're no good to me,' I said, and placing a shoe on his backside I launched the Nigerian over the side.

Prometheus hit the water with a loud splash and then disappeared.

As soon as he was in the water, I sat down at the steering wheel and moved the boat away from him – just a few metres, so that it was just out of reach and the lesson might be learned, properly.

'What the fuck?' he said as he emerged, thrashing the water angrily with his arms. 'What the fuck d'you do that for? I lost my sunglasses. And my fucking phone. And my hat.'

'I didn't like the hat,' I admitted. 'To be honest you're better off without it. And you won't need a phone out here. There's no signal anyway.'

He started to swim towards the boat; I edged it away from him.

'Hey! What you doing, man? What's the big idea? This isn't funny. That phone was a Vertu Signature with Bang and Olufsen speakers, its own concierge and everything. It cost me nearly seven grand.'

'For a phone? They saw you coming, son.'

'Fuck you, man.' He swam towards the boat a second time and I moved it again.

'Stay the fuck where you are,' I said. 'Or I'll leave you here. I'm serious.'

'You crazy nigger,' he said but now he was just treading water; and he had one of the many crucifixes around his neck in his fingers as if he was going to pray.

'You think so? Bad news for you if I am. You see I'm the nigger in the boat. And you're the nigger in the water. To be quite precise, you are in the Straits of Salamis. To the west, behind you, we have the island of Salamis. And to the east, behind me, is the Greek mainland and the port of Piraeus. You could probably swim to either one, if you're lucky. I don't know what the currents are like here but you might make it, depending on what kind of a swimmer you are. However, I should tell you that contrary to what most people believe, there are sharks in the Mediterranean Sea, including the big predators like the great white, the bull shark and the tiger shark. Either way you're in dire straits, motherfucker. And that isn't a joke but a simple statement of fact.'

'All right, I get that you're mad at me. But I said I'm sorry about Bekim. What more can I do to prove that?'

'You can listen to what I've got to say – not that you have any choice about that.'

'All right, I'm fucking listening.'

'Shit, I know I am.' I lifted my ear into the breeze. 'It could be that I can hear something out here at sea. You see, this is the site of a great sea battle. The Battle of Salamis. Some historians have argued that it's one of the most significant battles in human history. Hard to believe, isn't it? This bit of deep blue sea, covered in blood and pitch and oil. Men screaming in agony. But it happened all right, in 480 BC, around the same time as the Battle of Thermopylae, and that's some local history you do know about. According to your Facebook page, *300* is your favourite movie.'

A big wave hit the Nigerian, and for a second he disappeared. When he came up again there was fear in his eyes.

'Hey, the next time you put your head under the water tell me what *you* can hear. Maybe it will be the voices of all those men who met their end in these waters – drowned, stabbed with a spear, shot with an arrow, burned to death with Greek fire. Thousands and thousands of men who never saw their families again, whose bones make up the seabed a hundred metres below your feet.'

I hit the throttle and moved the boat in a circle round the Nigerian's head; it looked very small in the water, like a floating coconut.

'Now then. Xerxes, the Persian king – you know about him, I guess – he sailed up here with the largest fleet that ever put to sea, in a hurry as usual. Twelve hundred ships, it was said, against about three hundred and seventy Greek ones, called triremes. And pretty much the same thing happened here as at Thermopylae. There were just too many Persian ships trying to get through these narrow straits and, much like we did the other night against Olympiacos, they lost their formation. But Themistocles, the Greek commander, he made sure that the Greeks kept theirs. Not to mention their discipline.

'On board each Greek ship were the hoplites, armoured infantry who fought in hand-to-hand combat. These men carried a sword and a spear and, most important of all perhaps, a shield on their left arm with which they protected not just themselves but also the soldier to their left. In other words, one man relied on another for his protection. So, just as the ships kept their formation, so the hoplites kept theirs. Not all of the Greeks were friends. In fact as far as I can see the Spartans and the Athenians were old rivals and probably hated each other. But against the Persians they were united and despite overwhelming odds, the Greeks prevailed.

'There's your lesson. You look after the guy to the left – because the guy on your right is doing the same for you. The Greeks were a superstitious lot but when a Persian was trying to stab them in the neck with a fucking spear, they didn't put much faith in their gods. In a battle it was the guy to your right who was going to look after your arse, and all the lucky charms and fucking prayers in the world weren't going to alter that fact. That's teamwork, son. That's something you *can* believe in. Be it war or football, it amounts to much the same thing. You look out for the next guy; that way, when the game is over you can look your mates in the eye and know that you did everything you fucking could. Otherwise your team isn't worth shit.'

I cut the engine and sat down near the stern.

'Which brings us to the last part of the lesson: you, Prometheus. Now I think you could probably pray to God to pull your arse out of the sea and who the fuck knows – maybe a ship would come along and rescue you. Or you could put your trust in your fellow man, namely me. So which is it to be?'

I leaned over the side and held out my hand. 'Me, or God?'

238

Prometheus grinned and took my hand.

A few minutes later he was lying on the deck of the Regulator, staring up at the sun and laughing.

'What's so funny?' I asked.

'I was thinking. That's the most interesting history lesson I think I ever had. Maybe if I'd had a teacher like you at my school, then I might have passed a few exams instead of jail-breaking stolen smartphones.'

I shook my head. 'Don't worry about that, son. If you'd ever passed an exam at school, you wouldn't be what you are now: one of the most naturally talented centre forwards I've ever seen. Seriously. You're a star in the making.'

He sat up, still grinning. I had to hand it to him; he was a good-natured kid.

'You really think so, boss?'

'I know so. All you have to do is learn how to play for the team. There's no limit to what you can do on the football pitch provided you don't mind who gets the credit.'

He nodded.

'Besides, you've passed the best exam there is, my friend. You're playing Premier League football at one of the best teams in the country. You pay attention to what I tell you and you'll go all the way, son. If that's what you want.'

Prometheus held out his hand. I took it again. And this time there were tears in his eyes. 'It's all I've ever wanted.' He grinned again. 'That and a new phone.'

'I'll buy you one.'

'No, it's all right. I've got a couple of cheap burners in my hotel room. Just in case.'

CHAPTER 38

'Where have you been?' asked Eva Pyromaglou. 'I've been calling you for the last hour.'

I was back at the Astir Palace, back in my bungalow, with an hour to kill before I went on the team bus to see the Panathinaikos game, answering emails and examining the contents of Bekim Develi's Louis Vuitton Keepall. I don't know why I should have found it shocking that Bekim had worn Frigo No. 1 underwear, but I did; actually, I know perfectly well why I found this shocking: Frigo No. 1s are a hundred quid a pair.

'I was on a boat,' I said.

'Me, I've spent the whole morning in the lab on this when I should have been looking after my son.'

I didn't answer; I was getting used to Greeks complaining about one thing or another. If you let them they'll even complain about the Romans and how they nicked everything from Greece – and that was two thousand years ago.

'What have you got for me, doctor?'

'You mentioned a bonus, Mr Manson?'

I laughed. 'You should play football.'

'Like I told you, I have a son who needs expensive medication.'

'Actually, you didn't tell me that, but what the hell. I said another five hundred if you found something. Did you find something?'

'Yes.'

'I'll send the money round by courier. This morning. All right?'

I was beginning to see the problems you might have if you lived in Greece. Everything in the country had a barcode and the only unexpected item in the bagging area was something for nothing.

'That would be quite satisfactory,' she said, briskly. 'So then; I have a name for you. Nataliya Matviyenko, aged twenty-six, bra size 32AA. Her implants were done at a clinic in Thessaloniki about two years ago. She paid cash.' Eva sighed. 'About five thousand euros.'

'Did you find an address?' I said.

'Yes. It's in Piraeus, at an apartment building on Dimitrakopoulou. That's less than a kilometre from where her body was found in Marina Zea. There was seawater in her lungs consistent with drowning, also some diesel. Again that's consistent with where she was found. I found traces of a lubricant in her anus – but no semen – and cocaine in her blood. If there had been any traces of semen in her mouth or her vagina the seawater would almost certainly have destroyed it; saltwater has a radical pH and is a highly effective antibiotic. I also found traces of epinephrine. My guess – and it's just a guess – is that she was probably on antidepressants. Lots of these girls are. Although why I don't know; they should try working in a Greek hospital.'

'Anything else?'

'About her? No, that's it, I'm afraid. I'm emailing you all this right now. My address is on this email, so please remember what I said. I don't want the cops having sight of any of my findings.'

'If only you knew how much I disliked the police, you wouldn't worry about that, love.'

I glanced at my Mac as an email with a Greek suffix appeared in my Inbox.

A moment later I heard a knock at the door of my bungalow.

'I've got to go. Thanks a lot, doc. I'll send your money right away. But call me if you think of anything else that might help.'

I tapped the call off and opened the door, half expecting the maid, but instead it was Simon Page with his training report and a list of possible injuries. His eyes were as bright as marble in his tanned face.

'There's a slim possibility that Ayrton Taylor will be fit again for Wednesday. I fucking hope so because the Nigerian lad, Prometheus – he just doesn't seem interested in playing football right now. I've tried putting a rocket up his arse, but he just gives me such a look of dumb insolence that it makes me want to smack him in the mouth. At least I think it's dumb insolence. I've got a terrible feeling that he's just dumb. Seriously, I watched him trying to pull his fucking jeans on this morning and he managed to get his feet caught in all those bloody chains on his belt and fall flat on his arse like a right spaz. If he struggles with getting his kegs on, how's he going to understand the difference between 4-4-2 and 4-3-3? He'll think they're both fucking ten and leave it that.'

'Don't worry about him,' I said. 'We've had a very constructive talk about everything, he and I. I talked, and he listened. I could be wrong, Simon – and I sometimes am – but I think everything will be fine with that lad now. At least it will be when he finds out which fucking pocket I put his bollocks in. Anyway, he's not as dumb as you think he is. I think he might actually be quite smart.'

'Let's hope you're right,' said the big Yorkshireman.

My phone rang again. I didn't recognise the number, but I answered it anyway. In retrospect, I wish I hadn't; Simon heard every word.

'Mr Manson?'

'Yes.'

'This is Francisco Carmona. From Orientafute.'

Orientafute – or Representação Sports e Agência de Orientação – was the largest agent-servicing company for footballers and football managers in Europe; and Francisco Carmona was its rapacious Brazilian founder. He'd made deals with all the big clubs and was rumoured to have made a twelve million euro fee on the summer transfer of Getúlio to Real Madrid for 125 million euros – the largest fee ever pocketed by a football agent.

'I was very sorry to hear about Bekim Develi. He was a great player. A good man.'

'Yes he was.'

'Look, I'm going to be in Athens on Monday and if you're still there I was wondering if we might meet up and have a talk.'

'Mr Carmona. I don't know how you got this number but I have no interest in speaking to you now or at any time in the future. I have an agent already, thank you.'

'No problem. But if you change your mind, I'll be staying at the Astir Palace hotel.' I ended the call and shook my head.

'Fucking Frank Carmona. I'll bet he's here to try and tap up some of our lads.'

'Aye, there's nothing players like more than someone telling them how much they could earn at another club.'

I could tell Simon thought that this might include football managers as well, but for once he was too diplomatic to say so.

'Nothing we can do about it,' I said. 'The transfer window doesn't close for another week.'

'Did you speak to Vik about replacing Bekim?'

'Not yet.'

'Christ, I'm fed up of being here,' said Simon. 'I never thought I'd say this, but I wish we were back in London.'

'I'm working on that.'

'With all due respect to you, boss, that doesn't exactly fill me with fucking optimism. Finding Zarco's killer back home was one thing, but this is Greece. They do things differently here.'

'Just as often they don't do them at all, Simon. That's really the point of what I've been up to these past few days. Or maybe you thought I was just seeing the sights. Checking out the Acropolis and the Parthenon. Setting up a secret meeting with Francisco Carmona, perhaps.'

'It's none of my fucking business what you do in your spare time, boss.'

'Well, I'm not. Really. I've never spoken to that shite hawk before.'

'I believe you. Listen, boss. There's something I have to tell you. Last night I was chatting with this English bloke at the hotel who's got a mate who has a local radio show. Fellow called George Hajidakis. I think it's the Greek equivalent of TalkSport. Anyway this bloke – Kevin, his name is – he told me that Hajidakis had said that Olympiacos aren't taking any chances next Wednesday. He reckons they've already bought the referee. He's Irish.'

'Look, Simon, the Greeks are always calling foul. About the only thing they can agree on is that someone else's club are a bunch of cheats.'

'Yes, but this bloke told me that George Hajidakis was going to mention the bent Irish ref on the show till he had the shit beaten out of him by two heavies with brass knuckles. He's in hospital now.'

'Saying it and knowing it are two things. But proving it to the satisfaction of UEFA is something else. Christ, those bastards fined José Mourinho more than fifty thousand euros when he was at Madrid just for suggesting that you've got no chance of a fair match against Barcelona. So you'll excuse me if I keep my fucking mouth shut, Simon. If your friend *is* right and they have bought the ref then we'll just have to play around that, like a dog turd in the goal mouth.' I shook my head. 'Forget it. I don't need this right now.'

'You're a cool bastard, Scott Manson, and no mistake. I tell you the referee has probably been bought and you just shrug it off like a cheap raincoat. So you're saying we just ignore it, or what?'

'Seriously, Simon, we've got enough grief in Greece without adding to it. In case you'd forgotten we're not allowed to leave the country. The team is effectively under open arrest with one of our number suspected of having had a hand in a girl's murder.'

'The tart. Right.'

'Now keep this to yourself but I managed to find out her name. I'm going to call that lawyer now and tell her.'

'I see. Want me to leave?'

'No. I'd rather you didn't. If something happens to me then it's best there's someone else who knows her name, too. Someone English.'

'What do you mean by that?'

'Only that I don't really know what the fuck I'm doing, or what the fuck I'm getting myself into here. It could be that this is more dangerous than I thought it was.'

I called Dr Christodoulou on speakerphone so Simon could hear our conversation, and told her the name of the girl; but I didn't tell her what I had in my mind to do next.

'How did you find this out?' she asked.

'Never mind.'

'You know that it's a crime to withhold information in a murder inquiry,' she said. 'Even in Greece. By rights I should really inform Chief Inspector Varouxis. I could be disbarred.'

'Just hold off for a little while,' I told her. 'At least until I've had a chance to follow up on this.'

'All right. But only until Monday, right?'

'Sure. How is it going with your own enquiries? Did you manage to find out anything about Svetlana Yaroshinskaya?'

'Not yet. Like you said, it's the weekend. Most Greeks don't work on a Saturday.'

I was half inclined to ask her on which particular day they did work but thought it would have sounded rude.

'All right. Give me a call when you have something.'

I hung up and looked at Simon.

'That gives me less than forty-eight hours.'

He frowned.

'To find out who killed her and why.'

'Maybe you should leave this alone,' he said. 'We don't need you getting yourself murdered, boss. Right now you seem to be the only one who's in with a shout of getting us all home. Just be careful, okay? I've already had one bugger die on me while we've been here. I don't want another.'

CHAPTER 39

Panathinaikos arranged for a coach to take us to their match against OFI at Leoforos, which was what the locals called the Apostolos Nikolaidis Stadium. As it pulled away from the Astir Palace hotel I walked to the back of the bus and peered out of the back window to see if there was a silver Skoda Octavia on our tail. When I saw that there was I smiled; it's always nice to be proved right about something. Especially when it's the cops.

I sat down and closed my eyes. It felt fantastic to be going to a football game, even one we weren't actually playing. The only pity was that I wasn't going to see the game itself. I had other plans that afternoon. The mood on the coach was boisterous to say the least, with Gary Ferguson leading not just the team these days but its sense of humour, too, even though his jokes were more obvious than any new hair on the front of his head.

'Look at the state of this country,' he complained as the coach roared north. 'Shops boarded up. Roads left unrepaired. Squeegee guys everywhere. People say it's the credit crunch, whatever the fuck that is. I've been watching the Bloomberg Channel every day in my room since I got here to find out what happened to this bloody place.' The idea of Gary glued to Bloomberg got a laugh all of its own. 'That's the financial channel with all these wee numbers on the bottom of the screen. To be honest when I first saw them I thought they were the final scores but it turns out they're stocks and shares, shite like that. Anyway, take it from me, lads, you won't find any of the answers on Bloomberg as to why they've had such a bad recession here. You want to find out what went wrong take my advice and watch some Greek porn channels. They explain everything. Quite simply everyone in Greece is fucked.'

More laughter.

'As a matter of fact, that's why I feel so at home in this shithole. This country makes the coffee for fucking Germany in the same way that Scotland makes the tea for England. But I reckon the Greeks could teach the Scots a few things about doing fuck all for a living.'

I always loved listening to Gary riff about stuff. Maybe he did have a future career in television after all, as a comedian. But after a while, something else began to creep to the edge of my mind and crouch there like a guy in a high-viz jacket at the end of a match, as if he was expecting trouble, and, much as I would have preferred it, I could hardly ignore it. I got up and sat behind the coach driver. He was in his sixties, I thought; lots of white hair, big sunglasses, skin like leather, Nikos Galis T-shirt (Nikos Galis was a Greek basketball player), BO like the last towel in a sauna and tobacco-plantation breath.

At the next red light I put a slightly damp twenty on the dashboard in front of him.

'I was wondering if you knew Thanos Leventis.' I paused, and then added: 'Hannibal Leventis?'

'I knew him.' He shook his head. 'It was really terrible what he did. I'll be honest with you, sir, I didn't think he was the type. I mean, you have to be crazy to do what he did, right? But he wasn't crazy at all. Not even bad. He was just ordinary.'

I stayed silent for a moment as he manoeuvred the coach around a difficult corner. Then I said: 'There was some talk that Leventis didn't act alone. That he had an accomplice.'

'Yes, sir. That's what one of the victims said. But the police judged her evidence to be unreliable, apparently. She was badly beaten up, of course. I suppose it's why they didn't think she could be relied on as a witness.'

I knew a bit about unreliable evidence myself.

'And what do you think?'

'I heard she said the other guy worked for the United Nations because he was wearing a UN T-shirt or something like that. That's why the cops discounted her evidence. After all, who wears a UN T-shirt? And what kind of UN worker goes around raping and murdering people? They're supposed to stop that kind of thing, not take part in it.'

'I guess you're right.'

'But you know, if there was another guy, then they'll catch up with him sooner or later. After all, if you do that kind of thing once, you'll almost certainly do it again.'

'Unless he already has.'

We turned onto Leoforos Alexandras. Some of our players hadn't yet seen the stadium and they were surprised at how dilapidated it looked.

'It's not exactly Stamford Bridge,' said Xavi Alonso. 'Or Silvertown Dock.'

'It looks ready for demolition,' observed someone else.

Ayrton Taylor had the SP on why this was:

'In fact,' he explained, 'it was supposed to have been demolished more than a decade ago. Panathinaikos moved out of Leoforos in 1984 to play in the new Olympic Stadium. But they had to move back here in 2000 while renovations to bring the place in line with UEFA requirements took place. Cut a long story short, the money ran out and now they're stuck here for the foreseeable future.'

'It's just like I was saying,' said Gary. 'The country is fucked.'

'And to think people in Britain are still bellyaching about the cuts,' said someone else. 'They don't know how well off they are.'

'Come to Greece and then vote Tory,' said Ayrton. 'Makes perfect sense to me.'

Antonis Venizelos, our liaison from Panathinaikos, greeted us at the main entrance. He wore a short-sleeved green shirt and a green and white tie; with all the hair on his arms he looked like an Iranian surgeon.

He handed out some tickets, lit a menthol cigarette and we trooped after him and into the ground.

'So,' I said, making polite conversation, 'the other team. OFI. Where are they from?'

'The island of Crete,' he said, 'where English whores go on holiday to get laid by a nice Greek boy.'

'I'm sure that's not the only reason,' said Simon, stiffly.

'English whores and sand monkeys.'

'Sand monkeys?' I frowned. 'Who or what are they?'

'The island of Crete is where all the illegals from Libya and Egypt make for on their cargo boats.' Venizelos shrugged. 'It's a real problem for them and for us and the EU does nothing about it. As long as they stay out of Germany and France no one gives a damn. Every week our coastguard has to rescue boatloads of them. Just the other day they picked up 408 in one boat. That's 408 people we're now going to

250

have to look after. In my opinion we should have let those bastards drown. Then maybe someone would help us to do something about it.'

The crowd began to applaud as they saw us take our seats and Venizelos left us. The stadium may have been falling down but our welcome was holding up; and the pitch looked to be in excellent condition.

'I'm glad he's gone,' said Simon. 'For a man who smokes menthols he says some very sour things. Sometimes I've half a mind to stick one on him, boss.'

'Don't do that, for Christ's sake. These are the only friends in Greece we have.'

'You do know he's a bloody Nazi, a member of the far-right Golden Dawn? At least that's what he told me.'

'Lots of people are, I think. They've got eighteen seats in the parliament.'

'That doesn't mean they're right.'

'No, of course it doesn't.' I looked at my watch. 'Listen, I've got to go somewhere, and I probably won't be back in my seat until the end of the match. It suits me for the cops to think I'm here for the next hundred and five minutes. So don't worry. I'm not about to disappear, like Zarco.'

'Where are you going, boss?'

'It's probably best I don't tell you,' I said. 'Just enjoy the game. And if anyone asks you later on, I was here all the time.'

Simon nodded. 'Right you are, boss. And remember what I said: be careful.'

I went out of the south entrance where, outside the official Panathinaikos store, Charlie was waiting in the Range Rover. We drove fast and west for a while before turning south in the direction of Piraeus.

'I never thought I'd hear myself say this,' said Charlie, 'but it's a pity you weren't watching Olympiacos. It'd be nearer and we'd have more time.'

'Can't be helped. But if we miss full time it won't really matter that much. The important thing is that we've given the cops the slip again.'

Charlie glanced in his mirror as if just making sure and then nodded.

CHAPTER 40

Dimitrakopoulou was the north street on a little square of neat gardens with tall trees and a playground where several children were having noisy fun on the swings under the watchful eyes of their mothers.

Charlie got out of the car and fetched an old blue police sweatshirt and matching baseball cap from a plastic bag in the boot.

'I brought these from home,' he said, putting on the sweatshirt and the hat. 'They wouldn't convince a real policeman, of course, but for anyone else they'll do fine. Let me do the talking. And don't speak to anyone. It's probably best if you seem bad-tempered and overworked and keep your sunglasses on; that way, you'll look like a real detective.'

Nataliya Matviyenko's apartment was on the top floor of an ochre-coloured building with so many green canvas canopies shielding its several balconies from the strong afternoon sun it looked like it was under sail. There was a pharmacy on the ground floor that, according to the plastic clock on the door, was about to close for the afternoon and, next to the pharmacy, a modern glass door with several bell buttons.

'There's a Nataliya Boutzikos here,' said Charlie, 'but no Nataliya Matviyenko.'

'Has to be her,' I said. 'Don't you think?'

Charlie nodded and rang the bell; it was always possible someone else lived in the same apartment – Mr Boutzikos, perhaps – but there was no answer.

'Now what?' I asked.

'Now we wait for the cavalry.'

'Holy shit,' I said. A police car was coming slowly along Dimitrakopoulou with its blue light on.

'Relax,' he said. 'This is them now. The cavalry, I mean. These guys are nothing to do with the GADA. They're friends of mine. I put a call in to the Piraeus Police for a squad car to turn up and make things look a bit more convincing, at least for the benefit of people who live around here. They'll keep watch for us while we break into her flat. Have you got a couple of twenties?'

I gave him four tens and watched as Charlie went over and leaned into the driver's window. I didn't see him hand over the money but I suppose he must have done because the police in the car switched off their blue light, lit up a couple of cigarettes and settled down to wait for us to do what we wanted to do. Charlie returned to the door as the pharmacist came out of his shop, still wearing a crisp white coat, and curious to know why the police were in his neighbourhood.

Charlie started talking to him and, after a while, the pharmacist went inside the shop again. In an effort to contain my nerves I took out my phone, checked the recent calls list and then rang Francisco Carmona, from Orientafute.

'Frank? It's Scott. Sorry I couldn't talk earlier.'

'That's okay, Scott. I'm used to people pretending they don't know me.'

'I was a bit taken aback to discover you're coming to Athens, Frank. When I called you before it was because

I wanted to speak to you about a player at another club. Someone you represent. Hörst Daxenberger, from Hertha.'

'You're looking to replace Bekim Develi?'

'That's right. Why don't you cancel your flight to Athens and get on a flight to Berlin and see how much that German lad wants to come and play in London instead of trying to upset some of my players with some of that Orientafute bullshit.'

'It's not your players I'm interested in, Scott. It's you. You're the reason I was coming to Athens. I want to represent you. From what I hear, you might need an agent.'

Charlie came back from the police car.

'Look, I can't talk now. Just speak to that German lad and find out if he's interested.'

I finished the call and looked at Charlie.

'That's a stroke of luck,' said Charlie. 'Mr Prezerakou is Nataliya's landlord and he's gone to fetch some keys for us. I told him we were looking for illegal immigrants and naturally he's only too keen to help. No one around here likes illegals. He hasn't seen her in days but that's not unusual at this time of year. He says she often goes on vacations to Corfu. Apparently, she's a good tenant and always pays her rent on time and he insists he saw all of her paperwork before he rented her the apartment. Originally, the apartment was rented to her husband, Mr Boutzikos, but he's working in London now and Nataliya manages the place herself.'

Ten minutes later we were inside Nataliya's apartment and nosing around her belongings which, for me at least, felt oddly transgressive. Charlie didn't look remotely bothered by what we were doing although we both wore latex gloves and it wasn't for the sake of appearances: Mr Prezerakou had stayed downstairs in his shop but the cops already had my fingerprints and it wouldn't have done for them to have discovered my dabs all over Nataliya's flat.

Everything was neat and tidy and furnished with that Ligne Roset sort of stuff that people on the continent seem to think is smart and contemporary. There was a large, signed Terry O'Neill photograph of Faye Dunaway lounging by the pool of the Beverly Hills Hotel that prompted me to think that Nataliya might reasonably have supposed she resembled the Oscar-winning actress. Otherwise the place spoke of a person who loved reading and not films – there was no TV and her shelves were groaning under the weight of books in Greek, Russian and English. Her closet was full of designer labels and in her tiny bathroom was a make-up trolley that could have supplied a large girls' school.

Charlie had found her passport in the door of a small desk. 'She was Ukrainian,' he said. 'Born Kiev 1989.'

He handed it to me and I placed it on the kitchen table before I stepped onto the balcony and looked out at the rooftops of the surrounding buildings; with their numerous water tanks, washing lines and satellite dishes it was not a particularly inspiring view but it was a typical one.

On the balcony itself was a yoga mat and a number of carefully arranged weights, including some kettlebells, and I wondered if Nataliya's murderer had helped himself to one of these to tie to her feet before dropping her into the nearby marina. I took a picture of them with my iPhone camera. Meanwhile, Charlie had found her handbag – or at least the bag she had probably been using on the night of her death; I had a vague idea that it matched the one I'd seen her carrying on the CCTV footage Varouxis had shown me of her visiting Bekim Develi in his bungalow at the Astir Palace hotel. Like everything else it was designer-made and expensive.

Charlie emptied the contents onto the kitchen table beside the passport and we both sat down to go through these. There was a make-up bag, a purse containing a thousand euros in new one hundred notes, credit and identity cards, a driving licence, a mobile phone, a small scented candle, some eyedrops, some earrings, some shoe clips, a bunch of keys, a picture of a man we took to be Boutzikos, several condoms, some lubricating gel, a pair of handcuffs, a vibrator, some antiseptic hand gel, a packet of wet wipes, a change of underwear, a pair of stay-up stockings. The pharmaceuticals were, said Charlie, more interesting: four epinephrine auto-injectors, a bottle of ceftriaxone and a bottle of flunitrazepam.

I took a picture of everything – including the passport and licence – on my iPhone.

'It looks as if she was allergic to something,' I said, taking one of the auto-injectors out of its box. It hadn't been used. None of them had.

'Not necessarily,' said Charlie. 'Epinephrine is a vasodilator. A lot of hookers in Greece use epinephrine as a fast-acting substitute for Viagra when clients can't get it up. It's just adrenalin after all. And unlike cocaine, epinephrine won't get a girl busted if a cop finds it in her possession.'

'What is ceftriaxone?' I asked.

'That's her just-in-case,' he said.

'Just in case of what?'

'Just in case of gonorrhoea. A lot of VD is penicillin resistant in Greece, so they prescribe ceftriaxone. Or azithro-mycin. If you can get it. Looks like she wasn't about to take that chance.'

'And Levonelle?' I asked examining a small pharmaceutical box with Greek writing. 'What does that cure?'

'Unwanted babies. It's the morning-after pill.'

'And the flunitrazepam?' I emptied out some little blue and white tablets on the palm of my hand. 'That's a sedative, isn't it? For depression.'

Charlie laughed. 'If you could read Greek you would see that the trade name for flunitrazepam is printed on the box, also. This is Rohypnol. The so-called date-rape drug. A lot of hookers slip it into the drinks of their more badly behaved clients. No, this little girl looks like she was prepared for anything.'

'Except the thing that happened. She wasn't prepared for that.'

'No, I guess not.'

Charlie swept everything back into Nataliya's handbag. 'No one is ever prepared for a trip to see Persephone,' he said.

I picked up Nataliya's iPhone 4, which was in a neat little plastic case with a gold chain that made it look like a girl's evening bag, took off one of my latex gloves and tapped the screen. The battery was in the red but there was enough juice left in the thing to see that, like my own phone, a security code was needed to access its contents.

'We need to get into this,' I said. 'We can use it to find out who she saw that night. So we'll keep it for a little while. At least until Monday when our lawyer will have to tell the police about this place.'

'Then we'd better take the handbag as well,' said Charlie. 'Otherwise that detective will think it looks strange. We can always bribe some Roma people to hand it in to your lawyer for the reward when you're done with it. They can say they found it in a wheelie bin on the marina.' He shook his head. 'He'll think it looks strange anyway when the apothecary downstairs tells him about the police having been here already. But cops in Greece are used to other cops doing a bit of freelance work. He'll know it was you, of course; or someone you paid to do it.' He looked at his watch. 'So we'd better get you back to the game and your alibi for this afternoon.'

As I put the phone in my pocket, Charlie added: 'But as to how you're going to get past that code, your guess is as good as mine. I don't know anyone who can break into these things.'

'Don't worry,' I said. 'I know just the man.'

CHAPTER 41

About a minute after I took my seat again Panathinaikos scored the only goal of the match. It wasn't a great goal; the OFI back four defended like they were wearing ankle weights and the goalkeeper managed to go the wrong way even though the forward in the green shirt had already telegraphed where he was planning to kick the ball. But none of that stopped the crowd from partying like it was 1999: a huge green firework exploded at the Gate 13 end, so loud it had every one of the London City players and staff – myself included – ducking down like a missile had been fired into the stadium by an Apache helicopter.

'Christ's arse,' yelled Simon. 'What the fuck was that?'

A cloud of green smoke drifted across the pitch, turning everything in the stadium opaque and, for a minute, it looked as if we were at the bottom of the sea, like those drowned sailors from the Battle of Salamis.

'I think that was just the beautiful game, as celebrated by Zorba the Greek,' I said.

'Makes you wonder how they kicked off back here when they won Euro 2004. I tell you what, if I could speak Greek they'd think I was fucking Plato. Each one of those Greeks thought that someone else was going to make the tackle. Four players in the box and not one of them marking his man. Whenever another team get anywhere near our box, you know what I want? I want our back four to die in a ditch to defend those eighteen yards. That's the way you used to defend and it's the way I used to defend. It takes heart to play football like that, boss. And those lads just didn't have it. Look at them: all those fucking tattoos they have on their bodies. There's only one tattoo, only one slogan that should be inked on every great centre back's chest: ¡No pasarán! They shall not pass. That's what I'd have tattooed on me if I was a defender today.'

I took the coach back to the Astir Palace with the team and sat next to Prometheus.

'What did you think of that?' I asked.

'Not much. And they're racists, too. I could hear monkey chants every time one of the black players got the ball. I thought Greeks were supposed to be civilised.'

'Whatever gave you that idea?'

'It's the birthplace of democracy.'

'Perhaps. But it certainly didn't count for much even then, I reckon. If you hear monkey noises on Wednesday night, here's what you're going to do. Score a goal. And then score another. That's the best way to shut these bastards up. But as a matter of fact, if you'd been on that park you'd have scored three. Before half time.'

Prometheus grinned a big grin.

'That lot we just saw are the Greek champions,' I said. 'By default, maybe. But they are a top side. Same as Olympiacos. And when we play *them* on Wednesday night, I want you to go and score a hat-trick, not for Bekim Develi but for yourself. As Aristotle says, "Blessed is he that opens the eyes of the blind." So, I want to see the player I know you can be.'

'Okay, boss.'

261

'This morning you were telling me that you used to jail-break stolen phones,' I said. 'When you were a kid.'

He shrugged. 'Still do. Just to keep my hand in. I love knowing about that shit.'

I handed him Nataliya's iPhone.

'Could you sidestep the passcode on this one? Only you'll have to do it quietly, without talking about it, because what I'm asking you to do could get us both arrested.'

'Wouldn't be the first time that's happened, boss.'

'I don't doubt it. But this is serious stuff now. And these are serious people. If we get caught it'll be six months in a Greek nick.'

Prometheus took the phone from me and tapped it awake.

'Leave it with me, boss. I'm from Nigeria. If I don't know how to do it I can just as soon call someone at home who does.'

Back in my bungalow at the Astir Palace I checked my emails and then took another look at the contents of Bekim Develi's Louis Vuitton Keepall and matching toilet bag; I already knew what kind of underpants he wore but I was looking for something else – a key to understanding Nataliya's death that was going to enable me to steal a further march on the police. I guessed that just having her name and her phone wasn't going to be enough; it seemed to me that you couldn't have too much information when you were investigating a crime like murder.

I spread the contents of the Keepall on the floor, the same way ex-cop Charlie had done with Nataliya's handbag. I'm a quick learner that way. I was still looking at these as if I was playing a memory game with objects on a tea tray when Skype gurgled its watery ringtone. It was Sara Gill, the Englishwoman who'd been raped and almost murdered in Athens. I'd Skyped her earlier and left a message to Skype me back.

I clicked on the little green bubble for a video call and found myself looking at an Asian woman with short brown hair who was probably in her thirties; a little overweight, she wore a white T-shirt and a grey jacket. The room she was in was typically Cotswolds, with a big fireplace and a dog sleeping on the floor behind her.

'Hello, Mr Manson,' she said. 'I'm Sara Gill. You Skyped me earlier. I was in the garden at the time. Detective Inspector Considine explained your situation on the telephone. And I read about that unfortunate young woman in the newspapers, of course. So I'll help you if I can.'

'Thanks for calling me, Sara. It's a long shot, I know, but I wondered if there was a possibility that her death might be connected with what happened to you and a number of other woman in Athens only a few years ago. You see the woman who died this week was a prostitute and it struck me as a little odd that the police didn't mention that the other women who were murdered were also prostitutes. Nor did they think to mention that there might be a football connection; Thanos Leventis drove a bus for the Panathinaikos football team, didn't he?'

She listened patiently while I stumbled around my explanation like a flat-footed drunk. I tried to explain, with all the diplomacy of the England rugby team, that there was no suggestion that she herself was a prostitute; no more was I comfortable asking her about what had happened, but even on Skype she could see this and tried to put me at my ease. Then she told me her story clearly and patiently and it was several minutes before I realised that a slight tremor had crept into her voice. When she got to the end of her harrowing account she swallowed an egg and I saw her hands were shaking.

'Thank you,' I said. 'That can't have been easy for you.'

'It wasn't,' she said. 'But I've decided that it's only by talking about it that I will ever get justice.'

'Why do you think the police didn't believe what you said – that there were two men who attacked you?'

'For one thing, they had a confession from Thanos Leventis. And what's more Leventis said he had acted alone. I don't think they wanted to risk anything to mess up his story. For another, I'd been beaten to the point of unconsciousness and it was several days before I was thinking straight again. I was in shock, of course, which meant I contradicted myself during the initial interview. But they had already decided I was unreliable as a witness. By the time they caught Leventis I was back in England, and no one was much interested in what I had to say. I called the police a few times and reminded them that there was another man but they didn't seem to care very much. That's when I called the Greek newspapers and told them. But I think most people were happy to sweep it all under the carpet and forget about it. And let's face it, this was when the Greek economy was collapsing around everyone's ears. There were riots in the streets as people tried and failed to get their money out of banks. The newspapers had bigger fish to fry. The police didn't even ask me to attend the trial as a witness. It was all over before I knew it and I didn't even get a chance to confront Thanos Leventis in court.'

She wiped the corner of an eye with a handkerchief.

'I'm sorry to make you talk about this again, Sara.'

'Don't be,' she said firmly. 'If there's any chance that what you're doing might help to catch this man then you have my thanks, Mr Manson.'

'Can you give me a description? Of the second man.'

'Yes. He was older than Leventis. In his late thirties, I should say. Tall, with dark hair and a very hairy body, like a lot of Greeks. I know that because he made me perform oral sex on him. I do remember that he had very sweet breath, like he'd been eating mints.' She laughed. 'Not like a Greek at all, if you know what I mean.'

'Oh, I do. I do.'

'And here's the bit I think made the police think I was deluded; it was like he had three eyebrows.'

'Three eyebrows?'

'At least that's how it seemed to me.'

'Would you recognise him again?'

'I think so. Yes, I'm sure I would.'

'What was he wearing?'

'Jeans and a T-shirt, with a sort of UN logo on it. Again, I'm not sure about that. Sort of . . . sort of like a wreath made of olive branches? Except that it wasn't a map of the world within the branches, but it looked more like a sort of labyrinth.'

'A labyrinth?'

'Like the one in the story of Theseus and the Minotaur. Only I don't think this one was as complicated as that. I sometimes think that's the key to everything, not metaphorically, but in reality. If I could work out what that sign meant it would help me find the man who raped me. Not Leventis. Because the truth is, Leventis couldn't get it up, if you'll pardon my French. That's why he knocked me out. And that's why I'm alive today. Because they thought I was already dead. They dumped me in the harbour and the water was so cold that I woke up. But when they left I'm sure they thought I was already dead.'

'They dumped you in the harbour? I didn't know that. Where, exactly?'

'I'm not sure exactly. Somewhere in Piraeus, I suppose. The actual assault took place on a piece of waste ground next to a football stadium. Which wasn't very far away from the harbour, because that's where I'd been walking when I was attacked. I do remember that the people who fished me out took me into the lobby of a nearby hotel.'

'Can you remember the name of the hotel?'

'Yes, it was the Hotel Delfini. They were very nice to me, and called the police. From there they took me to the Metropolitan Hospital, which was right next door to the stadium where I'd been attacked. I could see it from my hospital bed. Only it wasn't the one where Panathinaikos play; it was the other Athens team that plays there: Olympiacos. Yes, I remember now; that was the other football connection. Besides the fact that the driver of the coach worked for Panathinaikos.'

'What day of the week did the attack take place, Sara?'

'It was a Saturday night in September.'

'And would you happen to remember if there'd been a football game that day?'

'No, I don't. But it was the last Saturday in September, so you could probably find out.'

After we finished our Skype conversation I called up Google Maps and saw that the Karaiskakis Stadium where Olympiacos played was exactly 3.5 kilometres from the Hotel Delfini in Marina Zea; and there was a large patch of waste ground immediately to the southwest of the ground, on the Piraeus side. Given where she'd been dumped after the attack, it was beginning to look like a real possibility that Nataliya's death might be connected with the attack on Sara

Gill and others. In view of the racism of the Greeks, had she been attacked because she was Asian? The Greek newspapers were often reporting attacks on Romas and Pakistanis by the far-right Golden Dawn organisation. And I knew from my own experience that a dark skin was enough to bring hatred and contempt down on your head. I was equally intrigued by Sara's description of the logo on her attacker's T-shirt: the word labyrinth had of course reminded me of the tattoo on Nataliya's left shoulder. Was this a connection, too?

Absently I stared at Bekim Develi's belongings laid out on the bungalow floor, thinking about Sara Gill's closing remark. At the back of my head, a half-perceived thought began to gain clarity. After a moment or two I realised that perhaps the key that *I'd* been looking for was staring me in the face. I bent down and picked it off the floor.

It was the key not to a suitcase, or a car, or a hotel room, or a left-luggage locker, but to Bekim's house on the island of Paros.

CHAPTER 42

The next day I caught the lunchtime flight to Paros aboard a DHC-8-100, a propeller plane with more vibrations than the Beach Boys and none of them good. Paros was just one of a group of islands known as the Cyclades which, from the air, resembled a betting slip torn up and its pieces scattered on a bright blue carpet. Paros wasn't the smallest island of the group although you could have been forgiven for thinking that it might have been when you saw the tiny airport with its postage stamp of a runway.

I hired a little Suzuki 4x4 at Loukis Rent-a-Car immediately opposite the sleepy little airport terminal, and using the directions from the guy in the office I set out for the southwest tip of the island, where Bekim's house was to be found. The island itself was like a large links golf course – scrubland with drystone walls and very few trees. But for the omnipresent noise of cicadas you might almost have thought yourself in a remote part of Ireland suffering an unusually severe heat wave. The locals were just as wizened and peasant-like. Nearly every building I saw was made of white stone with all of the doors, window frames and shutters, balcony railings, and gates painted the same shade of blue, as if only one colour could be obtained at the local hardware shop. Either that or everyone on the whole island was an Everton supporter.

Less than fifteen minutes later I was driving up a rutted track to a collection of rectangular white buildings surrounded by empty rough land that bordered a perfect little private beach. Bekim's house resembled an outpost in some forgotten French colony. I parked my car around the back in the shade and tried to call Prometheus, to see how he was making out with Nataliya's iPhone, but I couldn't get a signal.

Inside, the house was much less traditional, with open-plan rooms, polished wooden floors and the sort of Eames furniture that belonged in an episode of *Mad Men*. On the wall, in pride of place opposite a huge fireplace, was a wonderful painting of a football match by Peter Howson which, instantly, I coveted. In the dining room was another picture by Howson, this one a portrait of Henrik Larsson painted during his seventh season for Celtic in 2003–2004; again I wanted it. Elsewhere I found numerous modern sculptures in white marble and polished black granite by an artist called Richard King that were as beautiful as they were tactile. As far as I could see there was no television and no telephone, and very little post on the doormat, or anywhere else, for that matter.

In the kitchen I made myself some Greek coffee, sat down at the kitchen table and flicked through some old copies of the *Athens News*, an English-language newspaper. It made depressing reading. On most of the front pages there were colour pictures of the Hellenic police taking on rioters outside the Greek parliament building. On another front page I saw a thuggish-looking man holding a big black flag with a symbol that looked a bit like the UN logo; inside the branches was a sort of small golden labyrinth. Except that this wasn't really a labyrinth at all, but a sort of simplified swastika. I turned the page and found another photograph, this time of a man wearing a black T-shirt with the same sign. According to the caption the man belonged to the Order of the Golden Dawn, the far-right political party. And suddenly I knew the kind of T-shirt that Sara Gill's attacker had been wearing. He was a neo-Nazi; a fascist.

I finished my coffee and then conducted a thorough search of the house which yielded precisely nothing else of interest except that Bekim had a peculiar fondness for tinned Heinz soups and spaghetti hoops. There were cupboards full of the stuff. I was on the point of concluding that the whole trip had been a waste of time when the back door opened and a small hobbit of a woman came into the kitchen, carrying a basket of cleaning things. She gave a scream and dropped the basket to the floor when she saw me and, having apologised for giving her a fright, I explained that I was a friend of Mr Develi's.

'He no here right now,' she said and it was quickly obvious that the woman – whose name was Zoi – had no idea that her employer was even dead. I thought it best not to tell her, at least for the present: it was information I wanted, not tears. 'He is playing football in London.'

'Yes, I know,' I said dangling the door key. 'It was Mr Develi who gave me this key.'

She nodded, still suspicious.

'I've been staying on the mainland, in Athens, and Bekim said I should come and stay here if I got the chance.'

That much was true at any rate.

'You stay here tonight?' she asked.

'Yes. If that's all right. Just until tomorrow.'

'You want me to fix a bed for you?'

'No, I think I can manage.' I looked around. 'Have you worked for him long?'

'I clean this house for Mr Develi since he came to the island. Eight years ago. He like it here very much because Paros is quiet and people leave him alone. Most locals don't even know that he is such a famous footballer. He very private here. Like other rich people who live on Antiparos.'

Antiparos was the neighbouring smaller island to the west.

It felt strange to hear Bekim described in the present tense; as if he wasn't dead at all. Of course, in this woman's mind, he was still very much alive.

'Bekim Develi. The Goulandris family. Tom Hanks. His wife, Rita Wilson, she is Greek. Everyone like it here because nobody knows they're here. Is a big secret.'

I couldn't help but wonder about that, given the alacrity with which Zoi had told me of their presence on the island.

'Do you cook for him, too? Bekim, I mean.'

'No. He say he very fussy. He doesn't like Greek food. Only Greek wine. Just very plain English things. Eggs, bread, salad. I bring him these things but always he prepares his own food.'

It seemed strange to have a holiday home on a Greek island if you didn't like Greek food; then again most English tourists in Greece seemed to subsist on a diet of hamburgers and chips.

'I can cook for you if you like, Mr . . . ?'

'Manson. Scott Manson.' I picked up a photograph on one of the kitchen shelves and showed it to her; it was a team photograph taken at the end of the last season when we'd just learned we'd made it to the fourth spot and had qualified for Champions League football. I couldn't help but wonder what might have happened if we'd come fifth. Would Bekim still be alive? 'That's me there,' I said.

'Yes,' she said, more reassured now than before. 'That is you.'

'I'll probably go into town tonight and find something to eat in a local taverna,' I said. 'So there's no need to trouble yourself.'

'Is no trouble. I like to cook. But as you wish, mister.'

'Otherwise I can make do with a plate of tinned spaghetti. Like Mr Develi.'

She pulled a face at the thought of that. 'Ugh. I don't know how he can eat things out of a tin.'

'He sounds like a difficult man to work for,' I said.

'Mr Develi?' Zoi frowned and shook her head. 'He is a wonderful man,' she said. 'No one ever had a better person to work for than him. He is kind and generous like no one I ever met. Other people who know him will tell you this, too.'

'Really? I thought you said he was very private here.'

'He has friends on the island. Of course he does. There's the artist lady in Sotires, who knows him best, I think. Mrs Yaros. She and Mr Develi are very good friends. She's a sculptor. Lots of sculptors live on Paros. They used to come here for the fine marble but now all the best marble is gone, I think. I think maybe she know him better than anyone around here.'

'I'd like to meet this Mrs Yaros. Do you think she's at home?'

Zoi nodded. 'I saw her this morning. In the supermarket.'

'What's her address?'

'I don't know the address. But her house is easy to find. You drive away from here, turn left, go for three miles, past old garage, turn right and her house is at the top of a steep hill. Is grey and white. There is a big blue gate. And sometimes a dog. The dog isn't friendly, so you'd best wait in the car until she comes to fetch you.'

'Thanks for the advice.'

I finished my coffee and then got back into the car. Even though I'd parked it in the shade the little Suzuki felt as hot as a crematorium. I switched on the air conditioning, started the engine and drove back down the track towards the garage. A few minutes later I was through the blue gate and driving up a steep, paved slope which had the little Suzuki straining to reach the top. But for the tip about the dog I might almost have got out and walked. The slope levelled out at the edge of a terraced garden and, above the sound of the engine, I heard what sounded like a dentist's drill. For a moment I thought I might have got the wrong house. Then, in an open workshop/studio, I caught sight of a slight figure in a mechanic's blue overalls, covered in a fine white dust. It was hard to make out if this was a man or a woman because of the protective mask he or she was wearing. I steered under the shade of a carport and waited for the dog or its owner, but when neither came I opened the car door cautiously and called out.

'Mrs Yaros? Forgive me for dropping in on you like this. My name is Scott Manson. And I'm a friend of Bekim Develi.'

By the time I had walked to the workshop the figure in the overalls had switched off the compressed air cylinder that powered a tiny drill being used to fashion an impossibly beautiful spiral of marble that looked like a piece of material falling through the air, removed her mask and tossed a mane of blonde hair from one shoulder to the other.

I recognised the woman immediately. It was Svetlana Yaroshinskaya, better known to me as Valentina.

CHAPTER 43

'What on earth are you doing here? I don't understand. This is private property. Did Bekim tell you how to find me?'

Somehow the woman managed to look more beautiful in her dusty overalls, although that could have had something to do with the fact that she had already unbuttoned them to reveal her generous cleavage. I opened my mouth to account for my presence but she wasn't yet in the mood for explanations.

'I must say that was very unkind of him, to say where I was. You can tell him from me: I'm very angry. He's betrayed my trust.'

The pink sandals she was wearing and her painted toenails were about the only concessions she'd made to her own femininity; that and the diamond stud I could see glinting in her belly button.

'It wasn't Bekim who told me how to find you,' I said. 'It was Zoi. His housekeeper.'

'How did you even know I was here?'

'I didn't. I came to see a Mrs Yaros. And instead it's you, Valentina. Frankly, I'm as surprised as you are. I had assumed Mrs Yaros was a Greek. I mean, it sounds Greek.'

She nodded. 'That's how I like it. Yaros is short for Yaroshinskaya – my real name. And please don't call me

Valentina. Not on Paros. I'm never Valentina when I'm here. My first name is Svetlana.'

'All right.' I raised my hands in surrender. 'No problem.'

'So why *are* you here?'

Like Zoi, Valentina clearly had no idea that Bekim Develi was even dead. For a moment I considered telling her I'd come to buy a sculpture, to spare her feelings a little, but in her dusty overalls she looked tough enough to hear what I had to say without a lengthy team talk.

'I'm here because Bekim is dead,' I said, bluntly. 'Last Tuesday night, during a football game against Olympiacos, he collapsed and died on the pitch in front of twenty-five thousand people.'

'Oh my God,' she said. 'Poor Bekim. I didn't know.'

'So I gather.'

'You'd better come into the house.'

She led the way around an odd-shaped swimming pool to a small back door, and stepped over a sleeping dog.

'Zoi told me he was fierce,' I said, hesitating.

'He used to be. But he's too old to offer much in the way of defence now.'

'I know the feeling.'

I followed her into a sparsely furnished house that was more of a museum to work I presumed must be her own. We went through a drawing room and into the kitchen where she lit a cigarette and started to make Greek coffee. Next to the cooker was a photograph of Svetlana in St Petersburg standing next to an enormous equestrian statue of Peter the Great. I'd seen it from the bus on the team's pre-season tour of Russia; at the time the tour had seemed like a disaster but of course that was before I knew what a real football disaster felt like.

275

'What was it?' she asked. 'A heart attack, I suppose.'

'Something like that. We're still awaiting the autopsy, I'm afraid. Nothing in Athens moves quickly, it seems. Especially when everyone seems to be on strike.'

She sighed. 'I'm so sorry. I had no idea.'

'I'm beginning to see why Bekim liked it here so much,' I said. 'Anyone would think televisions and the internet and the newspapers had never been invented.'

Svetlana answered with a shrug, and then: 'Most people who come to live on the island want to get away from the world,' she said. 'We're a bit like the lotus-eaters in Homer's *Odyssey*. You know? Once you eat the fruit you lose the desire to leave? I don't know – like most islanders I just want to live in peace and quiet. These days it's only bad news on TV and in the papers. On Paros we try not to pay attention to what happens in Athens. It's nearly always depressing.'

'I suppose Alex is too upset to come to Greece and sort things out. Which is why you're here.'

I turned my attention to a framed drawing on the opposite wall; a good drawing of a young woman who resembled Nataliya.

'I'm not here for him or even her. I'm here for me. And for the team. You see, none of us is permitted to leave Athens until the police have satisfied themselves that Bekim had nothing to do with the death of a girl with whom he had sex on the night before he died. A Russian girl I believe you know.'

Svetlana let out a sigh that filled the kitchen with cigarette smoke and made me want one myself. 'Nataliya.'

'Is this a drawing of her?'

'Yes.'

'She was found in the harbour with a weight tied to her feet.'

'Oh, God.' Her eyes filled with tears for a moment and tearing off a square of kitchen towel she dabbed at them for a minute. 'The poor kid.'

'Until now I've been trying to keep your name from the police. As a favour.'

'Thank you.'

'Your name, your phone number, your Skype address, your email. Not that I can see it would have made much difference. You never seem to answer them, anyway.'

'My phone doesn't get a signal here. I don't have a landline. My computer is in the repair shop right now. Something's wrong with it.' She frowned. 'And the police think what? That Bekim had something to do with Nataliya's death?'

'Something like that.'

'Impossible. He was always very kind to her. And she was fond of him. Almost as fond of him as I was.'

She took the drawing off the wall and contemplated it sadly.

'I'm glad to hear that,' I said. 'Not least because I'm checking out a few leads myself in the hope of clearing his name. You might say I've turned detective on the assumption that I couldn't achieve any less than the Hellenic police. I came to the island to look for something that might offer a clue as to how or why she met her death. And it looks as if I was right. I have found something.'

'Oh? What's that?'

'You, of course.'

'Me? I can't tell you what happened to her.' She put the drawing back on the wall and rubbed one of her breasts absently.

'Perhaps not. But you can help to colour in my drawing. If you do that, I'll try my best to keep your name from the police.'

'I need to wash and then cool down.' She unbuttoned her overalls, let them fall to the ground and, naked, sipped some of the delicious coffee she'd made. The cup, and more especially the saucer, made the informality of her appearance all the more alluring.

'You've no idea how hot it is in that studio. The air conditioning has broken down. And I have dust in every part of my body.'

Wet or dry Svetlana was the best thing to look at for miles around. While she showered, I took a few minutes to admire some of the sculptures that surrounded the pool: elegant pieces of marble and granite that had the quality of natural objects – plants, shells, marine life – which, given that they were carved from stone, were all the more impressive.

I turned as Svetlana stepped out on to the deck, towel in hand and glistening. She draped the towel over the back of a basket chair then dived into the water, swam a couple of lengths and then came to the water's edge. I sat down on a chair near her.

She sank below the surface for a moment and then came powering up again, lifting herself onto the side with arms that were more muscular than I remembered, and sat there in the sun like the Little Mermaid.

'So, tell me what you *think* you know,' she said.

I told her. It didn't take very long. I was almost embarrassed at the sudden realisation of how little I did know. Perhaps that's how it is with detective work. You know nothing; and then, a few minutes later, you think you know almost everything.

'I last spoke to Bekim about two weeks ago,' she said. 'He emailed me from London with the intention of hooking up in Athens. I said I couldn't come because I was working. And he understood that. So, naturally he'd have called Nataliya. No, wait. I need to go back to the beginning, about six years ago. It's not that I feel the need to justify myself to you, Scott. I don't. It's just that when you said you'd kept my name from the police I realised that you'd done me a huge favour. I think that in return I need to tell you absolutely everything.'

CHAPTER 44

'In 2008, when the recession hit this country really hard, some of the banks looked like they would fail. Like a lot of Russians I had money in the Bank of Cyprus and it seemed for a while that I was going to lose it all. For a while my work stopped selling. Art is always the first thing that most people cut back on. But not Bekim, who has a good eye for paintings, and for sculpture, too. He saved me from going under. He bought several pieces of mine and then came up with a suggestion of how I could earn some regular money. He said that even in Greece there were lots of guys in football who would be prepared to pay for a GFE – a girlfriend experience – with someone who wasn't a professional escort.

'I thought it was a joke at first. But then he introduced me to an English woman at the Hellenic Football Federation, Anna Loverdos, and some Greek guy from UEFA she was into. Anyway, they were hot for Bekim's idea. The whole thing was Bekim's idea. He said we'd be doing a favour to a lot of guys who would otherwise just go and get themselves into trouble on Sofokleous, which is the red light area of Athens. Bekim was the first, of course. The man has a libido like a goat.

'The first time I went with another man it was some old guy from FIFA. Something to do with the World Cup in

Qatar. I was the cherry on top of the money he'd been paid for his vote. The sex was lousy but the money was great. I got paid five thousand euros for spending the weekend with him because some of that was mouth-shut money. The guy gave me a thousand-euro tip. He could afford it, of course. Later on I read in the newspaper that he got over a million US dollars for his vote.

'Then Anna called me again and before I knew it she was calling once or twice a month. She would tell me to contact some footballer or perhaps an official from FIFA or UEFA. I'd get paid as much as a couple of thousand euros a night, cash. I told myself that turning tricks wasn't such a bad thing for an artist to do. Fucking a few guys didn't seem as bad as some of the things that Caravaggio and Cellini had done.' She shrugged. 'You can justify anything to yourself, if you want to. I figured that all I really cared about was my work and that if I had to fuck some rich guy in order to keep doing it, then that's what I'd do. I won't deny that there were plenty of times when I even enjoyed it. Especially when it was a player. There are worse things to do than sleep with fit and handsome young men.

'Like I say, the work was part-time, at first. Maybe a couple of times a month. I paid off all my bills; I even had enough to buy a small flat in Athens. Then Anna started to telephone me a bit more often. It seems that there's no shortage of guys with money in football. Agents, managers, players, officials, even a few match referees who someone wanted to fix before a big game. So I found another Russian girl to help me out when I was busy. Nataliya. She was much more of a professional than I was; and much better at it, too. I'd either see the client myself, if I needed the money, or I'd give the work to Nataliya and take ten per cent. That seemed fair. It's less than my art dealer charges. I think Bekim preferred her to me, anyway. She was more adventurous than I am. If he was coming to Athens he'd call me or Nataliya direct. He meant well, of course. And he'd recommend us both to a few people. You included.

'After a while I didn't want to do it any more. I sold some of my work to a cruise ship company and I was a lot less inclined to fuck guys in football for money. You might find this hard to believe but as a matter of fact, you were my last client. Really, I only did it as a favour to Bekim. He paid me in advance and said I didn't have to fuck you if I didn't want to but you were a nice guy, and you'd behave yourself. Anyway, just so you know, I did it with you because I wanted to. But I've never done it here on Paros. Not even with Bekim. When I'm in Athens I'm Valentina. When I'm here I'm Svetlana Yaros, the sculptor. And that's never been a problem until today.'

She gathered her hair in a ponytail at the back of her head and squeezed some of the water out.

'Stay there,' she said.

She got up for a moment and went to fetch not her clothes or a robe but a cigarette from the kitchen and I wasn't sorry about that. Calypso herself could not have looked more seductive.

'Tell me about Hristos Trikoupis,' I said.

'Did he tell you about me?'

'No. It was Jasmine.'

'Ah, Jasmine. You have been thorough. For a while I had a regular thing going with Trikoupis. He wanted me to be his mistress, but I wasn't interested in something like that. He was too hairy for me. Too much like an animal. What is more he has terrible breath.' She wrinkled her nose with

282

displeasure. 'We'd have dinner at Spondi and then I'd go to his apartment near the stadium and have sex with him. But I'd stopped seeing him and more or less got out of the football VIP escort business. When you and I went to the game against Hertha he saw us and was furious about it. I didn't mean to make him angry. But he was so jealous of you. Like, he really hated you.'

'That explains a lot,' I said. 'He said a lot of nasty things in the newspaper about me I figured were just mind games, ahead of the match. But maybe I was wrong about that.'

'I don't know. Maybe.'

'When did you last see Nataliya?'

'In May, I think. We had a drink together at the Grande Bretagne with two black guys. A Panathinaikos player and his agent. We all went to dinner at a place called Nikolas tis Schinoussas where we met another player, a Romanian guy. He plays for Olympiacos. Then we went back to the Romanian's place in Glyfada. The agent went back to the hotel by himself.' She frowned. 'You're going to make me try to remember names, aren't you? I'm not much good with names.'

'Try.'

'The Romanian guy was Roman someone or other.'

'Roman Boerescu?'

She nodded.

'And the others? The two black guys?'

'Let's see now. The player was called something angelic. Yes. It was Séraphim.'

I nodded. 'Séraphim Ntsimi. Panathinaikos bought him from Crystal Palace in the summer.'

'If you say so. I wouldn't know anything like that. I just sleep with them.'

'And the agent?'

'Tojo. At least I think that was his name. Tall guy. Head like a bowling ball.'

I nodded. 'Yes, I know who that is.'

I was silent for a while.

'How am I doing?' she asked.

'Good.'

She closed her eyes and held her face up into the sun.

'Are you planning to stay at Bekim's villa tonight?' she asked.

'That's the idea.'

'What are you going to do for dinner?'

'I thought I might go into town and find a little taverna. Not to mention a telephone signal and a Wi-Fi signal.'

'You won't get into anywhere good. Not in August. Everywhere reasonable will be booked up. Why don't you have dinner here?' She shrugged. 'I already made something. I generally cook for two and that lasts for two days. So you're in luck, really.'

'I'd like that. But on one condition. That you put on some clothes.'

'Are you sure about that? There are some men who would pay a lot of money to have a naked woman cook for them. Besides, I never wear clothes at home, apart from my overalls. And I wouldn't like to wear those while I'm serving dinner.'

'Perhaps we can excuse them on this occasion,' I said vaguely. 'It is very hot, I suppose.'

CHAPTER 45

Svetlana was a good cook and had prepared a variety of delicious Greek dishes.

'It's nice to have someone here for dinner,' she said bringing one plate and then another out onto a terrace that overlooked a small yard that was full of blocks of stone. 'When I'm here I tend to live like a nun.'

She poured me a glass of cold white wine and then went back into the house, leaving me to think a while. For some reason I was thinking about Sara Gill. At the same time I was thinking about football. The truth is, of course, I'm nearly always thinking about football; and quite often when I'm thinking about football I remember something that João Zarco used to say. He was much more of an original thinker than most people ever knew. I could almost hear him now:

'I've been reading about this Greek philosopher called Zeno,' he said. 'You know? That story about the arrow in flight? It's an argument against motion. That time is entirely composed of instants so that at every instant of time there is no motion occurring. I was wondering if his thinking could be applied to football, and I think it can. Everything in football can be broken down into distinct passages of play like the movement of the arrow; and every passage of play can be broken down into transitional moments, when a game turns decisively: a tackle, a poor clearance, a penetrating pass. These transitional moments can have the force of revelation when you see these moments of revelation for what they are. So that you can act on them. That's all the future is, too.'

At that point I wouldn't say I had a revelation, but I did stand up from the table and make a fist. Something Svetlana had said – I wasn't even sure what this was – had made me guess the probable identity of the man who had helped Thanos Leventis attack Sara Gill; the man who had raped her and left her for dead in the harbour.

When Svetlana came back onto the terrace she was wearing an elegant pair of black slacks and a matching long-sleeved T-shirt, and she smelt of perfume.

'You look pleased with yourself,' she observed.

'If I do it makes a change on this trip,' I said, sitting down again. 'I've never been one to sit around congratulating myself. I guess all football managers are like that: beset with thoughts about what could have been. Sometimes it seems that there's a guy inside my head who's always cross with me.' I sighed. 'Poor Bekim. This might have been his best season ever.'

We sat down at the table and started to eat.

'I certainly admire your appetite,' I said, watching her eat a large plate of moussaka. 'It's not many women who can eat like that with a clear conscience.'

I knew I didn't have to make a cheesy remark about what a good figure she had – we both knew it was superb – but I was anxious to secure her continued cooperation. Svetlana had told me quite a bit, however I felt I needed to know everything.

When we finished dinner she lit a cigarette and since it was Sunday night – the only night when I allow myself to smoke – I had one, too.

'Thank you for an excellent dinner,' I said. 'And for saving me from an evening on my own. It was the local taverna or tinned spaghetti.'

'Tinned spaghetti?'

'Bekim's kitchen cupboards are full of the stuff.'

'Yes, of course, it would be. He loved English food. You know, I think the last person I cooked for was probably Nataliya. She came out here to stay for a few days about six months ago. She was going through a bad patch, poor kid. She was depressed. I'm not exactly sure but I think there had been an attempted suicide when her boyfriend had cleared off to England.'

'This would be the guy called Boutzikos.'

'Nikos Boutzikos. Yes.'

'You were friends then? You and she.'

'It wasn't just business. We were – well, let's just say we were close.'

'No, let's just remember that you agreed to tell me everything,' I said. 'For keeping your name from the police. So I need it all, if you don't mind.'

'All right.' For a moment she exhaled smoke from each nostril, like a dragon about to breathe fire. 'If you really must know we went to bed together. It was her idea. She wanted me more than I wanted her, and I only did it because I thought it might make her feel better. As a matter of fact it was me who felt better. She made me come like a train. Which is odd because I have very little experience with women.'

I shrugged. 'Then I guess she knew what she was doing. Professional girl like her. After all, that was her job, wasn't it? Threesomes. Foursomes, for all I know. That kind of thing.'

'You make that sound ugly.'

'I don't mean to. But in retrospect that's how she seems

287

to me: professional. How else am I to describe someone who was prepared to dope her clients?'

'Nonsense. She wasn't that kind of girl at all.'

'What do you think these are? Breath fresheners?'

I tapped the Photos app on my phone and showed her the picture of the Rohypnol pills I'd found in Nataliya's handbag.

'These were found in her bag,' I said.

But Svetlana was still shaking her head.

'You've got it all wrong. Nataliya didn't use these for knocking out clients. That's not how this business works. Not at our sort of level, anyway. No, these pills were for her. They're antidepressants. A girl on Omonia Square might have done what you're suggesting but not someone like Nataliya. At a thousand euros for a two-hour GFE she wasn't exactly a hooker off the street.'

I showed her the next picture. 'And I suppose the ceftri-axone was just in case she caught a cold.'

'Accidents happen. It's best to be prepared.' She frowned. 'How do you know all this anyway? About the Rohypnol? I thought you said the cops hadn't found anything.'

'They didn't find it. I did. With the help of my driver, Charlie. He used to be a cop with the Hellenic police. We persuaded her landlord in Piraeus to let us into her flat and then had a nose around. I took her bag away for safekeeping. And I photographed the contents, as you can see.'

I handed her my phone and let Svetlana look at the pictures I'd taken.

'For the moment I still have the bag although our team's lawyer in Athens reckons that I will have to hand it over to the police sooner than later.'

Svetlana paused when she saw the picture of Nataliya's iPhone.

'So, the cops are going to want to speak to me after all. I mean they'll almost certainly find my number on her phone. Not to mention a few texts, perhaps.'

'Not necessarily. One of my players used to knock off phones for a living. He's trying to break the code. It might be that I can erase one or two things before I hand it over.'

'I see.' Svetlana swept the screen of my phone to view the next picture and then frowned. 'Wait a minute,' she said.

'What?'

She turned my phone around to show me a picture of one of Nataliya's four EpiPens.

'These EpiPens. I don't think she was allergic to anything. In fact, I'm sure of it. I cooked for her. She'd have mentioned something like that.'

'Charlie says that's not why she had the stuff. He says Viagra is in short supply in Greece and that a shot of adrenalin will help some guys get it up.'

'Nonsense. Believe me, there's no Viagra quite as powerful as a twenty-five-year-old girl like Nataliya.'

She pinched the screen of my iPhone and enlarged the picture of the EpiPen.

'Besides, look at the writing on the side of the box. It's in Russian. This wasn't even hers. This EpiPen was prescribed in St Petersburg. *To Bekim Develi.*'

'What?'

'She must have taken it. *Them.*'

For a moment I considered the possibility that Bekim had been using epinephrine as a performance enhancer, like ephedrine, for which Paddy Kenny had been busted while playing for Sheffield United back in 2009. Suddenly the heart attack started to look like it might have been self-inflicted.

'Christ, the idiot,' I muttered. 'Bekim must have been using the stuff as a stimulant.'

'Well, he was but not like you think,' said Svetlana. 'Bekim might have been a lot of things but he wasn't a cheat. But surely you must know he suffered from a severe allergy?'

'An allergy? To what?'

'To chickpeas. He never travelled without at least one of these pens.'

'Are you sure?'

'Of course I'm sure. He told me himself.'

'I've seen the medical report that was carried out prior to his transfer. There was no mention of any allergies.'

'Then he must have lied to your doctor. Or the doctor agreed to cover it up.'

'Our guy would never have done something like that.' I shook my head. 'But chickpeas. Surely that's not very serious.'

'Not in London, perhaps. But it is serious in Greece. They use chickpeas to make hummus. And for curries, of course.'

'Christ. That explains the spaghetti hoops.'

Svetlana nodded. 'As long as I knew Bekim he was always careful about what he ate. Especially in Greece.'

'Then no wonder he didn't let Zoi cook for him.'

'If he'd accidentally ingested chickpeas, he'd have suffered anaphylaxis.'

'And without the EpiPen that would have been potentially fatal.'

She nodded.

'But surely someone at Dynamo St Petersburg, his previous club, would have known about this?' I wasn't asking her, I was asking myself.

'And if they didn't mention it?' She left that one hanging

290

for a few seconds before saying what was already in my mind. 'That would have affected the transfer fee, wouldn't it?'

'It would have affected the whole transfer,' I said.

'I know Russians much better than I know football,' said Svetlana. 'They certainly wouldn't allow the small matter of medical disclosure to affect a big payday. Not just his previous club, but Bekim, too. He was really delighted to go and play for a big London club. Russians love London.'

'So they must have colluded in the deception,' I said. 'Him and Dynamo.'

'Why not?' said Svetlana. 'Your own doctor probably just asked him a simple question. Are you allergic to anything? And all he had to do was answer was a simple "no".'

I took a long hit on the cigarette and then put it out; the flavour brought back strong memories of prison when a single fag can taste as good as a slap-up meal in a good restaurant. I said: 'The more important question now is what Bekim's EpiPens were doing in Nataliya's handbag?'

Svetlana didn't answer. She lit another cigarette. We both did. There was much to think about and all of it unpleasant.

'This is serious, isn't it?' she said after a while.

'I'm afraid so. If Nataliya took his pens it must have been because she was paid to do it.'

'By who?'

'I don't know. But forty-eight hours ago this guy from the Sports Betting Intelligence Unit – part of the Gambling Commission back in England – asked me if Bekim could have been nobbled. In spite of what I told him, it's beginning to look as though he might have been.'

'Nobbled? What does it mean?'

'It means fixed. Interfered with. Doped, like a horse. *Poisoned*.'

I tried to remember the late lunch we'd all had at the hotel, prepared by our own chefs according to the guidelines laid down by Denis Abayev, the team nutritionist: grilled chicken with lots of green vegetables and sweet potato, followed by baked apple and Greek yoghurt. Nothing to worry about there. Not even for someone with an allergy to chickpeas. Unless someone had deliberately introduced some chickpeas into Bekim's meal.

'He must have eaten something with chickpeas in it before the match,' I said. 'There's no other explanation.'

'Okay, let's work this out. How long before the match did you have lunch?

'Three or four hours.'

'Then that can't have been it. When you have an allergy it's almost instantaneous. He'd have gone into anaphylaxis the minute he ate the stuff. On planes they'll sometimes tell you that they're not serving nuts just in case a person who suffers from an allergy should inhale a tiny piece.'

'Yes, you're right. Which makes you realise that for someone who has got an allergy a nut or a chickpea can be as powerful as a dose of hemlock.'

'And anyway,' she asked, 'why would someone do such a thing?'

'Simple. Because on the night that Bekim died, someone in Russia took out a very big in-play bet on the match we played. These days, people will bet on anything that happens during a match: ten-minute events, the time of the first corner, the next goal scorer, the first player to come off – anything at all. It means that someone from Olympiacos, or someone from Russia, must have nobbled Bekim somehow. A ten-minute event like Bekim scoring and then being taken off. That must be it.'

'Nobbled. Yes, I understand.'

I looked at my iPhone but as before there was no signal. 'Shit,' I muttered. 'I really need to make some calls.'

'You can't,' she said. 'Not up here. But I could drive you into Naoussa where there's a pretty good signal at the Hotel Aliprantis. I have a friend there who'll let us use the internet, as well. If you think it's necessary.'

'I'm afraid I do. Svetlana, if I'm right, it wasn't just Nataliya who was murdered, it was Bekim, too.'

CHAPTER 46

Naoussa was a very typical little Greek town by the sea, with lots of winding, cobbled streets, low white buildings, and plenty of tourists, most of them English. The air was humid and thick with the smell of cooked lamb and wood smoke from many open kitchen-fires. Jaunty bouzouki music emptied out of small bars and restaurants and in spite of the English voices you would not have been surprised to have seen an unshaven Anthony Quinn step-dancing his way around the next corner. A line of Greek pennants connected one side of the little main square to the other and behind a couple of ancient olive trees was a taverna belonging to the Hotel Aliprantis.

The minute we entered the place I got a five bar signal on my iPhone and the texts and emails started to arrive like the scores on a pinball machine; before long there was a little red 21 on my Messages app, a 6 on my Mail app but, mercifully, fewer voicemails. As Svetlana led me through the restaurant and into the little hotel's tiny lobby I uttered a groan as life began to catch up with me again. But worse still, I'd been recognised by four yobs drinking beer and all looking as pink as an old map of the British Empire. It wasn't long before the innocent holiday atmosphere of the Aliprantis was spoiled as they struck up with a typically English sporting refrain:

He's red,
He's dead,
He's lying in a shed,
Develi, Develi.

and, just as offensive, although I'd heard half of this one before:

Scott, Scott, you rapist prick,
You should be locked up in the nick,
And we don't give a fuck about Bekim Develi,
That red Russian cunt with HIV.

Svetlana spoke Greek to the hotel manager, a big swarthy man with a beard like a toilet brush, and then introduced me to him. We shook hands and as he led us both up to his office where I could make some calls in private and send some emails I was already apologising for what I could very clearly hear through the floorboards. Somehow, in the frustrating week I'd spent in Greece, I'd forgotten that when they wanted to be, a few English supporters could be every bit as unpleasant as the worst from Olympiacos or Panathinaikos. That's football.

'I'm sorry about that,' I said.

'No, sir, it is me who is sorry that you and your team should have had such poor hospitality while you are in Greece. Bekim Develi would often have a drink in here. And any friend of Bekim Develi's is friend of mine.'

'I ought to have realised I might be recognised. I should go. Before there's any trouble.'

'No, sir, I tell *them* to leave. You stay here, make your telephone calls, get your emails, I fix those bastards.'

'All right,' I said. 'But on one condition. That I pay for their meal.' I laid a hundred euro note on the desk in the office. 'That way, when you tell them to leave, they'll think they had a free meal and just clear off without any trouble.'

'Is not necessary.'

'Please,' I said. 'Take it from me. This really is the best way.'

'Okay, boss. But I bring you something to drink, yes?'

'Greek coffee,' I said.

The manager glanced at Svetlana who asked for some ouzo. I picked up the iPhone and started to read my texts.

Peter Scriven Have managed to persuade Astir Palace hotel manager to let the team remain until Friday. But then we HAVE to leave; no fail. Still trying to find alternative hotel.

Frank Carmona I spoke to Hörst Daxenberger and he IS interested in a transfer to London City; think I can get him for 35 MILLION EUROS. But you will need to move fast as Dortmund also keen on him.

Jim Brown, Daily Express Would you care to comment on a rumour in El Pais that Sheikh Abdullah has made you an offer to manage Malaga FC?

Louise Considine Have arrived Grande Bretagne; lovely room; but where are you? xxxx

Simon Page Good news: Ayrton Taylor will be fit for Wednesday. And Prometheus excelled in training today. On the down side, Kenny Traynor has a dodgy thumb. Could even be broken. Am organising X-ray for tomorrow a.m.

Charlie Have located Roma man who will 'find' Nataliya's handbag for us and hand it in to Dr Christodoulou when you give the word. 100 euros.

Lookers Land Rover Land Rover Battersea has moved while we rebuild, to 44 Weir Road, Wimbledon SW19 8UG. Call 02072283001 for move info. TXT OPTOUT TO 66777

Kojo Ironsi I spoke to Phil Hobday about St Etienne goalkeeper Kgalema Mandingoane and he is interested; says you should call him today and set up a meeting with Vik. From what I hear Kenny is injured!

Maurice McShane Tottenham lost; Arsenal lost; Crystal Palace lost; West Ham lost; Burnley top of the BPL. I must be on drugs.

Sara Gill Thanks for trying to help. Let me know if I can be of further assistance. Sara Gill.

Bastian Hoehling Sorry to hear about all your troubles; call me if there's anything I can do. Better still, when all this is over, come to Germany for a weekend; we'll go to Oktoberfest in München.

Prometheus Spoke to mate in Lagos and got into that phone. More difficult than I thought. Basically you hold power button down until slide to power off function appears; press cancel but don't let go of power button, see? Then place emergency call but don't let it go through; then you release the power button for just a moment; next you hold it down again; now it goes back to the slide to power off; so you press Cancel and the whole screen goes black, OK? Now you press the home button and let go of the power button at the same time. There's a flash and now you're in the phone, right? You double press the home button and the phone is yours. You can access pictures, everything. This girl had an email stuck in her outbox that's too long to text. Will send it. Simon says I trained well today. Can't wait for Wednesday, boss. Won't let you down. P

Dr Christodoulou Chief Inspector Varouxis called me; he wants to speak to you; I think tomorrow the doctors' strike will finish and we can get the autopsy done on both Bekim Develi and Nataliya. Don't worry. I didn't tell him anything.

Louise Considine Where are you, Scott? I'm getting worried. Love you. XX

Sarah Crompton Can you do an interview in the next couple of days with Daily Telegraph's Football Correspondent, Henry Winter for his online blog Henry Winter's Google Plus Hangout? I like Henry. He's smart. And it's high time you did some publicity.

Phil Hobday Kojo says there's a goalkeeper we should buy. Mandingo. What do you think? And what's this story about you going to Malaga CF?

Detective Chief Inspector Byrne John and Mariella Cruikshank go to trial a week tomorrow; are you going to be back in London by then, to give evidence at their trial? Please let me know ASAP

Viktor Sokolnikov Come to dinner tonight on The Lady Ruslana; bring Louise; I saw her at the Hotel Grande Bretagne. I had no idea she was in Athens. Call Russell Gordon, the ship's captain and he'll send the tender for you.

Paolo Gentile Malaga FC looking for new manager. Owner Sheikh Abdullah would like to meet you. His yacht, the Al Mirqab, currently moored in Hydra. Will send helicopter to pick you up. Sheikh has big plans for the club and wants a new manager with vision.

Dad I have to go into hospital for some routine tests; don't worry, I'm fine; just wanted to let you know. Rangers now top of the Scottish Championship. Next year they'll be back. x

Chief Inspector Varouxis I have more CCTV I need you take a look at; can you contact me? I will send a car, or come to your hotel.

Downstairs, the singing in the restaurant had stopped and moved outside where it continued for a while longer. I went to the window and looked out on the square and watched the four culprits as they sat on the edge of a fountain in front of the Blue Star Ferries office, drinking beer and smoking cigarettes. One of them was wearing a T-shirt with a *Keep Calm and Carry On* slogan; another was wearing one that I'd seen almost as many times: *Lookin' to Score BRAZIL*. They stayed there for a while and then, to everyone's relief, left.

I picked up the iPhone and started to listen to my voice-mails but these were just some of the same people and messages – more or less – as the ones who'd texted me already. There wasn't enough bandwidth to download the document that Prometheus had attached to his email; the rest were unimportant. I called my dad to reassure myself that he really was okay; then I called Louise.

'Hey, I'm sorry I wasn't there when you arrived,' I said. 'I should have met you at the airport.'

'That's all right. Where are you? I was getting worried.'

'On the island of Paros.'

'Paros? What are you doing there?'

'I came to Bekim Develi's house to check out a few things. I'm glad I did because things are a lot clearer to me than they were before.'

'So are you finished down there, Sherlock?'

'Yes, but I'm sorry, baby, I'm not going to be able to get back to Athens until tomorrow morning. There just isn't a flight.'

I heard some laughter in the background.

'Where are you anyway?' I asked.

'On Viktor Sokolnikov's yacht,' she said. 'He invited me for dinner. Wait a minute. He wants to speak to you.'

There was a longish pause and then Viktor came on the line.

'Scott? What are you doing on Paros? You should be here with your girlfriend.'

I told him what I'd just told Louise.

'Paros is only half an hour away from here,' he said. 'I'll send the helicopter for you right now. Drive to the Hotel Astir on the north coast where I happen to know there's a helipad we can use. I'll have it come and pick you up. You can be here within the hour.'

'There's no need to go to all that trouble.' I was keen to see Louise again but somewhat mortified that I'd forgotten that she was coming to Athens; I was also nervous about the idea of taking a night-time flight in a helicopter. 'I can catch the plane back to Athens tomorrow.'

At the same time I knew it was wiser to return to the mainland as soon as possible. I could hardly delay telling the police what I knew for much longer. Not only that but the Wi-Fi on *The Lady Ruslana* was as quick as any on the mainland and I was keen to read the email from Nataliya's outbox. I had a feeling it would be a key piece of evidence in identifying her murderer.

'Nonsense,' said Vik, 'it's no trouble at all.'

'Are you sure?'

'Of course, I'm sure. Look, you can both spend the night here on the yacht. And the tender will take you back to shore in the morning. Okay? Besides, I want to talk about this German guy, Hörst Daxenberger. And Kojo's goalkeeper, Mandingo. And then you can tell me everything you've discovered since you put on your deerstalker hat and lit your favourite Meerschaum.'

CHAPTER 47

We got back into Svetlana's car and drove slowly out of the town of Naoussa, west around the bay, towards Kolymbithres and the Astir Hotel's helipad. There was plenty of time. The hotel was less than five miles away and the only thing causing traffic on the road were the geckos.

'I know the guy from Loukis Rent-a-Car,' she said. 'I'll drive over there in the morning and tell him to come and fetch the car from my place. Zoi will lock up, of course. She's very reliable.'

'I'm afraid I didn't have the guts to tell her that Bekim is dead.'

'Don't worry. I'll tell her. What's going to happen, do you think? To the house?'

'I've really no idea,' I said. 'I'm sorry I have to leave so suddenly. I haven't been here for very long, but I can easily see why you are. It's a beautiful island. And look, I promise to do everything I can to keep your name from the police, Svetlana. But to do that I may need to speak to you again. So, tomorrow and for the next few days, will you make sure you go back to the Aliprantis, or somewhere that you can collect your texts and emails?'

'Okay. I promise.'

I squeezed her hand on the gear stick.

We had driven about two miles from Naoussa when I recognised two men on the road, trying to hitch a lift. I glanced at the big Hublot on my wrist; it told me there was just enough time for a bit of payback.

'Pull up,' I told her. 'I know those two guys.'

'They're the hooligans from the town?'

'Two of them, anyway.'

'Please, Scott, I don't think this is a good idea.'

'Actually, it's an excellent idea,' I said. 'All the same, stay in the car and if they come after you, don't wait for me, just drive away. Okay?'

Svetlana said nothing.

'I mean it. Just drive off. Don't think twice about it.'

I took off my watch, laid it carefully on the dashboard, buttoned my shirt to the neck and got out of the car; the road was empty and there was no one about, which suited my purpose. In the distance I could just make out the blue glow of what was likely the Hotel Astir's floodlit swimming pool. And somewhere far away – possibly the same place – there was music: it sounded like Pharrell Williams. The two men were already running to where we were parked under a twisted olive tree thinking that they'd landed a ride home. But they stopped when they realised exactly who and what they were hurrying to.

I walked towards them in the moonlight, clapping my hands and singing a song to the tune of 'Cwm Rhondda'; a joyous, taunting song you could hear at every football ground, on any match day in the season.

'You're not singing any more. You're not singing any more.'

The one wearing the *Lookin' to Score BRAZIL* T-shirt was about six feet tall, heavy-set, with a gold chain around his pink neck and so much golden stubble on his mug it looked like a newly harvested wheat field. The other one – the one wearing the *Keep Calm and Carry On* T-shirt was taller and thinner, his mouth as thin as a slash in a potato, his forehead curled up into a knuckle of irritation and concern. He tossed away his cigarette without a thought for the forest fires that often ravage that part of the world; he deserved a smack just for that. The best and the brightest they weren't; but they looked tough enough.

'We're not looking for any trouble, mate,' he said.

'No?'

'No. We're not.'

'You should have thought of that when you were back in the town,' I said. 'I didn't like what you were singing. It's fuckers like you that give English football a bad name. Who spoil it for decent people. But I'm not here for me. I'm here for my friend, Bekim Develi. My friend didn't like your singing either.'

'Listen, Manson, get back in your fucking car and drive on, you stupid black cunt.'

I grinned; any doubts I'd had about what I was going to do were now removed.

'That's exactly what I'm going to do.' All this time I kept walking towards the pair. 'Just as soon as this black cunt has sorted you out.'

The one thing I learned in the nick was how to fight like you mean it; that's the only way you *can* fight when you're in the nick. It's not the kind of fighting that you see hooligans getting up to in the street, if that can even be called fighting at all. That's the same way chimpanzees fight and most of it is just for show; they run at each other, shove a bit and shout and then stop, take a few steps back and then run at each other again, egging everyone else on, looking to see

304

who's really up for it, where the weaknesses are and, as a corollary, where to attack first. But in the nick you go in fast – before a screw has a chance to interfere and put a stop to it – and hard – hard enough to inflict real pain; and you don't fucking care if you get hurt because there's no time to think about that. Once you're committed to it, you have to stay committed no matter what. The other thing you learn about violence in the nick is to keep your feet firmly on the ground and use your head and your elbows to aim at something small, because there's not a lot of room in a cell or on a landing when you're handing it out to another con. And there's nothing smaller or more effective to aim at than another bloke's nose.

Without a moment's hesitation I launched a battering ram of a head-butt at the centre of the taller man's face, and I felt something give like the sound of an egg breaking and heard him utter a loud cry of pain; it meant the fight was already half over because he collapsed onto the road and lay there holding his face. Les Ferdinand would have been proud of me; it was a great header.

One down, one to go.

Now the other man came at me and threw a big right hand which, if it had connected, would certainly have caused some damage; but he was tired, and probably drunker than I was, and the punch seemed to come all the way from Luton, on an EasyJet Airbus; delayed, of course. I had plenty of time to block it with my left forearm, which left me ample opportunity to bring a right elbow hard through my centre line against the left side of his face. Probably I didn't have to hit him again, but I did – a hammer blow on the side of his nose that felled him like a pile of cardboard boxes, intended to render him every bit as ugly as he'd sounded in the Hotel Aliprantis. In spite of what I'd told these two guys, I hadn't just struck a blow for Bekim: I'd also hit them for every banana ever thrown at me and for every racist epithet or obscene taunt yelled my way during a game. I kid you not, there isn't a guy in the Barclays Premier League who wouldn't like to hand out some grief to a bunch of fans now and again. Just ask Eric Cantona.

It was all over in less than sixty seconds; neither of them showed any intention of getting up and carrying on. I thought about kicking them both when they were on the ground and immediately rejected the idea. Knowing when to stop is as important as knowing when to start. I didn't even say anything. I'd said all there needed to be said. I figured it would be a while before they sang anything again, least of all some crap about a man's death.

I got back into the car, unbuttoned my shirt collar, calmly put on my watch again and then checked my appearance in her rear-view mirror; I wasn't injured. I didn't even have a headache.

'Drive,' I told her.

'Feel better now you've done that?'

The wind took hold of the distant music and hurried it to our ears. Pharrell Williams.

'I feel. . .' I grinned. 'I feel happy.'

And the truth is I felt great. Like I'd scored a winning goal in an important match. Even the local cicadas seemed to be cheering.

CHAPTER 48

As the helicopter rose into the air above the Hotel Astir I took off my shoes and socks, tightened the belt on my cream leather seat and pushed my bare feet into the thick pile carpet in a futile effort to relax. On the flat-screen TV above a polished walnut cabinet I could see a map of Paros, and an altitude and speed indicator. In a few minutes the island itself had disappeared into the sky's thick, purple blanket and we were flying just below the aircraft's fifteen thousand foot ceiling and heading northwest at a speed of 150 mph. Cocooned in a four-million-dollar helicopter equipped with every conceivable luxury, I ought to have felt more comfortable; instead I was as nervous as a white rat in a laboratory. Already I was opening the drinks cabinet and generously helping myself from a bottle of cognac. After a few moments studying our progress on the map I picked up the remote control and found a BBC channel with a football match to watch instead; Burnley playing someone or other. I didn't really care; it was a very good cognac.

About forty minutes later the Explorer's skids were on the deck of *The Lady Ruslana*, although these were probably not as big as the ones in my underpants. I stepped gingerly out of the helicopter and onto the deck which felt reassuringly solid. Inside the ship I was met by one of Vik's crew and she ushered me down to a lower deck where I had a quiet moment alone in a luxuriously furnished state room with Louise.

'I've missed you so much,' she said.

I folded her in my arms and kissed the nape of her neck and then her mouth.

'You seem tense,' she observed. 'Preoccupied.'

I shook my head but this was true, of course. Some of my mind was still up in the air with my stomach, but mostly it was on my iPhone: before I answered the text from Chief Inspector Varouxis I was keen to read the email from Nataliya's phone that Prometheus had forwarded to me.

'And I know what it is,' she added. 'I see that face almost every day. It's a cop's face. It tells me you have a dark secret you really wish you didn't know, or an important question you're struggling to answer. If you were more interested in me you might have seen the same thing in my own face, sometimes. That's all right. It's my fault, actually. I should have realised before I came to Athens that your head would be somewhere else.'

'I should have known you'd be able to see what's inside my head.'

'I'm a detective, remember?'

I kissed her again. 'I'm very glad you're here. But I have to pee.'

But the first thing I did when I went to the bathroom was not to pee but to take a quick look to see if I could open Nataliya's email now that I was near a better Wi-Fi signal. Irritatingly, I found the email was written in Russian and I realised that if I wanted it translated there were only two people on the boat who could do that: Vik or Phil. I hardly wanted to bother Vik and decided I would ask Phil to send me a translation of the email before breakfast the following morning when I would have to contact the Hellenic police again.

I came out of the bathroom and kissed Louise again, only this time like I meant it.

'That's better,' she said.

'Sorry.'

'Come on,' she said, taking me by the arm. 'Let's go and join the others. But I'm tired. I've been travelling all day. And the flight was delayed. So if you don't mind, I won't stay long. Besides, I'm just dying to go to bed in this room.'

Arranged around a horseshoe of cream-coloured sofas, enjoying the evening sea air and a magnum bottle of Domaine Ott rosé wine under the stars, were Gustave Haak, Cooper Lybrand, Phil Hobday, Kojo Ironsi, the two Greek businessmen I'd seen before and several rented girlfriends who were so young and fit they looked like they were crew members on their night off. Vik introduced me to the two Greek guys. Five minutes later I'd already forgotten their names. In view of the cognac I'd consumed earlier I asked for a bottle of water; I thought it best I try to clear my head a little. A lot of what I was going to say to Vik and Phil when we were in private wasn't going to be easy to hear and I certainly had no wish to spoil the evening for the others; so, for a while, I was happy to submit myself to being teased about the rumour that I was set to become the new manager of Malaga FC.

'You'll like the Costa del Sol,' said Phil. 'It has probably the warmest winter of anywhere in Europe. My boat is moored near there. In Puerto Banús. It's about the one part of Spain where you don't see any unemployment. Which is probably why I like it so much.'

'Forget the weather,' said Vik, 'what's the team there like?'

Phil shrugged. 'Arab-owned, I believe. Kojo? What's your opinion of them?'

'Malaga?' Kojo pulled a face. 'Underperforming. The Qataris bought the club in 2010 and Manuel Pellegrini was manager. He was doing well there and got them to fourth place in La Liga. He even managed to help them qualify for the Champions League for the first time in their history. But clearly something must have been wrong otherwise he wouldn't have gone to Manchester City.'

'It sounds as if they really do have need of Scott,' said Gustave Haak.

'He's a man of many parts,' said Vik.

'So I believe,' said Haak. 'The last time we spoke he was investigating the death of a prostitute in the harbour.' He left off playing with the hair of one of his girlfriends for a moment. 'That is true, isn't it, Scott? And near my boat, too, I believe.'

I thought it best to keep off that subject; I had the strangest idea that the idea of high-end call girls being found at the bottom of the harbour might have been the cause of some distress to at least two of his companions. Politely, I steered the conversation back to Malaga.

'I've no idea where this rumour has come from,' I said patiently. 'Paolo Gentile, probably. You know how it is with agents and narrative IEDs.'

'What's a narrative IED?' asked Louise.

'I was wondering that myself,' admitted Lybrand.

'That's the new buzzword phrase for a communications weapon: a rumour that's designed to disrupt the efforts of your competitors. Football is full of them. In a way they're almost as destructive as the ones in Afghanistan. The quickest way to get someone to join club A is to start a rumour that he's leaving club B and headed for club C. Unsettling football players is easier than waking a baby. All you have to do is gently rustle some money.'

'Equally, the best way to get a good price for a player is to say he's not for sale under any circumstances,' said Vik. 'Isn't that right, Kojo?'

Kojo nodded. 'If you're going to do something in business it's always best never to say that you can do it until you've done it. And sometimes not even then.'

'You know, Scott, we're very happy with the way you've handled this football club,' said Phil. 'You enjoy our total confidence. Doesn't he, Vik?'

Vik laughed and lit a cigar. 'Now you've really worried him.'

'I know. That's why I said it.'

'You'll have to excuse us, Louise,' said Vik. 'When Scott is tired and at our mercy like this we tend to take advantage. It's rare we get a chance to get a word in edgeways. We're rather more used to the sound of him talking up our team's chances or playing down their inadequacies.'

'More often the latter,' said Phil, sourly.

Louise took my hand, squeezed it fondly and then kissed my fingertips.

'Well, I'm kind of tired myself so, if you don't mind, I'm going to bed. It's been a long day.'

'I'll be along in a short while,' I said.

Louise gave me a look and then grinned.

'No, really,' I said.

Politely, the men were standing up.

'You're going to talk about football,' she said.

'No, we're not.'

'Sure,' said Louise. 'See you later.'

But this was also the cue for Haak, Lybrand, the two Greeks and most of the ladies to take Vik's launch and go ashore or aboard Haak's own yacht, the *Monsieur Croesus*. And when the rest of the girls had also retired to wherever it was on *The Lady Ruslana* they had been detailed to spend the night, I was left alone with Vik, Phil and Kojo.

There was a long silence.

'Perhaps,' said Kojo, 'someone might like to tell me this: if we're not going to talk about football, what the hell are we going to talk about?'

CHAPTER 49

The cognac was wearing off. Or maybe the sea air was clearing my head; it certainly needed a bit of housekeeping. My mind felt like it was playing keepy-uppy with a golf ball.

From the boat the Greek shoreline looked like another galaxy; and for those in Vik's sphere of influence it might as well have been. Unemployment, financial crisis, striking workers – these were much further away from *The Lady Ruslana* than the mile or two of inky black sea that separated us from the mainland. But in spite of everything, I'd come to like the Greeks and I almost felt guilty just being aboard Vik's floating palace.

I was getting my second wind now and for a while we discussed the forthcoming game against Olympiacos and how I intended to approach this.

'I distrust tactics, even at the best of times,' I said. 'Football matches have a regular habit of making a nonsense of them. Remember the much-vaunted *trivote*? The high-pressure triangle that Mourinho used at the Bernabeu? It never really worked. Jorge Valdano, the Madrid sporting director, use to call it shit on a stick, didn't he? But I do have a strategy for the game. It's an idea I've used before. I don't have a fancy name for it – like Mou – but if I did I'd call it Football Darwinism. I've been looking at some of the Reds' recent games and

I've picked out the weakest player, their midfielder, Mariliza Mouratidis. He's younger than the rest. And his mother's in hospital. A Greek hospital. So I think his mind is elsewhere. I know mine would be if my mother was in a Greek hospital.'

I paused for a moment as I remembered my dad was in hospital, too; and then carried on speaking.

'But there's something else, I think. Most footballers want the ball. Mouratidis can't wait to get rid of it. It's like he doesn't want the responsibility. So what we're going to do is that when Mouratidis has the ball we're going to make the tackles twice as hard and twice as quick and, if possible, from more than one of our lads. In short we're going to gang up on him like a bunch of playground bullies and try to break him. You can see chickens doing it sometimes; they gather around the weakest chicken and peck it to death. My guess is that he'll either cave under the pressure or, more likely, hit back. With any luck he'll be sent off. After the first leg, we've got nothing to lose.'

Vik chuckled. 'I like it.'

'God, you're a ruthless bastard,' said Phil.

'No,' I said. 'But I do want to win this game very badly. Call it payback for the many inconveniences we've suffered since arriving here.'

After this we discussed the merits of buying Hörst Daxenberger and Kgalema Mandingoane; that was good as it meant delaying our conversation about Bekim Develi's true fate. Vik had known Bekim longer than anyone and had been fond of him. I wasn't looking forward to telling him that his friend had been poisoned.

Buying Daxenberger was a no-brainer: he was very strong on the ball, and equally strong off it – the kind of player who acts like a talisman. Thierry Henry was a bit like that;

Arsenal were always a different side when Thierry was on the pitch. It wasn't just the fact that he was skilful – all professional footballers are skilful – it was something else. Napoleon knew the value of having generals who were lucky; and luck was what Henry had in spades. Other players rubbed off that; you didn't need to cross yourself or recite from an imaginary Koran when he was on the pitch.

Mandingo – I didn't like that name but I could see it was pointless arguing against it – was a harder sell which was why Kojo had uploaded some of the lad's best saves onto his iPad, including the one I'd seen him make against Stuttgart the previous Friday night. I had to admit that I was impressed with his ability. And when I received another text from Simon to say that while he was sure that Kenny could play on Wednesday night with painkillers, he was now more or less certain that the boy's thumb was broken, that removed any lingering doubts I had about buying the African. The need for another keeper was now acute.

When eventually it was agreed that we should buy both of these players, I sent a text to Frank Carmona offering to pay something less than the transfer fee he'd mentioned, and a noticeably delighted Kojo, flicking his fly-whisk like it was his own tail, retreated to a remote corner of the boat to call Mandingo in Saint-Étienne with the good news that he probably had a new football club.

'He looks happy,' said Phil.

'I should think he bloody is,' I said. 'Just think how much commission he's going to charge that poor kid. Football, eh? It's the only legal way left to buy a black man.'

Vik nodded vaguely which seemed to tell me something. I asked, 'Did you decide to increase your share in his King Shark academy, Vik?'

'As a matter of fact I've decided to buy the whole shooting match. From now on we'll get first look on all the academy's players.'

'So this deal for Mandingo – effectively it means you'll be paying commission to yourself.'

'I suppose it does, yes.'

'We've got some news for you, Scott. News you might find a little harder to accept, at least in the beginning. But you'll get used to the idea. Vik?'

'Kojo is going to be our new technical director,' said Vik. 'He'll be making decisions regarding any new players.'

'His decisions? Or your decisions?'

'We're lucky to get him,' said Vik. 'He knows players better than anyone. And besides, he comes as part of the King Shark package. In a sense we're getting his services for nothing.'

'In the future,' added Phil, 'you should take all your ideas for signing new players to Kojo.'

I bit my tongue; I wasn't quite ready to talk myself out of a job.

'Tell me,' said Vik. 'What progress have you made with this murder investigation? That's why you were on Paros, isn't it? To search Bekim's house?'

Trying to overcome my irritation that Kojo was now doing something any manager might reasonably have expected to be doing himself, I nodded; but I still saw no reason to tell him about Svetlana.

'Good progress. I think I'm on the verge of a real break-through. Yesterday afternoon I discovered that the girl who was found in the harbour at Marina Zea was called Nataliya Matviyenko,' I said. 'She lived in Piraeus, with her boyfriend, or maybe her husband – a guy called Boutzikos. And she was an escort, a high-class call girl who was originally from Kiev.'

'Excellent,' said Vik. 'But how did you find this out?'

'It's probably best you don't know,' I said. 'For now.'

'I see.'

'After all, it's only the team and the playing staff who are forbidden to leave Greece right now. You and Phil can clear off whenever you wish. Not forgetting your new technical director of football. Probably best we keep it that way.'

'Yes, perhaps you're right.'

'Hopefully I'll know a lot more about Nataliya and possibly even who killed her when I've had a chance to translate her last email. A message that was stuck in the Outbox of her phone. For some reason it didn't send.'

'You have her phone?' said Vik.

'Not just her phone, but the contents of her handbag.'

'You have been busy,' said Vik.

'Look, I think you should both prepare yourself for a shock. I'm sorry to be the one who tells you but the fact is I'm almost certain that Bekim was murdered. In Nataliya's handbag were some EpiPens, auto-injectors containing a single dose of epinephrine for people who are severely allergic to something which leaves them at constant risk of anaphylaxis. *People like Bekim*. These EpiPens had been prescribed for him. For some reason this girl, Nataliya, took them when she went to Bekim's bungalow at the Astir Palace on the night before he died. It's my guess she was paid to steal them, by someone who got to Bekim on the day of the match and nobbled him. Probably the same person who put a hefty bet on the outcome of the match, or some in-play feature of the match. I've yet to find out what that was. Someone in Russia, it looks like. That's what my contact in the Gambling Commission has told me, anyway.'

'Wait a minute,' said Vik. 'Are you saying Bekim died from . . . from an allergic response? Not a heart attack at all?'

'No, what I'm saying is that a heart attack was most likely the result of anaphylactic shock. Which might have been avoided if his condition had been known.'

'But I knew Bekim for several years,' said Vik. 'He never mentioned any of this to me. What was he allergic to?'

'Chickpeas.'

'Chickpeas? You're joking. Are you sure?'

'Positive. And it was no joke. I'm not sure an allergy like that would have counted as much of a problem in England. But here in Greece – well, chickpeas are a menu staple. It beats me why he decided to have a holiday home here of all places, where he was at greater risk.' I shrugged. 'But that was Bekim.'

'It would probably explain why he would never come for a curry,' said Phil. 'They use them in Indian food, too. Remember? At the end of last season we booked the Red Fort for an end of season dinner? In Soho? And he declined to come?'

'I'd forgotten that,' I said. 'Anyway, I'm not sure how much of this the autopsy will reveal. An allergy produces symptoms that could easily be mistaken for something as ordinary as a heart attack. All the same I'm damned sure this is what killed him. Someone tainted his food with chickpeas. Perhaps as little as a couple of grams of the stuff. I'm afraid that for a man like Bekim this was every bit as lethal as if they'd poisoned his food with polonium.'

Vik shuddered. 'That's a word no Russian living abroad ever likes to hear,' he said.

I smiled to myself; my news had shaken them more than I might have imagined.

'Why didn't our own team doctors find this out?' said Phil. 'Did they fuck up, or what?'

'Not necessarily,' I said. 'It's not really something they'd test for. More like a question they'd have asked him during the medical. What I do think is that someone at Dynamo St Petersburg covered it up to make sure Bekim's transfer to London City went through all right when we bought him back in January. And that it was almost certainly done with the player's own connivance.'

'I can guess who that was,' said Vik. 'The club's part owner. Semion Mikhailov.'

I was glad I didn't have to say this myself; no one likes to tell his Russian billionaire boss that he has been sold a pig in a poke.

'Of course,' said Phil. 'That slippery bastard owed you money, didn't he? And you took Bekim as a player in part payment of that debt.'

Vik nodded sombrely. 'Which also makes him suspect number one for nobbling him, too. Semion Mikhailov is a big gambler. But like a lot of big gamblers he prefers a sure thing. Who better than him to take advantage of our having a Champions League match here in Athens? The girl's phone. Do you have it with you, Scott?'

I found the email I'd received from Prometheus on my own iPhone and handed it to Vik. 'No, but I have the email she sent. From the address bar it looks like there were several people it was meant for.'

'Would I be right in thinking that the police don't have any of this information either?' he asked.

'That's right, but only until tomorrow.' I glanced at my watch; it was almost 2 a.m. 'Or to be more accurate, today. I'll have to hand Nataliya's handbag and its contents over to Chief Inspector Varouxis later on this morning. Given that this is already a murder investigation, our lawyer, Dr

Christodoulou, thinks it would be ill-advised to hold back evidence from the police for much longer.'

'And she'd be right,' murmured Phil. 'You could go to prison for something like that. We all could. This is serious, Scott. By rights we should call the police right now. Don't read that, Vik. If you do you'll become complicit in whatever law-breaking has already occurred.'

But Vik was already reading the email.

'Look, Phil,' I said. 'I'm aiming to put a bomb underneath the Greek police and I'm hoping that this email will do that. After that I really need to concentrate all my attention on Wednesday's game. I want to walk into police headquarters this morning with enough evidence to put this whole investigation into the fast lane. Maybe even the name of the person that put her up to nicking his pens. Perhaps even the identity of the guys who dropped her in the harbour wearing a cast iron ankle bracelet. And he'll have to listen to me because I've also got evidence that perhaps connects this case with a series of older murders. It turns out that this isn't the first time that a local call girl got dumped in the marina. Back in 2008 they had something similar happen. The guy they nabbed for those had an accomplice who was never arrested. And I know who he is. With any luck his name is on that email.'

'Jesus,' said Phil.

'How about it, Vik? Have we got a result?'

'Yes and no,' said Vik. 'This email she tried to send – it appears to be a suicide note.'

CHAPTER 50

'So what did you talk about?' asked Louise. She was wearing a little black nightdress now that resembled the twilight of some erotic goddess and was leaning on one elbow examining my face carefully for clues. 'With Phil and Vik. It wasn't just football, I'll bet.'

I moved my head on the pillow.

'He didn't fire you, did he?'

'No, he didn't. But it's almost as bad.'

I explained that Kojo Ironsi was now the club's technical director.

'What does that mean?'

'For one thing I think we're going to have a lot more African footballers in the team. But I suspect it also means that Vik wants to make all the real footballing decisions himself. He probably thinks Kojo will be more inclined to do what he's told than I am. At least when it comes to buying and selling players.'

'But he's not wrong about that, is he?'

'How do you mean?'

'Oh, come on, Scott. You were against the sale of Christoph Bündchen; and you were against the purchase of Prometheus. I seem to recall you were even opposed to buying Bekim Develi, too. I bet there's probably someone else – someone else I don't know about – someone Viktor Sokolnikov wanted to buy or sell and you just pissed on the idea. Made him feel stupid. You're good at that, sometimes.'

I thought for a moment. 'I didn't want to sell Ken Okri to Sunderland, I suppose. Or lose John Ayensu.'

'There you are. It's Viktor Sokolnikov's money, Scott. You should try to remember that. London City is his plaything, not yours. Just like this stupid yacht.'

'What's stupid about it?' I said, although I knew she was right; it was a stupid yacht.

'As a way of losing vast sums of money there's not much that beats having a superyacht. Except a Premier League football club. It seems to me that a football club is the biggest white elephant any billionaire can buy. A white woolly mammoth, probably.'

'I don't know. The laws of economics operate differently when applied to football. I sometimes think that Maynard Keynes should have written a special chapter for football teams. In big clubs profit and loss don't always mean what they're supposed to mean.'

'Maybe, but you wouldn't be the first manager who couldn't buy or sell the players he wants, would you? Doesn't Mourinho have a similar problem with Abramovich at Chelsea? From what I've read it wasn't Man U who told him he couldn't have Wayne, it was the Russian.'

'You're very well informed, all of a sudden.'

'Listen, if you don't choose the player you can't be held to account when he fails to score. It wasn't Mourinho who bought Fernando Torres; ergo, he can't be blamed when Torres misfires. Think about it, in a sense it lets you off the hook from which managers are hanged by the newspapers.'

'Perhaps.'

'Sure it does. It'll give you a chance to focus on what's happening on the pitch. So you can do your real job. Not to mention my job.'

'I guess you're right.'

'By the way, how's doing my job coming along?'

'A true detective, I am not.'

'No one is. At least not the way it works on TV. You know? With clues and everything that comes with them: it takes time to find stuff out.'

'Actually, Louise, I've found out quite a lot. But you were right what you said earlier, when I'd just got off the chopper. There is something I really wish I didn't know.' I told Louise all that I'd learned. 'Now all I have to do is piece it all together.'

'It sounds like you've had a very productive long weekend. Most coppers rest on the seventh day. Even the ones on duty. But you seem to be almost on the point of solving the case. I'm impressed.'

'There's a lot I still don't know,' I said.

'Get used to it,' she said. 'Even when a case goes to court you'll find you still don't know everything. You never can. The trick is to know just enough to secure a conviction. More often than not it happens that we send a bloke down knowing only half the story.'

'Don't I know it,' I said.

Louise winced apologetically.

'I suppose the question is, did Nataliya really commit suicide, or did someone make her write that email? After all, it does seem rather extreme to tie a weight around your ankles and drop it into the harbour just because you were depressed about having played a part in his death.'

'All suicide is *sui generis* extreme.'

'If I knew what that meant, I might agree with you.'

'Unique in its own characteristics. Besides, you said Nataliya was given to depression. And her hands weren't tied. And she did nick his pens. She betrayed him. So she felt guilty. That doesn't strike me as wholly improbable. Just sad. The real question is, who put her up to the theft? And by the way, I think before you go and see that Greek copper you should get someone to translate the email properly. Getting Vik to translate it is a bit like asking the fox to mind the chickens.'

'You mean just because he and she were both Ukrainian?'

Louise shrugged. 'You said it. And after all, it's not like he's a stranger to rentals. Those girls on the boat tonight. They didn't come from the Greek Red Cross, you know. You don't think he's just a tiny bit suspicious?

'I don't know what to think about him. But I do know I'm never doing this again: trying to solve a crime while managing a team. It's not like anyone seems at all grateful for what I've done. On the contrary, it was like I was the one who'd brought them a fucking problem.'

'I told you: get used to that. As a policeman, sometimes your only reward for trying to do your job is to be treated like a criminal. Just look at the way Hillsborough got reported; seriously, you'd think that it was the Yorkshire police who killed all those poor fans. Sure, they fucked up. Yes, they were stupid. But they're not murderers.'

'You don't suppose I could end up in a Greek nick for anything I've done, do you?'

'It's a bit late to start thinking about that now, darling.' She shrugged. 'Conducting an illegal search, suborning a witness, withholding evidence – which is what you've done – that's a serious business, Scott. They might even argue that doing what you did has obstructed their own inquiry. And they might just be right about that, too.'

'Jesus. Help me out here, Louise. You're a copper. Give me some advice. What *am* I going to tell this Greek detective?'

'You mean how are you to avoid the possibility of making him feel like a complete dick?'

'Exactly.'

'I think less "it seemed to me that you guys really weren't doing anything very much to solve this case, so I decided that I should step in and help you poor idiots out", and a little more "I'm sorry but I seem to have stumbled across some information that I think might just be relevant to your inquiry and I thought I should tell you about this as soon as possible". Something like that could work. You've got a Greek lawyer, haven't you? So take her with you. Get her to say it in Greek.'

'No. I don't think that's a good idea. She doesn't much like the police.'

'Nobody does. Or had you forgotten?'

'Yes, but she's a lawyer. They're supposed to be on the same side.'

'I'm afraid that's true only half the time.'

'My biggest problem is this: there doesn't seem to be any way of telling Chief Inspector Varouxis that Nataliya committed suicide without also revealing that Bekim Develi was probably murdered. I mean, he's just as likely to continue the team's detention in Greece for his murder as for hers. So I'm providing an alternative narrative that really doesn't seem to help us in the long run. It fucks us in the mouth instead of the arse. But either way we're still fucked.'

'That's a bit legalese, but I think it puts it very well.' She thought for a moment. 'Look, I could come with you if you like. I don't speak Greek but I could show him my warrant card. One professional talking to another. I could even offer to suck his cock if he gets heavy with you.'

'That might work.'

'He's Greek. Of course it will work. These people invented arse fucking and cock sucking.'

'Sounds like a plan.'

I yawned and she leaned across me, dropped a breast onto my mouth and let me suck her nipple for a while. It was odd how I'd forgotten just how comforting that can be in moments of real stress.

'Here's some good advice,' she said, 'from one detective to another. It's something that always works for me when I'm working a case. Get some sleep. Things will seem a lot clearer in the morning.'

CHAPTER 51

Nataliya's bag and all its contents, including Bekim Develi's EpiPens lay in evidence on the table in front of me next to an ashtray that contained my still-smoking cigarette. I'd needed a couple of hits off it while I'd been telling Chief Inspector Varouxis my story and the smoke was now drifting towards him. I reached forward and stubbed it out.

'So, let me get this straight,' said Varouxis. 'You say that a Romanian gypsy found a lady's handbag on the harbour quay at Marina Zea and, recognising that it might have belonged to the girl who was drowned there, he handed it in to your lawyer, Dr Christodoulakis, for the ten-thousand-euro reward.'

'That's correct,' I said. 'His name is Mircea Stojka and he lives in the Roma encampment at Chalandri.' I pushed a piece of paper across the long table on which was written the man's address.

Varouxis regarded the address at arm's length as if he had forgotten his glasses.

'I know it. The camp is by the Mint. Where we make the money, ironically enough. You should take your boss there sometime. To see how some people live in this country since the recession bit.'

I was in the top floor conference room of the GADA on Alexandras Street, with Varouxis, Louise and a junior detective I hadn't met before who was also the shortest person in the room. His name was Kaolos Tsipras and he was examining Nataliya's purse from which I had previously removed the banknotes; it was impossible to imagine that anyone would have handed in a thousand euros in cash, even for a substantial reward. Since I'd last seen him Varouxis had shaved off the ridiculous little tuft of a beard underneath his bottom lip revealing a Harry Potter sort of scar on his chin. He was leaning on the windowsill, smoking a cigarette of his own, arms folded, his blue shirtsleeves rolled up and his top button undone; he looked as if he'd been working all night. His iPad lay on the windowsill beside him. From time to time he glanced out of the grimy window at the Apostolis Nikolaidis stadium where City were soon to be playing Olympiacos, as if wishing that he could have banished me to sit in the dilapidated stand.

'And you also say that when you looked at her phone you found what appears to be a suicide note stuck in the outbox of her email app? Which you've already had translated from Russian into English.'

'Yes. And Greek. Well, of course, I knew I was coming here today and I thought it might expedite your inquiry.'

'That was very thoughtful of you, sir.'

I shrugged. 'Of course, I know I shouldn't really have touched the phone at all, Chief Inspector. And I'm very sorry about that. But honestly, there didn't seem to be much point in worrying about any fingerprints. It was quite clear that Mr Stojka had already handled the phone quite extensively. I know that because he told us he had done so to sidestep the passcode, intending to sell her phone on the black market.

He only handed it in to us because he knew we were paying a lot more as a reward than he could have got for a new one.'

Varouxis nodded, patiently.

I'd met enough policemen in my time to know that the Greek believed not a word of my story; a weary sigh and a look of doubt is the same in any language. But having made so little headway with his own investigation he wasn't about to challenge me, not yet anyway. All the same, I still felt obliged to follow Louise's previous advice and eat some more humble pie.

'It would seem that I owe you another apology, Chief Inspector. You were quite right: Nataliya Matviyenko was well known to Bekim Develi. At least that's the impression you get from her suicide note. Wouldn't you agree?'

'Would you be kind enough to read her email out again please, Mr Manson?'

'Certainly, Chief Inspector.'

'Let me,' said Louise, and collecting another sheet of paper off the tabletop, she started to read aloud in a posh, butter-wouldn't-melt voice.

'Everything is horrible and hopeless. I thought I knew what it was to feel low but I now see I was wrong. I have now reached a very dark place in my soul from which there can be no return and I just want to go to sleep and not wake up again, ever. So, I am writing this email because I want to explain a few things and to apologise to everyone who's helped me in the last few months. You all tried very hard to make me feel better but I know now I can no longer go on with my life. I'm at the end of what I can cope with. I'm so very, very sorry for what's happened. I feel so guilty. Please

forgive me. It was me who killed Bekim Develi. If I hadn't taken his EpiPens then he might still be alive. I didn't mean to hurt him at all because he was always very kind to me, and a good friend. I was told that he might feel a bit ill and that was all. I had absolutely no idea that he could actually die. If I had known that this was even possible I would never ever have done it. When I saw what happened during the football match I was horrified. And when I heard that he was dead I wanted to die myself. Nothing I can do could ever bring him back. As usual I've made a big mess of things. But worse than that I keep thinking about Bekim's girlfriend, Alex, and his beautiful baby boy, Peter. Bekim was so proud of him. He showed me so many pictures of him that his face is now imprinted on my brain. I am responsible for taking away Peter's father. Peter will never know his father. The simple fact of the matter is that I cannot come to terms with it. Not now. Not ever. I'm sorry but I can't live with the memory of what I've done.'

Louise sighed and put down the sheet of paper from which she had been reading. I could see that it had affected her.

'In spite of what Nataliya writes,' I said, 'she obviously didn't kill him. But she seems to have held herself responsible for doing what someone else obviously did: the person who put her up to this, and who must have doctored Bekim's food here in Greece.'

'It's a pity she didn't say who that someone was,' observed Varouxis.

'The curious thing is,' I added, 'I've spoken to our team nutritionist, Denis Abayev, and he insists that the only thing

Bekim consumed before the match was a banana protein shake that Denis made himself and using ingredients that he brought on the plane from England. That was at least two hours before the match.'

'Which means it can hardly be the source of the substance that caused him to suffer an allergic reaction that cost him his life,' said Varouxis. 'But in the light of this new information I shall certainly want to speak to your team nutritionist again.'

I nodded. 'Naturally.'

'You don't suppose it could just be a coincidence,' suggested Sergeant Tsipras. 'That Mr Develi's death was natural after all. And that it had nothing to do with her stealing his pens.'

Varouxis looked at his subordinate with weary disappointment. 'Policemen don't believe in coincidence any more than they believe in the kindness of strangers. Not when there is – as Detective Inspector Considine has told us – the evidence of a substantial bet placed on the outcome of the match. By a Russian. In Russia. Quite possibly by the same person who owns the team for which Bekim Develi used to play, Semion Mikhailov, who had probable knowledge of his condition. No, someone got to him all right. Someone who was in league with this man, Semion Mikhailov. I think we can agree on that.'

'Yes, of course,' said Tsipras.

'There's something I'd like to show you,' said Varouxis.

He collected his iPad off the windowsill and switched it on with a sweep of his forefinger. A moment or two later Louise and I were looking at a short, grainy black and white film of what looked like a Mercedes Benz leaving the team's hotel in Vouliagmeni.

'This is CCTV footage that was taken from a camera near the main gate to the hotel, which has only just come to light. We are almost certain that Nataliya is the person sitting in the back seat of the car. Unfortunately you can't actually make out the number plate of the car, the driver or the figure sitting next to Nataliya, who might indeed be the someone she mentions in her suicide note: the man who put her up to stealing the pens.'

I watched the little bit of film several times before concluding that it left me none the wiser about what precisely had happened to Bekim Develi.

'I don't suppose you have an idea as to who this person in the car might be, Mr Manson,' said Varouxis.

I was close enough to him now to smell his aftershave, which reminded me of a very pungent air freshener of the kind you sometimes smell in taxis; like the scent of an artificial flower.

'No idea.'

'You're not aware of any of your players who might have hired a Mercedes limousine to go somewhere that night.'

'Like I told you before, they were supposed to be having an early night before a big game.'

'Yes, of course.'

'You might ask all of the limousine companies in Athens if they can remember collecting a Russian woman from the hotel that night,' suggested Louise.

'Yes, we will certainly do that, thank you,' said Varouxis. 'Anyway, as it happens we now believe that the person in the car might more probably be Nataliya's pimp, or some sort of sexual pervert who could even have been her next client.'

'Why do you say that?' asked Louise.

Varouxis ran the film again and then stopped it with a tap of his forefinger.

'If you look on the back shelf of the car you'll see – there, if I can enlarge this a little more – it's a little grainy but you can see what appears to be a whip. It is what I believe is sometimes called in English a cat of nine tails.'

'So it is,' said Louise.

'Again, I have to ask this,' said Varouxis. 'You don't have anyone in your team who might be into this kind of sadistic behaviour?'

I shook my head. 'No one.'

'Were there any signs on Nataliya's body that she'd been whipped?' I asked, knowing full well that there were none. The sight, sound and smell of Nataliya's mortal remains during Dr Pyromaglou's midnight autopsy were going to linger in my mind for a long time. 'I mean, you didn't mention any, before.'

'No signs at all,' said Varouxis. 'At least none that we know of. But now that the doctor's strike is over we shall at last be able to organise a proper autopsy for both Bekim Develi and Nataliya Matviyenko. Today, I hope.'

'Perhaps the whip was just a toy. All part of a sex game.'

'Beating someone doesn't sound like much of a sex game to me,' said Louise. 'Unless of course she used it to whip him. Now that's something I can understand. A woman beating a man with a whip. There are several of my so-called superiors at Scotland Yard I'd like to take a whip to.'

'I hadn't thought of that,' confessed Varouxis. 'Perhaps he got whipped, not her.'

'That would explain why there were no weals on her body,' said Louise. 'Which there certainly would be if she'd been whipped. It would seem impossible to participate in that sort of sexual activity without it leaving marks. Perhaps, Mr Manson, you should keep a lookout for the tell-tale marks the next time you see your team in the shower. Which will be on Wednesday night?'

'I'll certainly bear that in mind,' I said.

CHAPTER 52

'There's something else we need to tell you, Chief Inspector,' I said, carefully, 'and well, it relates to an old case of yours. Well, perhaps not that old. The Thanos Leventis case.'

Varouxis stiffened. 'What about it?'

'I think there might be certain similarities between that particular case and the death of Nataliya Matviyenko.'

'Principally the fact that one of Leventis's victims was thrown into the harbour at Marina Zea,' added Louise. 'Namely Sara Gill. An English woman.'

'I spoke to Miss Gill,' I said. 'About the attack on her in 2008.'

'You did?'

'We both did.' Louise spoke firmly. 'In an effort to establish if there might be a connection with the death of Nataliya Matviyenko.'

'And what did you conclude?' asked Varouxis.

'There isn't any connection,' said Louise. 'Nevertheless, I believe I am now in a position to make a formal request through the British Ambassador to your government that the Special Violent Crime Unit here in Athens reopens that case.'

'May I ask why?'

'From what Miss Gill has told me,' said Louise, 'you came to the entirely understandable conclusion that because of the severity of her injuries she wasn't likely to make much of a witness. She herself admits that she was confused. And that her story didn't seem to make sense.'

Varouxis nodded and lit another cigarette, calmly. 'Actually, it wasn't my decision not to pursue her story,' he said. 'It was the decision of my police general. But please go on.'

'Things are very different now,' said Louise. 'She's much recovered and remembers a great deal more about what happened to her. In particular, we now believe that she's in a position to identify the second attacker.'

'We?'

'During a Skype call I had with her on Saturday evening Miss Gill gave me a description of the man who attacked her,' I said. 'A very detailed description. From what she's said I'm more or less certain that I've met the other man who attacked her.'

'And who might that be? No. Wait a minute. Tsipras?'

'Yes, sir?'

'I think it's best that you leave the room,' said Varouxis. 'I think if Mr Manson here is going to utter a libel against someone it's best he does it in front of only one witness. For the sake of diplomatic relations between our two countries. I wouldn't like Mr Manson to get into any more trouble.'

'Very well, sir.' Tsipras stood up and left the room.

'All right,' said Varouxis after his subordinate had left us alone. 'Who do you have in mind?'

'His name is Antonis Venizelos, and he works for—'

'I know who Antonis Venizelos works for. Everyone in this building knows Antonis Venizelos. He's a very popular man. Venizelos supplies us with free tickets to all Panathinaikos matches. He's in and out of police headquarters like it was an extension of that stadium across the road.' He nodded out of the window and sighed. 'All right, tell me what makes you think that he's the other man who attacked Miss Gill?'

'She told me the man was hairy. Very hairy. Like Venizelos. A man with very sweet breath. Venizelos eats a lot of cardamom seeds and smokes menthol cigarettes. She also described a man who was wearing a T-shirt with a sort of UN logo on it. She told me that it was sort of like a wreath made of olive branches? Except that it wasn't a map of the world within the branches, but what looked more like a sort of labyrinth. I'm certain that what she was describing was a Golden Dawn T-shirt. A neo-Nazi organisation of which Venizelos is or used to be a member. At least that's what he told my assistant manager. But most tellingly she described a man who appeared to have three eyebrows. This was the detail that at the outset makes her seem unreliable. However, Venizelos has a very defined scar through one of his eyebrows that leaves one with the distinct impression that he has not two eyebrows but three. Considering Thanos Leventis drove the coach for the Panathinaikos B team, there exists a strong possibility he knew Antonis Venizelos. Also I know from my own conversations with him that Venizelos holds some very misogynistic views. Frankly, I think he hates women as much as he hates Pakistanis and Roma gypsies. I can't say that I am a hundred per cent certain it was him, Chief Inspector. And you have my word that I certainly haven't spoken to Miss Gill about my suspicions. However, I do think there is a very good chance that she would be able to pick him out of a police line-up.'

Varouxis lit another cigarette and thought for a minute.

'But then I suspect you already knew the man I was going

to name,' I said. 'That's why you asked Sergeant Tsipras to leave the room, isn't it?'

Varouxis remained silent.

'If you'll permit me to say something,' said Louise. 'Surely it's better that you should reopen the case yourself than at the behest of the British ambassador and your own Ministry of Justice.'

'In spite of what you say, the only way I could reopen this case would be if I had the kudos of solving the death of Miss Matviyenko, or the death of Bekim Develi. No one could argue with my decision to reopen Miss Gill's case under such circumstances as those.'

'Might I ask why anyone would argue with it?' said Louise.

'My superior, Police Lieutenant General Stelios Zouranis, is the cousin of this man Venizelos. He is also a member of Golden Dawn. I dislike both the man and the organisation, but my hands are tied, at least until I crack this particular case. The minister would have to listen to me then, you understand. He could not resist it.'

Louise nodded. 'We understand.'

'Antonis Venizelos has that scar through his eyebrow from an injury he sustained in a football match against Thessaloniki back in 2000,' said Varouxis. 'Venizelos stamped on the ankle of another player, for which offence he was head-butted by a third player and received sixteen stitches in his head as a result. He was always a very dirty player. And I say that as a Panathinaikos supporter. Indeed, for a while after that incident his nickname was Minotaure.'

He opened the window and waved some of the smoke out of the conference room.

'I tell you frankly that I always suspected that he was involved. And I would dearly love to put this man in prison.

And not just because he is a rapist and a murderer but because his kind represents the worst in our society. His kind of hatred and intolerance are not the true Greek way. We might have invented democracy but we are beginning to forget what it means. In order to convict him I will need to make my voice louder and solving this case will certainly do that.'

'Yes, I can see that.'

'I am impressed by what you've been able to discover, Mr Manson. Impressed but perhaps not that surprised after the way you were able to find out who killed João Zarco. I should have realised that you were not the type of man to sit on his hands and do nothing. I give you my word that if you help me now that I will help you.'

He held out his hand for me to shake; I took it. Then he shook hands with Louise.

'Perhaps the three of us can bring things to a satisfactory conclusion,' he said. 'In fact, I am quite sure of it.'

CHAPTER 53

After the pre-match chat with ITV – why do these guys always ask such stupid questions? – I went to find my players.

For the match against Olympiacos at the Apostolis Nikolaidis Stadium, across the road from the GADA, I chose to wear my own plain black tracksuit, matching T-shirt and a pair of black trainers. A Zegna linen suit, white shirt and silk tie hardly felt appropriate for what was certain to be a long and frenetic evening, and I wanted all of my players to fully understand what I had to say to them in the dressing room: that the game in front of us was going to require a die-in-the-ditch performance of real substance and very little style.

Not that there was much style on offer to us that night; the dressing room at Apostolis Nikolaidis was as shabby as the outside of the stadium had suggested it would be, and a sharp contrast to the shiny, brushed aluminium perfection of the facilities we enjoyed at home in Silvertown Dock. Some of the coat hooks on the walls were loose or non-existent and there were only wire hangers for shirts and jackets; the floor was uneven and it was strewn with spent matches, cigarette ends and bits of chewing gum. The chiller cabinet for water bottles wasn't switched on but that hardly mattered since it was also empty. There was a strong whiff of drains in the air and mould growing in the corners of the dripping showers which were missing more tiles than an old Scrabble set. Nor was there any air-conditioning either, just a couple of industrial-sized fans that blew Simon Page's player notes around the place and made me glad that I'd only brought my iPad.

'Right, you noisy sods,' said Gary Ferguson throwing his man-bag onto the bench, 'stop complaining and get your fucking kit on. Just remember, if this shithole is for the home team then imagine what the away team dressing room looks like. There's probably a turd in the bath. In fact, I know there is because I left one floating there yesterday.'

That got a big laugh.

'Are you going to eat that banana?' said Zénobe Schuermans.

'Actually, I was thinking of throwing it into the crowd,' said Daryl Hemingway. 'Just in case they run short during the game.'

'Count yourself lucky they just throw bananas here,' said Kenny Traynor. 'When Hearts used to play Hibs the cabbage bastards threw fucking coins.'

'At Anfield they used throw toilet rolls,' said Soltani Boumediene.

'I swear,' said Ayrton Taylor, 'if someone throws a coin at me I'm going to throw it back.'

'Listen, son,' said Gary, 'if someone throws a coin on the pitch at this place it's more likely to be an offer to buy the fucking football club.'

'When are those illiterate Scouse fuckers going to realise that it's "a field" not "an field"?' asked Jimmy Ribbans.

All this was just nerves and I let them have a few more moments of levity before settling them down.

'Right then,' I said. 'Could I have your attention please, gentlemen?'

I waited for a long minute and outlined my strategy – the one I'd described to Vik and Phil on *The Lady Ruslana*. Then I told them the hard truth about our chances. Like a lot of truths this one contained an important constituent that wasn't required to make any sense. That's a manager's job; to remind players that football is one of those magical places where the truth is often stranger than fiction.

'It's no small thing to turn over a 4–1 deficit,' I told them. 'This would seem difficult even on our own ground at Silvertown Dock. But here, in Athens, in this third-world slum that Panathinaikos call a stadium, in the dilapidated capital city of a shit-stormed country that's going to the dogs but which still manages to bark very loudly indeed?'

I paused for a moment so we could all hear the noise of the capacity crowd, which was mostly Greek; about fifty per cent Olympiacos, thirty per cent Panathinaikos hoping to see their old rivals beaten, ten per cent City fans, and ten per cent impartial tourists come to watch what they hoped might be a fascinating game of football.

'You hear that? That's the sound of those dogs barking now. All that barking means the same thing: no one expects us to win tonight. No one here in Greece. And no one back in England, either. Everyone has written us off. I just got a tweet from Maurice in London: on ITV Roy Keane has just said our chances of going through to the next round are less than they were for the blokes in *The Guns of Navarone*. Which is almost true; it certainly seems to me we've been through our own Greek tragedy, gentlemen. They used to give a goat to the Greek poet who could tell the best story. Well, you can keep the goat; this particular tragedy could have won you the fucking Booker prize.

'For ten days we've had to endure being away from

homes and our families; we've had whole armies of TV and press all over us like jock-rash; we've had the local filth asking us questions about hookers and drugs and all kinds of shit that were nothing to do with football. They've thrown bananas at us on the pitch and brickbats in the newspapers. Our champion, our Ajax is dead and yes, they think it's all over. Would you believe that *Proto Thema* – the biggest selling Sunday newspaper in Greece – said that this match we're about to play had been reduced to the status of a mere testimonial? That we were just turning up to give us something to do in Athens while we were under effective house arrest? To which I say, fuck off. We're made of stronger stuff than that. This team doesn't just "turn up". We turn up to play. And when we play we play to win.

'Certainly we can win tonight. I look around this room and I see faces that are serious about winning this game. Which is all that I would expect of the men I pick to defend the reputation of this team. So let's forget the rumours about bent referees, shall we? Maybe we are playing twelve men plus the crowd but that isn't going to stop us playing our game.

'However, I don't expect us to overcome a 4–1 score line. I'm not stupid. None of us are. The fact is that if we win overall on aggregate tonight it will be the biggest miracle in this part of the world since they found the lost treasure of Troy. A solid-silver fucking miracle. But since I happen to be talking about miracles let me also remind you of this, gentlemen: we are in the country of three hundred Spartans; where myths and legends, and yes, even bloody miracles, come to life. But you know, the day I went to see the statue of Zeus and the mask of Agamemnon in the National Archaeological Museum, the place was more or less empty of Greeks. Which made me think that maybe the Greeks have forgotten the power of their own myths, that maybe they don't remember the stories of Perseus, Theseus, Jason and Orpheus.

'Did anyone think Perseus stood even half a chance of slaying the Gorgon? Not the Greeks. Who thought that Theseus could go into the labyrinth and slay the Minotaur? Certainly not the Greeks. And Jason, remember him? Did any of the Greeks really think that he and his Argonauts stood even a snowball's chance in hell of even finding let alone bringing back the Golden Fleece? No. Of course they didn't. And what about Orpheus? When he descended to the underworld in an attempt to bring back his wife, Eurydice, the Greeks wrote him off, too, just like those other heroes. But against all expectations he came back from the dead. That's why they're called heroes. They were endowed with great courage and strength and did things against all the odds that is the stuff of legends. That is why they are remembered.

'You know, *The Guns of Navarone* is one of my top ten favourite films. I can't begin to tell you the number of bank holidays I've given up to watch it. But I rather think maybe Keano has forgotten that at the end of *The Guns of Navarone*, Gregory Peck, Anthony Quinn and David Niven actually manage to pull it off, after all. Against all the odds and on a warm Aegean night such as this, they manage to destroy those big, impregnable guns in an explosion of spectacular drama.

'And I remembered something that Jensen, the guy who sends them on the mission – something he says at the very beginning of the movie that I want to share with you now: Anything can happen in a war.'

CHAPTER 54

'Good luck.'

Kojo Ironsi was standing immediately outside the dressing room door when I opened it. A large part of me wanted to tell him to go and fuck himself but I fixed a smile onto my face like a stupid false moustache and shook the big hand that was outstretched in front of me.

'Thanks,' I said.

'This game – it means a lot, doesn't it?' he said.

'No, right now it means everything.'

'Vik and Phil are up in a box with Gustave,' he explained. 'I'm going to join them in a minute but given my new position as Technical Director I thought I'd come down and say hello. See if there's anything I could do.'

'Kind of you.'

'I know you weren't exactly thrilled about my appointment, Scott, but I sincerely hope we'll be able to work together.'

'I'm sure we will. Just give me a little time to get used to the idea, okay?'

'Sure, anything you say.'

Kojo's big gold Rolex caught the light as he flicked the air with his fly-whisk. He was wearing a light brown linen Safari suit and open-toed sandals; all he needed was a leopard skin *karakul* hat and he'd have looked like a minor African dictator.

'It's pretty hot out there,' he said. 'Almost sub-Saharan. And probably just as unpredictable.' He paused for a moment and then added, 'You should make sure the players are all properly hydrated, don't you think?'

I bit my tongue and nodded. 'Thanks for the useful advice, Kojo. I wouldn't ever have thought of that myself. Not in a million years. But then what do I know? I'm just the fucking manager.'

But Kojo didn't hear this; he was already glad-handing both of his King Shark players: Prometheus, of course; and then Séraphim Ntsimi who was the other, only he was playing for Olympiacos. Kojo also shook hands with another Olympiacos player, their saturninely handsome full back, Roman Boerescu.

I don't know why but in spite of the animosity I was feeling towards him I was impressed to hear Kojo speaking Greek, and with some fluency too. Which was probably why, briefly, I pictured him and Séraphim with Valentina and Nataliya at Roman's place in Glyfada. Who had been with who? Kojo with Valentina? Or Kojo with Nataliya? Or both? The dirty bastard, I thought, at least until I remembered that, according to Valentina at any rate, Kojo hadn't actually fucked either of the girls; which wasn't something I could say myself.

For a minute both sides waited impatiently in the tunnel; and then a minute longer. It was so warm that Kenny Traynor was fanning his face with one of his gloves. The twenty-two child mascots holding hands with the players already looked almost as warm as him and thoroughly overawed by the whole occasion. I could hardly blame them for that. I hate the players' tunnel before a match. Most of the time you have no idea who half of the people are or what they're even doing there.

Out of the corner of my eye I saw Kojo speaking to the handsome-looking woman who a minute before I'd seen kissing the Romanian on the cheek, which struck me as odd: WAGs weren't normally allowed in the tunnel. Then I saw that she was in charge of the child mascots, all of whom were now looking up to her for their cue, as if she'd been their mother. And perhaps in a way she was; from what I gathered she'd just given the kids their tea, or whatever Greek kids have when they're in a Champions League football match. As I watched she smiled and reached across a small head and gently placed the hand of a shy little girl in one of Kenny Traynor's enormous paws.

Kenny leaned towards me. 'I wouldn't mind, boss,' he said, 'but her little hand is so sticky.'

'Put your gloves on,' I said.

'It's so hot in here,' he said.

'I've heard everything now,' said Simon. 'A goalkeeper complaining his hands are too sticky. Find out what the kid had for tea, son, and then rub some more on your gloves. Sticky fingers will make a change from your usual buttery ones.'

Kenny thought that was very funny. And so did Gary; but for just a moment my sense of humour seemed to have deserted me.

'What are we waiting for?' I heard myself say, impatiently.

Kojo repeated my question to the woman who answered him in Greek.

'According to Mrs Boerescu they can't find the CD with the classical music for the PA system,' said Kojo.

'That's his wife?'

Kojo nodded. 'Beethoven, or whatever it is.'

I looked at Boerescu and then his wife. For a fleeting moment I considered going over to Roman Boerescu and saying, in earshot of his wife, 'Valentina says hello.' I guess if I'd been Greek I would have done it.

'It's not Beethoven,' I told Kojo. 'It's Handel's *Zadok the Priest*.'

'That doesn't sound like it's got much to do with sport,' said Kojo.

'I think it's just meant to be awe-inspiring,' I said. 'The kind of music you'd want for the anointing of a king or a priest. Or the best team in Europe, I suppose.'

'What kind of priest was he? This Zadok.'

I shrugged and shook my head. 'Haven't a clue.'

'I think maybe he was the first high priest of the new temple at Jerusalem,' said Soltani Boumediene who, despite being an Arab, had once played for Haifa in Israel and knew about stuff like that. 'The one built by King Solomon back in the day, before the Romans turned up and sacked the place.'

'You surely don't mean that this Zadok guy was a Jew?' said Kojo.

'I suppose he must have been,' answered Soltani, 'if he was in the Old Testament.' He laughed. 'I mean, I doubt he was a bloody Scientologist.'

Kojo pulled a face. 'Better not tell the Muslims the guy was a Jew.'

'In which case,' I said to him, quietly, 'better just shut the fuck up about it, eh?'

'If they had any idea that they were walking out onto that pitch to a piece of music about a Jewish rabbi,' said Kojo, 'they'd have a fit. Seriously. Who knows what these guys are offended by these days.'

'So shut the fuck up,' I told him again.

'I'm a Muslim,' replied Soltani, 'and really, I don't have any problem with it at all. It's just a piece of music.'

Mohamed Hachani, one of the Olympiacos players, said something to Soltani in Arabic but Soltani just shook his head and stared down at his own boots; so Hachani addressed what I assumed must be the same question, in Greek, to Kojo, who answered him just as the music finally started and the referee waved us forward. The players and the children started to shuffle towards the end of the tunnel. But Hachani stood still and spoke to Soltani in Arabic again; and again Soltani just shook his head as if he preferred not to answer which now drew an angry response from the other man. Hachani took hold of Soltani Boumediene's shirtsleeve and shouted, this time in English.

'What kind of a Muslim are you, anyway?' he demanded. 'This bloody music is an insult to all Arabs. And you are a disgrace to Islam, my friend. If I had known that the Champions League music was really about a fucking Jew I would never have agreed to play in this competition. And you should feel the same way about it.'

'Get over it,' said Soltani. 'And please, don't swear or use racist language like that in front of the children.'

Tugging Hachani's hand from his sleeve, Soltani smiled kindly at the mascot whose hand he was still holding, and started towards the end of the tunnel again.

But Hachani was not so easily brushed off and, irritated that Soltani seemed to be making light of something he himself regarded as very serious, he started to shout in Arabic; but still ignored by our long-suffering player, it seemed that he could think of no other way to make his anger felt than to throw a water bottle at him. To my relief Soltani continued to ignore Hachani and, for a while, things between them seemed to simmer down; but in retrospect I should have anticipated that there might be more trouble between them and substituted Soltani right then and there.

I followed the players out of the tunnel and onto the pitch where the air was so thick and warm it felt like soup, but because of the many green and red flares burning in the stands it smelt and tasted like something else; civil disorder, most likely. There were so many flares my first thoughts were of another Bradford City disaster, when fifty-six fans were killed after the rubbish underneath a stand in what was probably better condition than the one at Apostolis Nikolaidis was set alight by a carelessly discarded cigarette end. That was another major difference between English stadia and those in Greece. Smoking was not permitted anywhere at Silvertown Dock – or for that matter at any other stadia in the English league – but in Greece, where everyone smokes, everyone smokes at football, too. And frankly it's better when they do smoke; when they're pulling on a fag they can't shout racist abuse.

The players lined up patiently, and then trooped past each other, shaking hands like we were all gentlemen on the playing fields at Eton College. I myself made a point of shaking hands with Hristos Trikoupis, who even managed an apology for his previous behaviour when I told him that his secret was safe with me; but all of that was lost when it kicked off between Mohamed Hachani and Soltani Boumediene again.

Simon Page told me later on that when Soltani lifted his own hand to shake Hachani's hand, the Olympiacos player spat on it. But I didn't actually see what happened and unfortunately neither did anyone on TV or the dozy Irish referee. All he saw was Soltani's fist make its probably well-deserved connection with Hachani's hooked nose.

The referee didn't hesitate. First he showed Soltani a yellow card; and then he showed him a red.

CHAPTER 55

Mohamed Hachani was making a three-course meal of it with wine and coffee. He was still lying on the pitch with his hands pressed to his face as if he might never again get up, which might have been a more satisfactory outcome. Even his own team mates were smiling awkwardly as if they knew the play-acting was going on for too long; perhaps they were embarrassed and if not they ought to have been. After all, everyone but Hachani knew that the last time we'd seen a player prone for so long, he died. What he was doing now seemed disrespectful to the tragedy of what had happened to Bekim Develi.

The Irish referee, Blackard, was, of course, well within his rights to send Soltani Boumediene off, and all the protests in the world – that the boy had merely retaliated after being spat on – weren't going to change his decision. Referees in the modern game take a dim view of retaliation as anyone who saw what happened to Beckham after he kicked that bloody Argie in the 1998 World Cup will no doubt remember; Diego Simeone went down from that tap on the calf as if he'd been shot with a rifle. Hard to believe he's now the manager of Atletico Madrid. Besides, I agreed with the sending off. If players retaliated to every foul no one would ever kick a ball.

But that was one thing; what happened next was something else altogether. When we brought on Jimmy Ribbans as a substitute, Blackard ordered him to leave the pitch and then, when I asked why, he informed me that City could not substitute another player for the man he had sent off. The actual laws of the game, however, say differently and things quickly descended into farce as I ran after the referee like a blue-arsed fly as he moved towards the centre spot, trying to explain to him the meaning of rule five, and all of this under a storm of whistles and jeers from at least half the spectators in the ground.

'You can't do this,' I yelled at him.

'I've sent the player off the field,' he said, 'and that's the end of the matter, Mr Manson.'

'I'm not disputing that, you idiot.'

'And I shall be reporting you to UEFA for your abusive language and behaviour.'

'And I shall be reporting you for not knowing the laws of the game. Take the pig shit out of your ears and listen to me. I'm trying to stop you from looking like a complete idiot in tomorrow's newspapers. Which you will do unless you pay attention now. Since you hadn't actually blown the whistle to start the game, the normal rule that applies to sendings off just doesn't apply. Whether you like it or not, those are the rules of football. All your decision to send off Soltani Boumediene means is that we're down to two substitutes instead of three. And that he can't take any part in this game, or – if by some miracle we should qualify – the next one.'

'Well, that makes absolutely no sense at all. Look here, I would hardly have sent the player off if I thought he was just going to be subbed by you, now would I?'

'That's for you to say, referee. Nevertheless, the law is the law. And there's no room for interpretation. Consult your own officials. Go and find the UEFA guy and ask him if you like. But if you ever want to referee a game outside a potato field in Galway again I should pay attention to what I'm saying now. What you're doing is not within the rules of the game. And if you're not careful your name will be a byword for stupidity before the end of the week.'

After much heated argument, during which time I was ordered to sit in the stands not once but three times, I finally managed to persuade him to read the rules now displayed on my iPad. Mr Blackard then went to consult with his five match officials and I walked back to our dugout to the usual shrill Greek chorus.

'What's he say?' asked Simon.

'He's still standing on his dignity.'

'What did I tell you?' said Simon. 'I told you that bastard Backward, or whatever his fucking name is, was bent.'

'I don't think he's bent,' I said. 'I think he's just stupid. And ignorant. And pig-headed. And scared of looking like a twat.'

'It's a bit late for that, I'd say. Why did Mohamed Hachani gob on Soltani's hand anyway?'

I explained about the Champions League music and how Hachani seemed to have taken offence to its subject.

'People as sensitive as that lad have got no business playing football,' observed Simon. 'Next thing we'll have Hindus refusing to throw in the ball because it's made of cow leather. Or Muslims refusing to run onto a pitch because the fucking grass is fertilised with pig shit. Christ, when I was playing for Rotherham we used to leave a turd in someone's fucking shoe. For a laugh, like. I'd like to have seen Hachani's face then.'

354

'This confirms what I've always suspected. That Yorkshire men have a sophisticated sense of humour.'

'Happen that's true, aye.'

'But technically this is all Kojo's fault. If only he'd kept his fucking mouth shut, then none of this would have happened and Soltani would still be on that pitch. It was him who kept on pointing out that Zadok was a Jew.'

'That's why he's the Technical Director, I suppose,' observed Simon. 'Because technically he's a cunt. We both agree about that, boss. But now he's in place at this club it's going to be very hard to get rid of the bastard. Anything you say to Vik about him is going to look like sour grapes.'

'I'd like to stick that fucking fly-whisk up his arse.'

'Is that what it is? I was wondering why he was walking around with that thing. I thought it was a sort of feather duster. You know? Like Ken Dodd.'

Blackard finished talking to his officials and now waved Jimmy Ribbans onto the pitch and for the first time that evening I smiled, although mostly I was smiling at how anyone could have mistaken a fly-whisk for a feather duster.

'Thank Christ for that,' said Simon. 'It seems like the Irish cunt has seen sense. Now maybe we can get on with the fucking game.'

I glanced behind us up into the stand and met the faces of several thousand hostile Greeks who proceeded to tell me that I was a *malakas* and other interesting epithets to do with the colour of my skin. I wondered if any of them could even read the many *Respect* and *No To Racism* slogans that appeared in Greek and English on the perimeter advertising hoardings.

A minute or two later, the referee checked his watch and, fifteen minutes later than scheduled, he blew his whistle for the game to start.

CHAPTER 56

After everything that had happened before the match, it was a relief to watch a game of football, even though that wasn't the way I'd decided we were going to play it. Because right from the kick-off our players were quickly on their weakest player – the midfielder, Mariliza Mouratidis – like they held him personally responsible for keeping us all in Greece, and closing him down like they were a bunch of liquidators.

'I hope this works,' said Simon. 'You know what European refs are like. They hand out cards like Japanese businessmen. And after what just happened with that Irish bastard, Backward – he's probably dying to send another of our lads off.'

'On the contrary,' I said. 'I think that what happened might just work in our favour. Backward already looks stupid because he didn't know the rules. He'll know that in his bones now. There's no point in looking like a cunt as well.'

But two extra-hard tackles in the first fifteen minutes stood out from the rest. Mouratidis ran at speed onto a long ball from Roman Boerescu which landed just inside our box, with the ball bouncing just a little too high for him to control; he looked up, waiting for it drop a little so he could perhaps head it onto his foot, with no idea that Kenny Traynor – all six foot three of him – had already taken off and, like Mercury himself, was now heading through the air, fist first.

Kenny punched the ball cleanly and fifteen yards clear of his box, at least half a second before his trailing knee caught Mouratidis on the side of the head and clotheslined him. Fortunately the inevitable Greek howls and demands for a penalty were wasted on the Irish referee and the officials who'd had an excellent view of what had happened. Anyone looking at the incident would have said that Kenny had touched the ball first and behaved with an almost foolhardy lack of concern for his own safety, so much so that everyone in the City dugout was relieved to see him get up again. Everyone but the Olympiacos supporters, that is, who were outraged that a penalty was not going to be given.

'Nice one,' I said. 'That should give the lad plenty of pause for thought.'

'You fucking Irish *malakas*,' someone not very far behind me was shouting at the ref. 'You want to wear your glasses instead of keeping them up your arse.'

Mouratidis stayed flat on his back for at least two minutes; and after treatment off the field, returned to the game with no obvious signs of injury. It was perhaps unfortunate for him that the next incident involving the boy was to compete for a fifty-fifty ball with Gary Ferguson, who has the hardest head in British football. The man could head a wrecking ball and still walk away with a smile on his face. The two players jumped for a high ball, with the difference between them being that the later slow-motion replay showed Gary's head arriving with more energy and malice aforethought than a rock from a trebuchet; it was almost as if he had regarded the football as an unfortunate impediment to the delivery of a real Glasgow kiss. And Gary knew what he was doing; he seemed to head his way through the ball, before his head connected with the young Greek's forehead.

Once again Mouratidis went down as if felled by a Tyson uppercut only to find that Gary, who knew very well how appearances can influence weaker-minded referees, had already beaten him to the deck and was now holding the crown of his head and writhing on the ground as if trying to roll himself up in turf.

Anxiously I glanced at the linesman and was reassured to see his flag had stayed by his side.

'Christ,' muttered Simon as both physios sprinted onto the pitch amid a virtual storm of whistled air. 'I hope that crazy Scots bastard is all right.'

'He's not injured,' I said. 'A head like Gary's could breach a castle wall. He's just wriggling his way clear of a potential yellow, that's all. You mark my words, Simon. Just as soon as he sees the ref's hand is staying away from his top pocket he'll be on his feet again, like nothing happened.'

A minute later my prediction was fulfilled and, still holding his head as if he could feel his hair transplant starting to work, Gary came back to the line with Gareth Haverfield. I got up from the bench, grabbed a bottle of water from the kitbag and stood beside them. Gary took the bottle from my hand and, with the plastic tit between what few teeth were left in his head, muttered back me, 'I'll be very surprised if the fucker gets up from that, boss.'

'We don't want the bastard off the field,' I said. 'I told you. We just want him nervous when he's on the ball. Like it was filled with fifty thousand volts. So that the next time Prometheus runs at him he'll think it's better just to stay the fuck out of his way.'

To my relief, Mouratidis got up and started to hobble back to the line. I glanced anxiously at Trikoupis to see if he was about to send another man on in the young Greek's place, but none of the Olympiacos players were even warming up. 'Got it,' said Gary, and tossing the bottle behind him he ran back onto the pitch.

'If this carries on,' observed Simon, 'it won't be Mrs Mouratidis who's in hospital, it'll be her son, too.'

'That's their problem,' I said. 'Ours is winning this game.'

Once again Mouratidis went back onto the field, apparently still none the worse for wear. I stayed at the edge of my technical area shouting instructions, most of which were lost under the noise of the crowd; but when I saw Gary speak in the ear of Prometheus the African kid turned, caught my eye, and then nodded very deliberately as if he understood exactly what to do.

A minute or two later he ran onto a powerful roll-out from Kenny that looked more like a snooker shot it was so well placed, and a split second later Prometheus was sprinting straight up the centre of the pitch like Wayne Rooney on ketamine – the raging bull way he used to run straight at people when he first joined Man U after leaving Everton. Mouratidis kept pace with Prometheus for ten or fifteen yards before making a futile, almost childish attempt to get his arm in front of the young Nigerian who wasn't having any of it and even seemed to shrug him off like an old overcoat, whereupon the Greek fell beneath the feet of another chasing player and didn't move again until Prometheus had completed his run, by which time the ball was in the back of the Greek net.

The goal was so quick I didn't even see it. The best goals are often like that, over before you know it, which is why managers often look so dozy in the dugout. Sometimes you can't see the very thing that you're looking for. With the Olympiacos crowd behind their goal carrying on regardless with their Neanderthal chants, it was only the Panathinaikos fans going wild with delight to see their greatest rivals a goal down after just twenty minutes that tipped us off that we were now one-up on the night.

'He's only fucking well scored,' yelled Simon.

I turned away from the pitch and double-punched an invisible dog at my knee before I found myself held around the waist by Simon Page in a bear hug of alarming power and then lifted high into the air. He put me down just in time for me to catch Prometheus as he launched himself into my arms, and it was fortunate that I'm a fit man as the combination of these two celebrations would surely have injured someone weaker.

'Thanks, boss,' yelled Prometheus. 'Thanks for believing in me, and for making me believe in myself.'

'Now go and score another and remind these Greek bastards how good you are,' I yelled back at him.

Slapping the club badge on the breast of his shirt Prometheus sprinted back onto the field and I told myself that it was me and not our new technical director who'd helped the boy find his winning streak again. This is all football management's about: making players feel good about themselves enough to play the best they can. To do that you need a bit more than just a hairdryer, and anyone who tells you different is full of shit.

'Four–two,' yelled Simon.

Twenty minutes later, on the edge of half time, Prometheus struck again when Jimmy Ribbans's powerful twenty-yard strike ricocheted off their goalpost and, without a moment of hesitation, the Nigerian boy launched himself headfirst at the rebound and scored – an astonishing diving kamikaze of a goal that was every bit as courageous as it was spectacular: 4–3.

'I don't know what you said to him on that fucking boat,' said Simon. 'But it worked.'

'All I did was give him a history lesson.'

'He's like a different player. Now if he can do it once more I'll have his baby.'

Trikoupis was looking rattled now. Summoning his team captain, Giannis Maniatis, to the touchline, he gave him some animated instructions, seemingly unaware that half time was just minutes away and that he had actually moved several feet beyond his technical area and was now standing on the pitch. The sixth official, William Winter, pulled at the Greek manager's shirtsleeve, trying to bring him back into the technical area, but the Olympiacos manager was having none of it. He wrested his arm away from Winter who pulled at him again, and, perhaps because he was English, Trikoupis turned and shouted in his face.

I'm pretty sure that Winter didn't speak more than one word of Greek; but then he only needed to know one word; *malakas* is a word that all of the officials are well aware of and while they had been briefed by UEFA to be on the lookout for it from some of the players and of course from the crowd, none of them had expected to hear it from the Greek manager himself.

Calling the sixth official a wanker to his face would have been bad enough but Trikoupis now shoved him away. Winter took a couple of tiny steps backwards, and then fell flat on his back. Now it's a fact of the modern game that nearly all players will, from time to time, take a dive in the hope of a foul or a penalty, but it's rare in the European game that you see an official go down as easily as Winter did. I'll always remember watching a match between Newcastle and Southampton when Mohamed Sissoko put the referee on the deck and, to all the world, it looked like it was the ref who had taken a dive. Fortunately on this occasion the lino was right beside William Winter and immediately raised his flag to summon Backward who, advised of what had happened – or at least appeared to happen – and doubtless pleased that he could send someone else off who wasn't actually playing, ordered Trikoupis to the stands.

Trikoupis kicked a plastic water bottle away in disgust. The bottle flew through the air and struck a uniformed policeman in the face. At which point the cop took Trikoupis by the arm and led him off the pitch. The Olympiacos fans went wild with anger, while those of Panathinaikos went wild with delight.

'Is he arresting him, or what?' I said.

'I fucking hope so,' admitted Simon. 'I would love it – love it if that bastard spent the night in the cells.'

He and I tried to contain our glee but it wasn't easy; while the Greeks came pouring out of their dugout to remonstrate with Mr Backward and the cop, Simon and I retired to our own dugout, occupied our mouths with chewing gum and water bottles and observed the proceedings from a safe distance. This was just as well as a red flare came sailing through the air and landed close to the corner flag in our half.

'You can tell a lot about a country by the way they protest against the inevitable,' mused Simon. 'I mean, it's obvious that referee isn't going to change his mind about that one. But the bastards seem determined to argue it.'

'You can tell why Zeus got so pissed off with these people and was so fond of throwing thunderbolts about the place,' I said. 'They'd try the patience of a pope.'

By now the referee was surrounded with Olympiacos coaching staff and players and it wasn't long before the assistant manager, Sakis Theodoridou, had been sent to join Hristos Trikoupis in the stands.

'That's their half-time team talk well and truly fucked,' said Simon. 'I guess the physio will have to do it now. Or maybe that Mrs Boerescu who did the kiddies' tea before the match. Christ, that's a nice-looking woman. She can give me a bollocking any time she wants. Just as long as my bollocks are in the right place, which'd be resting comfortably on her chin.'

Another burning flare came sailing through the air as if somewhere a ship was in distress and, completely recovered from his severe fall, Mr Winter walked away from the mêlée that was still berating the referee, and kicked the flare off the pitch, where a security man attempted to put it out with an extinguisher.

'This is beginning to look serious,' I said. 'Let's just hope that twat Backward doesn't abandon the match. Not with us two-up on the night.'

'He wouldn't do that, would he?'

'He just might, you know. Last time a match between the Greens and the Reds was abandoned was as recently as March 2012 when the Greens set fire to the stadium.'

'Fuck me,' said Simon. 'I know it's important, football. And I know you want players who will fight when there's nothing at stake, but that shouldn't ever apply to the fucking fans.'

CHAPTER 57

Somehow the match restarted and a couple of minutes later the Irish referee blew his whistle for half time, which managed to calm things down a little. Air conditioning and about a ton of Valium would have been more effective, probably. As we trooped down the tunnel I heard an enormous, deafening bang that someone told me was an exploding fire extinguisher; sometimes the Greek fans set them alight, I was told by someone, which seemed so fucking crazy and dangerous I almost considered pulling out of the game then and there. What kind of a country is it where they set fire to extinguishers? One way or another I was looking forward to going home to London, where – thank God – hooliganism of this order was a thing of the past and the biggest bang you'll ever hear is when David Beckham shuts the door of his Rolls-Royce in anger.

In the malodorous slum of a dressing room I told our players only that there was nothing I could tell them that would improve the way they were playing now, except for one thing:

'Just imagine what's happening right now, in the Olympiacos dressing room. Fucking chaos, that's what's happening. Total meltdown. Let's hope Trikoupis is in jail. Giannis Maniatis is probably having to do the team talk. Giving them a piece of his mind. Which he probably keeps in that little space between his eyebrows.'

'What would you say, boss?' asked Gary. 'What would you say to them if it was you in there giving the team talk?'

'Yes,' said Ayrton, 'it'd be good to hear that.'

'Christ,' I said, 'I wouldn't know where to start. But I suppose the first thing I'd tell those guys in red would be this: you're a complete bunch of *malakes*.'

Everyone cheered with noisy good humour.

'Either that or a bunch of fucking mongs.'

More cheers.

'He said "mong",' squeaked Ayrton Taylor, in imitation of Ricky Gervais, who is quite fond of the 'm' word himself.

'But seriously, lads, Gianni needs to tell his team to keep a lot tighter at the back. That's the major problem. The way they defended those two set pieces we had – that was appalling; we were unlucky not to have scored from those as well. They seem more interested in trying to keep possession of the ball than in defending. I think that may have been the inspired team tactic of the night. Deny us the ball and play pass the bloody parcel and hope that we'll give up chasing the game. But it's not working. Nothing for them is working now. Not even the gods.

'In the air, well, they're just crap. A team of acrophobic pygmies could win more high balls than they did in the first half. And certainly I would take that child Mouratidis off. He's completely lost his bottle now that Gary has given him an old-fashioned Toxteth lobotomy.'

Prometheus grinned a huge grin and clapped Gary on the back of the head.

'Here, mind the fucking hair,' he said, which got another big laugh.

'Gary? You might not get the Ballon d'Or this year, but you'll certainly win the lead balloon for the best head-butt I've seen since Zinedine Zidane took out Marco Materazzi. Maybe they'll erect a statue to you in Qatar. But I really wouldn't know who I'd bring on in Mouratidis's place. Mrs Boerescu, probably. She couldn't do any worse than him. Maybe she could offer a free blow job for anyone of theirs who scores a goal tonight. That might get them going a bit. I know it would get Big Simon going. He's talked about nothing but her sucking his cock since he saw her in the tunnel.'

Everyone cheered again.

'Frankly, they're not playing like a side that went into this leg 4–1 up. They've lost every cube of the ice cool they should have had about this game. I mean, all they needed to do was keep their heads, but that's not happening. At the moment they're being ripped open by good old-fashioned running football. Not passes. Running. Real Roy of the Rovers stuff. When you run at them it's like you fillet them with a fucking fish knife. They don't know how to handle a fast-running game. And that's all I'd say to you. Run at the cunts. You get the ball and run at them like Prometheus did when he scored his first goal and I promise you we'll win this.'

We went back on the field to find that the local riot police had turned up in force bearing shields and batons and were now facing the Olympiacos fans, on the basis, I suppose, that the Panathinaikos fans were less likely to burn down their own stadium. An acrid cloud of smoke hung like a net curtain and the match restarted with everyone wondering if it would be finished that night.

Mouratidis was still on the field, which struck me as a serious mistake, but I hardly paid this much attention after what I'd just seen in the tunnel. *Because surely William Winter*

366

had winked at me. Was it possible that he was on our side? I was still trying to get my head around what this meant when the referee blew his whistle. Immediately Olympiacos were on the attack and thanks to Giannis Maniatis they enjoyed their best chance of the night. It should have been a goal, such was the quality of the Greek captain's effort, with a brace of superb strikes: the first came off Kenny Traynor's enormous fist and ricocheted straight back at the Greek's feet; the second strike ought to have been in the back of the net as soon as Maniatis put his boot through it, but somehow Kenny picked himself off the ground, dived again, and this time collected the ball cleanly with two hands. The most astonishing thing was not that Maniatis failed to score but that a man as big as Kenny Traynor could move so quickly; I've seen scalded cats move with less speed. And even the Greek captain was moved to go and shake our goalkeeper's hand after his awe-inspiring save.

This single sporting gesture did much to alter the temperature of the match; because having seen their captain shake Kenny Traynor's hand, the Olympiacos fans applauded him too, as if they realised not only that they'd seen a save of the rarest quality, but that they'd also seen a decent sportsman in the person of their own mono-browed captain.

Simon clapped his big hands and shook his head.

'Bloody marvellous,' he boomed. 'What did I tell you? Sticky fingers. That's what any great keeper needs. God only knows how that man didn't score. What a pity that Kenny Traynor isn't English and that he'll never grace a World Cup.'

I didn't say anything. Even as a Jock myself I couldn't have argued with that. But that wasn't what was making me silent. It was the realisation that after what Simon had said I knew exactly how Bekim Develi had been killed; it had been staring me in the face like the Zapruder film for the last hour; not only that but I knew who had killed him, too.

I stayed quite still for a moment, then walked back to the dugout and sat down feeling like a man who has suffered a stroke and for whom half the world has suddenly disappeared. If you had placed a mirror in front of me I would not have seen my own reflection. The noise of the crowd seemed to get sucked up in a vacuum, along with the oxygen in the air around me. On the pitch I could hear the worms crawling through the earth underneath the grass; they were surely better than the people who had killed Bekim. Above me the smoke seemed to roll like thunder through the stadium; it tasted sweeter than the sour flavour that I had in my mouth from knowing what I now knew, beyond any reasonable doubt.

'You're in charge,' I said. 'I'm afraid I need to go and speak to someone. Right now.'

'Can't it fucking wait?'

'No, it can't.'

'Speak to who?' asked Simon as I stalked off. 'Where the fuck are you going?'

'To speak to Mrs Boerescu. I want to ask her something. Maybe she'll give me a blow job if I talk to her nicely.'

CHAPTER 58

Charlie and two of Vik's bodyguards were standing at the end of the corridor that led to his box, watching the match through the open door of another box which was not occupied.

'Everything all right, boss?' asked Charlie.

'I'll tell you in a minute, Charlie, after I've spoken to *my* boss.'

'Mr Sokolnikov, right. Just let me know if you want my help for anything else. I like working for you, Mr Manson. You're a good guy.'

'Thanks, Charlie.'

The bodyguards nodded silently and I nodded back, wondering if they were armed and what they might have done if they had known what was in my mind; only it wasn't them who gave me pause for thought as I opened the door to the box, but Louise. I'd forgotten that Vik had invited her to watch the match with him and she was the only person in that room whose good opinion of me really mattered. About Vik, Phil, Kojo Ironsi, Gustave Haak and his diminutive toady, Cooper Lybrand, I couldn't have cared less.

'Scott,' said Vik. 'What the hell are you doing here?'

'Yes,' said Phil. 'Surely you must have missed the all-important goal.'

'What goal?' I asked.

'Ayrton Taylor just scored from thirty yards,' said Phil. 'While you were probably climbing all those stairs.'

'What?'

Kojo swatted something invisible with his fly-whisk. 'It was a beautiful strike,' he said, quietly. 'Almost as good as the one scored by Prometheus.'

I walked to the window and stared down from the gods at the pitch where Ayrton was still sprinting around the pitch perimeter, spinning an orange City football shirt in his hand like it was a lasso, and probably earning himself a yellow in the process. At last the Olympiacos fans had become silent. 'Bloody hell.'

'That's right,' said Vik. 'We're three–nil up. That's four all on aggregate. If things stay as they are we'll go through on the away goal we scored last week. Isn't it wonderful? I don't know what you and Simon have said to them this past week, but the boys are playing out of their skins. Congratulations. Right now, I couldn't be more happy.'

'That's right,' I said. 'We will. Jesus fucking Christ. We're going to qualify. I don't believe it.'

'Even so,' added Phil, 'don't you think you should be down there on the touchline supporting your team? Advising them? Encouraging them? With all due respect, it's a little bit early for a celebration. There are at least thirty minutes of the game left to play.'

My delight in the score line gave way to something much less pleasurable.

'I didn't come up here to celebrate,' I said. 'Or to look for any praise, Phil. Not right now.'

Louise stood up and tried to take my hand; she could see the anger in my face even if the others couldn't. I took my hand out of hers, kissed her fingers and tried to contain myself for a few moments longer.

'Then, I don't understand,' said Vik. 'What *did* you come for?'

'Louise,' I said, 'I think you'd better let us have the room for a moment. You, too, Mr Haak, Mr Lybrand. What I have to say is best kept among the people at this football club. Me, Vik, Phil and Kojo here.' I smiled a humourless smile. 'If you don't mind.'

'Be careful,' murmured Louise and went out of the door.

'I don't deserve you,' I whispered.

Looking more than a little bemused, Gustave Haak and Cooper Lybrand stood up but hesitated to follow her, looking to Vik for their proper cue to stay or leave.

'Scott, please,' said Vik. 'These gentlemen are my guests. You're embarrassing me. Whatever this is about, can't it wait until after the game?'

'I'm sorry, Vik, but no, it can't. You see, if I wait I might just lose a little bit of the anger I'm feeling now and then I might not be able to go through with this.'

'That sounds ominous,' said Phil.

Vik looked at Haak and Lybrand and nodded. 'Perhaps, if you guys were to wait downstairs. You'd better tell Louise to wait there, too.' He shrugged. 'I'll text you all when we're through in here, okay?'

'All right,' said Haak and went out of the door, with Cooper Lybrand close on his heels like a small dog.

'Soccer's not really my cup of tea, anyway,' he said. 'I prefer baseball.'

'Wanker,' I muttered, after they'd gone.

'Your timing stinks, Scott,' said Phil.

'You're right. But you can't always time these things to

371

perfection. One minute you don't know something and then the next it's like the light goes on and you see everything really clearly but you just can't wait until the time seems right to do something about it.'

'You're a jealous bastard, if ever I met one,' he added.

'Why do you say that?'

'I assume this display of petulance is all about Kojo here. And his appointment as the club's new technical director? He told us about your swearing at him in the tunnel before the game.'

'That was thoughtful of him.' I decided to say nothing about his role in Soltani's sending off; that seemed hardly important beside what I had to say now. But it told me something important about the kind of treacherous colleague Kojo would have made.

'If you are going to offer us your resignation,' said Phil, 'then it could easily have waited until after the game.'

'Yes, it is about Kojo.'

Kojo put down his cigar and stood up. We were all standing now.

'But it certainly isn't about his appointment as the club's technical director. And it's not about me offering you my resignation. At least it wasn't. Although now that you've mentioned it, Phil, then we'll have to see how things pan out, won't we? But why don't you tell them why I'm here, Kojo? I assume you must have guessed.'

'Me?'

'Yes, you. You may be unscrupulous but you're not stupid.'

'I've no idea what you're talking about, Scott. Like I said to you before, I sincerely hope we can work together but I'm beginning to have my doubts about that. Seriously, Vik, this man seems a bit unhinged.'

'I wouldn't work with you Kojo. Not in a million years. Not if you managed every player in the world. And I'll tell you why. I mean, quite apart from the fact that you are a fucking crook—'

'Of course he's a fucking crook, Scott,' said Vik. 'Do you seriously think I don't know that already? I know everything about this dodgy bastard. How do you think he got the bloody job at the club in the first place?'

'What?'

'He twisted my arm, that's why I employed him. He threatened to reveal an important business deal I have concluded with Gustave Haak and the Greek government. A deal that's been cooking for months. A deal it's best that no one knows about. Especially here in Greece. At least not right now.'

'Vik, please,' said Kojo. 'You make it sound like blackmail. It wasn't like that at all. All I did was point out that I could hardly talk about your deal if I'd signed a confidentiality agreement, which I could only do if I was actually employed by you. I was actually trying to protect you and our relationship. I explained all this to you before.'

'Shut up, Kojo,' said Vik. 'When I want you to speak again I'll press a button. That's what I've paid for, right?' Vik looked at me with narrowed eyes; it was the first time I'd seen him looking angry. 'There was a deal being cooked which he overheard while he was a guest on my boat. And which I don't want anything to disturb. Anything at all. You understand?'

'And perhaps the less Scott knows about that deal the better,' Phil told Vik. 'Don't you think?'

'His salary as technical director and what I paid for King Shark are a drop in the ocean compared to the deal I've just done here. So, whatever it is you've come to tell me about him, I really don't give a fuck about it. D'you hear? He could have embezzled Oxfam and I wouldn't give a damn. Okay? So why not forget about whatever this is about and go and watch the rest of the game from the dugout, *where you belong?*'

I nodded. And I might have done exactly what Vik had suggested I do – at least until after the match – if Kojo had not put that fat cigar in his greedy mouth and smiled at me.

The last time I punched someone in the face as hard as that I'd been on C wing – the induction wing – at Wandsworth Prison; I don't even remember his name, all I know is that the guy had it coming DHL. It was some white bastard with more body art than a tattoo parlour window, who hated Arsenal and who kept calling me a coon; and that would have been all right except that on this particular day he'd gobbed on me, too – a great green Gilbert of a gob that was the slimy straw that broke the camel's back, so to speak. According to the medical orderly in the prison hospital I broke his nose so badly it looked like a belly dancer and they had to put so many bandages up his nostrils that they thought he was Paul fucking Daniels when they pulled them all out again.

Kojo could take a punch though and for a minute or two he and I went at it, trading punches and kicks as if we were matched in a cage at the Troxy in east London's Commercial Road. Finally, after a couple of hard ones on the side of my head that left my ears singing like a kettle, I felled him with a short uppercut and he didn't get up again.

By now the bodyguards had appeared, guns in hand, but with the fight very obviously over, Vik waved them out again.

'Out, out,' he yelled. 'Get the fuck out. We'll deal with this ourselves.'

I bent down, retrieved the silk handkerchief from the top pocket of Kojo's safari jacket, wiped my face and my knuckles with it and threw it away.

'I need a drink,' I said. 'I need a drink very badly. D'you mind if I help myself?' I poured a glass of champagne, drained the glass, sat down and breathed a sigh of relief.

'I feel so much better now that I've done that.'

CHAPTER 59

Vik and Phil looked at me with a mixture of fear and horror, so much so that I laughed out loud. Then there was a big roar outside and I jumped up to look out of the window, but it wasn't a goal, just the Greeks bellyaching about something else. I turned back to face my employers and shook my head.

'I thought we scored again,' I said. 'But it was nothing.'

'Jesus, Scott,' said Vik. 'Have you gone mad?'

'Maybe. Now ask me why I smacked him.'

Vik rolled his eyes and shook his head. 'I already told you,' he said, raising his voice. 'I know he's a crook and I really don't care what he's done.'

'Oh, he's a bit more than a crook, is our technical director. He's a murderer. It was him who was behind what happened to your friend and mine, Bekim Develi.'

Kojo pushed himself up on one elbow and leaned back against the wall. 'It's not true, Vik,' he said, reaching for the handkerchief that was no longer in his breast pocket. 'I never murdered anyone.'

'You know,' I said, 'I have to hand it to you, Kojo, that's almost true. Almost.'

'Here.' Phil picked the handkerchief off the floor where I'd dropped it and tossed it to him; Kojo wiped his bleeding nose with it and stayed silent.

Vik poured himself a glass of champagne, set down an upturned chair and sat on it. 'Why don't you just calm down, Scott?' he said. 'Calm down and tell us what this is all about.'

'I guess I am pretty stoked,' I said. 'All right. Here it is – the whole ninety minutes. On Sunday, when I was on your boat, I told you that someone put Nataliya Matviyenko up to stealing Bekim's EpiPens from his bungalow at the Astir Palace Hotel, on the night before he died. That someone was our friend Kojo, here. Kojo actually drove her away from the hotel in a chauffeur-driven Mercedes after she'd nicked the pens to order. I know that because on Monday morning the police showed me some new CCTV footage.'

'It wasn't me,' said Kojo.

'It's true that no one can see your face on that film, Kojo. The Greek cop, Chief Inspector Varouxis – he thinks you were another punter, one who was into some kinky sex, on account of the fact that there was a whip lying on the rear shelf of the car. Except that it wasn't a whip at all; it was that stupid fly-whisk you always have with you, wasn't it?'

'I don't know what the hell you're talking about,' said Kojo, dabbing at his nose with his handkerchief. 'And I didn't know anyone called Nataliya.'

'We can easily check with the local limo companies to see if you hired a car that night. No? And you already knew Nataliya from a trip you made here to Athens just a few months ago. I have a witness who was with you. Another hooker.'

'That's your witness?' Kojo laughed. 'Another hooker?'

'Kojo had dinner with her and this other girl, one of his players – Séraphim Ntsimi, who plays for Panathinaikos – and Roman Boerescu, who plays for Olympiacos, of course. In case you weren't paying attention, he's the one who almost scored against us tonight. Oh, and if you've forgotten Nataliya, she was the hooker who drowned herself in the harbour, because she was so upset about what happened to poor Bekim. They were good friends apparently. She has my sympathies. I'm pretty upset about it myself. But then you've probably guessed as much by now.'

I took a deep breath and tried to overcome the adrenalin coursing through my body that was making me tremble a little. A big part of me wanted to really go to town on Kojo for what he'd done; a bloody nose didn't seem like nearly enough.

'Why would Kojo do such a thing?' asked Vik.

'Exactly,' whispered Kojo.

'*Money*. That's why Kojo does everything, right? For money. In case you didn't notice he's spent the last few months desperate for money. On account of the fact that he has some largish gambling debts. Remember when we met him at that restaurant in Paris? Taillevent. He said then that he was going to Russia to look for a partner – trying to offload the King Shark Football Academy to someone with very deep pockets. Anyway, it turns out that he found a partner. Only it wasn't exactly the kind of partner he was looking for. He and your old friend, the owner of Dynamo St Petersburg, Semion Mikhailov, made a very substantial bet on the unlicensed market to do with the outcome of our first match against Olympiacos. Mikhailov knew about Bekim's allergy and persuaded Kojo that he should help make the bet against London City a sure thing. By putting the fix in on our best player. A player who Mikhailov just happened to know was also our most vulnerable.'

'Vik,' said Kojo. 'You have to believe me. This is all pure fantasy. I never made any such bet.'

'Maybe you didn't make it yourself, but you were in on it. And you had a good excuse to be here in Athens and do Semion Mikhailov's dirty work, didn't you, Kojo? City had just bought Prometheus and we were playing Olympiacos for a place in the Champions League. And you were looking to sell us another player, too. You were even invited on Vik's yacht to talk about it. Which was also very convenient as you didn't have to stay on the mainland and become a potential suspect like the rest of us.'

Vik looked pained for a moment. 'It's one thing stealing his pens,' he said. 'But that's not what why Bekim died. As you said yourself on Sunday night, someone tainted his food with chickpeas. Perhaps as little as a couple of grams of the stuff. I can't see how Kojo could have done that. On the day of the match Kojo was with Phil and me all day. Plus we have a team nutritionist. Everyone was very careful about what they ate before the match. On your own instructions.'

'Yes, I didn't understand that part myself. Until tonight, when I was in the tunnel before the match and I saw Mrs Boerescu. It turns out that she's employed by Olympiacos to look after the kids before the match. You know? The ones who walk onto the pitch with the teams. I spoke to her just now. Nice woman. According to her it was Kojo who paid for the tea tonight. And who generously paid for the tea last week – on the night Bekim Develi died. Normally those kids don't have any tea. On account of how everyone in Greece is short of money. But Kojo thought that was too bad and decided to take on the cost himself.'

Kojo was silent now. Painfully, he picked himself off the floor and sat down on a chair. He looked at me with tired, bloodshot eyes, and then dropped them again like I was on the way to the truth.

'But he didn't just pay for it. He actually provided it. Again, according to Mrs Boerescu, he phoned up a restaurant in Piraeus and ordered the food personally. Wasn't that kind of him? Apparently he's even thanked for his generosity in the match programme. In Greek, of course, so none of us would have noticed it. And nothing fancy, you understand. Just the sort of stuff all Greek kids like. Lots of fizzy drink, of course, but with just one dish on the menu: crisps and pitta bread *and hummus*. That's right, hummus. It's made of chickpeas. So that when the kids joined our lads in the players' tunnel their hands were sticky with the stuff. I ask you: getting children to effectively poison a guy, how cynical is that? And when he scored a goal in the first five minutes of the game – that one all-important away goal – Bekim celebrated in the way he'd started doing only very recently: he sucked his thumb. In celebration of the birth of his baby boy, Peter. But even if he hadn't sucked his thumb just touching his mouth and his nose would have caused him to go into hypoallergenic shock. How am I doing, Kojo? Does any of this ring a bell?'

'Is this true, Kojo?' asked Vik.

Kojo said nothing.

'Maybe I should ring some more bells for you?' I kicked him hard on the thigh. 'How about it, Kojo?'

'All right, all right,' he yelled. 'Take it easy, will you? Look, nobody intended the guy to die. It was an accident. It certainly wasn't murder, like Scott says it was. Bekim Develi was only supposed to be unable to continue the game. If he hadn't sucked his thumb, if this country wasn't in such a shit state he would still be alive, and none the worse for wear. And that stupid girl wasn't told to steal *all* his pens; just one. So I could verify that Semion was right about Bekim's allergy. But even if she did steal them all it's not like he could have taken any of those pens onto the pitch, is it? Taking the pens was just us making sure of the facts regarding his condition. Drowning herself – that was a complete overreaction. No one could have foreseen such a thing. But for that you'd all have been back in London and Bekim's death would have been just another footballing tragedy. Another Fabrice Muamba.'

'Except that Muamba's still alive,' I said.

'Is that it?' asked Vik.

I shrugged. 'Jesus, what else would you like?'

Vik took a deep breath, drained his glass and went to the window of the box where he took a money clip out of his pocket. I'd seen it before and for a moment I thought he was going to pay someone off. Instead he slipped it off the wad of notes he was carrying and began to rub the piece of gold in his fingers.

'I don't have many friends,' he said quietly. 'When you're as rich as I am friendship is something that always comes with its cap in its hand, head bowed, touching its forelock, soliciting a loan or a favour or a business deal. But Bekim Develi was my true friend, and from way back – Scott's right about that. He never wanted anything. In fact, he was the only guy who never let me pay for anything; who even bought me presents. It was Bekim bought me this money clip. I don't know how he got hold of this little object. It's eighteen carat gold, Cartier, and it was a gift from President Nixon to Leonid Brezhnev in 1973 when the two leaders met in Washington. Bekim knew I loved little things like this one, objects with history in their DNA.

'He was very thoughtful in that way. He really seemed to like me for myself, you know? That's a rare thing for me, gentlemen. Unheard of today. And it really upsets me to hear that this is how he died and why. Not to mention what's happened to Bekim's girlfriend, Alex, as a result. Semion Mikhailov, I can deal with that bastard in my own way. The question is, what are we going to do about you, Kojo?'

'We hand this cunt over to the police, that's what we're going to do about it,' I said. 'It's true, most of the evidence is must-haves, could-haves and probablies; but with his confession in front of three witnesses I don't doubt for a minute that I can make a pretty convincing case to that copper when next I see him.'

'I'm sure you can,' said Kojo. 'But the minute you do that, of course, I'll have my lawyer release a very detailed statement about the plans Vik and that guy Gustav Haak have put into motion in this country. You think I won't do it, Vik? Oh, I will. I can promise you that.'

Vik said nothing; he exchanged a look with Phil and then let out a sigh.

'But let me explain what they would prefer you not to know, Scott,' said Kojo. 'Let me tell you about the Erytheian Islands. Your boss and Gustav Haak, they just bought a chain of islands from the Greek government, for one euro. Those were the Greek guys on the boat the other night. I know that one euro doesn't sound like a lot of money and it isn't, but you see Haak and Sokolnikov represent a group of international investors who already own the whole country. Quite literally. They've been buying up Greek sovereign national debt since 2012 and they own most of it which means they *do* own the country, in all but name. If they dumped all their bonds now Greece would go down the toilet. So the Greek government are just going to do what they're told out of fear that Vik and his friends flush this country away. And what they've been told is this: that the Erytheian Islands, somewhere just north of Corfu, are going to be run as a tax-free zone for your boss and his friends. Eventually it will be like a Greek version of Monaco, I suppose. These things are all the rage these days. In China they call this a Freeport. In Cuba it's a Special Economic Zone. Imagine it, Scott. You're worth twelve billion quid, like Vik. Or twenty billion, like Haak; and you don't pay any tax, anywhere at all. Wouldn't that be nice? Not only that but if they have their way no one will ever know a damn thing about it until it's all up and running. Except you and me, of course. We'll know about it.'

Vik said nothing.

Outside there was a roar as the match ended; Panathinaikos fans were cheering the humiliation of their hated rivals. There was another very loud explosion, the sound of several air horns and in the distance a police siren. Phil glanced anxiously out of the window as something bounced off it.

'It would seem that London City just qualified for the next round,' he said.

That hardly seemed important now; at least not to me; not any more.

'Tell me you're not going to sweep this shit off the beach, Vik,' I said.

Kojo grinned; he could read the runes of what was about to happen even if I couldn't. 'Yes, Vik, go on,' he said. 'Tell him that friendship means more to you than dollars and cents.'

'Maybe Kojo didn't mean to kill Bekim, Vik,' I said, 'but in my book this bastard did something almost as bad: he helped to bring about the death of your best friend, for profit. A man I knew and admired a great deal. He should be punished. Justice needs to run its course with him.'

Vik turned away from the window and grimaced.

'Don't be a fool, Scott,' he said. 'Frankly I'm a little surprised to hear you of all people talk about justice. There's only the law and we both know what that's worth in Greece today. It takes authority to make law and I'm afraid that authority – real authority – has ceased to have any meaning in this country. Take a look out of that window. The Olympiacos fans are now attacking the riot police with Molotov cocktails. But is anyone surprised? When even the courts and the lawyers are on strike there's certain to be disorder and chaos and anarchy in plentiful supply. You can read it painted on the walls. You can smell it burning in the air. And you can see it washing your windscreen at the traffic lights. Why argue about that? We both know I'm right.

'So. Here's what's going to happen. Kojo, you and I still have a contract of employment and a watertight non-disclosure agreement. You'll continue to be paid by me, but I don't ever expect to see you again. And certainly not at my football club, or any other club for that matter. I expect you to disappear, Kojo. Go somewhere you can really use that fly-whisk – somewhere in Africa would be good, I think – and draw your salary. But don't ever think of working in football again. And always remember this: my arm is long; but my memory is even longer.'

Kojo stood up. 'What about my things on the boat? My laptop? My clothes?'

'I'll have my ship's captain bring your luggage to shore at the Astir Palace tomorrow morning at eight o'clock. Now get out.'

Kojo Ironsi picked up his fly-whisk and smiled. 'Congratulations, Scott,' he said. 'You won tonight. Then again, maybe you didn't win anything. Like the man once said, a game is not won until it's lost.'

After Kojo had gone there was a longish silence, mostly from me since I didn't know what to say although I now knew exactly what I had to do.

'Four–nil,' said Phil, eventually. 'Incredible.'

He looked at me and then at Vik. 'What about Scott?' he asked. 'I believe he has the same kind of non-disclosure agreement in his own contract, if he bothers to read it.'

'Scott Manson?' Vik spoke my name as if he was trying it out to see how loyal it still sounded in that room. 'I don't know, Phil. It's really up to him, isn't it? He's been very clever. Maybe he's too clever for football. Perhaps that's his problem as a manager. But really, there's not much hard evidence here. If you ask me, that cop Varouxis will be satisfied with the suicide of the girl and the name of that other guy. The one who murdered those hookers back in 2008, or whenever Scott said it was.'

'The Hannibal murders,' supplied Phil.

'Precisely. Him. And that's a good collar, I'd have thought – solving an unsolved crime that no one even knew was unsolved. Every policeman dreams of doing something like that. Yes, he'll have to make do with that. Because I certainly didn't hear any confession from Kojo. Did you?'

Phil shook his head. 'No. Nothing at all.'

Vik thought for a moment and then wagged a finger at me. 'Everything else we've heard here tonight is just speculation,' he continued. 'The girl – Nataliya – committed suicide; we knew that already from that unsent email we found on her iPhone. And now that the police know that they can hardly keep us here any longer. But we'll probably never discover who poisoned Bekim Develi. You might almost say it was the hand of God. That's how the insurance companies describe these things, isn't it?'

'I think that's called an act of God,' said Phil.

'Yes,' admitted Vik, 'you're right. It's slightly different in Russian, of course. But better the hand of God than the hand of an innocent child, don't you think? After all, I'm sure Scott here wouldn't like it to become known that it was a little child's hand that was used by unscrupulous, greedy men as a murder weapon in this case. Imagine what it would be like to be that child; to go through life knowing that you were the person who killed Bekim Develi. No, that's not a cross that any child should ever have to bear. Wouldn't you agree, Scott?'

I sighed a deep sigh and unzipped my tracksuit top; I was feeling hot from all my exertions; and not just those, perhaps. I was maybe a little sick, too, only this had nothing to do with heat, or smacking Kojo around the room. Having just qualified for the next round I should have been feeling on top of the world. Instead I wanted to find a hole and crawl into it.

I picked up the bottle of Krug, drank from the bottle for a second in a way I calculated was insulting to them both, burped loudly and then shook my head. 'The trouble with rich people. . .'

Vik groaned as if he'd heard this lecture before; and very likely he had.

'Be careful,' he said, 'you're not exactly poor, Scott.'

'No, I'm not. And you are quite right to remind me of that fact, Vik. I guess that's the difference between your kind of money and mine. You see, I've never really had to deal with the idea that, under the right circumstances, there might be absolutely nothing I wouldn't do and nobody whose face I wouldn't step on to keep a hold of that money, or to accumulate even more. Does that make any sense to either of you? No, I didn't think it would somehow.'

I nodded at them both.

'You'll have my written resignation in the morning, gentlemen. But right now I'm going to say goodbye to my team before spending the rest of the evening with my girlfriend.'

CHAPTER 60

Even when you're winning and on top you never know when the whistle may blow. Just ask Roberto Di Matteo, the caretaker manager of Chelsea who steered the club to a memorable double in 2012, and was promptly sacked following a mildly shaky start to the 2012–13 season. Or Vincent Del Bosque who got the bullet from Real Madrid just forty-eight hours after they won La Liga in 2003. Now that was harsh. Success in football rarely breeds more success, merely great expectations; and like the story goes, great expectations are often disappointed.

Already I had a few grey hairs on my head where none had existed before and that was after just seven months in charge – one less than Di Matteo. The fact is, after a week of combining football management with amateur detective work I was knackered and looking forward to a good rest.

Of course, most football managers get the sack or leave because another club makes them an offer they can't refuse; but it's perhaps rare for a manager to walk away from a club having just secured qualification for the next round of Champions League football, and the English press were all over the story like a colony of ants when Louise and I flew back to Heathrow's Terminal Five without the rest of the team. And not just that story, either.

To my girlfriend's credit she hadn't ever repeated what she'd told me on Vik's boat when I seemed to be on the verge of finding out exactly what had happened to Bekim Develi: nothing in this world gets solved the way you think it should – the way it ought to be solved. But she was right. It doesn't. I felt absolutely no satisfaction in having discovered how Bekim Develi had been killed and who had been behind it; and I could never have predicted that solving the case could feel so utterly pointless. Most of the time I wondered why I'd ever bothered. She got that right, too.

As for me I could have said a lot about what happened in Athens to the mass of reporters at Heathrow but I hardly cared to spend any more time involving myself in the murky financial affairs that had prompted my resignation from London City. That was all behind me now and I felt as if a great weight had been lifted off my shoulders. Instead I chose to confine all of my remarks to football, which suited me a lot better. That's the nice thing about football. There are moments in life when only football seems important. When everything else seems trivial and inconsequential and sometimes you think it's probably the only reason why fields are flat, why grass is cut short and why gravity was invented. Besides, I honestly wouldn't have known how to explain Greek sovereign national debt.

'I didn't resign to go and manage another football club,' I told the waiting reptiles. 'I didn't resign because I wanted more money or more power to buy the players I wanted. I didn't resign because of the Leicester City result or because we lost the first leg to Olympiacos in Athens. I didn't even resign because the police chose to detain our whole team in Greece for no good reason. Contrary to the suggestions of some papers, I resigned because I had a profound difference of opinion with the owner of the club as to how it should be run but, with no disrespect to Mr Sokolnikov, that shouldn't be a surprise to anyone who loves the game. After all, football is something about which a lot of men and women feel very passionately and sometimes that passion means that people find they can no longer work with each other. It's as simple as that. It's just the way the balls come out of the bag, right?

'I wish everyone at Silvertown Dock every success. They richly deserved the result in Athens. On the whole, it was a privilege and a pleasure to work with all those guys and I like to think that many of them were also my friends. Still are, I hope. But most of all I'll miss the fans. It's them who are in my mind most of all. After the death of João Zarco they took me to their hearts and gave me their unqualified support. For which I humbly thank them.'

'Scott?' asked one of the reporters, 'did your resignation have anything to do with the death of Bekim Develi?'

'Yes, it did but only to the extent that it has made me re-examine my priorities. Bekim Develi was a man I liked and admired enormously. I think everyone did. As a result of that tragedy I've decided to focus on what's important in my own life and what I want to achieve. I think that's normal. I don't think anyone should be surprised when someone chooses to make some life changes as a result of something awful like that. I've always been able to look after myself and really that's just what this is now; me looking after myself.'

'Since you mention looking after yourself,' said another reporter, 'perhaps you'd like to comment on the story in the *Sun* that you beat up two Englishmen on the Greek island of Paros. It's rumoured they're going to sue you. Did your resignation have anything to do with that?'

'Was it only two geezers? I forget. Listen, I had a small falling out with some yobs who thought Bekim Develi's death was a proper subject for comedy. At least that's what the songs they were singing seemed to suggest. Maybe I don't have a very good sense of humour, I don't know, but if you ask me they both needed a bloody good hiding.'

'What does the future hold for you, Scott?'

'I'm not sure you were listening, friend. Which of us can honestly say what the future holds? Isn't that what Bekim's death tells us? That nothing is certain? After all he was only twenty-nine, for Pete's sake. And that's rather the point of what I was saying just now. So I don't intend to go back into football management right away. Frankly, I'm not so sure that anyone would have me, anyway. I think maybe my half-time team talks are a bit more Gordon Ramsey than Henry the Fifth. My father has a sports apparel company and I'll be spending a little more time helping him with that for the moment. But this is not to say I've fallen out of love with the game. Not at all. Football means everything to me.'

'May I ask what your next move is going to be, Scott? Spain? Malaga? There's a strong rumour that you're going to take up a job in Spain. You do speak excellent Spanish.'

I sighed, grinned, and shook my head. 'I also speak German, Italian and French. But it seems my English isn't so good. Didn't I already say I wasn't immediately going back into management? However, since you asked so nicely, I will tell you what my next move is.'

I looked at Louise, smiled warmly, took her hand in mine and kissed it fondly.

'It's simply this. Me and my girlfriend, we're going to walk down the King's Road tomorrow afternoon and, if we can get tickets, we're going to go to Stamford Bridge and watch

Chelsea play Tottenham Hotspur. It has all the indications of being a cracker of a game. But for once I'm happy to say that I really don't give a damn who wins.'

PHILIP KERR

A SCOTT MANSON THRILLER

FALSE NINE

CHAPTER 1

Whenever I want to feel better about life I go on Twitter
and read some of the tweets about myself. I always come
away from this experience with a strong feeling about the
true sporting character and essential fairness of the great
British public.

> You're a useless bastard, Manson. The best thing
> you ever did was resign from this football club.
> #Cityincrisis

> Did you really resign Manson? Or were you
> sacked like every other overpaid cunt in football
> management? #Cityincrisis

> You left us in the lurch, Manson. If you hadn't
> quit we wouldn't have that stupid bastard
> Kolchak in charge and we might not be 4th from
> bottom. #Cityincrisis

> Come back to the Crown of Thorns, Scott.
> Mourinho did it. Why can't you? All is forgiven.
> #Cityincrisis

I suppose you think that what you said about
Chelsea on @BBCMOTD was clever, you stupid
black cunt. You make Colin Murray look good.

Most @BBCMOTD pundits are the walking dead.
But if Darryl Dixon ever needed to put a crossbow
bolt in a someone's eye, it's yours.

Just because you've been on the cover of
GQ doesn't mean you're not a black bastard,
Manson. You're just a black bastard in a nice suit.

We miss you, Scott. The football is rubbish
since you left. Kolchak hasn't a fucking clue.
#Cityincrisis

When are you going to explain why you quit
City, Manson? Your continued silence about this
is damaging the club. #Cityincrisis

I'm only on Twitter because my publisher thought it would
help to sell more copies of my book before Christmas. There's
a new edition out in paperback with an extra chapter about
my short reign at London City. Not that it says very much.
I'd already signed a confidentiality agreement with the club's
owner, Viktor Sokolnikov, which forbids me from saying why
I left the club, and mostly it's to do with the death of Bekim
Develi. Or at least as much as I can say about that. The new
chapter had to be read by Viktor's lawyers, of course. Frankly,
it's really not worth the paper it's written on and all the tweets
in the world aren't going to alter that fact.

I'm not a fan of social media. I think that we'd all be a
lot better off if every tweet cost five pence, or you had to

put a postage stamp on it before you sent it. Something like that. Most people's opinions aren't worth shit, mine included. And that's just the reasonable ones. It goes without saying that there's a lot of hate on Twitter and a great deal of that hate is to do with football. Part of me isn't surprised. Back in 1992 when a programme cost a quid and a seat no more than a tenner, I expect people were a bit more forgiving about football-related matters. But these days with a ticket at a top club like Man U costing six or seven times as much, you can forgive the fans for expecting a bit more from their team. Well, almost.

The funny thing is that while I never pay a lot of attention to the nice things people tweet about me, I can't help but pay attention to the insults and abuse I get. I try not to but it's hard, you know? To that extent, Twitter is a little like air travel: you don't pay it much attention when it's going well, but you can't help but pay attention when it's going badly. It's curious but there's a small part of me that thinks there's an element of truth to the unpleasant tweets. Like this one:

> If you were any good, Manson, you'd be at another club by now. But for the death of Joao Zarco you'd still be picking up cones.

And this one:

> Deep down, you always knew that the boots you were wearing were much too big for you. That's why you fell, you stupid fuck. #Cityincrisis

Then again, just occasionally you read something that seems to have something interesting to say about the game itself.

> You never understood that the purpose of
> passing is not to move the ball but to find the
> free man.

And perhaps, this one, too:

> The trouble with English football is everyone
> thinks he's Stanley Matthews. Don't dribble the
> ball, run with it; run to provoke.

For anyone who calls himself a football manager, being unemployed is probably your default position. Losing your job – or leaving it because you find it's just untenable – is as inevitable as scoring a few own goals if you're a good number four. As Plato once said, shit just happens. It's always painful to leave a football club you've been managing but the high rewards for success mean there are also high risks for failure. It's the same with investment; whenever I see my financial advisor for lunch he always reminds me of the five levels of risk appetite. These are: Averse, Minimal, Cautious, Open and Hungry. As an investor I would describe myself as cautious, with a preference for safe options that have a low degree of risk and may only have a limited potential for reward. But football is very different. Football is all about the last level: if you're not risk-hungry you've no business being a manager. Anyone who doubts that should look at the colour of Mourinho's hair or check the lines on the faces of Arsène Wenger and Manuel Pellegrini. Frankly, it's only when you've lost your job that you can truly say you've made your bones as a manager. But let's face it, today's managerial pariah can quickly turn into tomorrow's messiah. Brian Clough is the best example of a manager who failed badly at one club only to succeed spectacularly at his next.

It's tempting to imagine that Leeds United might have won two European Cups, back to back, if only they'd kept faith with Clough. In fact I'm sure of it.

Even so, it's hard being out of football management. It wasn't so hard during the summer, but now that the season is well under way I just want to be on the training ground with a team – even if I am just picking up the cones. I miss the game a lot. I miss the lads at London City even more. Sometimes I miss the team so much I feel physically sick. Right now I feel ill-defined as a person. Like I have no meaning. Etiolated. Which is a good word for what it's like to be an unemployed manager: it means someone who's lost their vigour or substance, and it also means pale and drawn-out due to a lack of light. That's exactly how I feel: etiolated. Just don't use a word like that on *MOTD* or they'll never ask you back. I can just imagine the tweets I'd get about using a word like that.

The fact is that you're only a manager when you're managing, as Harry Redknapp might say. When you're not doing it – when you're appearing as a pundit on *MOTD*, or a guest on *A Question of Sport* – you're what, exactly? I'm not sure that I'm anything at all. But here's another tweet that puts it very well, I think:

> Now that you've left City, Manson, you're going
> to find out that you're just another cunt in
> football.

Yeah, that's exactly right. I'm just another cunt in football. It's worse than being an actor who's working as a waiter because no one knows when you're a 'resting' actor. But when you're a manager who's out of work the world and his fucking dog seem to know about it. Like the bloke who sat beside me on the plane to Edinburgh this morning.

'I'm sure you'll find another job in management soon,' he said, encouragingly. 'When David Moyes was sacked from United I knew that it wouldn't be long before he was back at a top club. It'll be the same for you, mark my words.'

'I wasn't sacked. I resigned.'

'Every year it's the same old game of musical chairs. You know, Scott, I think people should bear in mind that it takes time for a manager to turn things around when a club is not doing well. But if you give a manager that time, then quite often he'll prove his gainsayers wrong. Nine times out of ten, the manager's just the scapegoat. It's the same in business. Take Marks & Spencer. How many CEOs has Marks & Spencer had since Sir Richard Greenbury left in 1999?'

'I wouldn't know.'

'The problem there is not the manager, but the whole retail business model. The fact is that people don't want to buy their clothes where they buy their sandwiches. Am I right, or am I right?'

Looking at my travelling companion's clothes I wasn't too sure about that. In his brown suit and salmon pink shirt he looked exactly like a prawn sandwich but I nodded politely and hoped for a moment when I might get back to reading Roy Keane's riveting book on my Kindle. It never came and I got off the plane wishing I'd thought to wear a cap and a pair of glasses, like Ian Wright. I don't need glasses. And I don't like caps. But I like chatting about football with strangers even less. Looking like a cunt is a lot better than spending a whole flight talking to one.

It was very strange being back in Edinburgh after so many

years away. I ought to have felt more at home here – after all, it was the place where I'd done the larger part of my growing up – but I didn't. I couldn't have felt more alien or out of place. It wasn't just the past that made Scotland seem like a foreign country to me. Nor was it much to do with the recent referendum. I hadn't shared the Scots' dislike of the English as a boy and I certainly didn't share it now, especially since I'd chosen to make my home in London. No, there was something else that made me feel separate, something much more personal. The truth was I'd never really been permitted to feel like a proper Scot on account of the colour of my skin. All of the kids in my class at school had been freckle-faced, green-eyed Celts. Me, I was half black – or, as the Scots used to describe me, 'a half-caste' – which was why I'd been nick-named Rastus. Even my Edinburgh schoolmasters had called me Rastus and although I wouldn't ever have shown it, this hurt. A lot. And it had always struck me as amusing that the minute I arrived at a school in England – with a Scots accent long since scraped off the bottom of my shoe – my nickname should have become Jock. Not that the boys of Northampton School for Boys weren't racist, too, but they were a lot less racist than their Scottish counterparts.

I'm lucky in that I have a seat on the board of my dad's company to fall back on, but that certainly didn't stop me from putting myself around a bit to see what was out there. My agent, Tempest O'Brien, was firmly of the opinion that it was important for me to see as many people as possible.

'It's not just your achievements that make you eminently employable,' she'd told me, 'it's you, the whole *GQ* package. You're one of the most articulate and intelligent men I know, Scott. Christ, I nearly said in football, but that's not saying much, is it? Besides, I think it's crucial that people see you're not just sitting back and living off your earnings – which according to the newspapers are substantial – as a director of Pedila Sports. So it's important you play that down. If people think you don't need to work then they'll try to buy you cheap. So the first place I'm going to send you is Edinburgh. There's a job going at Hibs. No one is going to try and buy you cheaper than a side in the Scottish Championship. I know your father was a Hearts man through and through but you should go and talk to them because it's a good place to start. Better that you should make your mistakes and hone your interview skills there where it won't matter than somewhere more important where it will, like Nice, or Shanghai.'

'Shanghai? Why the hell would I go to Shanghai?'

'Did you see *Skyfall*? The Bond movie? Shanghai is one of the most futuristic cities in the world. And the place is just rolling in money. It might be good experience for you to work there. Especially if they start buying football clubs in Europe. And the rumour is they're looking to do just that. The Chinese are a can-do people, Scott. Can do and will do, probably. When the Russians get tired of owning clubs or when the rouble finally collapses and they have to sell out, who are they going to sell to? The Chinese, of course. Within twenty years the Chinese are going to be the world's number one economic superpower. And when China rules the world, the capital of that world is going to be Shanghai. They started building a new tram in December 2007, and it was open less than two years later. Contrast that with Edinburgh's tram. How long did that take? Seven years? A billion quid spent on it and still they're bitching about fucking independence.'

The tram – which was supposed to run from Edinburgh Airport to a stop just across the road from my hotel – was out of action that particular morning; a power cut, they said. So I got the bus. It was an inauspicious start. And Tempest was right about something else, too: they were still bitching about independence.

I checked into the Balmoral Hotel, ate some oysters at the nearby Café Royal and then went down Leith Walk towards Easter Road to see Hibs play Queen of the South. The ground and the pitch were better than I remembered and I guessed there were between twelve and fifteen thousand there – a big difference from the record attendance of sixty-five thousand in 1950, when Hibs played their local rivals Hearts. It was a cold but beautiful afternoon, just right for a game of football, and while the home side had the better run of the play for most of the match they were unable to take their chances. Paul Hanlon and Scott Allan both went close and Hibs lost a chance to go level on points with a side they ought to have beaten with ease. The Queens looked happy to have come away with a point in a goalless draw that did not please the Edinburgh fans. Jason Cummings was about the only player who impressed me when his swerving thirty-yard shot was saved by the Queens' goalkeeper Zander Clark, but it was a less than memorable game and on the evidence of what I'd seen, Hibs, who were more than ten points adrift of the league leaders, Hearts, seemed destined to be spending another year out of the SPL.

I went back to the hotel, ordered some tea which never came, had a hot bath, snoozed my way through the football results and *Strictly For Morons*, and then went around the corner to a restaurant called Ondine, where I'd arranged to meet Midge Meiklejohn who was one of the club's directors. He was an affable man with a large head of red hair and green eyes. In his lapel was a Hibs crest which served to remind me just how old the club actually was: 1875. And of course this proud tradition was a major part of the club's problem. Of any old club's problem.

We talked generally about football for a while and drank our way through an excellent Sancerre before he asked me what I'd thought of the game and, more importantly, Hibs themselves.

'If you'll forgive me,' I told him, 'your problems aren't on the pitch but in the boardroom. You've had how many – seven? – managers in ten years? Who've probably done the best that could be done, in the circumstances. The manager you've got is doing a great job, and things aren't going to get any better until you address the fundamental problem which is that football clubs are like regional newspapers. There are simply too many of them. Prices are going up and readership is declining. There are too many papers competing for too few readers. The same is true of football. There are too many clubs competing not just with each other but with television. Your gate today was maybe twelve thousand, while some of your players are on two or three grand a week, maybe more. Your wage bill must take two thirds of your gate. Which leaves running costs and the bank. Your business is dying on its feet. Full-time football is just not a viable option for you or, for that matter, for nearly all of the Scottish clubs, bar two.'

'So what are you saying? That we should just give up?'

'Not at all. But the way I see it you have two choices if you're going to survive as a club. Either you do what some Swedish clubs do – clubs like Gothenburg – with most of the players taking part-time jobs as painters and decorators. Or there's what a French philosopher speaking about something else calls "the detestable solution". A solution which makes total business sense but which will have the supporters crying out for your head, Midge, and everyone else on your board.'

'What's that?'

'A merger. With Hearts. To form a new Edinburgh club. Edinburgh Wanderers. Midlothian United.'

'You must be joking. Besides, that's been considered before. And rejected.'

'I know. But that doesn't mean it's not the right solution. Edinburgh isn't Manchester, Midge. It can barely support one good team, let alone two. You use the assets of one club to pay off the debts and build a future for them both. It's simple economics. The only problem is that tribes don't like economics. And Hibs and Hearts are two of the oldest tribes in Scotland. Look, it worked for Inverness Cally Thistle. In less than twenty years they've merged two failing clubs and gone from the Scottish Third Division to being second in the SPL. The case for a merger is irrefutable. You know it. I know it. Even they know it – the supporters – in their heads. The only trouble is that they don't think with their heads, but with their hearts. If you'll pardon the expression.'

'These people aren't like other people,' said Midge. 'They know how to hate and more importantly they know how to hurt. I'd probably have to seek police protection. Leave the city. We all would.'

'Then to quote Private Fraser, you're doomed. Doomed, I tell ye. It's the same for most of the clubs in the north of England. It's history and tradition that are holding them back, too. There's this singularity called the Barclays Premier League that deforms everything that comes close to it and which is sucking everything in English football into its mass. The big clubs get more successful and the poor ones disappear. Who wants to go and pay twenty quid to watch Northampton Town get stuffed when you can support Arsenal in the comfort of your own home? That's the physics of football, Midge. You can't argue with the laws of the universe.'

'It's only a game,' said Midge. 'That's what these bloody people forget sometimes. It's only a game.'

'But it's the only bloody game as far as they're concerned.'

I went back to the hotel to watch *MOTD* but it hardly seemed worth it since the matches were all Scottish ones. Not that there would have been any English Premier League matches anyway because of international duties, which meant I was at least spared watching Arsenal throw away a three goal lead, as they'd recently done against Anderlecht in the Champions League. That had grieved me a lot less than it might have done. The fact is that since I started to watch football with the eyes of an ordinary fan I've come to appreciate something genuinely beautiful about the beautiful game. It's this: learning how to lose is an important part of being a fan. Losing teaches you – in the words of Mick Jagger – that you can't always get what you want. This is an important part of being a human being – perhaps the most important part of all. Learning to cope with disappointment is what we call character. Rudyard Kipling had it almost right, I think. In life it helps to treat triumph and disaster with equal sangfroid. The ancient Greeks knew the importance that the gods placed on our ability to suck it up. They even had a word for it when we didn't: hubris. Learning how to suck it up is what makes you a mensch. It's only fascists who will tell you anything else. I prefer to think that this is the true meaning of Bill Shankly's oft-quoted remark about life and death. I think that what he really meant was this: that it's character and sand that are more important than mere victory and defeat. Of course you couldn't ever say as much while you're the manager of a club. There's only so much philosophy that anyone can take in the dressing room. That kind of shit might work on centre court at Wimbledon but it won't wash at Anfield or Old Trafford. It's hard enough to get eleven men to play as one without telling them that sometimes it's all right to lose.